A JOURNEY CAST IN FIRE

THE ANCIENT CHRONICLES OF EMPYREA BOOK 2:

A JOURNEY CAST IN FIRE

B. H. PRESTON

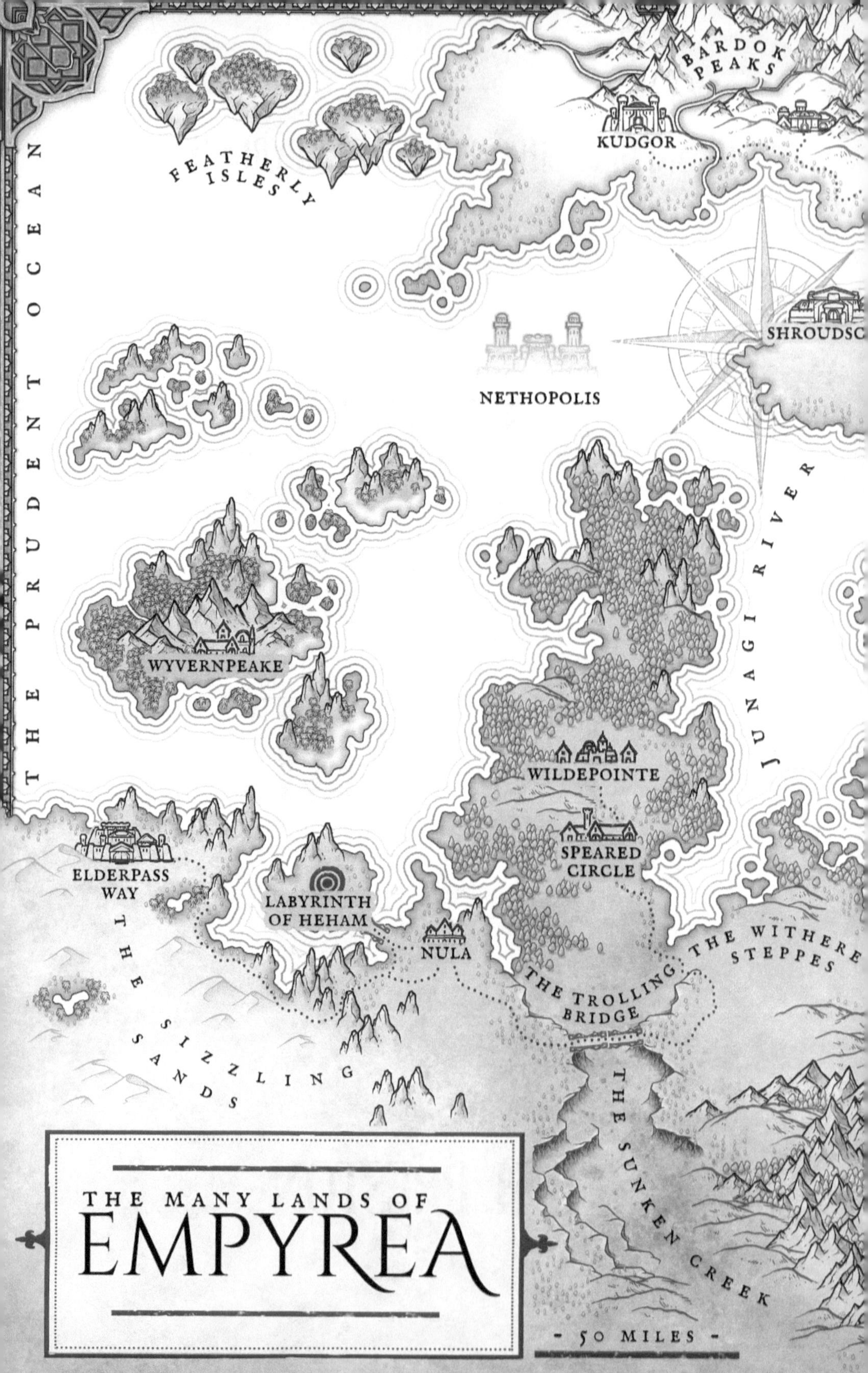
BARDOK PEAKS
KUDGOR
FEATHERLY ISLES
NETHOPOLIS
SHROUDSC
THE PRUDENT OCEAN
JUNAGI RIVER
WYVERNPEAKE
WILDEPOINTE
SPEARED CIRCLE
ELDERPASS WAY
THE SIZZLING SANDS
LABYRINTH OF HEHAM
NULA
THE TROLLING BRIDGE
THE WITHERE STEPPES
THE SUNKEN CREEK
THE MANY LANDS OF EMPYREA
- 50 MILES -

TO THE VAST TUNDRA WILDS
RAGMAW
HINGTAGA
WHALDALF LANDING
THE PEACEFUL EXCHANGE
THE MYSTICAL CITY OF LUMHAGEN
EL TYRION
OAKREST
BINICORN'S FARTHING
FAYSPIRE
THE FORGOTTEN FOREST
BRANCHY OAKS MARKET
BRIGHTSHIRE FOREST
KARNERGRIEN
THE LAMPI GLADE
ASHLAND
WESTRAMORE
THE DESOLATE FIELDS
THE BARREN BADLANDS
DARKVALE VALLEY
TALAIFOTIA
DEEPER INTO THE INFERNAL BARRENS

ALSO BY B.H. PRESTON

The Ancient Chronicles of Empyrea
A Hero Forged in Blood
b.h.prestonbooks.com

For my mom, Otherine Preston.
You nurtured my love of books and supported me always.
May you rest in peace.
April 3, 2024

A JOURNEY CAST IN FIRE
PRONUNCIATION GUIDE

Acantha – /ah-KAN-thah/

Adena – /A-DEE-na/

Agalus – /AH-gah-lus/

Agwin – /Aug-win/

Aelunara – /AY-loo-NAH-rah/

Alpheon – /AL-fee-on/

Amphisbaena – /AM-fuhs-be-ah-nah/

Andaluria – /An-DA-lu-ria/

Anika – /AH-nee-kah/

Aspis – /AH-spis/

Asitra – /AH-sih-trah/

Asiz – /Ahh-ZEEZ/

Ashland – /Ash-land/

Bardicus – /BAR-da-cus/

Bhalla – /BAH-laa/

Binicorn – /Bi-na-corn/

Blakenshield – /Blay-KIN-sheeld/

Bonberry – /BON-beh-ree/

Branaloy – /BRAH-nah-loy/

Briskly – /BRI-sklee/

Bristlekamp – /BRI-sl-camp/

Brightshire – /Brite-SHAIR-ur/

Bug – /bug/

Choralight – /KOR-ah-lite/

Chum – /Ch-UM/

Cimetes – /SIGH-me-tes/

Craig Diávolos Castle – /KRAYG dee-AH-voh-los KAS-ul/

Daneyel – /DAH-nee-el/

Daven Jones – /DAY-vən jones/

Deimanus – /DAY-mah-nus/

Dinereus – /di-NEER-ee-us/

Doran – /DOH-rən/

Dratonium – /drah-TOH-nee-um/

Drubata – /droo-BAH-tah/

Duke – /Dook/

Dunntaika – /dunn-tie-ka/

Ellawyn – /EL-ah-win/

Echethier – /Eh-KAH-theer/

Eldrin – /EL-dren/

Elaena – /eh-LAY-nah/

Empyrea – /Em-PEER-ri-ah/

Evias – /EH-vy-ahs/

Fayspire – /FAY-spai-ur/

Faelish – /FAY-lish/

Fluteds – /FLU-teds/

Gadar – /GAH-darr/

Gangor – /GAN-gor/

Garth – /Gaarth/

Guktash – /GUK-tash/

Hintaga – /Hen-TAH-gah/

Ititken / Itik – /IT-it-ken/ / /IT-ik/

Junagi – /JOO-nah-gee/

Kaden – /KAY-den/

Kaledio – /kah-LEH-dee-oh/

Karatheas – /kah-rah-THEE-us/

K'Lani – /kuh-LAH-nee/

Kel Tyrion – /kel-Teer-ee-un/

Khekül – /KHEH-kool/

Khesza – /KEZ-ah/

Kili – /KEE-lee/

Kugdor – /Cug-DOOR/

L'eldrian – /el-DRI-an/

Liasti – /lee-AHS-tee/

Lucient – /LU-see-ent/

Lumhagen – /LOOM-hay-gen/

Luna – /LOO-nah/

Malacheen – /mah-LAH-cheen/

Malech – /mah-LEKH/

Megalos – /MEH-gah-lows/

Mercalyptus – /MER-cah-lip-tus/

Millicent – /Mil-LAH-cent/

Mosswhisper – /MOS-whis-per/

S'Durnen – /s-DUR-nen/

Sdurne – /sdurn/

Muk Muk – /MUK-muk/

Nethopolis – /na-THA-poe-lis/

Nosegye – /NOWZ-guy/

Omak – /Oh-MAHK/

Orealus – /OR-real-us/

Parrotlets – /PAIR-ra-lets/

Pepper – /PEH-per/

Petey – /PEE-tee/

Regar – /REH-gar/

Rosenhelm – /ROW-sen-helm/

Sadunia – /SAH-doo-nee-ah/

Scruffenfoot – /SKRUH-fin-foot/

Shroudscar – /SHROWD-scar/

Seward – /SOO-ərd/

Serenya Larethian – /seh-REN-yah lah-REH-thee-ən/

Soothsage – /SOOTH-sayj/

Sozonos – /soh-ZOH-nos/

Talaifotia – /TAH-lay-foh-tee-ah/

Ta'la – /TAH-lah/

Tha'lassa – /THAW-lah-sa/

Thalgrem – /THAL-grem/

Threlka – /THREL-kah/

Trophorus – /TRO-for-us/

Truthorium – /TROO-thor-ee-uhm/

Tuskarion – /tus-KAR-ee-on/

Valmyr – /VALL-mear/

Varun – /VAH-run/

Vynthium – /VIN-thee-um/

Waptoo – /Wop-TOO/

Wap'Too – /WAP-too/

Westramore – /Weh-STRAH-more/

Weylyn – /WAY-lin/

Whaldalf – /WALL-dalf/

Woo'apma – /WOO-op-maa/

Wildepointe – /WILL-da-point/

Wyrmtongue – /WIRM-tung/

Yah'zaval – /Yaah-sha-val/

Yew – /yoo/

CHAPTER 1

After the death of his foster father, Kaden Sheppard had thought he knew what hard was. It was a beautiful morning, the sunshine bright overhead in a way it had refused to be for the past week of travel, the moody fog melting off quickly thanks to the heat. Dew glistened on the pine needles all around the camp, and Kaden could hear a robber jay singing—more like squawking—in the distance. His friends all surrounded him, alive and mostly well, and he didn't have to help cook breakfast.

He wished he could appreciate it all a little more, but after the terror and exhaustion and elation of yesterday's battle in the goblin fortress of Shroudscar, Kaden mostly just felt tired, sore, and strangely empty. It wasn't how he wanted to feel, but it seemed too hard to reach for anything more.

Maybe he was unwell. He should talk to Bhalla about that… once he finished waking up and found the old wizard. Even sitting up out of his bedroll and putting on his boots felt hard right now, so much more difficult than such a simple task warranted.

His enormous hunting hound, Duke, who'd been stretched out beside him on the ground, leaned over and helpfully licked his ear.

"Ugh, Duke." Kaden pushed the big dog's head away, giving him a scratch behind the ears as he did so. The prospect of avoiding a tongue bath from his enthusiastic but very smelly dog made getting up a little bit easier, actually.

Even so, he'd learned since then that "hard" came in many shapes—grief, doubt, leadership, and the fear of losing the people he loved.

Getting one of them back on his journey to reclaim the land from darkness? That was a blessing from Orealus, and Kaden gave thanks from the depths of his heart even as he watched Petey, his first and best friend—other than Duke—bicker with Chum as he brewed tea.

Turned out, you could be thankful and still be annoyed when your friends weren't even *trying* to get along.

"That's too much!" Petey said, jerking the bag of loose tea leaves away from Chum as the sharp-horned satyr added another pinch to the kettle. Bug, Petey's adoring hopping toadstool companion, let loose a puff of yellow pollen in matching consternation. Some of it got into Duke's nose, and he sneezed, spraying pollen and mucus all over Kaden's boot. *Gross.* "You'll use it all up before the week's out, at that rate!" His bright yellow eyes—goblin eyes—were narrow with irritation, and the corners of his long green ears twitched like nervous mice.

"Better no tea at all than the pale, tasteless stuff you brew," Chum retorted. He was the first satyr Kaden had ever met, and apparently, the only one he ever would since Lucient's forces had wiped out the rest of his people. Being the only one of his kind didn't make Chum any more eager to get along with others, though. He thought of himself first, Weylyn second, and everyone else was a very distant third. "You'll have to keep it on the fire for half the day just to make it palatable!"

"I'll keep it on for as long as it needs to be on." Petey rolled his eyes. "Honestly, I was only dead for a minute, and you went and declared yourself keeper of the tea?"

"Don't joke about that," Ada said from where she was sitting closer to the fire, checking the pot to see how the porridge was coming along.

Porridge. Again. Yuuuuum.

"Nobody wants to think about you dying," she continued as she brushed one of her long black braids back from her face. Ada Davenrich, or Adena as her mother called her, was a little older than Kaden, with bright green eyes and warm brown skin. She wasn't the first person to answer the call of his quest, but she had already proven her worth despite her youth and inexperience.

In truth, Kaden felt a little better about his own inexperience with her; having someone else to learn and discover things with, rather than already being an expert at them, made confronting his own limitations a bit easier.

"*I* don't mind it," Chum said snappishly.

"Yes, but we all know what a reprobate you are," Weylyn called out from the other side of the fire, where he was painstakingly tapping out a dent in one of his massive steel pauldrons. Kaden could still barely believe he'd convinced Weylyn, Son of the Wolf, the greatest mercenary in the land, to join his crew. How did someone as green as Kaden command someone as experienced as Weylyn? His stomach dipped in that familiar, unwelcome way. Being "chosen" still felt like wearing armor two sizes too big, a role he hadn't grown into, no matter how hard he tried.

With care and deliberation, he was learning. He hoped those would be enough to help him justify his next decision, because he still needed to figure out where they were going next. Duke shifted closer at his side, his tail thumping once against the ground as if he sensed Kaden's unease.

A faint tug stirred beneath his sternum again, subtle but persistent, as if something deep within him were trying to point the way forward. He tried to ignore it, but it lingered like a compass needle seeking north.

A drop of dew dripped down onto the top of his head from the tree above, and Kaden flipped the hood of his cloak up with a silent huff. Honestly, he would have liked nothing more than a break from travel for a while, a chance for his mind and body to catch up with the events they'd been through, but that wasn't going to happen. Not now that Bhalla the Bright was here.

Here, but not *here*. Where had the wizard gone now? He'd arrived last night, with little fanfare, and listened to Kaden talk all through his watch, telling him of their adventure so far. Bhalla had laid out the next step in the quest—to find the blessed armor of Orealus, which Kaden would need if he were going to survive a confrontation with Lucient and unite the nations as king.

Kaden pressed to his feet, holding in a groan at the way his muscles balked and complained at getting up. He shook his head as Ada caught his eye, her unspoken offer to join him turned down. He needed to find Bhalla, needed to get some things straight before he could make his next big decision. The less he shared his uncertainty with the others, the better. Duke stretched out on the ground with a doggy smile, then got up and trotted after him as Kaden headed into the trees. He ranged ahead a few steps, nose low to the forest floor, then circled back with a quiet huff, satisfied the path was clear.

A hundred yards or so away from camp, Eldrin was shooting arrows into trees. Kaden watched his elven friend's face tighten with focus, staring out at a target only he knew before he loosed. A second later, Kaden heard "Got it!" and Redfern flew out of the dense pine forest, waving the arrow in one small hand. She flew it back to Eldrin with a grin, her bright red hair bounding in a braid between coppery wings. "You can fire it harder than that; I'll still be able to catch it."

"Will you? Or will I end up perforating one of Queen Pepper's bodyguards like a piece of ripe fruit and get punished for it?" Eldrin replied haughtily, but Kaden could see it was just a front. Amazing that he noticed those things now about the prickly elf prince. There had been a time when Kaden was convinced they'd never understand each other. Time and togetherness had worn their sharper edges down, though.

"Sounds like you're making excuses to me," Redfern singsonged before looking at Kaden. "If it's my lady you seek, she and Millicent are with Bhalla. There's an overlook about a quarter-mile's distance that way." She pointed deeper into the forest. "They should be there."

"Thank you," Kaden said, then added, "Try not to embarrass Eldrin too badly."

"Hey!"

"Can't promise it, sire!"

At least someone's having fun, Kaden reflected as he headed deeper into the trees. He moved slowly, listening to the sounds around him, checking the ground for signs of those who'd passed this way before him. He was still pretty green as a tracker, but he'd been working on it with his foster father, Daneyel, before… everything, and was working even harder now that he had people relying on him.

Eldrin is better at it. Redfern is better. Weylyn is better, uke brushed past him, his shoulder warm and solid against Kaden's leg, and the contact steadied him more than he liked to admit.

Kaden knew he could count on his friends to do their part, that he didn't *have* to be great at tracking, but he felt compelled to be as good as possible. What if something went wrong, and he couldn't fix it because he couldn't find the right path? How would he move forward?

Your thoughts are spiraling. Get ahold of yourself. It was easier said than done. The miracle that was Shroudscar—the miracle of beating the goblins, of killing their vile leader Garth, and saving Petey, the miracle of him coming back to life—should have freed Kaden from so many of his worries. He'd done it, led his people through battle, and come out the other side with everyone hale and hearty! Shouldn't he be *less* worried now?

Why did he feel even more uncertain instead?

Kaden saw the trees start to clear a few hundred yards away, and heard the sound of Queen Pepper's bright, happy laughter. Duke slowed behind him, paws scraping softly over stone as the ground turned rocky beneath their feet. He stopped, closed his eyes, and tried to calm himself. *Orealus, be with me. Help me make the right choices. Help me do your will, and keep my friends safe.*

There was no answer this time. Maybe Kaden had used up all of Orealus's goodwill for the time being. Kaden took a deep breath, then headed for the overlook.

It was little more than a rough, rocky outcropping that was too stony for even the gnarled pines to get their roots into, but he had to admit that the view was spectacular. To the west, he could see the vast green, purple, and golden plains of the centaurs, and he could almost imagine that the blue blur beyond that was the sea and not just the edge of the sky.

Bhalla was sitting on the rocky overlook, his legs folded, wrinkled face creased with a smile as he chatted with Queen Pepper Shinyfawn, mistress of the Enchanted Woods, leader of the fairies. Millicent, her other guard, hovered a few feet away, her close-cut blue hair waving in the breeze. She glanced at Kaden as he stepped out onto the rocks, then relaxed her grip on the spear in her hand. Pepper turned and noticed him at the same time.

"Kaden!" She was smiling, and her long white hair was braided with flowers for what seemed like the first time in ages. They were little yellow-and-blue mountain tansies, not the big, bright blossoms he'd first seen her with, but they suited her. "Good morning," she continued. "Did you get any sleep at all?"

"A little," Kaden replied. It was technically true if you counted "dozing between fretting and tossing and turning" as sleep.

"I imagine you want to speak with Bhalla again."

"Oh, I wasn't—" He didn't mean to kick her out of the conversation. "Please, you don't have to leave for my sake."

"It's all right," she said. "I've got things to stay busy within the camp, and plenty to gather for my medical stores if we're going to be off on the next leg of our adventure soon."

"Ah, yes. Right." *Off on an adventure, sure. But where are we going?*

Queen Pepper and Millicent flew by Kaden, carrying the scent of sweet tansies with them. Only Bhalla was left, his legs folded beneath him as he sat on the rocky perch he'd found for himself. His white hair was wild around his head, his beard thick enough to obscure all but the edges of his smile. "Come," he said. "Sit with me. There are still things for us to discuss, and I'll have to be leaving soon."

"Leaving?" A hope Kaden hadn't even realized he held in his heart sank to nothingness, leaving him feeling somewhere between numb and panicked. "You can't go with us?"

"Orealus has other tasks for me, I'm afraid," Bhalla said, and there was genuine regret in his tone. "I would like to be there for you, to guide you as I wished I'd been able to guide your father, but prayer and experience have both taught me that that's not my role."

"But why not?" It didn't make sense to Kaden. "Surely our chances of success would be greater if you came with us. You're the most powerful wizard there is!"

"I am," Bhalla agreed, his smile gone. He looked out over the land spread out in front of them, his gaze as distant as the sea. "And that power brings many dangers along with it. While I'm honored to be one of Orealus's chosen wielders of yah'zaval, it doesn't come without a price. The power of Orealus rings across the land like a holy bell, and those who are attuned to hearing it can follow it. If I were to come with you, I would have to curtail almost all use of my power, for fear of bringing the forces of Lucient, primed for battle, down upon you."

Kaden swallowed hard. "Is that what I did in Shroudscar?" he asked. "Gave us away to Lucient? Could we be attacked at any moment?" At the time, it had felt transcendent to use the power of yah'zaval to destroy Garth and half of the filthy fortress of Shroudscar along with him, sending its goblin inhabitants running. But if he'd endangered his friends' lives…

Bhalla shook his head. "Goblins are fiercely territorial. The likelihood of them allowing anyone else into their domain is slight, and you sent all of them running for the deepest, darkest caves in all of Empyrea, so I think you're all right for now." He looked out at the horizon again for a moment, consideringly. "I'm not trying to say it's wrong to use the power of yah'zaval. Orealus bides in us for his own reasons, and to deny his power would be to deny him. You will need to become used to your new capabilities, and that means using them. But I doubt you'll be blasting goblin fortresses into oblivion very often."

Kaden felt his face flush. "I, ah… no. Probably not."

Bhalla clapped him on the shoulder. "Well, there you are! And I think you'll be all right without this old man dogging your steps, Kaden. You've assembled quite the company here."

"I didn't get everyone," Kaden confessed. "Bardicus wouldn't make an alliance with me, and my terms with King Varun of the merfolk and Chief Cimetes are… well, I think they might have agreed to help me more to shut me up and get us out of their kingdoms than because they really believe we have a chance against Lucient."

"Oh, I think they might come around," Bhalla said reflectively. "Bardicus in particular appreciates a good tale of adventure, and you've got a lot more of those now than when you started. Many more coming, too. Now!" He pushed to his feet, using his staff to help lever himself up. Kaden quickly joined him, and Duke made him laugh as the enormous hound shamelessly pushed his head under Bhalla's hand in his quest for pets. "Speaking of your quest, where are you going next?"

That was the whole problem! "I don't know yet. I don't know where any of the pieces of armor are, and everyone has their own idea about where we should look for support next, and… I just don't know!" Kaden exclaimed.

Bhalla frowned. "What about the map I gave you? That should help. It's got all the locations marked out on it, after all."

Kaden was completely confused. "What map?" he asked.

"Didn't I give it to you when you came to Lumhagen?"

Kaden frowned, searching his memory. He tried to picture scrolls, weapons, frantic escapes, but nothing surfaced. Too much had happened too quickly, and there had been far too many crises to remember every artifact they should have taken with them.

"No." Kaden indicated the massive sword across his back. "You gave me Vrangar, and you gave Petey Loyal Dwingent, but there was no map."

"No map? Sacred Orealus, how forgetful of me." Bhalla shook his head and began patting at the front of his robes. "I'll be losing my own head next," he muttered. "Map, map… perhaps in the bag of expansion…" He pulled a tiny pouch out of his inner robe, untied the top of it, then stuck his entire arm inside. Kaden's mouth dropped as he watched Bhalla's arm vanish into what looked like thin air.

"It's got to be in here somewhere!" Bhalla's head followed his arm. Kaden waved a tentative hand in the air right in front of the bag, half expecting to bump into Bhalla's unseen arm if it extended beyond the pouch— but his hand moved unimpeded.

Wow. That's got to be handy.

A second later, he heard Bhalla shout "Ha!" followed by his quick reappearance, gripping a stained, slightly tattered piece of paper in one hand. "I had it stuck between two pages in one of my books," he said with a sigh. "Ridiculous, I tell you. Well… here." He handed the paper to Kaden. "Take good care of that, and may it be a guide for you when you need help finding your place. And now…"

The air around Bhalla shimmered as if heated, the edges of the world bending with a soft hum. A sharp tang of ozone tingled at the back of

Kaden's throat, an unmistakable sign that yah'zaval was gathering and bending space at the wizard's command.

He lifted his staff and spun it in a slow circle, like an enormous sign of Orealus in front of him. A glow followed the tip of the staff, connecting the ends of the circle, and a moment later, the center of it filled with the sight of Bhalla's observatory.

"I must be gone," he said. "There are many tasks for all of us to do, and less time to accomplish them in with every passing moment. But Kaden." He lowered the staff and set his hand firmly on Kaden's shoulder, looking up at him with a serious face. "Know that no matter how dark the path ahead seems, Orealus is with you, and so am I. Listen to your heart, listen to your dreams, and don't forget." He tapped Kaden's crystal Amulet of Orealus. "You always have a light to brighten your path."

Before Kaden could speak, before he could even nod an acknowledgment, Bhalla had stepped through the glowing circle and into another place entirely. The glowing portal vanished a moment later, leaving Kaden alone with Duke. Kaden clutched the map to his chest like it contained the answers to every question in the world.

He hoped it did. Otherwise, he wasn't sure what they'd do next.

CHAPTER 2

Kaden returned to his friends alone and found them eating a hearty breakfast and bickering quietly over small, mundane things as they all tucked in. That was good. Better that they bicker over those than the next step in their journey. Kaden was hoping that there wouldn't be any fighting, but he knew the chances of that happening were about as good as Duke going a hundred feet without sniffing a tuft of grass or peeing on a stand of trees.

"Here." Ada handed him a bowl as he sat down, and he smiled his thanks at her before beginning to eat. The porridge was a little different today, at least—someone, probably Queen Pepper, had found a cache of tart, yet sweet purple berries to enhance the bland meal with. Kaden ate faster than normal, which, in hindsight, was too bad because as soon as he was done, he looked up and found the eyes of almost everyone on him. Some were calm, others excited, but all of them were expectant.

"So," Eldrin said as Kaden stalled by taking a drink of icy mountain-stream water from his cup, "where does Bhalla say we should go next?"

"Who cares where that fraud of a wizard says we should go next?" Weylyn demanded with a frown. "We don't answer to the whims of someone who can't even be bothered to join the quest he says he supports."

"Actually, there's a reason for that," Kaden began, but he was immediately talked over by Petey, of all people.

"He's not a fraud! Bhalla is the greatest wizard in the world! Kaden and I saw him do powerful feats of magic when we were in the city of Lumhagen. You should be more respectful of him."

"I respect those who earn respect, little one," Weylyn retorted. "And I haven't seen anything from that old man yet that makes me want to kowtow to him."

"Did *he* fight off a terrible sea monster?" Chum chimed in officiously, snub nose in the air. "Did *he* do battle with a hideous forest golem? Was *he* there when Weylyn beat Chief Cimetes's champion into a bloody pulp? Did *he*—"

"Did *you* do any of that either?" Petey snapped. "No! You didn't!"

Chum braced his hands on his hairy hips. "I did plenty! I certainly did a lot more than *you* down in Shroudscar, I'll have you know, since the best you could come up with was getting captured and then getting almost dead."

"You—"

"That's enough." Queen Pepper's voice was clear and carrying and silenced the argument as swiftly as a hand smothered a candle. "Perhaps we should refrain from speculating and let Kaden tell us what he and Bhalla spoke about." She turned back to Kaden, a gentle smile on her face.

Oh, boy. "Well, obviously, the next step is reassembling the Armor of Orealus," he said, trying to pull his thoughts together. "The sword Ruach, the helmet Sozonos, the breastplate Justicia, the shield Aspis, the boots Paz, the greaves Megalos, the gauntlets Deimanus, and the belt Liasti."

"We knew that already," Redfern said with a sigh, and was nudged into silence by Millicent.

"And we know who has most of them," Kaden went on, rubbing his temples. Their arguments felt sharper than usual, or maybe his nerves were simply stretched too thin. Leadership was harder on quiet mornings than on battlefields.

"Ogres, trolls, dragons. How, exactly, are we meant to choose between such scintillating options?" Eldrin asked dryly. "Didn't Bhalla have *any* opinion on the best place to start? He must have given you some direction, because while each race generally keeps to their own territory, if we have to search every creek a troll might have nested near to find the helmet Sozonos, then I might be ancient by the time we assemble the entire thing."

"If only time brought you wisdom as well," Weylyn said. "Too bad you'll probably be as puerile with white hair as you are with that yellow mane of yours."

"Too bad by the time my hair turns white, you'll be dead," Eldrin shot back.

"Neither of you will get a day older if I have to kill you myself because you're so annoying!" Ada said, momentarily silencing the group. She wasn't one to make threats, much less violent ones, and it was surprising to hear such things come out of her mouth. "Give Kaden a moment to speak, for the love of Orealus."

"Oho," Chum said with a chortle, "does the little lord need a woman to speak up for him?"

"Do you have a problem with women speaking up?" Millicent asked, sounding calm, but Kaden could see how tightly her hands were gripping her bow.

"Bhalla gave me a map!" Kaden interjected before the discussion could come to blows. Blessed Orealus, if this was how his company got when they were at loose ends, then it was probably best for them to pick a destination as soon as possible. "It shows where each of the pieces are."

"Well, so he was good for something after all," Weylyn said in a pleased tone of voice. "Show it to us, then."

Disaster averted. Kaden felt relieved and a little proud as he pulled the folded piece of paper out from between his vest and his shirt. He unfolded it and took a long look.

Wait.

What?

There was nothing written there. The paper, about as long and wide as two of his hand lengths, was old and weathered, dotted with stains and sporting tatty edges. But there was nothing on it.

"What does it show?" Weylyn pressed.

"Um." Speechless, Kaden could only turn the paper around so that everyone else saw the blank face of it.

"Is this some sort of joke?" Weylyn's tone promised that if it was, he didn't find it funny in the least.

"This is what he gave me," Kaden said. "It ought to be a map, labeled with the locations of the Armor of Orealus. I... I don't know why it looks like this."

Weylyn grimaced. "Maybe because a useless old charlatan of a wizard gave it to you!"

"Bhalla is not the type to do that," Queen Pepper assured him, but her calm assurance had no effect on Weylyn this time.

"I think he's exactly the type to do that. He's a trickster, admit it, good for nothing but making people dance to his tune and watching them suffer from afar."

"That isn't true!" Eldrin protested, standing up abruptly. Weylyn stood up to match him, the two of them squaring off for another argument even as Pepper flitted into the air between them, trying to intervene.

Kaden knew he should be concerned by them, knew that he probably ought to try and stop them, but instead, he stared at the paper in front of him. *It cannot truly be blank.* Bhalla wouldn't do that to him. Kaden believed the wizard when he said he wished he could help more. He certainly wouldn't try to lead Kaden astray by giving him something useless and setting him up for failure. He *wouldn't.*

I have faith in Bhalla. I have faith in you, Orealus. Show me the way. Reveal the map to me. The paper remained stubbornly blank, but Kaden wasn't about to give up. He took a deep, calming breath, then raised his hand to his chest to make the sacred *O* of Orealus over his heart. As he did so, the backs of his knuckles brushed the crystal pendant around his neck. For a split second, the pendant glowed, and in that same fragment of time, the paper seemed to...blur. Or perhaps...

Light spilled across the page like sunrise over mountains, forming rivers, forests, and ancient runes with a living, breathing precision that made Kaden's skin prickle.

Aha! A light to brighten his path, Bhalla had said! It wouldn't be the first time the pendant's light had helped save him, either. Kaden gripped the crystal tight in his fist and made the sign of Orealus again. A moment later, brilliant white light poured forth, nearly blinding him and everyone else in camp. The argument stopped. Everything seemed to stop for a moment as they all basked in the glow of the power of Kaden's faith. Once the light finally died enough that Kaden could see again, the piece of paper in his hand had completely transformed.

"It *is* a map!" Exultant, Kaden thrust the paper toward Weylyn, who took it warily and held it at arm's length while he examined it. "Look at it! It shows us where the pieces of the armor can be found, doesn't it?"

"It seems to," Weylyn replied after a moment. He didn't sound totally convinced, but at least he wasn't actively arguing against its existence anymore. "Who's to say that it's accurate, though, after appearing out of nowhere like that?"

"Oh, please." Eldrin seemed to be trying to be scornful, but the sharp edges of his temper were softened as he looked over the map himself. "Now you're just being recalcitrant for the sake of it. Pepper uses yah'zaval every single day. Kaden literally blew up an entire city not twenty-four hours ago with the power of yah'zaval. You've never had any problems with them, so don't make exceptions now just because you don't like the providence of this map. Hmm." He scanned it more carefully, his gaze lingering in spots. Redfern and Millicent both peeked over his shoulders to see for themselves. "This… is going to be a challenge."

"Hand it back to me," Kaden said, and Eldrin complied. He spread it out in front of him, finally taking a moment to really *look* at it since he'd passed it off so quickly once the picture appeared. Kaden frowned, wishing he'd paid better attention to his study of geography with his foster father. "Where are we, exactly?"

Queen Pepper came over to sit next to him and gently tapped the right side of the map. "We're here. In the Bardok Peaks."

"Huh. We're actually not that far from Kugdor, then." Those were the northern mountains where they had first met Bardicus, the king of the dwarves, a doughty race of warriors whom Kaden had tried to win over to their side for the upcoming war with Lucient the Deceiver. Bardicus had been relatively gracious in his welcome of them—he'd only fought Kaden a *little* and everyone had survived, which counted as friendly these days—but he'd turned down Kaden's request for an alliance. His people were already in a constant battle for survival against the creatures who shared their mountains, and he didn't fancy pledging himself to a fresh conflict led by someone who had seen so little of it.

Kaden had seen far more conflict since he last spoke with Bardicus. "I wonder…" He checked the fine print on the map, next to a dark star which indicated the location of one of the pieces of armor. "Omak…" He frowned. "Why does that name sound familiar?"

"Omak?" Weylyn clarified. "In Cragmaw?" Kaden nodded. "If I recall correctly, that's the name of the current alpha leader of the largest ogre tribe in those mountains. Word has it that the battle between him and the former leader lasted for three full days and nights, and only ended when Omak finally got the upper hand long enough to crack his opponent's head between a boulder and his mace, notoriously known as Skullcrusher. I hear he wears the broken skull around his neck."

"Where do you learn such things?" Ada asked, her face a bit sallow, eyes wide. "What person could get close enough to witness a battle like that and survive?"

"In a place like Westramore, news and gossip were valuable commodities," Weylyn said with a shrug. "I heard the tale from a merchant who makes regular cargo runs to the foot of the Bardok Peaks, who heard it from one of the dwarves who came down to collect a cartful of fresh vegetables they couldn't grow for themselves. He'd apparently heard it from an ogre they'd fought earlier that month, who had boasted that their new leader, Omak, would split the skulls of every dwarf in the mountains just like he'd split the skull of Og."

"It sounds like he's causing problems for the dwarves," Kaden said.

Eldrin chuckled, but it wasn't a happy sound. "Ogres and dwarves have been at each other's throats since before the last war against Lucient, and they'll surely be at each other's throats until the end of days."

"Still. Perhaps Bardicus would agree to help us go up against Omak." The more he thought about it, the better Kaden liked the idea. "After all, if he's got the piece of Orealus's armor known as Liasti, we'll need to confront him one way or another."

"Will we, though?" Chum sounded dubious. "Or could one of us just very quietly and carefully sneak into the ogre cave, steal Liasti, and then sneak out with no ogre the wiser?"

"No one sneaks up on an ogre, not like with the goblins," Eldrin said. "They might look like big dumb brutes, but they've got excellent hearing. In their caverns, they can feel every footfall, hear every whisper. Unless Queen Pepper has a gift for complete concealment…" He glanced at her, but she shook her head.

"I'm afraid not. Yah'zaval has the faintest scent to it, and a creature so attuned to their surroundings would notice one of us passing, even if we kept to the air." She looked at Kaden. "It certainly can't hurt to visit Bardicus again and make the request. Even if he doesn't want to aid us in recovering Liasti, he might be willing to loan us some guides to improve our chances."

"I agree." When no one immediately spoke up against it, Kaden nodded and stood up. "Then our first move will be to return to Kugdor and seek another audience with Bardicus. Hopefully, he'll be in a more helpful mood this time."

"Even if he isn't," Petey added, "at least we'll get to sample some more of his grog!"

Eldrin laughed and clapped Petey on the shoulder, knocking him forward a step. "Way to keep your eye on the horizon, friend. Get enough grog into Bardicus, and who knows what he might agree to this time around."

"It's settled." Kaden looked around at his company. "Everyone, pack up. We leave within the hour."

CHAPTER 3

It felt strange to be going back to a place he had been before. For months now, Kaden had been focused solely on going forward, moving on to the next step, the next challenge. Everything had been new, and now he was returning to something familiar.

A flicker of unease stirred inside him, a fear without shape or name. Returning to familiar places meant risking seeing them changed or destroyed, and part of him suspected he would not like what waited for him.

It made him wonder how it would feel to go someplace else he had been before, to see another long-missed face… perhaps the face of his mother.

How would she react when she saw him? Had she ever found her husband's grave? Would she ever be able to forgive Kaden for not being able to protect his foster father?

"—den? Kaden!"

He snapped out of his fugue and turned to look at Ada, who wore a worry line between her eyebrows. "You were grinding your teeth," she said. "I could hear it. When I called you the first time, you didn't seem to hear me."

Kaden did his best to shake off the sadness that threatened his composure. "Just thinking about something, that's all."

"Must have been something serious."

"Not too serious. Do you need something?"

Ada looked a little taken aback by his bluntness. Kaden didn't want to come off as rude, but he also was in no mood to discuss his complicated feelings surrounding his family. "Not *need*," she said at last. "I just thought you could use some companionship, that's all."

He swallowed. Ada always seemed to sense the fractures he tried so hard to hide. It unsettled him and comforted him in equal measure.

"Oh." Kaden made an effort to clear the cobwebs from his mind. No one deserved to be snapped at when they were just trying to help. "Are you looking forward to meeting King Bardicus?" he asked.

"I hardly know," Ada said. "I mean, I've heard tales of him, of course. My village was close enough to Kugdor that we got the occasional dwarves coming through from time to time. They were always very interested in our herbs, especially anything that could be used to flavor grog." She rolled her eyes playfully. "They were very singular in their pursuits."

Kaden had learned that among the dwarves, brewing was a solemn craft, bound tightly to tradition. Their recipes carried victories, losses, and oaths too important to forget.

Kaden chuckled. "Any flavor would be better than what they ended up with. My only memory of it is that it's very… strong. And foamy. And the smell, *whew*, it could make your eyes water if you looked into a tankard of it for too long."

"My mother is one of the dwarves' favorite trading companions," Ada said with a grin. She hesitated, then added, "She supplies more than flavoring. My mother oversees the Alchemists Guild for this region. Medicines, poultices, and antidotes. When plague or war comes, it's her people who keep villages standing long enough for faith or steel to matter.

"She says it's because her herbs are the best, but I heard the dwarves talking about it amongst themselves, and *they* were saying it's because she brews the most potent rotgut on the far side of the mountains."

Ada's firm and proper mother had brewed alcohol on the side? It made sense, given her trade in herbs and medicines, but still, Kaden was a bit surprised. "So you like them?"

Ada hummed consideringly. "I like them as… individuals. The most we ever had at our stall at once was five, and that was nearly too many to keep track of. We lost eight jars to breakage that day, and one of them tried to pay for his goods with a hand axe. Mother said no."

"She should have accepted," Eldrin said from a few feet back. "Dwarven crafts sell for a lot of money. Your mother could have bought fifty jars to replace her eight with what she'd have gotten for them."

"My mother has never been overly fond of weapons," Ada demurred.

"Who says you have to be fond of them to get a good price for 'em?" Chum called over from where he was striding next to Weylyn. "Money is money, no matter where it comes from. That was poor business sense on her part."

"It would be poorer business to try and sell something she had no sense of the value of," Ada shot back. "That's a clear path to being taken advantage of, and would damage her reputation for knowing the rest of her trade, which she absolutely does."

Was this level of bickering normal in a group this large, or was it just Kaden's luck that he'd brought together people who largely seemed to have little interest in getting along? He opened his mouth to speak, but Weylyn beat him to it.

"You two should save your breath for the climb," he said, pointing up the slope at where the trail they followed got lost in the rocky ground ahead of them. Their path was little more than a game trail now, but up there it practically disappeared. "We're coming at Kugdor from the way less traveled, and it's going to take every bit of stamina we have just to make it to the entrance of his kingdom. We'll be lucky if we make it there by nightfall."

"Have I ever mentioned how grateful I am that I can fly?" Redfern said, fluttering in a lazy circle above their heads. "Because I am. So grateful. Orealus be praised for his perfection in making us, the fairy people."

"Although it's harder for us to fly in the mountains as well," Queen Pepper interjected with a quelling glance at her bodyguard. "The air is thinner there, and colder. The chill saps our wings of energy and strength, and we work more for a lesser result."

"Anyhow," Chum said with a haughty sniff, "it's clear that Orealus reached the peak of perfection when he designed the satyr. Wisdom, elegance, beauty—we have… have…" He sniffed again, a long, nostril-flaring scenting. "Goblin," he said sharply, poking Petey and getting an indignant "Hey!" for it. "Use that nose of yours for something other than looking ugly."

"What am I supposed to be smelling for?"

"Just smell!"

Petey rolled his large yellow eyes and took an exaggeratedly deep breath. "I don't smell anything but your—wait." He sniffed again, and Bug quivered where he was perched on Petey's shoulder. "Is that… smoke?"

"Smoke?" Kaden held up his hand, and everyone stopped. "Millicent, Redfern, go look from above," he urged them. "See if you can tell where the smoke is coming from. We don't want to walk into a camp of ogres if we can help it." The two fairies flew up past the tops of the thick, gnarled trees, but Chum was already shaking his head.

"This isn't the smell of a campfire. It's too strong for that, too… *powerful*, if that makes any sense."

"Too many things other than raw wood mixed in with it," Petey agreed. "I can pick out a hint of bitterness, like camphor, and seasoned pitch, and…" He and Chum looked at each other. "Meat," they said in tandem.

"Orealus save us when the two of you agree on anything," Weylyn muttered, but his expression was serious. "We're close to the entrance to Kugdor. Do you think—"

The fairies swooped back down before Weylyn could finish his sentence, their hands wrapped tight around their weapons. "Kugdor is on fire!" Millicent exclaimed. "You can see the flames pour out from between the entry pillars. All about the clearing in front of it, there's a battle between dwarves and ogres."

"I saw King Bardicus," Redfern added worriedly. "He fights like a hurricane, but he'll soon be overwhelmed."

"Then we have to help him," Kaden said.

"If he's vastly outnumbered, there might not be much we *can* do to help, especially against ogres," Eldrin cautioned. "Ogres have sharp hearing in the open," he added. "They can pick up movement from far off."

The warning dragged Kaden back to the goblin caverns of Shroudscar, every drip and scrape booming through the stone around him. But ogres were worse. Bigger lungs. Bigger ears. Bigger consequences.

"We have to try," Kaden insisted. "What if Omak is there? We might be able to take Liasti from him right now!" It pained him to stand here arguing when he knew that his ally was the wrong term, friend was even less accurate, but Bardicus was someone he respected. If he didn't at least try to help in the dwarves' time of need, then he wasn't worth much as a leader. "Move fast but stay together as a group. Redfern, keep watch from above!"

"Aye, my lord!" Redfern flew away again, while Millicent positioned herself next to Pepper with a fierce look on her face.

They moved as quickly as they could without tumbling over themselves, but it was hard—the ancient granite crumbled underfoot after years of frost and heat, and the carpet of pine needles only made the climb slicker. The sun was sliding toward sunset, casting long, jagged shadows across the mountainside.

High on the ridge above them, a lone figure kept pace, silent where they stumbled. He moved with sure, practiced steps across the broken stones, always far enough back to stay hidden, always close enough to intervene if the ogres ahead broke from their lines too soon. His eyes never left Kaden, watchful and measured, aching with the effort of staying unseen.

Within five minutes, Kaden caught the first bitter scent of smoke. Moments later came the shouts and clamor of battle.

"We're almost there," he called back to his friends. "Get ready, and if we get separated, at the very least pair up so that one of you is ranged and one in close combat. We can—"

His directives were cut short when a dwarf, his beard smoldering at the tip, expression crazed, charged through the underbrush straight into their group. He bellowed and swung his double-edged axe around in a mighty arc, then cried out, "I hear you, vile ogrekind! Come close enough to taste the kiss of my axe, you coward!"

How was he mistaking them for ogres? Kaden opened his mouth to explain, but Pepper forestalled him. "No," she murmured, her expression pained. "Look at him. He's been blinded."

Blinded... Kaden hadn't seen it at first in the dim light, but now he could make out the dark stains on the dwarf's face right beneath his horned metal cap.

"Where are you?" the dwarf bellowed. "*Where?*"

They would have to go around him, but the way he was swinging that axe, wilder and wilder with each passing second, made Kaden wonder if they even could without hurting the dwarf—or being hurt themselves. "I'll knock him out of the way," Weylyn said, pulling his wolf-headed helm down, but Pepper stopped him, too.

"Allow me," she said. She flew forward, dodging two whirling strikes, and touched the dwarf on the face. The bright light of her yah'zaval ability flared in her hands, and she murmured, "Quiet. Rest now." It took a few seconds, but eventually the dwarf dropped his axe, then let himself fall to the ground. In sleep, the agonizing pain he had to be in softened, and he looked only sad.

"Come on," Kaden said grimly. "We've got to move."

When they finally cleared the tree line outside of Kugdor, Kaden barely recognized the massive mountain entrance he'd remembered from last time. Flames were erupting from its mouth, like it had been transformed into a dragon instead of a home, and the clearing was thick with bodies—some still moving, but many grievously injured or dead. Here and there, pockets of dwarves fought with half a dozen ogres, barely managing to hold their own—the ogres were more than three times the size of the average dwarf, and for all that their weapons were usually simple clubs, they were also terribly effective.

But the ogres relied more on smell and sound than vision, and with the crackle of the flames and their terrible heat overwhelming almost everything else, they were floundering, stumbling over bodies and into trees. It was clear the worst of the fight had already been fought, and equally unclear who was winning.

"There!" Eldrin shouted, pointing at the knot of warriors closest to Kugdor. "I see his hammer!" Bardicus wielded the Great Hammer of Retribution, a massive stone-headed weapon nearly the size of an ogre's own and far deadlier. They watched as he smashed it into an ogre's knee, the brute screaming as it collapsed. Once it hit the ground, Bardicus delivered a final, crushing blow to its skull—so brutal that Kaden understood immediately how ogres had come to fear him.

Bardicus was so focused on the enemy in front of him that he didn't notice the massive ogre coming up behind him, mace raised and ready to end the dwarf king's life. Kaden surged forward with a shout, already knowing he'd be too late, but—

The ogre stumbled and nearly dropped the weapon when an arrow pierced the inside of his wrist. Out of the corner of his eye, Kaden saw Ada pull another arrow from her quiver.

"Go!" Kaden shouted to his party. "Go now!" He led the way into the field of battle, aiding dwarves where he could and avoiding sprawling attacks by ogres, but mostly focused on getting to Bardicus before it was too late.

"I'll cover your back!" he heard Weylyn yell, and then all specific sound was lost to the fury of battle. Kaden had never experienced anything quite like this—the battle was pitched and hot, utterly deadly, and seemingly unending as combatants went at each other with no care for anything other than killing their enemy. The scent of burning filled the air, and Kaden did his best not to look at the bodies that he had to move around—so many of them, how could there be so many of them?

He was almost to Bardicus when an ogre with a rattling necklace of skulls came barreling through the smoke, a massive bludgeon raised high above his head, his mouth gaping in a roar that showed off sharp, bloodstained teeth. Kaden jerked to the side to avoid the blow and felt the ground shake beneath his feet as the weapon struck nearby. He whirled and closed the distance before the ogre could attack again, bringing Vrangar's keen edge down on the beast's arm with all his might.

Kaden cut right through it.

He stumbled—he'd expected more resistance, not the gushing stump that his cut had left behind. He stared at the severed limb in a daze, only coming out of it when he saw the ogre grab his fallen weapon with his other hand and send it toward Kaden in a wide, crushing arc.

Kaden ducked and closed the distance again. This close to the ogre, he could smell the stench of it, practically hear the beat of its powerful heart as it raised a boulder-sized foot to stomp on him. Kaden didn't pause this time, simply firmed his footing and jammed his sword straight up through the ogre's diaphragm and into his ribcage.

He must have hit the beast's heart, because the ogre suddenly collapsed in a heap, his eyes rolling back in his head even as his teeth gnashed against the empty air. Kaden stared at the corpse, the body of someone who had been trying to kill him, and shuddered.

How much killing would he do over the coming months? Would he ever get used to it, used to the smell and the heat and the terrible emotions? Should he even *want* to?

Bardicus. Focus on Bardicus.

Kaden moved forward again, but Eldrin was already there. He'd abandoned his bow in favor of his long, deadly knives and was slicing at the legs of the ogre wielding the mace with all the precision and grace of an elf. Bardicus was there as well, still holding his hammer, but it was clear his energy was nearly sapped—it was all he could do to keep his shield up, but the dwarven king wouldn't retreat.

When Kaden joined the battle, the ogre in front of him finally seemed to reconsider his prospects. Rather than pressing his attacks, he swung his mace in a large circle over his head, bellowing something incomprehensible to Kaden, then turned and ran with surprising speed into the trees. Kaden heard the other ogres disengaging and pursuing their leader, although not all of them seemed happy about it, judging from their snarls and the way they glared back at the jeering dwarves. In less than a minute, the fight was over.

In the battle before that, from what Kaden could see, over a hundred dwarves had been killed.

"Curse those beasts to the foulest pit," Bardicus said hoarsely, setting the head of his hammer down to use as a cane. "And curse *that one* especially." He gestured toward the entrance to Kugdor, which was still pouring out flames, although not as fiercely as it had been. "They poured barrels of pitch down our chimneys along the mountain ridge, then lit the whole works on fire. I didn't think they were *clever* enough to see through the disguises we laid over those holes." He coughed into his hand. "More the fool me. We're lucky we caught on quickly enough to get most of our people to safety. Deep caverns, with clear water and clean air," he said for Kaden's benefit.

"Why didn't you take cover with them?" he asked.

Bardicus snorted, then spat a bloody mouthful to the ground. "What, and let an ogre band get away with setting fire to my home? Are you mad?"

"But…" Kaden gestured helplessly at the bodies all around them.

"Aye, the glorious dead," Bardicus said, and the other nearby dwarves hummed their agreement.

"Your arrival was timely, though," he added in a generous tone. "Would have been better if we'd finished off Omak the way you did that one over there, but no matter. You can help us hunt him down."

Kaden was dumbfounded. "Really? *That* was Omak?"

"In the rotten flesh. What, you thought he'd let someone else lead a raid on Kugdor and take the credit, with his influence among his people already waning? This was his effort at regaining control of his tribe, and likely getting any news on a certain, notorious *someone* that he could. That's the only reason I can think of that he didn't work harder to kill me—he wanted information about *you*." Bardicus shook his head grimly. "How does it feel to be infamous, 'Crownling'?"

Heat prickled the back of Kaden's neck. Being known was one thing, but being hunted was something else entirely.

CHAPTER 4

"But…" Kaden stared around at his companions. "How could he have heard about me already? We've never even met! I've hardly… there's scarcely been…"

"Oh, forgive me," Bardicus said with obvious sarcasm. "Is there some other long-limbed human lad who recently imploded the goblins' ragged excuse for a kingdom? Tales are passing faster than the wind about the young man who, with his sword of fire, brought Orealus's purifying light to that particular darkness."

"Who is passing such tales?" Kaden demanded.

"Birds, mostly." He shrugged. "Not that I speak their languages, but several of my people do."

"Birds." Kaden turned to stare in consternation at Queen Pepper.

"Many species share a rudimentary sort of language," she agreed. "It's simply a question of accustoming yourself to it. I understand it, of course."

Kaden suddenly wondered how many of the forest's endless chirps and calls had been messages passing from beak to beak, sharing warnings, secrets, and stories all happening around him without his notice.

"Why didn't you say anything?"

She frowned. "You seemed so burdened already, I didn't want to make matters worse by telling you that some idle gossiping crows were chatting about you to a passing hawk."

"But that's—" *Something I needed to know!* Kaden would have to be *so* much more careful about what he said and where, after this. Pepper was starting to look concerned, though, and the last thing Kaden needed was to argue with her now when there was so much left to do. "Never mind," he said at last. "We need to go after Omak."

"You want to go after the creature who set fire to Kugdor just so he could find out information about you?" Ada said.

Well, all right, it sounded a little bit mad when she said it like that.

"Excellent idea!" Bardicus hefted his hammer into the air, and all the dwarves within range shouted approvingly. "The night's not over yet, lads!" he yelled over the crackle of flames. In the terrible orange light that was the ravaging of his own home, Bardicus's broad, blunt face took on almost sinister shadows, and the blood that drenched him made his armor seem dark and forbidding. "We aren't going to let those Orealus-damned ogres slink back to their caverns after this! We'll hunt them through the night, track them down wherever they choose to lay their filthy, villainous hides, and exact our vengeance with the edges of our blades and the flats of our hammers! What say you?"

"*AYE!*" every dwarf still standing before the gates of Kugdor roared, echoed by some of the ones on the ground, too.

"You've done it now," Weylyn muttered to Kaden. "There's no way out of a night march at this point. Lucky for us that ogres don't see well in full light—Omak will try to find a place to hunker down come dawn. And their fearsome size actually makes them fairly slow in a tight-packed forest like this, so he won't be able to move very quickly."

Kaden thought fast. "How many ogres survived, do you think?" he asked Bardicus.

"The old brute brought at least eight others with him, as far as I could see," Bardicus replied. "And we've got five corpses on the ground."

Nine ogres? Nine ogres had wrought this much damage on the dwarves? Kaden tried not to let on his dismay, but he must have failed because Bardicus sighed. Rather than get angry at Kaden, though, he reached out, clasped his shoulder, and shook him gently.

"This is what we dwarves are made for, Kaden," he said, his voice unexpectedly soft. "Some people are made with beauty in mind, others with speed. My kind is as solid as the mountain rock beneath us, though, and we fight to defend it as fiercely as anyone ever could. I lost track of that once," he added, his expression regretful. "Thought it was more important to close ourselves off and hunker down than it was to fight the enemy to the death and beyond. I might have saved my people by doing it, but part of me will always regret not taking a stronger stand against Lucient when it could have made a real difference."

Kaden swallowed hard, not knowing what to say to that. Bardicus held his gaze a moment longer, then let go and turned to the blind dwarf who'd managed to stagger out of the woods and find his way over to them. "Regar! Look at you, not dead yet."

"Not from lack of trying," Regar said proudly. "Got the scars to prove it, I'd say."

"Pretty they'll be, once they close up. Your eyes might not work, but are your ears yet undamaged?"

"Aye, sire." He nodded. "They'll do just fine for cleaning this lot up."

"Good. Save who you can, give the rest an honorable burial. If I'm not back with this lot of outsiders by tomorrow night, I expect you'll need to send someone after my corpse."

"Understood," Regar replied with a grin. "I'll see that you don't molder out there for too long, my king."

"You won't see anything, you cheeky cave rat," Bardicus shot back, taking a swipe at the other dwarf, who somehow dodged it.

Bardicus turned once more toward the fallen, his expression hardening into something older than anger.

"Aye," he said quietly, resting his hammer head against the stone. "The glorious dead."

The nearby dwarves bowed their heads, a low hum passing among them, not a song, but an acknowledgment.

Barrels were rolled out from the deeper halls of Kugdor, their seals etched with runes older than the gates themselves. Among the dwarves, remembrance came before revenge. Even as the wounded were gathered and the fallen counted, members of the Brewers Guild moved through the smoke-darkened clearing, distributing small clay mugs filled with a bitter, black brew. This was not grog for celebration. Each recipe bore the weight of a name lost, a battle endured, a promise sworn. The living drank in silence so the dead would not be forgotten, for a people who let their stories fade were already half defeated.

"Get on with you, then," Bardicus said, lifting his hammer once more, "and see that the names are remembered. Hammertoe, Malacheen, you come with us," he called out. A pair of familiar faces popped out of the shadows, and Kaden felt a surge of relief that at least some of the dwarves he'd met here had survived. "I want one of you to the front, one of you to the back! The last thing we need is to be taken by surprise after the day we've had."

"Aye, sire!" They split up, fading from view, and Bardicus turned his expectant gaze on Kaden.

"Well then, Crownling? Shall we hunt down Omak together, and you can tell me why you happened to show up when you did at the same time?"

Kaden looked down at himself, taking a moment to assess and just breathe. He was still trembling from the aftereffects of the fight, the surge of ferocity in his blood replaced with fatigue. He'd been marching all day already; he was tired, hungry, and wanted nothing more than to clean up, lie down somewhere safe, and sleep.

If he did any of that, he would lose all chance of gaining Bardicus's respect forever. "I'm ready," he said firmly. "And so are my friends."

"Aye." Bardicus beamed as he looked out over them. "So you seem, my prince. So you seem."

* * *

The walk through the woods took place in silence, partly out of wariness for their enemy and partly because, well… no one really had the heart to talk after the terrible fight that had just happened. Bug rode silently on Petey's shoulder, his soft cap shedding only a thin halo of spores that faded quickly in the dark. Their party was down by two members after Pepper offered to stay behind and help tend to the wounded, and Millicent stayed behind with her.

Kaden had been surprised that Bardicus agreed to it. Then again, as rough as he was on the surface, Kaden was beginning to realize that there was incredible depth to the dwarf king's soul. He was a warrior through and through, but he wasn't immune to the suffering of his people either.

He does what he must while extending all the care he can toward those left behind. There was a lesson in this for Kaden if he wanted to face it. Right now, wasn't the time, though. Right now, was for breathing and stepping; breathing and stepping, breathing and stepping. If he could do that, if he could just do that and keep it steady, then he'd be able to keep going. He was so tired—weariness lapped at the edges of his mind, trying to coerce him under, but he fought against it with grim repetition. Breathe, step. Breathe, step. Breathe, ste—

"Careful there, lad." Kaden jolted as a strong arm across his midsection jerked him to a halt. "We're coming up on the caverns. And the sun…"

The sun had almost crested the horizon, Kaden realized. It had been coming on so gradually he hadn't even noticed it, but now that the sunrise was nearly here, Kaden felt like he was stepping out of a dream back into the real world. Everything around him sharpened, his blurry vision cleared, and he could feel his own body again rather than forcing himself to ignore every discomfort.

Ugh, his feet *hurt*. How far had they hiked? Five miles, six? And there was the broken undergrowth and trampled bracken that so clearly indicated something massive had barreled through here not long ago.

Drip. Drip. Kaden turned toward the noise and saw dark droplets slowly falling from the tip of a leaf. Even in the faint morning light, he could tell the drops weren't dew. They were too dark and smelled far too pungent for that. Duke lifted his head to sniff at the leaf, having spent the battle barking himself hoarse and lunging at ogres twice his size, then sneezed.

Too foul even for you? Wow.

Redfern flew to a halt in front of Bardicus and Kaden. "He's in there," the fairy reported, nodding her head toward the cave fifty paces ahead of them. "Alone, and muttering to himself nonstop. He's moving a bunch of rocks around, too. Might be trying to barricade himself inside until reinforcements come. If you're going to get him, you're going to have to do it soon, before he closes himself in completely."

"Rock-sealing," Bardicus growled. "Son of a—"

"I didn't know they really did that," Eldrin said curiously.

"Ogres and trolls both can do it," Bardicus replied, freeing his hammer from where he'd stowed it against his back for the march. "They don't often, ogres especially, because they can lose face from it. If one of ol' Omak's competitors found him rock-sealed, he could claim cowardice and take the kingship from him."

"What exactly is rock-sealing?" Petey asked plaintively. Kaden silently thanked him for saving him from having to ask the question himself.

"It's a defense these big brutes have, a kind of torpor they can go into once they're tucked deep away in a cave," Bardicus said. "Anyone else wouldn't be able to survive an airless, lightless cave with no food or water or warmth, but an ogre can put themselves into a survival state and go for days, even months, like that without issue."

"Why not just let him seal himself up, then uncover him and attack when he's in a torpor?" Weylyn suggested.

"Because if we let him seal the rocks, it's going to take more time than we've got to open 'em up," Bardicus snapped. "This is more than slinging a pile of boulders in front of yourself! Ogres can fuse the rocks they touch into a solid wall if they put enough of their Lucient-damned spirit into it. I don't want to waste time unburying Omak just so that we can face a horde of his people again. No, we go in now and finish it before he has time to tuck himself away." Bardicus shook out his arms and stamped his feet. "I'll lead the way! Malacheen, Hammertoe, you watch our backs out here!"

"King Blakenshield—"

"Maybe it would be better if—"

"No arguments from you!" Bardicus shouted fiercely, and his subjects quieted down, clearly unhappy about it but not willing to gainsay their king. Bug huddled closer against Petey's neck, the faintly glowing spots on his cap dimming as if he sensed the tension.

Bug's whiskers twitched, and the faint glow beneath his cap brightened in anticipation. "We need more light!" Ada interjected.

"By the time the light's high enough to be of use, he'll be buried," Bardicus said. "Sunlight won't be much help in a cave anyhow, and we haven't any torches. Now, no more wasting time. We need to—"

"Wait," Petey said. "Bug can help with that."

"*Bug?*" Bardicus laughed incredulously as Petey took the hopping mushroom from his shoulder and carried him out into the little clearing in front of the cave. "What's that wee beastie going to be able to do to light up the darkness we'll find in there, eh?"

"Anything is better than us blundering in there and accidentally chopping each other when we're meant to be attacking Omak," Weylyn said.

"Of course, you soft creatures can't see as well as you should in the darkness," the dwarf king sneered. "Stay out here, then, and I'll take on Omak by *myself.* You can—" He stopped speaking as a cloud of phosphorescent spores suddenly erupted from Bug, spreading like a fast-moving cloud into the mouth of the tunnel and beyond, so that every inch of rock glowed like it was covered in brilliant blue stardust.

It was stunningly beautiful as well as bright, and Kaden couldn't help himself from whispering, "Wow," as he stared at the bejeweled cave. Bug sagged against Petey's shoulder afterward, his glow dulled and his fluffy tail drooping as the last motes of spores drifted away. From inside, a deep voice bellowed in consternation.

"Ranged and small-arms weapons stay outside, in case he gets past us," Weylyn said, coming forward to stand next to Kaden.

"Aye, good call," Bardicus agreed. "Hammertoe, you're with me at the front. Malacheen, you take the rear—nothing gets past you, understood?"

"Aye, sire!" Hammertoe barked.

"Aye, my king!" Malacheen replied, giving a sharp, respectful nod. Her hand briefly touched her heart in a traditional dwarven salute.

"And I'll go first." Bardicus cast a hard glare across the party, daring anyone to gainsay him.

No one did.

"Right, then." He strode into the cave at a fast march, hammer held aloft as though it weighed no more than a twig.

"Let me go next," Weylyn said quietly to Kaden. "I've got more experience fighting in tight quarters like this."

"Have you fought in a lot of caves?" Kaden asked with a tired laugh.

"You'd be surprised where the mercenary life can take you. I had to fight my way out of an *outhouse* once." Weylyn followed Bardicus, and Kaden and Eldrin went next after Kaden firmly told Duke, "Stay, boy."

"Good luck," Ada called out softly. Kaden glanced back at her. She looked ethereal in the faint morning light, misty around the edges, like a dream. It would be so easy to get lost just staring at her…

Omak bellowed again, this time sounding enraged. Kaden slipped out of his brief reverie and ran after Eldrin into the glittering depths of the cave. It went back farther than he'd anticipated, and while the first fifty feet were relatively easy to find his way down, things got much more challenging after that. Apart from the stench of the ogre, the air was filled with rock dust, and freshly hewn boulders littered the ground, making it difficult to find a solid footing. On top of that, Bug's spores hadn't spread as evenly back here. The phosphorescence was patchy, and Kaden had to stop himself from using his amulet to light up the way ahead. Doing so would ruin his party's night vision, and he couldn't fight with one hand on the amulet anyhow.

"*Graaaaaarrrr!*" Omak let out a bone-chilling roar, and a moment later, Kaden saw a shower of sparks erupt from where the ogre's mace impacted Bardicus's hammer. The Hammer of Retribution and its master held firm, but in that brief moment of light, Kaden could see the strain in Bardicus's face.

Omak filled the entire back of the tunnel, a half-finished rock wall protecting his lower half while he swung his terrible weapon in tight, devastating circles from above. The mace was too big for him to raise it high, but the studded head was still terribly dangerous as he spun it so hard it almost looked like a whip.

Weylyn stood on the left side of the cave, trying to time Omak's blows so he could dart past and strike at the ogre's body. Judging from the fresh dents in his breastplate, he'd attempted that several times already without success. Meanwhile, the ogre just kept whaling on Bardicus, as though he could drive the dwarf king straight into the ground. And Bardicus, being who he was, refused to retreat from the onslaught, bearing it and waiting for an opening that he was less and less likely to be able to take advantage of.

"We'll never get Omak like this," Eldrin said grimly. "He's tucked back there as tight as a tick. We need to make room to harry him somehow." He shook his head. "Of all the times for us to decide we could handle things without Queen Pepper's yah'zaval."

True, it would have been much easier to fight Omak if Pepper could have dissolved the ground beneath him the same way she had with the ogres they'd encountered outside of Kugdor before. But...

Kaden glanced at his sword. He might not have Pepper's fine control and understanding of yah'zaval, but he had blown a whole wall apart just a week ago. Could he do the same thing here?

"Maybe I—"

Clang! They both looked over to see Bardicus fall abruptly to the ground, dazed from a blow to the head that got past his defenses. Omak roared in bloodthirsty delight and raised his weapon to deliver the killing blow.

Weylyn, who could have used this moment of distraction to attack Omak when he wasn't expecting it, instead stepped in to defend the fallen king. He set his feet and bent his knees and absorbed the ogre's mighty blow against his shield as Eldrin darted forward with both knives out.

Omak was ready for him by the time he got there, though. He redirected his mace's flexible head from Weylyn to Eldrin and back again. Eldrin, who had none of Weylyn's heavy armor, was forced to dance back to evade strikes that would likely kill him if they landed.

It was now or never. Kaden focused his thoughts on his sword, making the circle of Orealus in front of his heart. *Be with me now. Lend me your power so that I might do what's right and protect my friends. Help me, Orealus. Help me.* Then, without letting himself take the time to second-guess any longer, he dropped down to one knee even as he swung

Vrangar in a high circle overhead, finally bringing it down against the stone floor of the cave with a tremendous *crash!*

A blow like that should have broken his blade. Instead, the power of his strike traveled along the ground and to the stone wall protecting Omak, shattering it into a rain of pebbles. Kaden gaped. His hands didn't even hurt…

"Get up and fight!" Eldrin yelled at him, already striking at Omak's cramped legs and drawing blood across the ogre's burly, corded thighs. Kaden got to his feet and stepped forward into the fight, leaving Weylyn as much room as he could for his longer weapon.

Omak was shaken by the loss of his protection, and it showed. His swings were wild, crashing into the walls of the cave more often than not. He garbled vociferously in his own tongue, and his eyes glowed with malice as he finally dropped his mace and pulled out a long-bladed knife with a bone handle, thrusting the point directly at Kaden.

Eldrin took that moment to stab one of his daggers straight through Omak's wrist, twisting it on the way out and severing tendons and arteries as he did so. Omak screamed with rage and pain, but he didn't turn his attention to Eldrin, staying intently focused on Kaden. He reached down and picked up a rock the size of Kaden's head.

"Crownling," he snarled. "My god has spoken of you to me. For destroying you now, he will honor me above all others!" Omak drew his hand back as far as he could, ready to throw the rock at Kaden. Eldrin and Weylyn both attacked him, but neither could reach high enough to dislodge the rock from his hand.

There was nowhere to hide. Kaden would have to try to dodge it. Omak reared back a little harder, opening his mouth to yell, when—

SMASH! From seemingly out of nowhere, Bardicus's mighty hammer sailed through the air, the edge of its heavy steel head striking the very center of Omak's face. It hit with such incredible force that the rough flesh and sharp fangs beneath it seemed to deflate on themselves with a horrible, wet sucking sound.

Omak groaned, dropping the rock and bringing his hands up to his ruined face. By then, Bardicus had retrieved his hammer. As Omak bent in two from the pain, Bardicus swung a blow as hard as he could right at Omak's temple. The ogre collapsed a moment later, all the fearsome life in him gone in a flash.

Bardicus grinned and wiped blood from his face. "That's the way of it," he said with satisfaction. "With him down, the rest of these beasts will think twice before returning to Kugdor." He reached down and grabbed Omak's fallen mace, propping it over his shoulder. "War prize," he said when he saw Kaden's quizzical look. "Get the one you came for, too, lad."

"I—I didn't—"

"I know the legend as well as anyone," Bardicus snapped. "You didn't come back to these mountains just to drink grog with me. You came for him, and for the belt he carries. Powerful magic in that, or so they say. It unified his people when I thought nothing but the lash of Lucient himself could do that, but it was never meant for Omak." He nodded his head toward the body. "Go on, take it."

"Take it," Eldrin encouraged.

"It's your birthright," Weylyn agreed.

Kaden took a deep breath, then walked up to Omak's corpse. A belt, a belt… but a belt that would fit a human would never be long enough to go around an ogre. But maybe…

Ah. Kaden could just barely make out a golden glimmer beneath the skulls on the "necklace" that Omak wore. He pulled it off, with difficulty, found the clasp, and let the skulls clatter to the stone floor noisily, and beneath it all…

A golden belt. The belt is known as Liasti.

The first piece of the Armor of Orealus.

CHAPTER 5

Kaden wasn't sure exactly what happened between when he stumbled out of the cave, Liasti clutched in his hand, and when he next woke up. Exhaustion, fickle beast that it was, struck him like a blow from Bardicus's hammer the moment they were safe.

For a heartbeat, he didn't know where he was. The battle replayed behind his eyes in jagged flashes: Omak's roar, the cracking stone, the wet crunch of bone. Nausea rolled through him, sharp and unwelcome.

He vaguely remembered hands on him, laying him onto a surface too soft to be the forest floor, while a voice in his ear murmured, "You pushed yourself too hard, you should have…" Then it drifted away with his consciousness, and the next thing Kaden knew for sure was the flickering warmth of dappled sunlight on his face, the crackle of a fire near his feet, and the sound of people arguing.

A dull ache pressed behind his temples. He wished waking up meant he could rest, but rest was something leaders never seemed to earn. Every choice he made followed him into sleep and waited for him again in the morning.

Of course. Because if they weren't arguing, he might actually start to believe they liked each other.

In this case, however, the voice doing the majority of the arguing was Bardicus.

"—told you a dozen times already I'm fine, so leave it be!"

"Wounds don't turn into nothing just because you ignore them like they're nothing!" another voice snapped, and—ah, that was Ada.

Her voice cracked at the end, barely noticeable unless someone knew her as well as Kaden did. Fear, not anger, trembled beneath her words. She had almost lost people she loved too many times already.

Kaden watched them, the healer and the king, and wondered whether leadership ever stopped feeling like being pulled between duty and compassion.

"It's just a bruise!"

"From being hit in the *head*, you confounded old dwarf! At least let me make you one of my mother's blood tonics, so that if you *are* bleeding up there somewhere, it'll be less likely to pour into the gap between your brain and your skull."

Bardicus grunted. "Too much like Mistress Davenrich, you are. I've met the woman all of once, but you're her spitting image when it comes to being bossy."

"I'll take that as a compliment," Ada replied firmly. "Now, are you going to cooperate, or am I going to have the last laugh when your feet suddenly forget how to walk?"

"Cursed wench, fine! Make the bloody tonic already."

"*Blood* tonic," Ada corrected, but she sounded pleased as she began to rustle through her sack. At least, it sounded like that was what she was doing. Kaden, who both wanted to know more and also really didn't want to open his eyes yet, tuned in his other senses to what was happening around him. He heard the sound of a whetstone on metal— that was probably Weylyn. He felt the warmth of a large, shaggy body curled up next to him, where he lay—Duke, of course.

Duke nudged his hand gently, a soft whine humming in his throat, a reminder that even when everything felt broken, some things stayed loyal.

He also smelled the scent of freshly cooked meat, and that, more than anything, was enough to persuade him to wake up for real. It felt like it had been forever since he'd eaten more than vegetable stew.

He blinked and began to sit up, stifling a groan as his body made its many aches and complaints known to him. The fight with Omak had taken more out of him than he'd realized—even as hardened as he was to both travel and battle by now, Kaden had just graduated to an entirely new level of discomfort.

"Kaden!" A second later, a soft, squishy body landed right in the middle of his forehead. Even as light as it was, the sudden weight and impact were too much for Kaden. He fell onto his back again and stared up into the dark furrows of Bug's cap before the little creature shifted around enough that his beady black eyes were staring straight down at Kaden.

Kaden was probably the first person in the history of, well, *ever* to be subdued by the physical prowess of a hopping toadstool. It was kind of embarrassing, but it became way more embarrassing when Bug puffed a pink cloud into his face, evidence of his pleasure that Kaden was awake again.

"Bug! You stop that!" Petey was there a second later, pulling his pet off and Kaden up to sitting again. He handed over a rag to wipe off the spores even as he began chattering at a rapid pace. "Are you feeling all right? You probably are, Eldrin said you'd come through the fight all right, and Ada chalked your collapse up to exhaustion, but there's really no way to know for sure unless you're asking someone directly to their face, you know? Only I couldn't since you were asleep, and I certainly didn't want to wake you, but you've been asleep for six hours now, and Ada said you might be asleep for *another* six hours, and that would be a lot of waiting just to confirm that you're all right."

"Let the man get a chance to catch his breath," Weylyn said. He was sitting just a few feet away from Kaden, working—as Kaden had expected—on his sword's edge, but sparing a warm glance for Kaden himself. "Even for the best of us, battling ogres is hard work."

"But if he wasn't hurt, then why was he the only one to fall asleep before he could even take off his boots?" Petey asked, and *ugh*, had he really? Kaden felt a blush coming on that he hoped didn't show in his cheeks.

"None of the rest of us used yah'zaval in the fight, now did we?" Weylyn shot back, then set his sword aside and reached for one of what turned out to be three skewered rabbits cooking over the fire at his feet.

"Here." He handed the skewer to Kaden. "Get your fill while you can; these dwarves eat enough for half a dozen men."

"Because we're worth as much as half a dozen men," Bardicus said from across the fire, but there was no rancor in his voice. "Are ye well, then?"

"I feel fine," Kaden assured him, embarrassed by all the attention. "Just hungry and thirsty." And needing a trip to the nearest bush to relieve himself, but that could wait until his belly wasn't growling at him any longer.

"He's better off than you," Ada said from where she was grinding something up in her mortar. She sounded tart in addressing the dwarven king, but her eyes were all for Kaden. "You are, aren't you? No strange pains or injuries that we missed in the darkness last night?"

"No," Kaden said. "Really, I'm fine." To prove his point, he brought the skewer up to his face and pulled off a mouthful of crispy meat.

It tasted…oh, Kaden actually moaned, barely pausing to chew before digging into the rabbit again. It tasted incredible, and all of a sudden, his feeling of hunger had graduated to "utterly famished." He devoured the rest of the meal without pause, tossed the remnants of the carcass to an overly attentive Duke, then reached for the next skewer.

"That one's for Petey," Ada informed him before he could grab it.

"Oh, sorry."

"I'll share," Petey offered. He pulled the rabbit to pieces, his sharp goblin nails much better suited to the task than Kaden's human ones, and handed half the spoils to Kaden. He ate it up with as much relish as he had the first one.

"The elf lad should be bringing back more," Bardicus said once they were done. "Good to see he's useful for more than prancing around with his pointy little blades and getting in the way of a real dwarf's work."

"You were full of praise for him when it was your life his pointy blades were saving," Weylyn said, as even-tempered as ever. He'd finally put away his whetstone and was rolling his camp bed back up.

"Where's Chum?" Kaden asked, finally noticing the absence of the normally voluble satyr.

"Headed back to Kugdor with the other dwarves," Weylyn replied. "To let Queen Pepper and the others know what happened here, and get them started on preparing for the next leg of our journey."

"Which is…"

Weylyn looked at him sharply. "Well, that's up to you, isn't it?" he said. "But for my part, I note that we're getting low on essentials. A chance to restock would be good."

Kaden looked at Bardicus, who sighed and shook his head as he accepted a cup of water with the powder that Ada had ground up mixed in. "That's one thing I won't be able to do for you. With my mountain home damaged only Orealus knows how badly, every bit of food, cloth, and grog is going to have to go to those who do the work of rebuilding. Even then, we'll probably have to trade with others to get the supplies we need to make it through the next winter." He sipped at the water, then grimaced and glared at Ada. "Augh! This is fouler than a goblin's bottom! Are you trying to poison me, lass?"

"Sampled many goblins' bottoms, have you?" Ada asked coolly as she began to put her own supplies away. "Just drink it and don't fuss. Honestly, are you a king or not?"

"Cruel," Bardicus murmured, but he drank the rest of it down without complaint—verbal complaint, at least. Cup drained, he handed it back to Ada and continued, "What I can still offer you is tradeable goods. Ye've done me and mine a great service, coming to our aid in the fight against the ogres, and again in the killing of Omak. It will make my people safer for a long time to come, not having to worry about that skulking brute."

"Oh," Kaden said, feeling uncomfortable with the idea of trading services in such a way. "You don't owe us for that. We're happy to—ow!" A hard-shelled seed from a nearby tree pinged off his forehead.

As Kaden rubbed the spot, Weylyn turned back to Bardicus and said, "Don't forget your largesse in allowing us to keep Liasti. Surely that is payment enough."

"On the contrary," Bardicus growled, looking offended, "it was a pittance. I'd have *paid* ye to take it off his filthy corpse. No, I insist on paying you for your troubles."

"It's never a trouble to help friends."

"No one should ever work for free, not even an ally."

Kaden watched the conversation with a growing sense of confusion. What was going on here? What exactly were they bickering about?

"Agreed, but my prince endeavors to be more than your ally," Weylyn said, and suddenly the stakes were different. "If he is ever to unite the tribes and rally the forces of light against Lucient the Deceiver, he needs to be able to rely on you because you believe in him, not because you have paid him."

"I don't know if I *believe* in him or not," Bardicus snapped. "But I do believe in paying for services rendered."

"Not good enough. If you insist on paying us, then we insist on accompaniment on the next leg of our journey," Weylyn said coolly. "So that you can see for yourself the kind of person Kaden is and the kind of leader the only living son of Karatheas will be. And remember well the results of your recalcitrance last time, King Bardicus," he added ominously. "Because you can be sure that the rest of us do."

A strange sort of tension drew out between the two, one that Kaden could only watch and try to understand from the outside. Next to him, Petey was as stiff as a board, and even Duke had stopped crunching on the rabbit's bones, sensitive to the situation his human had found himself in. Only Ada looked the same as usual, if a little more admiring when she glanced toward Weylyn. She caught Kaden's eyes and winked.

What?

"Ten pounds of gold and gems from my own stores," Bardicus said at last. "A pittance to ease the path ahead, as well as accompaniment from my people's finest warriors." He looked at Kaden. "You want a chance to prove yourself to me, lad? You've got it now."

"I… thank you, but…" Kaden looked between them and pushed down the half a dozen questions he was wondering in favor of the most important one. "Who will be coming with us, then? Hammertoe?"

Bardicus scoffed. "I said the *finest* warriors, not the clumsiest ones. Hammertoe didn't get his grown name by being especially good with his weapon, if you follow me."

"Ah." That made a certain embarrassing amount of sense. "Well, we'd love to have whoever you decide come with us."

"I'm glad to hear it, since one of 'em's going to be me."

Everyone sitting around the fire went still for a moment, shocked by the insular king's pronouncement. "Are you sure?" Kaden finally asked.

"I wouldn't say it if I wasn't sure," Bardicus replied. "What, have I given you cause to doubt my words?"

"No, no, it's just… I assumed you would want to stay and lead the reconstruction efforts." *And the fact that you made it clear you have absolutely no interest in the outside world, the last time we were here.* Despite not saying the last part out loud, Kaden could see that Bardicus was reading between the lines.

"The world is coming to Kugdor, whether I will it or not," the king said grimly. "It doesn't help anyone for me to stick my head down a barrel of grog and pretend I can ignore it, especially not when it means leaving us vulnerable to our enemies.

"The truth is, I should have seen this attack from Omak coming. I didn't—didn't have enough patrols in the mountains, didn't talk enough with the beasts and our trading partners, ignored the signs that would have saved my people and my home. My kind never shy away from a fight, and I know they won't blame me for this one, but…" He sighed and shook his head.

"It's been years since I allowed myself to lose sight of my people to help someone else." Looking straight at Kaden, he added, "I'm talking about your father, King Karatheas, by the way—when I lost my wife and children."

Guilt and curiosity surged through Kaden in equal measure. "I'm so sorry," he murmured. "How… did you find out who…"

"It's impossible to know for sure," Bardicus replied grimly. "No one who stayed behind in Kugdor that day survived. If more of our families hadn't retreated to the deep caves, our future might have been completely lost. Of course, my wife would not retreat. Eilin was a warrior herself; she didn't rule from the rear. But the slaughter that I found on my return…" Were those tears glimmering in his eyes? "Almost five hundred defenders, all of them brutally cut down. I have not slept well for years, living with the agony of their deaths, but I thirst with an insatiable thirst for the hides of those who took them away from me.

"When I saw the devastation of my kingdom, I lost all hope and gave up. I took my people and returned to the mountain to rebuild. Your father called upon me again when he needed me, but I rejected him. At the time, I believed that he and his family deserved to feel how I felt when everything was taken from me." As he finished speaking, his expression tightened, as though the words had left a sour taste in his mouth.

The final battle between King Karatheas and Lucient had then occurred, and Kaden alone had been saved while the rest of his family was killed. Tear pressure increased in Kaden's eyes with a sense of understanding and anger. He was taken aback by the admitted selfish behavior of Bardicus that resulted in the loss of his family.

"Rumor has it General Vicitious and his army were responsible for what happened to your people," Weylyn put in.

"Aye, and what gives your claim any legitimacy?" Bardicus asked inquisitively while his anger started to rise.

"A young satyr at the time watched his entire village get razed enroute to your kingdom," responded Weylyn, alluding to Chum. Bardicus glanced over at Chum, his sad, broken body verifying the truth of the claim.

"I told myself I would no longer be in the business of helping others anymore and would look out only for my people," Bardicus stated. "However, may Orealus forgive me, I swear that I will spend the rest of my life hunting down Vicitious and his measly dogs, and they shall know my vengeance. Accompanying you on this quest of yours will be both an honor of mine and satisfy the need for vengeance in my heart." His small eyes narrowed as he looked at Kaden's face. "I won't let myself continue to be blind to the goings and comings of those around me. I can't, not when the price is this high. Accompanying you on this quest of yours will do me some good, I expect." He hesitated, then added, "Unless you'd rather not have me as a companion. If that's the case—"

"I'm honored to have you along," Kaden said firmly, and he saw Weylyn's shoulders relax out of the corner of his eye. "As long as you're willing to follow my orders when need be. I've got a lot to learn, and I listen to every one of my companions, but if things become dire, we can't have two people shouting different orders. Is that agreeable to you?"

Bardicus nodded easily. "Of course. I've gotten my revenge, lad—or prince, perhaps, if that's what you prefer. From here on out, I'm just another member of your party."

"Call me Kaden, then."

Bardicus grinned. "Kaden, then." He held out a massive hand, and Kaden got up, leaned over, and shook it. "Well met. If what happened with Omak is a sample of what I've got to look forward to with you, I expect I'll have a damn good time in your company."

Kaden ducked his head. "We haven't been in *that* many fights."

"Except against other goblins," Petey murmured. "And grawlers."

"Sea monsters," Weylyn added. "And centaurs."

"Golems," Ada put in mischievously.

"Don't forget the ambush when you were poisoned by the—"

"Okay, okay," Kaden said, sitting back down and holding up his hands. "Yes, there have been a few—a lot—of fights along the way, but we've come through them all right."

"All the more reason for me to look forward to the road ahead," Bardicus declared. "Speaking of which, where will that be?"

"If I might make a suggestion?" Ada said. Kaden nodded. "My village isn't far, and it would be a good place to resupply ourselves. I'd welcome the chance to see my mother again as well."

Oh, of course. *Of course, she wants to see her mother again.* For a moment, Kaden's heart ached, filled with the desire to see his own mother—foster mother—again. Did she still miss him? Had she tried to move on?

Those are questions for another time. "It's settled, then," he said. "When Eldrin gets back, we'll head back to Kugdor. Tomorrow morning, we make for Whaldalf's Landing."

Where they went after that... well, that would depend on the map. *It'll be all right, though. We managed Omak, despite everything. Surely the other pieces of armor can't be any harder to retrieve than a close-quarters battle with an ogre.*

Surely.

CHAPTER 6

It never got easier to traverse these woods, not for Kaden. Each patch of bramble felt like it reached for him on purpose, tugging at his cloak as if the forest wanted to test his patience. He didn't have the forestcraft of Eldrin or the flying ability of Pepper and her bodyguards to help him move quickly and quietly, and every snapped twig reminded him he was the weak link in terrain that seemed alive.

The forest breathed around them, warm and humming, as if aware of their trespass. Shafts of green-tinged light slid across the moss in shifting patterns that felt too deliberate to be wind. More than once, Kaden caught the faint, rhythmic pulse of something beneath the soil, like a heartbeat, but he couldn't decide whether it belonged to the land or something living inside it.

Bardicus wasn't the only dwarf tromping through the undergrowth. Thalgrem Thunderfist marched beside him, silent as a storm cloud, his heavy gauntlets catching on pine boughs and shedding sparks whenever metal scraped stone. He hardly spoke at all, but his presence was impossible to miss. The dwarves forged their armor for echoing caverns and firelit halls, not whispering pine forests. Even muted, their gear hummed faintly with runes meant to resonate in stone, reacting awkwardly to the greenery brushing past them.

The runes held ancient power, vibrating with the memory of deep caverns and mountain halls. Kaden wondered if the forest felt the dwarves the same way he did — like a foreign noise pressed into a quiet room.

He didn't have Weylyn's stamina either, or the light feet of Petey and Chum to help him navigate the fallen branches and slippery pine needles. The more he watched the others move with effortless purpose, the more the weight gathered between his ribs. A leader shouldn't be the slowest one in the line, and yet here he was, stumbling over every root.

Every misstep felt like a reminder carved into his bones. Leaders were supposed to guide their people, not slow them down. He tried not to think about how often Weylyn or Ada glanced back to check if he was still upright.

The only things that kept him from feeling like he was the most hopeless member of his party when it came to making his way through this forest were first that Ada wasn't faring any better than he was, and second, the dwarves.

Nothing about them was subtle, not the way their armor and weapons announced themselves with every step or the curses they let loose whenever one of them got snagged on a piece of thorny undergrowth. They didn't get snagged very often, thanks to their propensity to cut through anything that stood in their way. For all that their mountain was surrounded by forests, it was clear that they weren't in their element amongst the trees.

Thalgrem muttered something in Dwarvish that sounded like an apology to the trees themselves, though given the way he scowled at a snagged beard braid, it might have been a threat instead.

"It's a good thing we're not trying to sneak up on anyone right now," Eldrin announced rather loudly over lunchtime on the day they left Kugdor behind and headed for Whaldalf's Landing, their packs light but their spirits high. "You two rattle like a cook set in a cart."

Kaden managed a weak laugh. If Eldrin noticed how winded he was, the elf didn't mention it, which somehow made Kaden feel both grateful and embarrassed.

"We can't all spend our days prancing about the forest with nothing to show for it," Bardicus said, giving back as good as he got. "Some of us have more important things to do, like ruling our people. Not the sort of responsibility your father wanted to give you yet, eh?"

Eldrin's teasing expression darkened. "Don't you speak about my father, you—"

"Lunch!" Queen Pepper plopped a bowl of her constant stew—which was the name Kaden had come up with for it after eating it so constantly—into each of their hands. "Do let it cool before you eat. I'd hate for you to singe your tongues and lose your ability to speak for the rest of the day."

Kaden wasn't sure if there was an actual threat there, but both the elf and the dwarf treated it as if there was, and blew on their portions in silence before eating just as quietly. Queen Pepper nodded with gentle authority, then moved on to serving the next person.

Her willingness to do whatever work lay before her was one of the greatest lessons Kaden was learning from any of his companions. Sometimes it was hard to remember that Pepper was, in fact, a queen—the ruler of a secretive but thriving people in the Enchanted Wood. She had lived for centuries, and her grasp of yah'zaval was as profound as it was powerful. She deserved every honor imaginable, not the rough work of cooking, healing, and whatever else the quest demanded. And yet she did it all without complaint.

Even Millicent and Redfern occasionally grumbled about their duties, but Pepper was always there with a kind admonishment and a helping hand. She was exactly what a true queen should be—concerned, first and foremost, for the good of her people, in this case, the people with whom Pepper found herself entangled on an adventure.

She... actually, she reminded Kaden more than a little bit of his own mother—well, his adopted mother, Lydia. He couldn't remember the other one, but she was also a queen who'd fought to the last rather than retreating. Maybe Kaden could learn something about her from Pepper someday...

"What is that look for?"

"Hmm?" Too late, Kaden realized he was staring at Pepper instead of eating the food she'd offered him a moment ago.

She smiled as he rapidly spooned some stew into his mouth. "I know it gets tiresome," she said, patting his shoulder, "but we'll be at

Whaldalf's Landing in less than a week, and we'll resupply with all sorts of good herbs and seasonings there."

"Oh, I'm not complaining," Kaden assured her when he could speak again. And he really wasn't—certainly nowhere she could hear him. He took a few more bites and then, still fairly full from breakfast, put his portion within Duke's reach. As the big hound cleaned the bowl, Kaden continued, "I was just thinking about everything you've done for us on our journey so far. I never meant for you to need to take so much responsibility, and I don't want to be a burden to you."

Queen Pepper laughed brightly and drew everyone's attention, much like a single ray of sunlight through the tree canopy overhead would. "None of this has been a burden," she assured him, settling beside him on a fallen log with perfect grace as she shook out her long white hair. "Duty is never a burden, and there is no greater duty in the world than fighting against the evil that seeks to overwhelm us. I'm grateful to be a part of this effort, Kaden."

Kaden let her words settle in his chest. Pepper never needed to command respect; it flowed from her naturally, quiet and steady. He wondered if queens were born with that kind of grace or if Pepper had earned it through centuries of choosing compassion over comfort.

"I know you are, and I'm grateful to have you, but… did you never think that a quest like this might be below your station? I mean, you're not just some person off the street or willing member of your society, you're an actual ruler." In fact… "What are your people doing in your absence? How are they being governed?"

"Oh, they govern themselves," Pepper said. "We fairies are blessed by Orealus in many ways. In addition to having long lives, we also love our simple lives and the allure of our routines. Honestly, when it comes to ruling, I do very little as queen beyond my ceremonial role back home.

"However," she went on more somberly, "it is entirely within my duties to step up for my people when the outside world presses in on our realm. As queen, I am our chief diplomat; I must know what's going on beyond our borders to better keep us all safe. While this mission is certainly dangerous, I would never say it was below my station. I have some of the strongest magic in my kingdom—who better to come along than me?"

"Aye, that's the right attitude," Bardicus spoke up. "No ruler worth the skin they fill leads from behind. I'd have to step down in shame if I tried such a thing myself. Makes me wonder why the elf whelp's father sent him along rather than coming himself, but—"

"My father trusts me to represent our people on the battlefield and beyond," Eldrin said, a vicious edge in his voice. "I daresay if you still had a son, you would be honored to let him fight in your stead as well, to prove his worth to your house."

For all of Eldrin's polished confidence, the strain beneath his words was impossible to miss. His jaw tightened, his eyes briefly flicking downward as if bracing against something old and familiar. Kaden realized this wasn't pride speaking but a wound Eldrin carried quietly, one he refused to let anyone see unless they were paying close attention. The entire party seemed to hold its breath for a moment, waiting to see if Bardicus was going to take offense at the mention of his lost family. Fortunately, he only shrugged after a moment.

"True enough, I suppose. My boy never got old enough for that sort of thing, but you're right—I'd have welcomed his presence by my side."

Everyone exhaled with relief, and Pepper quickly picked up the thread of conversation again before it could be diverted into another potential argument. "My people all know their roles very well, and my regent is capable of handling anything that might come up while I'm away. Admittedly, if I die on this quest, things will become slightly more complicated, but that's why Millicent and Redfern are here."

Just the mention of their queen's potential death had both of her bodyguards airborne, spears gripped tight in their small but fierce hands. "I'm going to patrol," Millicent announced before flying off.

"I'm going to go stab things," Redfern muttered as she too vanished.

Pepper chuckled. "They do worry a bit, of course."

"Of course." From where Kaden was sitting, they were rather more than worried, but he kept his opinion to himself. "So…" A thought occurred to him. "Petey," he called out to his friend. "Is it the same for goblins?"

Petey looked up from his bowl, the tips of his ears twitching nervously. "Is what the same for goblins?" he squeaked.

"Ruling. Is the ruler expected to go out and fight, or can he or she sit back and let their underlings handle things?"

"Oh, no goblin would stay leader for long if he didn't fight," Petey said firmly. "It's a matter of respect. For goblins, respect is based on fear. You fear those who can hurt you, and that usually means the best fighters. You saw how it was, going up against Garth."

"Yeah," Kaden remembered his fight with the powerful, vicious goblin all too well. If Petey hadn't taken the killing blow meant for Kaden… "Yeah, I remember."

"Not for satyrs." Chum lifted his snub nose in the air. "For us, the best leaders were the wisest ones, those with great age and experience. Fighting was for brainless young bucks—thinking was what our chiefs did best."

"It's the same for humans," Weylyn put in. "Sure, some lead from the battlefield, but there are plenty who can afford to pay to get other people to protect their interests. Just look at what happened to Empyrea after King Karatheas died, then tell me his 'glorious' death was worth it."

No one spoke. There wasn't much to say to that, after all. They packed up pretty quickly and continued their journey toward Whaldalf's Landing.

Everyone who'd come this way the first time around was on edge, constantly staring out into the looming trees, keeping their ears sharp for the faintest sound of someone else rustling through the undergrowth. Kaden hadn't forgotten the ambush they'd suffered last time—well, he'd suffered the most, but he also couldn't remember much of it thanks to the fever that had overtaken him.

He found himself drawing closer to Ada, and when he was in speaking distance, he asked, "Do you have any of the medicine that your mother used to draw the dark elves' poison out of me?"

"I do," she said, patting the satchel at her hip. "She made a point of giving me some, and I had to memorize the recipe, because it tends to lose potency over time." Ada looked around warily.

"Why? Do you think we're being stalked?"

"I don't think so." Millicent or Redfern or Eldrin would surely have noticed by now if they were being followed… surely. "I just feel a little better having it around, if you know what I mean."

Ada smiled. "I understand. It makes you feel a bit braver, doesn't it? Just having it in case. I feel that way now that King Bardicus and his friend have joined us."

Kaden nodded. Ada had a way of naming the feelings he barely admitted to himself, and every time she did, it made him feel both exposed and strangely less alone.

"Right." Kaden glanced over at Thalgrem Thunderfist, who had marched with them in grim silence for the past two days. Even now, the dwarf walked as if carved from the same granite they hiked across.

Kaden had once thought Bardicus taciturn. Compared to Thalgrem Thunderfist, however, the dwarven king was as chatty as Petey. Thalgrem had barely offered more than a grunt or a sideways glance to anyone since joining them, his silence as heavy as the gauntlets he wore.

Petey was the only one who had managed to draw even a hint of interest from him. Last night, in a curious but respectful tone, Petey had asked where Thalgrem had gotten his surname. The dwarf had simply looked at him, lifted his gauntleted fists, and slammed his knuckles together at full force.

To everyone's astonishment, a shower of sparks flew from the impact, lighting up the trees and even starting a small brushfire—one Bardicus had been far too busy laughing over to help put out. Thalgrem had only grunted at the commotion, eyes fixed on the fading sparks as if remembering some other fire entirely. Kaden wondered what, or who, he saw burning there.

At least Kaden was learning more about other people involved in the conflict he'd thrown himself into. With so many tribal leaders with him now, there was plenty of information to be had on Lucient and his four dark generals of the apocalypse.

"They might be called 'generals,' but what they are is cowards," Bardicus opined moodily as he stared into the flames on what promised to be their last evening on the road. Kaden had noticed how the dwarven king became more loquacious at night, the tension he carried around inside of him eased by the darkness and quiet. Or maybe it was the grog he'd insisted on bringing as part of his rations. "They had their underlings do most of the actual fighting, beasts like Omak. I don't think Lucient himself ever showed his face on the field of battle."

"There was no purpose to it," Queen Pepper agreed sadly. "He had so many enthralled beneath him to do his bidding… so many that were once so bright and beautiful. Ozul, in particular, was once a powerful holy being, a source of light and hope for many of us throughout the land of Empyrea. Then he became corrupted and began to hunt down everything he used to hold up."

Yah'zaval was meant to draw people closer to Orealus, not tear them away. Trying to imagine that kind of fall made Kaden's skin crawl, as if some part of his own connection to the light recoiled at the thought.

"The Soul Reaper," Weylyn murmured. "I've seen the result of his devastation. He's burned entire towns to the ground, stolen all the souls that lived within them. It's hard to believe a creature like that was ever more than the thieving bastard he is now."

"He was," Pepper insisted. "He was beautiful. My dear husband and I once welcomed him into our own home, and the forest was lusher and more verdant for weeks after his brief visit. He was one of Orealus's chosen ones… the depths to which he's fallen now are truly inexplicable."

"It's the same with Thyriel," Eldrin put in. "He was blessed by Orealus with great beauty and purity of heart, held up as the epitome of everything we elves should strive for, according to my father. Now he is called Defyle, and he has the form of a huge maggot, and pestilence-carriers follow him wherever he goes. He creates sickness, hopelessness, and despair. All because… what, he couldn't resist the lure of being more than the perfection he already was?" Eldrin shook his head. "Whatever Lucient offered him and Ozul to betray their faith in Orealus, I sincerely doubt either of them found it to be worth it in the end."

"Too late by then," Chum said bitterly. "They've killed so many now that they'll never be able to redeem themselves. They don't deserve to."

"Everyone deserves a chance at redemption," Pepper said. There were head shakes and noises of dissent, but no one outright challenged her on it, preferring to change the subject.

"The other two were bad from the start," Bardicus mused. "Baal has been his underling for as long as I've ever heard of her. Beautiful and deadly, she is. Lucient's little pet."

"No general managed to destroy more troops than Baal during the war, from what I understand," Weylyn said. "A battlefield is chaotic enough without dark magic making it even worse."

"Bad as Baal was, Vicitious was the worst."

Kaden stared in amazement at Thalgrem. It was the first time he'd actually heard the grumpy, silent dwarf speak! His voice was rough and almost too deep to make out. "Why do you say that?" Kaden asked.

"Because he's Lucient's most dedicated bootlicker," Bardicus said, and Kaden couldn't help but feel a little disappointed that Thalgrem didn't answer himself. "A lying little snake, he is. Comes by his name honestly, too—vicious a brute as I've ever heard of. He could tear families apart, make brother fight brother with the poison he whispered in their ears. To lose faith not only in your god, but in your own flesh and blood…" Bardicus grunted and poked the fire with a stick. "I can't think of anything worse."

"Oh? Are his lies the reason your people backed out of the fight, then?" Eldrin asked acridly.

"Don't you speak of my decisions during a time of war like you know anything about them, stripling," Bardicus growled.

"Why not? Because you don't want to admit to being influenced by one of the dark generals of Lucient? Or because you're more ashamed of the fact that running away was your idea in the first place?"

Bardicus's hand went for his hammer, and Eldrin's went for his bow. Thalgrem and Kaden stepped in to stop them, but it was Pepper who brought everyone to silence.

"Shhh!" She held up a hand. "Something is watching us in the shadows."

The fire suddenly felt too small, its circle of light a thin barrier against the dark pressing in around them. Kaden's fingers twitched toward his weapon, heart thudding in time with the crackle of the flames.

Something? Maybe a dark elf? Kaden shivered unconsciously, one hand going to where he'd been wounded during the ambush in the woods, an injury that felt far older than it was. Before he could say anything, Pepper waved her hand and sent a swathe of light out into the sky, rays bouncing off each other and their surroundings with such brightness it seemed like she'd managed to capture and reflect the fiery surface of the sun itself.

The creature she had sensed in the distance was soon surrounded by the light. It lifted its head, dark eyes wide and glittering…

And then the deer took off into the forest like it had a grawler on its short white tail.

"Ha!" Petey clapped his hands over his mouth, but the laugh had already slipped out. After a second, Kaden began to laugh as well. Then Ada, then Pepper herself. Soon, even Bardicus and Eldrin were sharing in a chuckle.

"Perhaps my nerves got the better of me," Queen Pepper said placidly. "I must be overtired. We should all consider going to bed. Tomorrow is our final trek to Whaldalf's Landing, after all."

Kaden wasn't sure if she'd used the deer as the perfect distraction from the argument brewing among the company, or if Pepper really had been spooked by something out there in the forest.

Either way, he was happy to bed down and put the incident behind him. Tomorrow was a new day, a better day.

And no one could hide from Queen Pepper's abilities, surely…

At least, that was what he told himself as he closed his eyes. But even as he drifted toward sleep, he couldn't shake the feeling that somewhere out in the trees, something unseen listened to the forest breathe.

CHAPTER 7

The party's mood rose as they stepped out of the forest after seven long days of walking and finally began their descent toward Whaldalf's Landing. Ada in particular was in high spirits, which made her more talkative than she usually was. It wasn't that she was normally *shy*, certainly; she simply wasn't one of the people in the group who was either always bustling around to help, like Queen Pepper or Petey, or apparently in love with the sound of her own voice, like Chum or Bardicus. Now that she was back in familiar territory, though, her natural effervescence and joy made her hard to look away from.

At least, it did for Kaden.

"I can't wait to tell Mother all about our journey," she said, stepping around a tuft of dune grass as they marched downhill from the ancient pine forest into the sparser, sandier plain that led to the sea. "I mean, I'm sure she's already heard about some of it from Captain Herrington, but I know it's not the same as hearing it from the person you've been wondering about. I wish I could have written to her."

"Not a lot of couriers or friendly faces in Shroudscar or Nethopolis," Kaden said.

Ada laughed. "That's true, but mothers can be resistant to logic. You know how it is. Have you sent any messages to yours yet?"

Kaden's mood mellowed somewhat. "No. I don't want to do anything that will draw attention to her, and…" How could he put this next part? "I worry that she might not still… feel the way about me that she once did. I mean, I'm a foundling, not her own child, and after I got my foster father killed—"

Saying it aloud made the fear feel heavier, as though admitting it gave it shape. He wished he were brave enough to believe otherwise.

"You didn't do that," Ada said fiercely, placing a hand on his forearm as they walked. "Goblins did that. Your father wouldn't want you to marinate in your own guilt for the rest of your life, and I'm sure your mother wouldn't want that either. I bet she misses you."

The certainty in her voice steadied him more than her touch. Ada never hesitated when defending someone she cared about.

I bet she does, too. But thinking about it just made him sad, so Kaden shrugged. "Either way, it's best I leave her be for now. What are you most looking forward to when we get back to your home?"

Ada accepted the change in subject, although her arched eyebrow told Kaden that she knew that he was deflecting. "I can't wait to have some of my mother's crowned griffin soup. It's—"

"Crowned griffins?" Chum shouldered his way between Weylyn and Eldrin and trotted over to Ada's side, his eyes almost as wide as his mouth. "Really? Your mother makes crowned griffin soup?"

Ada grinned. "Better than anyone else. You like it?"

Chum puffed out his chest proudly as he adjusted the sling hanging from his belt. He called it *The Annoyer*— a simple but deadly hand weapon made of braided leather cords and a worn central pouch darkened by years of use. "Like it? I could fight a crowned griffin with this thing if I had to," he boasted, patting the sling as though it were a legendary axe instead of a weapon better suited to nuisance than execution, but no less dangerous in the right hands.

Then his bravado melted instantly into reverent hunger.

"*Like* it? *Like it?*" Chum moaned, one stubby hand rubbing his belly. "It's only the best food ever created by humankind! Delicate steamed crowned griffin, a rare delicacy of the sea, served with pumperkale peppers and garlic cloves, potatoes, and a hint of fermented wine, all those delicious herbs and that special secret ingredient that I *still* haven't been able to figure out… aaaaahhh." He smacked his lips, his expression dreamy. "It's bliss in a bowl. I met a man once who'd been blinded by one of those fish, and he said it was worth it just to have the pleasure of eating it afterward."

"Blinded?" What in the name of Orealus was this… fish, Kaden guessed… exactly capable of?

"They're very bright," Ada explained. "As in, blindingly so. You can only fish for them at night, and—"

"Stop."

Kaden, startled, looked over at Eldrin, who had frozen in place, one hand raised. His eyes were trained on the dark smudge that was Whaldalf's Landing in the distance, beside the even darker sea.

Eldrin rarely froze without reason. A prickle ran down Kaden's spine, the kind that warned him the world was about to shift beneath his feet.

"Care to share your reason for freezing us all in our tracks?" Bardicus asked sourly. "Because I don't know about you, but I'm ready for a share of that soup the satyr was talkin' about."

Eldrin glared at the dwarven king. "*Look* at it. See the smoke?" They all turned as one to peer at the distant town. There were numerous small plumes of black smoke rising from it. "The people who live there burn seagrass to heat their homes. Sea grass smoke is blue. *That* smoke is from something else being set on fire. Furniture, perhaps. Market stalls."

All of a sudden, the homely, welcoming town had taken on a darker and more sinister air. "They're being attacked?" Kaden asked, his heartbeat suddenly racing.

"I think so."

"But who?"

"We have to go help them, now!" Ada leaped forward, only to be stopped by Weylyn's heavy hand grabbing her around the wrist. She turned and raised a hand to hit him, furious, which he also caught. "Let go of me! Let *go of*—"

"You go running in there without a plan, and you'll be worse than useless," he snapped at her. "You haven't even freed your bow."

"I'll kill them with my bare hands if I have to!"

Weylyn sighed and looked at Kaden. "What are your orders?" he asked.

Kaden felt the weight of a pivotal moment on him. This would be his first true moment of command since Bardicus and Thalgrem had joined him, and he didn't want to appear rash. However, Ada might never forgive him if he didn't act quickly and decisively in defense of her home.

His pulse hammered. This was no practice council, no friendly debate—lives depended on him choosing correctly.

He turned to Redfern and Millicent. "Fly ahead and get us more information," he said. They nodded and left immediately. "Everyone else, arm yourselves. We're going to keep moving, but we need to make sure we're prepared for whatever might lie ahead."

"And if it's more than our little band can handle?" Bardicus asked with an assessing gleam in his eyes.

"Then we figure it out when we get there," Kaden replied. "But I'm not going to leave innocent people to fend for themselves if I can help it. Ada's mother, K'Lani, saved my life; I'm going to do my best to return the favor."

They spent a few moments arming and armoring themselves, Kaden making sure that Duke's armor was working as it should. He didn't pull out Liasti—it just didn't feel right to wear it when he didn't have the rest of the pieces of Orealus's armor, but he had Vrangar. That and his regular gear would be enough for now. "Come on," he said grimly, and moved forward at a jog.

It didn't take long for the sounds of fighting to reach them. Screams echoed off the surrounding dunes, and as they got closer, they could see the flames that were producing the black smoke—many of the village's houses, stone on the outside, were burning from the inside out. Ada darted forward again, but this time it was Kaden who stopped her.

"We have to stay together," he said firmly, even as they kept moving. "We don't know what kind of enemy is in there. Our best bet is to attack in numbers, not fall apart."

"Then go *faster*!"

A rush of air announced their return.

Millicent dropped from the sky first, landing lightly on a weathered rock, her spear already in hand. "The town's under attack," she said without preamble. "Serpent-men. Organized. Not a raid."

Redfern followed a heartbeat later, hovering just above the ground, her wings buzzing with agitation. "They're dragging people toward the harbor," she added, eyes flashing. "Not killing everyone. Taking them."

Millicent nodded once. "There's smoke from the market quarter. And magic. Strong magic."

Redfern's jaw tightened. "A portal. Big enough to move bodies through. And whoever's holding it isn't hiding."

Kaden's unspoken question was answered as soon as they got a decent view of Whaldalf's Landing's harbor. When they finally gained a clear view of Whaldalf's Landing's harbor, the scale of the attack became horrifyingly clear. People were throwing themselves off the docks and into the water, trying to escape whatever it was that was chasing them. For a moment, Kaden's eyes refused to identify exactly what he was seeing, but when he watched one of the pursuers throw its own sleek, muscular body into the water and drag a screaming young man out by the back of his jerkin, he knew it had to be right.

"Lizard men?" he asked, looking toward Weylyn. "Really?"

"Orphidians," Weylyn corrected, his face grim as he drew his sword. "Serpents who walk like men, servants of the dark general Vicitious. Don't let them get their teeth into you—their bite is venomous." He ran forward just in time to step in front of another Orphidian who was going after the people desperately swimming for boats that had already been launched into the safety of the sea.

The Orphidian, switching from up on two legs to down on all fours as soon as Weylyn appeared before it, didn't appear to be armed. It had feathers instead of hair, bulging reptilian eyes, and not one but two forked tongues emerging from its mouth as it hissed in fury. It attacked with open-claws, and terribly swiftly, dodging the first few strikes of Weylyn's sword as it tried to get close enough to—to—

"Orealus help us," Kaden whispered as he caught sight of the set of massive retractable fangs in the serpent-man's mouth, fetching up against Weylyn's massive pauldron as he turned just in time to keep the edge of them from touching his neck. The serpent-man hissed triumphantly and leaped for another strike—

Only to be cut clean in half by Weylyn's massive sword. "Get over here!" the mercenary called out to the rest of them, "I'm not killing all these snakes by myself!"

The daze that had briefly settled over them at the sight of such frenzied violence broke, and Kaden led the way forward, Vrangar at the ready in his hands. Eldrin and Ada's arrows shot ahead of him, wounding several more Orphidians before he even got within striking distance, and from there it was just a matter of cornering the wounded creatures and finishing them off.

Easier said than done. They moved like serpents, sinuous and smooth, and were hard to hit even when wounded. One of them leaped from its lowered position at Kaden, teeth bared, and the only thing that saved him from a potentially deadly impact was Duke running in between the Orphidian and Kaden with a snarl. The serpent-man's fangs broke against Duke's consecrated armor, and the creature whimpered in pain just before Duke's jaws closed around its neck.

"Good boy," Kaden panted, then ran on to the next one. It dodged his first strike, but he caught it on the second, slicing a deep wound into its chest. The Orphidian backed away, hissing and snapping, looking for a place to escape to.

Perhaps this is my chance to get some information out of it. Kaden lowered his sword and stepped forward with one hand outstretched. "I just want to—"

A red-fletched arrow found a home in the serpent-man's throat a second later. Kaden turned around to see Ada, already nocking her next arrow, a fierce light in her eyes. "Talk less, fight more!" she shouted at him before turning away to pick her next target.

There weren't many out here on the edge of town, though—perhaps most of them thought the people who'd escaped were as good as lost. But the ones Kaden had seen them dragging away... that poor young man, who was probably his own age, what had they done with him?

"To the center, to the center!" a heavy voice called out—Bardicus. He and Thalgrem Thunderfist were nowhere to be seen, but Kaden could hear the booming impact of their weapons. "They've got a portal up!"

A portal? Like the one Bhalla had used? Kaden ran along the street he remembered from his last visit here, the one that led from the tavern on the dock toward Ada's home next to the market plaza. Ada ran with him, breathing heavily. There was blood on her cheek—she'd already gotten close enough to have to use her knife on one of them. That or she'd been injured by an Orphidian, maybe edged with a fang…

No. She's fine. Focus.

They made it to the central market of Whaldalf's Landing, and Kaden's jaw dropped when he saw the size of the portal there. It made Bhalla's portals look tiny in comparison—this was a glowing blue oval as tall as a house, and it seemed to be a two-way street. While some Orphidians were still coming out of it, more were going back in… each of them dragging a human along with them.

"*Mother!*" Ada's scream was piercing, fear and fury warring in her voice as Kaden finally saw what she'd seen immediately—her mother, K'Lani, gripped around the waist by a serpent-man who was dragging her up to the portal.

"Ada!" her mother shouted back, her panicked expression going taut with terror as she set eyes on her daughter. "No, run! *Run!* While you still—"

Whatever else she was going to say was lost as the serpent-man pulled her through the portal. Ada screamed again, rage winning out, and began firing at anything reptilian she could see.

Kaden was more focused on the creature standing to the side of the portal. On the outside, he looked like another Orphidian—not too tall even on his hind legs, and wearing a dark cloak that almost covered up the bright gold feathers lining his head. But he stood out for another reason, too—the long staff he held in his hand, its point glowing the same color as the portal. Was this the wizard who was holding it open?

The Orphidian seemed to notice him at the same time. A sigh came from within his hood, and a moment later, he lowered it and stared directly at Kaden.

It was like all the chaos around Kaden stopped, every part of him transfixed by the arrogance and ferocity on that serpentlike face. The Orphidian's slender pupils flared with darkness as they focused on

Kaden, and when he opened his mouth to speak, his twin tongues darted forth like whips.

"Kadennnn Sheparddddd," he said, his voice a sibilant whisper that somehow sounded louder than all the noise of battle. Villagers fought and resisted, serpent-men attacked and dragged them toward the portal, but this creature paid no mind to any of it. "Sonnn of the dead king, enemy of my great lord. I am here for you. Surrender yourself to me now, or everyone you care about will dieeeee."

Before Kaden could react, before he could even blink, Queen Pepper flew forward, white hair floating like a corona around her head as she gathered the power of yah'zaval to her. She let loose with a wave of her nature ability, thorny vines pushing up out of the ground and wrapping the Orphidian in a tight, painful embrace. He still had a hold of his staff, however, and pointed it straight at Pepper with a hiss.

Pepper's wings suddenly stopped beating, and she fell to the ground, both hands going to her throat as though trying to pry something away from her neck. "Majesty, no!" Millicent screamed, and she and Redfern surged forward from where they had been holding position, flying to Pepper's aid as the Orphidian shrugged off her vine attack.

"Take her away from here!" Kaden called out, already moving forward. This creature wanted him? Fine. Kaden would fight if he had to. The Orphidian's snakelike face split apart in a hideous smile, elongated fangs on full display. Kaden swallowed hard. Could he possibly avoid being bitten? Even Weylyn had been too slow to escape an Orphidian's fangs, but he had full armor protecting him. Kaden wasn't… he couldn't…

"Too afraid to come closer?" the Orphidian asked with a hissing laugh. "Then allow me to come to you, lost prince." He stepped forward, staff at the ready, and Kaden braced himself against the terror rising inside of him. He couldn't run, and everyone else in his group was fighting desperately against the serpent-men already. How was he going to survive this?

"Back away, snake!" Bardicus swept a path clear of his unlucky enemies with his hammer as he fought up to Kaden's side. The Hammer of Retribution was caked with gore, but glowing with energy as well.

Kaden exhaled with relief and fresh determination as the dwarven king stood firm at Kaden's side.

"Vicitious, you festering filth," Bardicus said, his voice an awful snarl. *This is one of Lucient's four dark generals,* Kaden realized. "Face me now, and see your death delivered to you, just as you brought death to my family."

"The buzz of insects like you is no threat to me," Vicitious replied, "but if you want a fight, I will satisfy my blade with your blood." His staff vanished, and in its place appeared a short, curved sword that was glowing with runes. The runes flared red, like a blazing fire hungry for fuel. Kaden looked at it and was afraid all over again.

"Go with Thalgrem," Bardicus said to Kaden as he hoisted his hammer. "Close the portal before this snake escapes his fate!" Then he charged, and suddenly—

Kaden didn't know what to make of it. It was as though Bardicus wasn't there anymore, which didn't make sense—Kaden could still *see* him, just like he could see Vicitious. It was like looking at them through a mirror, though, or reflected in a calm pool of water—they were there, and yet they were apart. Vicitious had seemingly multiplied himself somehow, and three different versions of the dark general were attacking Bardicus all at once. He was barely able to defend himself. Kaden longed to go to him, to help him, but—

Thalgrem Thunderfist pulled on Kaden's hand, bringing him back to the present. He pointed to the portal, grunted, and smashed his fists together.

Right, close the portal. He needed to close the portal. Kaden focused on the power inside of him, the gift of Orealus that seemed so powerful at times, and so impossible at others. *Orealus, guide me. Hear my prayer. Allow me to do your will here today, and end Vicitious's reign of terror in this town.* Kaden felt the warmth that was yah'zaval spreading from his chest out to his arms. Around him, Thalgrem fought off serpent-men who were trying to break through to Kaden, and then Weylyn was there, and Petey.

I can do this. Kaden raised his sword, funneling the power into the blade, then—

"NO!" Desperate hands grabbed his arm and pulled it down. The power that Kaden had pointed toward the portal went into the cobblestones instead, and Kaden was knocked to the ground by his own power. Next to him, Ada groaned, downed as well, but clearly unrepentant for having thrown his strike off.

"My mother," she gasped, pushing back to her feet. "My mother is in there, I have to go to her, I have to get her back—"

Her voice broke on the last word, a sound full of terror and love all tangled together. Kaden had never heard Ada plead for anything before, and it shook him more than the battle raging around them.

A fresh blast of power pushed her down again as Vicitious suddenly came back into view, not ten feet from Kaden. "Too sssslow," he hissed with that terrible smile again. He strode forward, and Kaden had no one left to protect him now, not after his own power backfired. Vicitious raised his hungry blade over Kaden, ready to strike. "My lord will favor me above all when I bring him back your head."

Before his blade could drop more than an inch, Bardicus reappeared right in front of Kaden and hammered Vicitious so hard in the chest he knocked the serpent-man into the air. Vicitious flew backward with a scream, right into his own portal, which immediately began to close. His army stopped what they were doing and slithered as fast as they could for their salvation, clawing and snapping at each other as they fought to get through before it closed.

"Keep one for questioning!" Weylyn shouted, but it was too late. Just as the last serpent-man entered the portal, it closed for good, leaving only the back half of the hideous creature's body behind.

"No, please!" Ada screamed, reaching out toward where the portal had just been. "Please, not my mother, *not my mother!*"

"She's gone, lass!" Bardicus snapped, looking just as upset as Ada, but for an entirely different reason. "She's gone, and that *filth* got away from me again!"

Kaden swallowed hard. Grief and fury rolled through the group like heat off a forge, but he forced himself to stay steady, because they needed clarity, not collapse.

As Ada cried and Bardicus swore, Kaden looked around at the devastation. Whaldalf's Landing was in ruins, the plaza filled with the wounded and dead. People were crying, hurting, and as much as he regretted Vicitious's escape, he knew they had other things to focus on right now.

The fading warmth of yah'zaval pulsed weakly in his chest, a reminder that his power answered purpose, not panic.

"We need to help those who are left," Kaden said, getting to his feet. "Do what we can for the wounded. Then we can plan our next move."

What that could be, he didn't yet know, but he wasn't about to admit that yet.

CHAPTER 8

Clean-up was so much harder than making the mess in the first place.

It was a lesson Kaden knew well, both from his life as a farmer and his mother's stern reminders that he needed to tidy the wreck of his room before he could go out and play with Duke, but seeing it on the scale of an entire town… He and his company could help, but the truth of the matter was that it would take weeks, perhaps months, to rebuild Whaldalf's Landing. That was time they didn't have to dedicate, although Kaden wished they could.

It had been different at Kugdor. The dwarven city was burned, but Kaden hadn't been able to see the true extent of the damage. He'd seen the flames, he'd seen the ogres who caused the destruction, but the city itself had been hidden inside the mountain, and they'd moved on too quickly for him to comprehend the true damage done. But here, in the full light of day, he couldn't escape the sight of burned and blackened homes, of broken market stalls and shattered carts, of dead humans and dead livestock… oh, Orealus, there were so many dead.

He forced himself not to look away. If he wanted to lead, he had to be able to face the cost of failure with his eyes open.

"It could have been worse," was all Weylyn said when he caught sight of Kaden's face as he helped lay a body down in the town square. It was the seventeenth one they'd found, a young man probably no more than a year older than Kaden. "It could have been much worse."

"I know," Kaden murmured, but he didn't really feel it in his heart. Not when broken families were grieving all around him, weeping over the bodies of the dead or wailing at the thought of what was being done to their loved ones who'd been pulled through Vicitious's portal. Every single family in this village had been touched by violence today. It was a feeling Kaden wouldn't have wished on his worst enemy, much less…

Much less Ada, who had exhausted herself from crying an hour ago. Pepper had helped put her into a healing sleep, but from the frown on her unconscious face and the way she kept tossing and turning on the simple straw pallet, the sleep wasn't very restful.

Kaden kept finding his gaze drifting back to her, as if making sure she was still there and still breathing. Saving the town felt impossible, but failing her felt unthinkable.

"Thank you for your help," the mayor of the town, an older, salt-and-pepper-haired man named Daven Jons, said as the last body was laid out in the square—twenty in all. His dark brown skin was practically gray with fatigue and blood loss, and his eyes filled with tears as he looked over his dead neighbors. "For this, and for what you did to protect us."

"I wish we had done more," Kaden said, feeling helpless. Daven set a heavy hand on his shoulder, grief and gratitude plain on his face.

"You did what you could, and didn't shirk from it. What more could we ask of you?" He sighed and shook his head. "And yet I'm *going* to ask more of you. The same number of people who are dead were kidnapped by those Orphidians. I have no idea where they could have taken them, but perhaps you have some way of figuring it out?"

Kaden considered it for a moment. "Perhaps we do," he said at last, touching Bhalla's amulet where it lay under his vest. "We—I can't guarantee anything, though."

"Any help you can give us is appreciated," Daven said earnestly. "They took my youngest nephew. I've been looking after him since he was two. He was rising fifteen this year, and—" A sob caught in his throat. "His older brother didn't make it, but…"

"I'm so sorry." Kaden was more sorry than he could say. "Perhaps we could—"

"Mama?"

Kaden whirled around to see Ada sitting up on the pallet, looking around in confusion. As soon as her gaze found the bodies, her bleary eyes widened with horrible recognition. "No! My mother, she—" Ada pushed to her feet, stumbled, and caught herself just before she fell again. Kaden went to her side to support her, but she knocked his hand away.

"We have to find her! He took my mother. I have to get her back!" She began to move away from the square, blind to the damage around her—blind to everything except her singular goal. She needed her mother and would do anything to find her.

Kaden couldn't let her go after K'Lani, though. Not like this, without a destination, without even her bow in her hand.

"Wait!" Kaden reached out and grabbed her wrist. "Ada, you can't just run out of town, you don't even know where you're going!"

"Let go of me!" She fought against his grip, but he knew if he let her go, she'd try to leave even faster.

"*Ada!*" He pulled her into a hug, wrapping his arms around her tightly, both in an effort to soothe her and to keep her from running away. "We have to think this through," he said, trying to be firm but afraid he was coming off as simply frantic. "We can't just head into the wilderness and expect to find your mother."

"Kaden's right," Queen Pepper said as she flew in close, her voice warm and sympathetic. "I know how hard it is to lose someone you love, but we must also be clear in our next steps or risk exposing ourselves to more loss."

Ada made a harsh choking sound. "What do *you* know about losing someone you love?" she demanded. "You're a queen! You have a whole kingdom of people who love you! My mother is *all* I have!"

Pepper's gentle smile faded. "I'm very grateful for the love of my people and the life I have now, but the truth is that I lost my beloved husband during the Great War. We were together for more than a hundred years before he was killed." Her bright eyes turned even brighter with unshed tears. "He was the best of us and made my life so much brighter. Everything I do now, I do for the sake of his memory and to uphold the example he set for me."

Ada finally relaxed, the fight going out of her body as she stared at Pepper for a long moment. "I'm so sorry," she said at last. "I didn't know."

"It's all right," Pepper replied, stroking Ada's hair away from her face as Kaden gingerly relaxed his hold on her. "I've had time to adapt to the loss. It will always be part of me, but thank Orealus I've learned to cope. I pray that you won't have to, my dear. We *will* do everything possible to find your mother and the others who were stolen from this place, I promise you that."

"Thank you," Ada whispered, and the moment between the three of them stretched with poignancy.

For a heartbeat, it was just the three of them holding the square together: Pepper with her quiet strength, Ada with her raw grief, and Kaden with a resolve that still did not quite feel like it belonged to him.

That delicate thread was snapped by Weylyn, saying, in his usual flat tones, "Now that we've all bared our hearts to each other, can we get on with tracking down those serpent scum?"

Ada exhaled loudly, and Millicent, who'd been hovering a few feet back from Pepper, snapped, "You've all the delicacy of a falling tree, you big oaf."

"Do humans of your size not come with a sense of empathy, or is it squeezed out by all the muscles you pack on?" Redfern added.

Petey shifted his weight and muttered, "In my village, we at least waited until after the screaming stopped before poking at everyone's bruises."

Weylyn shrugged and looked at Kaden. "What?" he asked. "I was just asking if we could get back to work. Feelings are nice, but results are nicer, aren't they?"

"I hesitate to agree with you about anything," Eldrin said as he straightened up from laying a blanket over the last body in line, too small to be anything but a child, "but in this case, I do." His expression lacked any of the good humor Kaden was used to seeing in it. The mood was somber, and pervasive—even Chum hadn't cracked a joke or made an insensitive comment since they'd begun cleaning up the aftermath of the slaughter.

"The problem is finding Vicitious," Kaden said. He looked at Bardicus, who had his helmet off and was inspecting a dent in it with a deep frown. "Do you have any idea where he might be?"

"Would that I did," Bardicus growled, his bushy eyebrows practically meeting in the middle with the force of his glower. "If so, I would have hunted that snake down years ago. He's a slippery one, though—rarely bold enough to actually show his face in the light of day like this. He and his people operate in darkness and moments of chaos, appearing and disappearing as quickly as a morning mist. North is the best I can do, lad—somewhere to the north."

There was an awful lot of "north" to cover—too much. Kaden needed more specifics. He glanced at Pepper, then Weylyn, but both of them shook their heads.

All right, so… no one knew where Vicitious's lair was. But Kaden had already promised to help get Ada's mother back—her and Daven's nephew and everyone else who had been taken through the portal. He couldn't simply say, "Whoops, guess that's not going to happen," and continue the search for the Armor of Orealus. This was another testing point for his leadership, a moment of truth. This was a problem he needed to solve, not just for his people but for *himself*. He needed to be worthy of their faith, their…

Faith. Kaden might not be able to track Vicitious himself, but he knew someone who probably could. All he had to do was get in touch with Bhalla. Surely the wizard knew where Vicitious could be found, or could at least point them in a more specific direction.

Now… how to contact him?

Faith. Faith in Orealus, faith in his plan and his love, would help Kaden when nothing else could.

Bhalla had decades of training, ancient knowledge, and a mind sharp enough to bend the world with it. Kaden had none of that. What he had was trust, a direct line of faith, and the bond Orealus had placed in him. Sometimes that felt small, but right now it felt like the only thing that mattered.

Gently, Kaden disengaged his arms from around Ada and let her go. She blinked, shivering as her body processed the sudden lack of warmth, then wrapped her own arms around herself defensively. She didn't flinch away from Pepper putting an arm around her shoulders, though. Good.

"Let me try to get in touch with Bhalla," Kaden said. He was tempted to ask for privacy, just in case he failed, but to think about failure in this context was to tempt it. He needed to believe he was going to succeed, and there was no reason to think he wouldn't. Bhalla was smart—he must have foreseen that Kaden would need to contact him at some point.

Kaden took the crystal amulet off his neck, cupped it in both hands, then closed his eyes. Making the symbol of Orealus in front of his chest, he prayed.

Blessed Orealus, please, hear me now. Give me the knowledge and the strength to contact your servant Bhalla, so that I may rescue your faithful people. Let me do your will. Please, let me save them. Help me to save them.

Then he murmured, "Bhalla, I need you. Speak to me, please." He waited, holding his breath with cautious expectation. A second passed. Then another. Another…

Suddenly, the crystal flared with light, so bright that Kaden could see it through his closed eyelids. He blinked his eyes open just as everyone else was closing theirs against the brilliance of it, the flash of light slowly resolving into a full-size image of Bhalla. He was standing, and given how Kaden was holding the crystal, that put his head about five feet over everyone else's.

"Kaden, ah! Good!" Bhalla stared down at him. "But this will work better if you put the amulet on the ground, I think."

"Of course," Kaden said, setting it down. A second later, though, he regretted his decision as Duke ran forward, tongue lolling in a canine greeting as he attempted to jump up on Bhalla before—

He jumped right through the image of him and straight into Petey, who was easily bowled over by the enormous hound. Petey hit the ground with a thud and an "oof!" and Duke, still propelled by the momentum of expectation, ran right over him and into Chum, knocking him onto his back as well.

"Blasted beast!" Chum snarled, his furry legs kicking as he struggled to right himself. "I'm going to—*augh!*" Duke, who by now had realized he was going the wrong way if he wanted to greet Bhalla, had turned around and stepped on Chum's midsection with one of his huge paws in the process. Petey managed to dodge the dog on the way back, but a second later was driven to the ground again by Chum, who had lunged for Duke—and missed. Petey's head landed right on top of the amulet, which made it look like Bhalla was standing on top of one of his pointy ears.

"If he starts using my ear as a stepping stool, I am charging wizard rates," Petey groaned.

"I'm going to hogtie that dog of yours!" Chum shouted, scrambling to get off a wriggling Petey, whose bobbing head made the light in Bhalla's image flicker like a lantern being covered and uncovered in rapid succession. People, much to the chagrin of Kaden's two smaller companions, were actually giggling at the ridiculous sight, despite the pain that they'd just endured.

Kaden grabbed Duke, who was about to lunge at Bhalla again, and hauled him back onto his haunches. "No," he said sternly. "You stay." Duke's ears drooped, and he lowered his massive head between his front paws with a sigh. Weylyn, meanwhile, was pulling Chum to his feet and brushing him off.

"Stop bellyaching, you're all right."

"I'm not!" Chum insisted, pointing a stubby finger straight at Duke. "I have been assaulted, affronted, my dignity attacked by that—that—"

"He's just a dog," Petey said crossly as he sat up, finally out of Bhalla's image. "Whereas you're supposed to be a grown satyr, not a teething infant."

"I'll teethe *you*, you little—"

"Thank you for speaking to us, Bhalla," Kaden interjected before all shreds of dignity could be completely lost.

"Oh, of course, of course, my prince." The jovial light in his eyes faded as the wizard took in the solemnity of his surroundings. "Is this Whaldalf's Landing?"

"It is. They were under attack as we arrived." Kaden recounted the bare bones of the fight they'd just endured while Bhalla listened. When he finally got to the end, Bhalla's face looked drawn; all merriment fled.

"The counteroffensive has well and truly begun, then. And this is *only* the beginning," he cautioned. "Lucient's generals are barely contained by him when he's present—without him to direct them, they will descend to greater and greater depths of darkness and mayhem in their efforts to outdo each other and gain his favor. Vicitious… he's one of the worst. There was never any honor in him to begin with, and now that he is empowered by Lucient, his atrocities will only grow.

"Send out a warning to every town and city you can reach," he said for the sake of the villagers. "Let them know what's happened to you here, and tell them to be on their guard. I'm afraid more attacks like this are imminent."

"What about the survivors?" Ada asked, stepping forward into Bhalla's line of sight. She'd dried her face off, but her eyes were still swollen from her tears. "Where would Vicitious take them?"

Bhalla looked at her sadly. "I cannot look directly, for fear that he will sense my magic and move elsewhere, but there's only one place I can think of that General Vicitious would take the victims of a crime like this. He will be drawn to the site of his greatest sin and his greatest triumph in the name of evil. He will take them to Karnergrien."

Karnergrien… Kaden knew the name, vaguely, but he couldn't place it on the map in his mind. It seemed he was the only one with that difficulty, though.

"Of course he will," Bardicus snarled, his hands tightening so intensely on his axe haft that his knuckles blanched. "Nothing makes that snake happier than spoiling what was once beauty. Must make him right at home, ugly thing he is now."

"Where is Karnergrien?" Ada asked, confused. Kaden sent her a silent thanks.

"It's the former capital of Empyrea," Eldrin said. "I've never seen it myself, but my father said it was once the most beautiful city in the world."

"It was," Queen Pepper murmured. "I remember it well. The golden spires, the white marble buildings, and the songs the people sang… it was as lovely as a dream, and the castle was the heart of it. Now it is a city of waste and desolation. Its destruction was one of Lucient's greatest crimes, and Vicitious helped him every step of the way."

"Don't concern yourselves with the castle," Bhalla advised. "That's the domain of greater evils than Vicitious. During the last war, he built a fortress at the far end of the plain that leads to Karnergrien. He'll have any hostages there, within its dungeons. Getting to it will be a true challenge," he added. "Vicitious is linked to all fallen spirits, and his fortress is rumored to be guarded by the dead."

"Why bother with Orphidians, then?" Chum asked petulantly. "If he can command the dead."

"The farther you take the dead from the place of their death, the less power they have," Bhalla explained. "It's easier for Vicitious to animate the corpses of loyal Empyrean defenders for his fortress and use his Orphidians as shock troops."

He looked around at all the stunned, defeated expressions people were wearing and burst out laughing. "Don't be so glum! This isn't the end of your quest, my friends. It's not even a detour. You would have ended up there anyway," he continued with a meaningful nod at Kaden. "Check your map. It's not even that far, although you'll have to go carefully to avoid disturbing things that should not be disturbed. Binicorn's Farthing should offer a delightful respite from the chill, though."

Kaden cleared his throat. "Thank you," he said, determined to be gracious even if it wasn't exactly good news. "We'll go there directly. Do you have any more advice for us?"

"Better than that, my prince." Bhalla held up his hands, closed his eyes, and spoke in a language Kaden didn't understand. A second later, Vrangar began to glow. So did the weapons of every member of his party. Even Thalgrem looked mildly disconcerted by the sudden brightness of his metal gauntlets. As the glow finally faded, Bhalla opened his eyes again.

"There. That will equip you to deal with any undead you may encounter on your journey," he said cheerfully. "Cold steel is the best answer for a creature of flesh and blood, but the undead are different. You have to drive their animating spirits from their bodies. The blessing I put on your weapons will do that—for a time. You'll still have to work fast, though. Their spirits will be able to reinhabit their corpses, if they're determined enough."

Chum made a face and pulled out his sling. "Wonderful. Murder the same corpse twice. Exactly how I wanted to spend my week."

"On the bright side," Petey said weakly, "at least they will be too busy getting re-killed to chase us as much."

"Our great thanks," Queen Pepper said with a bow. Her response set the tone, and the rest of them followed suit.

"Thank me by staying safe and coming back alive," Bhalla said, weariness evident in the heavy slope of his shoulders. "Fare thee well, my prince."

His image vanished. A shuddering sigh seemed to go through everyone watching as they returned to the present moment, with all its chaos and despair. Several people began to cry, and as Daven went to comfort them, Kaden turned to his company.

"We leave first thing tomorrow," he said.

"Why not now?" Ada demanded.

"Because there are people right here, right now, who could use our help," Kaden replied. "The very least we can do is assist them with the bodies before we move on. Besides, I need to spend some time with the map to make sure I know where to go next."

"That's honorable of ye," Bardicus said with approval. "Come. Let's get some pyres built for these poor souls. Then I'm going to fix my armor. *Then* I'm going to imagine all the ways I could skin that scaly bastard, and where I'll hang his pelt when I'm done with him."

Whatever made the dwarf king happy. "All right," Kaden said, nodding. "Let's get to work."

CHAPTER 9

Binicorn's Farthing was no more than a day's hike to the south. Kaden was grateful for that—it gave him a clear-cut goal to focus on, something he could use to rein in Ada's desire to run ahead. He knew she was suffering, and he wanted to help her feel better as soon as possible. That meant getting to Karnergrien quickly, and the ancient city was just beyond the Farthing. At the same time, though… he dreaded the closeness.

Every step they took was a step toward the truth, and the truth might not be something that Ada was ready to face. Kaden remembered all too vividly how devastated he'd been when Daneyel died in his arms. He'd gone on because he *had* to, because if he didn't, he might have put his foster mother in even greater danger. He'd been driven onward by sheer necessity, but he still ached whenever he thought about losing the father he'd always known, who had been *his* all through his childhood. Ada couldn't remember losing her father, but if K'Lani was dead…

Kaden's throat tightened. He hated that leadership meant walking straight toward pain instead of away from it. Strength wasn't always swinging a sword; sometimes it was choosing not to run from the things that terrified him.

Kaden firmed his jaw. It wouldn't do for him to think too much about that right now, either. Worry wasn't going to keep his friends safe. For that, he needed to pay attention to his surroundings and make sure he was doing the best job possible of leading them through a place that, legend had it, was once one of the most beautiful sights the world had ever known.

Coming up over the last hill that led down into the valley of Binicorn's Farthing, Kaden couldn't see any of that beauty now. "Oh no," he whispered as he stopped at the apex of the rocky hilltop, his feet like stones.

Everywhere was the gray of ash or the black of burnt ground. The smell of it tainted the air, and the small trickle of water that was wending its way through the devastation was black and foul as well. Here and there were things that might have been the stumps of mighty trees, and the mountain that rose gently above it all could have once been beautiful. Now it was nothing but a blackened shell of a valley.

The air felt thin here, empty in a way that made Kaden's skin prickle. Even the yah'zaval energy seemed quieter in this place, its warmth pulled inward instead of flowing freely. It was as if Orealus himself had withdrawn his presence from the valley.

Even Ada was drawn out of her internal devastation to exclaim over what they were seeing here. "What happened?" she asked quietly, her eyes automatically turning to Queen Pepper.

"What does it look like?" Eldrin asked, his tone unexpectedly harsh. "Death. Just like everything that comes from that giant skyworm Morvar."

Kaden caught the tightness in Eldrin's jaw. This wasn't just anger; it was grief wearing sharper clothes.

"Eldrin," Queen Pepper began gently, but he was already moving away from the rest of them.

"I'll scout ahead," he shouted back, his voice angry. Queen Pepper sighed, then turned to look at the rest of them.

"This is where Binicorn's Farthing used to be," she said. Her voice was rich with both affection and dismay. "Not long ago, there lived the Agwhin—what we know of as binicorns. They were said to be among Orealus's first creations, and some of his most beautiful. They had the bodies of horses, but they also had two huge, spiraling horns coming out of the back of their heads. I remember being astonished by them when I first met a binicorn," she said with a little laugh. "I asked if they were for fighting, like the heavy horns of the mountain sheep or the antlers the deer sport. The binicorn—Vidalius, I think—he told me that they were instead made first and foremost for beauty. And they certainly were beautiful."

"Too gentle, those beasts," Bardicus put in, but even his normal terse tones were tinged with sadness. "I've met a binicorn or two in my day as well, and they were nothing but big, gentle fools. Blessed by Orealus, for sure, but not so smart when it came to being careful of their own lives. We *knew* something was going to happen; there was no way Lucient would let a place like this stand as a shrine to Orealus when he could destroy it so easily. We told them to leave, but…"

"This was the only place they knew," Pepper said. "I'm sure they couldn't imagine leaving it. Who *can* imagine the destruction of everything they know and love when they've never experienced that sort of loss before? And this place was…" She inhaled deeply, then winced. "Special. A fertile oasis in an otherwise inhospitable part of the world. There was a lake, fed by waterfalls from the mountain, and the most gorgeous, stately trees you've ever seen, the same type Eldrin's own home is made from."

Oh. Maybe that explained why he'd rushed ahead, then. He couldn't bear looking at the remains of a place that reminded him so much of Brightshire Forest. Kaden watched his elven friend stalk off into the distance and shook his head.

"Lucient sent Morvar after them," Queen Pepper went on, her eyes distant. "Lord of the Skies, bringer of death. Of all the dark powers gathered under Lucient's banner, Morvar must be one of the very worst. He is blacker than the darkest night, and glimmers like obsidian." Her voice was low, hypnotic—Kaden found himself visualizing Morvar with more and more detail as she spoke.

"His serpentine body moved as smoothly through the air as it did on the ground, with deadly grace and terrible beauty. His body was armored with spikes, his wings with talons. His horns were longer than three men laid foot to head, and sharp enough to cut flesh like gossamer. And the flames of his breath…" She shuddered. "They were hot enough to cook men in their armor, hot enough to turn anything living into ash.

I only ever saw him once on the battlefield, and we lost over a thousand soldiers that day. It would have been worse if he had more of a will to kill and was less susceptible to distraction."

"Speaking of distraction," Weylyn interjected, not ungently. "Morvar's a big, scary flying monster. Got it. Why does he matter right now?"

"He matters because you should know what you're getting into, ye daft human," Bardicus snapped.

"Morvar had been trying to destroy the binicorns for centuries," Pepper said, bringing the story back on track as they slowly descended into the valley after Eldrin, who was so far ahead now that Kaden could barely make out his silhouette. "He was held back by Andaluria the Windwalker, the oldest of the Agwhin. He was pure white and supposedly untamable by anyone except Orealus himself. But this last time…"

"Sounds like a tall tale," Weylyn said.

"Binicorns are real," Kaden protested, a half-forgotten memory playing at the edges of his mind. "Petey and I saw one in the forest outside my home. Just a glimpse, but it was beautiful." The creature had appeared as ephemeral as mist, but real.

"Good thing it never caught up to us," Petey muttered, looking around as they marched across the dead valley. The ends of his ears twitched anxiously. "And good riddance to all of them, I say. Binicorns don't like goblins."

"And why should they?" Redfern asked as she flew by, lightly slapping Petey across the back of the head. "Goblins and trolls and all sorts of dark creatures have hounded binicorns across all of Empyrea! Even men have partaken in the occasional binicorn hunt. If you escaped being skewered or trampled, you should count yourself lucky."

"I do!"

Chum shuddered dramatically and held up his sling as if it might ward off ancient spirits. "If a binicorn had charged us, this beauty would've slowed it right down. Annoyed it, at least. Probably right before it trampled me into a handsome satyr pancake."

"What about the dragon?" Kaden asked. Wind swirled around him, spotting his clothes with ash and dust. He glanced back at Ada, but she seemed unable to hear their conversation, walking stolidly along with her head down, hiding her red-rimmed eyes. He reached out and took her hand, drawing her back into the party. She gave his fingers a light squeeze of acknowledgment.

Her grip was steady, but her eyes were hollow. Ada wasn't really here. She was already running ahead in her mind, chasing a mother who might not be able to answer back.

"Should we expect to see him here?"

Bardicus shook his head. "Doubt it," he said, glancing at Thalgrem. The other dwarf just shrugged. "Dragons only come out when they're hungry or driven. They're powerful brutes, but they don't like to work if they don't have to. When they *do* come out, other dark creatures run for cover. I doubt the ogres and the Ophidians would have been so active over the past week if they knew a dragon might appear at any moment. Morvar would cut them down as readily as he does everything else without Lucient holding him back."

"Rumor has it that Morvar sleeps in a hidden cavern far to the north, blocking his treasure in with his enormous body so that no one else can see it," Millicent added in a tone of relish.

"I hope we do see him," Weylyn said abruptly. Everyone at the party turned to stare at him.

"Why?" Kaden asked, dumbfounded.

"I've got a bone to pick with that beast." Weylyn's eyes were unusually bright. "He's one of the reasons my father died."

"*Ugh*," Chum moaned, rolling his eyes toward the clouds as he picked his way across a rocky section of ground, hooves clopping noisily. "If I've said it once, I've said it a dozen times, you oaf! There's no 'bone picking' to be done with a dragon! The little ones, maybe, if you get them on the ground and hold them down long enough to shove a spear down their throat or through an eye, *maybe* you could walk away from that. But Morvar? No weapon's getting through that hide."

"And I've told you a dozen times, you're wrong," Weylyn said staunchly.

Unexpectedly, Bardicus chimed in. "Even a beast like Morvar can be killed with the right material. Takes a piece of the dragon you mean to slay to do it, and you have to have a forge capable of melding scales and dratonium together, but they *do* exist. We had a weapon like that in Kugdor, made many generations ago by one of my forefathers, an axe with a head as long as my own body. The dragon it killed was red, not black, but it was a mighty beast nonetheless."

Weylyn looked at him sharply. "Would that axe work on another dragon?"

"The unfortunate death of my grandfather tells me 'no,'" Bardicus replied sourly. "He thought to try his luck with one of the smaller drakes. He took the red-bladed axe, hunted the dragon to its lair, and set upon it there. The blade shattered with the first strike, and my grandfather was eaten shortly thereafter."

"Why did it shatter?" Kaden asked.

"Hard to say for sure. Perhaps because it was so old, or it might have to do with how the dragons grow their scales." He hefted his hammer for a moment, rubbing one of his broad, gnarled hands across the head. "Metal has its own sort of life within it, tones and threads that can leave it singing as it strikes or crack under the pressure. Hit the wrong thing with it, and even the finest forged steel can break. Strike a dragon's hide with a weapon that isn't attuned to the dragon's own song, and you and your weapon will lose your lives."

"We'll have to face Morvar eventually," Petey said glumly, glancing at Kaden. "He's guarding one of the pieces of armor. The, um, the breastplate, I think."

"Oh." Oh, great. Wonderful. Just what Kaden wanted to do, go up against a huge, almost-immortal dragon and hope for the best. His stomach sank like a stone.

He tried to steady his breathing. Facing ogres had been terrifying, fighting Omak had nearly killed him, but a dragon was something else entirely. A creature older than kingdoms. A beast even heroes whispered about. What was he compared to that?

Pepper looked at him with a gentle smile and patted his shoulder. "Let's catch up to Eldrin, hmm? A few more miles and we'll be out of the Farthing. Things will look better on the other side."

It was a sweet promise, but not one that could be kept. By the time they got to the other side of Binicorn's Farthing, a walk that took most of the day, they had left the ash behind in exchange for a wet, soggy depression of a field covered by mist. In the distance, Kaden could just make out what could have been the ruins of a great building.

Eldrin had already gathered firewood and hung his hammock. He was crouched over the logs he'd assembled, trying to get them to light, but the wood was damp, and the going was slow. "It might be a cold camp tonight," he said as they joined him, like he hadn't run ahead of them all day to be by himself. No one called him out on it, though. They were all too tired, their thoughts weighed down by the magnitude of what they'd just traveled through. Something that could lay waste to so much land, with such ferocity… how was such a creature to be handled? How could they hope to destroy Morvar, or even distract him long enough for Kaden to get the breastplate Justicia from him?

"Let me help," Queen Pepper said, and pointed her hand at the logs. Sparks of fire ran along them, pushing steam into the air, and a moment later the wood caught and began to burn merrily.

"Thank you." Eldrin nodded to her.

"It's my pleasure." She went to get the cooking items, and Kaden took a moment to speak softly with Ada.

"Are you all right?" he asked. She'd hardly said two words all day.

The silence that answered him felt heavier than the ash they'd walked through. Ada had never been quiet before and never withdrawn. Seeing her like this made Kaden feel helpless in a way battle never had.

"I'm fine," she said, not looking at him. She was looking at the ruins in the distance, her eyes avid. "Do you think my mother is there?"

"I think we're going to find out," Kaden replied. "Tomorrow, we'll—"

"Kaden!" Petey called from the edge of their campfire's light. His voice quavered, and he'd already drawn Loyal Dwingent.

"What is it?" Kaden asked, rushing over to Petey's side. The goblin's bright yellow eyes glowed as he stared out into the darkness, and his ears were stiff.

"There are things moving out there," he said.

The mist curled low over the ground, swallowing sound and shape alike. Yah'zaval felt muted again, distant, as if the land itself still tasted the blood spilled here and refused to forget.

"Figures. I can see them moving when the mist breaks. They're..." He looked somberly at Kaden. "They're coming our way."

CHAPTER 10

Of course they were. Of *course*. Kaden took a second to mourn the fact that the dinner he'd been looking forward to and the rest he'd been counting on were clearly not going to happen. Redfern, go scout it out," he said quietly. "We need to know what's coming at us. But stay safe!"

"I'm always safe," Redfern quipped before flying off into the night. A moment later, Kaden couldn't even see her anymore.

"Redfern is excellent at weaving yah'zaval into concealment," Queen Pepper said as she dimmed the fire with a gesture. "She won't be seen unless she wishes it."

"I'm not worried about any of you fairies," Chum said with a groan as he got back to his hooves. His round, fuzzy face was pinched with a mixture of disgust and fear. "You can all fly away when the danger becomes overwhelming. It's the rest of us I worry about. Me specifically."

Chum clutched his sling, The Annoyer, at his belt like it was a divine relic. "This little beauty was not designed for armies of dead people. It was designed for… mild inconveniencing." He glared at Weylyn. "This is all *your* fault!"

"That seems unfair. When have I ever let you get into trouble?" Weylyn asked, hefting his sword as he stared out into the darkness.

The mist pressed close around them, thick enough to feel against the skin. Even yah'zaval felt thinned here, drawn tight like a breath held too long. With the firelight low, it was actually a bit easier to see the figures slowly making their way toward them, thanks to the shreds of moonlight that filtered down through the clouds.

"Are you jesting?" Chum spread his hands. "Look at where we are!"

"Be quiet," Petey snapped, his ears hanging so low they nearly touched his shoulders. Bug shifted uneasily on Petey's shoulder, his faint glow dimming as the mist thickened around them.

"*You* be quiet, you—" Chum's comeback dissolved into coughing as Bug, perched on Petey's shoulder, sprayed a glittering veil of spores over the satyr's face. They smelled vaguely of mint. Duke, standing at Kaden's side, sneezed loudly.

"It's not poisonous," Queen Pepper assured them all. "Just irritating to those with very sensitive noses."

"If even the mushroom is tellin' you to shut yer gob, time to listen," Bardicus said, then looked at Kaden. "Well, are we going to wait for whatever these are to get to us before we strike? Eh? Seems cowardly to me."

Kaden resisted the urge to roll his eyes. Duke stood close at Kaden's knee, muscles taut beneath his consecrated armor, watching the mist with low, uncertain breaths. "I'd rather know what they are before attacking."

"Why?"

"Because if those are prisoners being forced to confront us by the Ophidians, I don't want to start killing them before we get a chance to figure that out."

"Ah." That prospect didn't seem to have occurred to Bardicus, if the way he was sheepishly scratching his ear was any indicator. Thalgrem knocked him in the shoulder with one of his gauntlets, hard, but it didn't even rock the dwarf king.

Ada had gone from placid to alert in a second. "Do you think it could be them?" she asked, the hand that had been resting on her bow now outstretched toward the distant invaders… who were becoming less distant by the second.

Her voice cracked on the last word, so quietly Kaden doubted anyone else noticed. Fear was hollowing her out from the inside.

"I don't know." Kaden didn't know anything; that was the problem. "That's why we're waiting for Redfern to get back before we—"

Whsst! An arrow hissed off into the night, striking one of the shambling figures square in the chest. It stumbled back but didn't quite fall to the ground, keeping its feet despite the enormous elven arrow that had pierced it down to the fletching.

"No!" shrieked Ada, turning furiously to Eldrin. "What if that's my *mother?*"

"It's not," Eldrin replied with certainty. "The breeze shifted toward us a few seconds ago. Can't you smell that?"

"Smell what?" Ada demanded, but… Kaden sniffed deeply and made a face. There *was* a smell in the air, something worse than dirt or human filth. It was the smell of rotting flesh.

The stench clung to the back of Kaden's throat, heavy and old, like something that had been waiting for them.

Redfern appeared a second later, casting off her shielding ability. "Fallen," she announced grimly. "The Ophidians have set the dead on us. We have to get past an entire field of these things to reach Karnergrien."

"The dead?" Kaden couldn't understand it. Once you were dead, that was it. Your soul was gone, passed on to Orealus—or somewhere else. "How can the dead rise?"

"It's a curse," Eldrin said, keeping an arrow at the ready. "These aren't the same people they were when they lived. The curse simply animates their bodies to move and attack anything living. Luckily for us," he added, "it's not a very clever curse. If we stay far enough away from them, we ought to be safe. We have to keep moving, though."

Yah'zaval recoiled from the Fallen. Kaden felt it—like the faintest tug of revulsion in his chest. Whatever animated these bodies was not of Orealus.

"We should just attack them all now and be done with it," Bardicus growled.

Redfern shook her head. "These ghouls have been raised from the battlefield between us and the city, Your Majesty. There are hundreds of them. We simply don't have the numbers to go through them all, and the more we fight, the slower we move."

"I think we should try to avoid them at all costs," Queen Pepper agreed, then looked at Kaden. "What do you wish us to do?"

Every set of eyes rested on him again. Leadership pressed on his shoulders like armor he wasn't sure he'd earned.

"Avoid them," Kaden said firmly, ignoring the disappointed groans he got from Bardicus and Weylyn. "We need to save our energy for the Ophidians when we finally reach them. Redfern and Millicent, you fly ahead and help us find the best path through them to the city. Queen Pepper, let the fire burn more brightly once we're away, to distract them. Eldrin, you're the vanguard. Relay their directions to the rest of us."

Eldrin smiled for what seemed like the first time in days. "As you wish, Your Highness."

He ran ahead before Kaden could thump him on the shoulder for teasing him. He focused his attention on Duke instead. "Soft paws," he murmured along with the gesture he'd used when training Duke to move quietly. Duke whuffed and lowered his head.

Duke's ears flicked forward, and his huge paws shifted into the slow, careful steps Kaden had drilled into him during months of training back home.

Kaden looked at the rest of the party. "Are you all ready?" Duke glanced up at Kaden once, tail low but steady, then turned his attention back to the darkness ahead.

The chorus of "yes" and a few "ayes was unanimous—except for Chum's "I never asked for *any* of this," which didn't count. Kaden led the way, keeping his eyes on Eldrin's back and waiting for some sort of directive, which… huh, maybe they should have worked this out a little more specifically, because they were getting pretty close to the Fallen now, and he didn't know if they should—

There. He saw the gleam of reflected moonlight on one of Eldrin's arrows, its head pointing to the right. Kaden complied, and slowly and steadily, they evaded the first line of the Fallen, most of whom kept heading for their abandoned campfire. They had to spread out at times, which Kaden didn't like, but it was worth it if they kept at least ten feet between them and the nearest Fallen. If they didn't…

A low groan was all that warned Kaden that something was amiss before a Fallen that had been shambling a second ago suddenly broke into something like a sprint and *launched* itself at the nearest member of their party. It was a surprise attack, and could have been deadly if the person it had launched itself at had been anyone but Thalgrem Thunderfist.

Its joints cracked like breaking branches as it lunged, faster than anything dead had a right to move.

The Fallen's middle completely disintegrated as Thalgrem punched right through it, his gauntlet sparking with power. The creature collapsed, and Thalgrem shook his hand off with a disgusted expression on his face.

"They get much faster when they're close," Kaden murmured. "Stay back from them, and keep your weapons at the ready at all times."

Their march was painstaking, but after an hour, they were nearly at the walls of Karnergrien, a once-noble city that had been overwhelmed by evil. A few more minutes and they'd be within the walls, that much closer to finding Ada's mother and the rest of the captured citizens of Whaldalf's Landing. Just a few—

"Maaaaahhhh!" Chum bleated in alarm as a Fallen they'd failed to notice attacked him from behind. It would have gotten its hands around Chum's neck if Duke hadn't lunged in from Kaden's side, throwing himself between them as his armor flared to life and the Fallen's skeletal dagger glanced off it. Duke smashed into the corpse, sending it reeling backward.

Unfortunately, it wasn't the only Fallen now alerted to their presence. More headed their way, their stumbling shambles gradually increasing in speed as their curse propelled them to the fight.

Kaden bit his lip as he drew his sword. "The Ophidians will hear the fight," he said worriedly to Pepper.

"I can keep that from happening," she promised him. "But I will need my bodyguards to focus on protecting me while I do. This use of yah'zaval must be carefully directed, and I won't be able to help you fight."

"Do it," he urged her. Queen Pepper closed her eyes, her wings beating so fast Kaden could barely see them, and brought her hands together in front of her chest. A ball of light gathered between her palms, dark blue and pulsing like a heartbeat. The rhythm was not magic but pure yah'zaval, a force of shielding woven from faith and intention. Each pulse smothered sound, thinning it until it vanished into the night.

It gave everything Kaden heard here an odd resonance, but at least he still *could* hear. He watched Pepper's fairies flank her protectively, then stepped into the fight.

The Fallen were odd opponents. They gave no heed to protecting themselves, leaving every target available, but likewise, they didn't react to blows that would have killed a living creature. Instead of stabbing them, Kaden found it was best to smash Vrangar against their heads, sending them crashing to the ground. In a few cases, he cut their legs out from under them, completely severing them several times. It didn't stop the Fallen from coming after him, but at least it slowed them down.

"This is useless," Weylyn grunted as he rammed one Fallen with a massive pauldron while headbutting another, sending it reeling back far enough that he could cut it completely in two. "They're alert to us now! More will come, and more after that, no matter how many we cut down. There's no telling how many dead were laid to an unquiet rest in this field. We need Queen Pepper to use some sort of yah'zaval abilities to push them back for good."

"She's already keeping us silent," Kaden said. "We don't want to let the Ophidians know we're coming."

"To hell with that, let them know! Let them know to fear us!"

"And get the captives killed before we even get close enough to rescue 'em?" Bardicus completely flattened the upper half of a Fallen with his hammer. "I'm all for stormin' the city, Wolf, but even I know that's a losing bargain."

"Don't you dare," Ada snapped. Her arrows were having no effect on the creatures, so she'd switched to a viciously sharp dagger. She and Duke were working together—the hound tripped the Fallen or sent them stumbling, and then she came in and cut their heads off. It was effective, but she looked tired. They were *all* getting tired, and Weylyn was right—the Fallen just kept coming.

Finally, there was a lull. Surrounded by the foul, rotting bodies of the dead, the last thing Kaden felt like doing was having a drink. King Bardicus, it seemed, thought differently.

"Ahh, lovely." He reached into his pack and hauled out a huge leather skin. "Been waiting for the right time to crack this open, and now's as good a time as any." He unscrewed the cap that had been worked onto it, and the harsh, potent smell of grog quickly spread, even managing to overwhelm the stink of the Fallen. Bardicus guzzled a few mouthfuls down, then passed it off to Thalgrem.

"Nothing better than grog to keep you warm while doing cold work like this," he said cheerfully when he caught Kaden staring at him.

"He's mad," Petey whispered to Kaden.

"He's *drunk*," Chum said enviously. "And I want to be, too!"

"Ahh, little goat man." Bardicus clapped Chum on the back so hard he almost sent the smaller creature to his knees. "You've got a true dwarven fighting spirit. Here!" He took the grog back from Thalgrem and thrust it at Chum, who took it with a grin. "Drink up!" Chum obliged with a grimace.

Eldrin coalesced out of the darkness, a look of impatience on his face. "What are you all waiting for? They're rising already! We have to get inside, now!"

"Rising?" Kaden looked at the Fallen by his feet, then leapt back when he saw it trembling, splayed limbs twitching as it struggled to get back up.

"We've got to get out of here!" Petey insisted.

"Go up the wall, there." Eldrin pointed at a half-collapsed stone tower a dozen yards away. The outside of it was tumbled down, but the inside half still stood, and contained a partial staircase they could climb. "Hurry! Before the curse compels them to follow you!"

Together, with Pepper finally coming out of her trance, they ran for Karnergrien.

CHAPTER 11

"Get up on top of the wall! Move fast enough, and they may not catch on to the ploy!" Eldrin chivvied them up the crumbling stairwell quickly until they were all perched up on the wall that had once protected Karnergrien from attack. Now it seemed to be more tumbled down than upright, but the section they were on appeared sturdy enough.

The air felt heavy in Karnergrien, thick with the remnants of ancient grief. Yah'zaval moved sluggishly here, as if burdened by the city's history.

Below them, the Fallen drifted through the ruins in slow, unfocused patterns—shambling patrols that never once lifted their hollow gazes upward. They moved like beasts following a scent, not like guards watching for intruders. Their distraction bought Kaden's group a brief, precious window to crouch low, whisper, and take in the city without being noticed.

From their vantage point, Kaden finally got a clear look inside Karnergrien. It was dark, but he'd grown used to seeing in low light. He squinted at the ruins below, trying to get his bearings. Almost none of the original buildings remained fully standing, but some areas were more heavily used than others. Long, low tunnel-like structures ran across the ruin-scape—Ophidian burrows, maybe? He wasn't sure.

"What do you see?" he whispered to Petey after a moment. Of all of them, Petey was the most used to living in the darkness.

"An encampment," Petey replied, his voice a bit shivery. "It looks pretty hastily put together—I doubt the Ophidians have been here long."

Goblins saw differently in darkness; the shadows sharpened for him, edges brightening into shapes the others couldn't parse. Karnergrien revealed itself to him like a half-dead thing.

"Makes sense," Bardicus opined.

"Why?" Ada asked.

"Because they risked a lot with that raid on Whaldalf's Landing. There's no history of Ophidians attacking anywhere near there, right? Only dark elves and the like." Ada nodded. "Probably means they're trying to expand their own territory. That portal they opened was likely the limit of the distance it could go. They're heading south, but they have to do it carefully."

"Why?" Her voice was bitter. "It's not like my village was able to put up much of a fight."

Bitterness cut through her voice, raw and jagged. Grief had stripped her down to nerves and instinct, and every explanation felt like an accusation.

"Oh, lass." Bardicus sounded tired. "It's not your village that would offer the fight. Don't you see how all these dark beasts work?"

"It's late, and we're all exhausted, Bardicus, don't tease her," Queen Pepper put in, then turned to Ada and patted her hand. "They're all clannish, dear. None of these creatures wants to work with others who aren't their own kind. It leads to them fighting amongst themselves as easily as them fighting against us. How Lucient kept them together for as long as he did in the Great War, I don't know."

"The point is," Bardicus continued, clearly irritated at the interruption, "that the Ophidians don't want to tangle with dark elves or trolls or ogres or any of that ilk if they can avoid it. So they're moving slowly and squatting in ruins like this whenever they can, taking what they need in quick-strike raids."

"Why…" Ada swallowed hard. "Why did they need people from my village?"

"Eh." Bardicus shrugged. "Labor, probably. Human work gangs preppin' what Lucient's armies will need for war. That, or…"

"Or they were taken to be used as food," Weylyn said, and Ada clapped both her hands over her mouth in an effort not to retch.

"Stop it!" Kaden snapped. He paused on the verge of losing his temper, knowing that he couldn't let himself do that.

Anger clawed at his throat, begging to be heard, but leaders couldn't afford to break. Not here. Not now. His temper was a luxury he didn't get to have anymore.

He *couldn't*. Someone had to keep control here; someone had to be in charge and have a level head. As unfair as it felt right now, as much as he wanted to just *scream* about it sometimes, that person had to be him. "Petey." He refocused on his friend. "What else do you see?"

"I think I see movement," he said, the tips of his ears twitching. "To the right side, there. I need to get closer to see what they're doing, though."

"We can probably move a little farther along this wall," Eldrin said with a dubious glance at it. "But if it goes down, we're going to be easy targets for the Fallen."

"Not to mention being buried under tons of rock," Chum muttered. "Not all of us are as light on our hooves as elves and fairies. Typical—nobody ever considers how hard these old stones are on a satyr's hooves. Or how hard falls are on a satyr's tail. Or how hard *everything* is when you're armed with nothing but a sling and goodwill!"

"Let's try it," Kaden said before Chum could really get going. They crept along the wall, doing a decent job of staying silent, although the occasional *clang* left Kaden wincing. He wondered if he should ask Pepper to silence them again… but he didn't want to rely too heavily on her abilities to get them out of scrapes, or risk her becoming exhausted. They needed to work on stealth, and this was as good a place to do it as any.

Ten yards… twenty… a bit beyond that, and they reached another turret, this one also falling, but the tumbled stone made a decent ladder to the ground. Better yet, from here they could actually see people.

"I count at least twenty humans," Eldrin said.

"Twenty-two," Petey added. "Half of them are doing some sort of digging in the rubble, the others are being held in cages in the back."

"Do you see my mother?" Ada's voice was thready with anxiety. "She's taller than most women, she usually keeps her hair wrapped with some braids down her back, she wears a silver bracelet on her left wrist…"

Petey squinted. "I… think so? I don't see the bracelet, but there's a woman with her hair up in one of the cages."

Ada leaned heavily against Kaden, the breath whooshing out of her like a gust of wind. He pulled her into a hug, which she accepted with a smile. "She's alive," Ada whispered.

Relief hit her so hard her knees shook. For the first time since Whaldalf's Landing, hope didn't feel like a lie.

"We'll get her out," Kaden promised.

"Um. There are… um. Some guards down there, too," Petey said, clearly reluctant to break the moment.

"Ophidians, or more Fallen?" Kaden asked.

"Fallen, I think. They're mostly just standing there."

Kaden nodded. "We can work with that."

Relief flickered through him—small, but real. A plan was forming, thin as thread but strong enough to follow.

If they were careful, they wouldn't have to deal with the Fallen until after they freed the people from the cages. Getting across the plains… that was going to be tricky, but…

"Ooh," Kaden heard Chum say, followed quickly by Weylyn's "Wait, don't—"

The wall they were standing on suddenly shuddered beneath their feet. Everyone turned to stare at Chum, who was holding something small and golden in his hand.

"What?" he demanded—at full volume.

The object shimmered faintly, runes etched across its surface—old Empyrean warding script, twisted from its original purpose. Kaden didn't know how he recognized it, only that yah'zaval recoiled from it.

"It's just a trinket, not a—"

The wall shuddered again and began to tilt. "It's not a trinket, it's a trap!" Kaden shouted. "Everybody, get ready to jump clear!" He held

Ada's hand as he looked around wildly for Duke. The wall tilted further and finally began to slide toward the ground.

Luckily, it slid in one piece, and they were able to jump off it before it fell apart. Unluckily, the Fallen were now very aware of the fact that they were here. There weren't nearly as many inside the city as there had been outside, but there was no time to waste now.

"Ada, go with Petey," Kaden said, reluctantly letting go of her hand. "The two of you ought to be able to open the cages and get the prisoners out. We'll deal with the Fallen who come this way. Once they're all down, we'll figure out the best route to take out of here." Ada nodded, then eagerly followed Petey toward the cages on a zigzag route that would steer them clear of the guards.

"How are we possibly going to move so many people safely?" Weylyn demanded, pulling his sword free as the Fallen began moving their way.

"If you have an issue with it, you should have brought it up before," Eldrin snapped. Everyone readied their weapons, and then—

A horn blew. The sound was clear and pure, surprisingly beautiful in the midst of such a dark place. The Fallen stopped advancing, all of them turning toward one of the few remaining buildings. A moment later, three heavily armored soldiers stepped out through the door.

Weylyn's breath hitched with surprise. "Those undead are wearing the armor of the Empyrean Royal Guard."

Kaden glanced at him. "What does that mean, exactly?"

"It means that these are the people who were responsible for protecting the royal family," Weylyn said. "The sword on the one in front—look at the hilt. And the insignia on the shield… those are the weapons of the captain of the guard. Captain Khesza." Weylyn's mouth tightened. "He served under my father. I trained with him as a boy."

The fog that had seemed semipresent out on the plain drifted inward, thickening the air between them and the Fallen. In a few moments, Kaden could barely make out the three corpse commanders they were facing, but the increasing sounds of movement told him there were plenty of enemies headed their way.

"The fog," Queen Pepper said suddenly. "It protects them in some way. There's something… something from the last war I'm forgetting, something about how to defeat these creatures…"

"It's called cutting their heads off," Weylyn snarled, striding forward toward his former teacher. "Khesza! I challenge you! Leave your ghouls out of this and face me like the man you once were!"

The captain stood just beyond the edge of the thickest fog, visible where the mist thinned around the ruined archway. He tilted his head for a moment, almost as though he was considering Weylyn's brash challenge. Then he raised his sword high, and dozens of Fallen burst forward out of the mist.

It was all Kaden could do to get Vrangar up between him and the first one before it literally ran itself onto his blade.

"Maybe we should try settin' the bloody brutes on fire instead," Bardicus said with a grunt as he smashed another Fallen into the ground. It was stirring not five seconds later. "Because we'll never make it out of here if they keep gettin' up, much less with a group of unarmed humans to protect."

"Then we'd have a bunch of *flaming* Fallen running around causing trouble," Eldrin replied. "Besides, dead flesh like theirs doesn't burn very readily."

A Fallen staggered past them, its jaw hanging loose, its limbs barely attached. Even half destroyed, the curse dragged it forward. Killing them felt like trying to kill the wind.

Thalgrim seemed to take this notion as a personal challenge. He banged his gauntlets together, building up a massive charge, before releasing all the energy in the direction of three Fallen who were running toward him. They fell, sizzling with residual energy. He looked on with satisfaction, but it was short-lived as the crackling corpses got jerkily back to their feet.

"Eh." Bardicus thumped his friend on the helmet. "A good effort."

"How good?" Chum shrieked as he dodged the grasping hands of one of the Fallen that was still sparking with electricity. "How is it *good*? It's just going to make it more painful when they manage to—*ow!*" The

Fallen touched his tail, setting off a static charge that made Chum leap into the air.

"Fallen… they were only called into combat at night," Pepper said from where she was hovering, protected by her fierce bodyguards as she racked her brain. "The sunlight was anathema to them… we need sunlight!"

"Brilliant." Bardicus smashed another Fallen back, pulverizing its head against the ground. "Only got to keep this up for another seven or eight hours then, eh?"

Kaden grimaced. There was no way they would last until sunrise. This was his fault—he should have thought it out better, made sure he had an actual plan before running in to try to save the day. He'd put his party and Ada's mother, not to mention all the other villagers, at even greater risk.

"Oh, there's a certain ability for that," Queen Pepper said. "It calls the light of Orealus into our weapons. It's not exactly sunlight, but the light of our God should be even more powerful. It's a difficult working of my abilities, though." She held her hand out to Kaden. "Help me," she entreated. "I need your strength working with mine."

Kaden cut down one more Fallen, then ran to Pepper's side. "I'm here," he told her breathlessly. The fight was raging ever more furiously all around them, more and more Fallen arriving and piling in, in some cases climbing over the bodies of their fellows as they struggled to get close enough to attack. Weylyn was the only one who'd run fast enough to reach the three leaders, and he had his hands more than full beating one back, then turning on the next who'd just risen from the last time he cut him down. He wouldn't be able to take much more of this.

"How do I share my strength?" Kaden asked as he held out his hand. She grasped it tight.

"Make the symbol of Orealus and pray for him to share his light," Queen Pepper said, then closed her eyes and began to chant.

Kaden followed suit, even though closing his eyes made him tremble with anxiety. He was counting on Redfern and Millicent to protect both of them while they tried this out. His hand itched to bring his sword back into position, but instead, he sheathed it and used his hand to make the circular symbol of Orealus over his chest. "Please be with us now," he prayed. "Orealus, father of light and life, guardian against the darkness, we need you now. Please share your light with us, and let me share my strength with Pepper. We come in your name to do your will, please, let us—"

A sudden warmth surged over him like a wave. Kaden opened his eyes and saw, to his astonishment, that the entire interior of the fortress was flooded with light. Light poured from Pepper's hands like dawn breaking through a storm. It wasn't magic. It was yah'zaval given form, Orealus answering. It felt like stepping from a cave into the brightness of midday, almost too hot to be comfortable for a moment before settling down.

Every single Fallen had gone stock-still, frozen by the light of Orealus. The glow was already fading, but it lingered in the weapons of every member of Kaden's party.

"Now that's more like it!" Bardicus shouted with joy. He hit a Fallen so hard with his hammer that it flew back into three others. None of them got up again. "Way to bring the power of yah'zaval into the fight!"

Pepper let go of Kaden's hand as the sound of fighting rose again. He went to reach for his sword, then forgot it completely as she collapsed into his arms.

"I'm all right," she insisted blearily. "It was a lot of power to channel, that's all. Go and fight, Kaden." Millicent joined them, protectively taking her queen from Kaden.

Kaden left them reluctantly, unsheathing his glowing Vrangar and laying into the nearest Fallen with furious, grateful energy. *Thank you, Orealus.* None of the Fallen they struck down got up again. Slowly, the fog itself began to lift, and as it did, the Fallen coming toward them in the distance actually began to collapse before getting within range of their weapons. The cleansing light of Orealus was working against the curse that had afflicted these poor people.

Eventually, the last ghoul standing was Khesza. The man who was once a captain of the Royal Guard was somehow holding his own against Weylyn's furious attacks, but finally Weylyn hit his head hard enough that he knocked his helm clean off his shoulders. As Kaden watched, the grimace marring the dead man's rotted face cleared. Rather than collapse like the others, though, he stepped back and lifted his gleaming short sword to his forehead, signaling his surrender.

The light of Orealus seemed to fill in the holes in the man's visage, repairing the damage wrought by time and violence until his face seemed whole and human once more.

Kaden had never seen death undone, not like this. It felt holy and wrong all at once, like watching a memory rise and take shape before his eyes.

"Well met, Son of the Wolf," he said warmly.

Weylyn let his sword drop a few inches. "Captain Khesza?" he asked warily.

"For the moment," the former Fallen agreed, and turned to look at Kaden. He smiled broadly. "The littlest prince! Look at how well you've grown, Your Highness. Daneyel did well by you."

Kaden's heart panged at the mention of his foster father, but he managed to nod. "He did his best."

"And that was clearly more than enough." The captain's eyes narrowed a bit. "You've the look of your father, King Karatheas. Your eyes are your mother's, but everything else... It's like seeing my lost lord in the flesh once more. You resemble him more closely than any of your siblings, even Ezrah."

"Truly?" Kaden wished he could remember his real father, but hearing about him from someone else was still satisfying.

"Indeed. Karatheas had the same height, the same breadth through the shoulders. He even fought similarly... although I assume that's because my protégé here is working with you." The look he turned on Weylyn was kind, so kind that Weylyn finally lowered his sword fully. "You've done your father and me proud, Weylyn. Stay with the prince. Protect him. He will need your strength in the face of what lies ahead."

"What *does* lie ahead?" Weylyn demanded before Kaden could. "What can you tell us about our enemy?"

Khesza shook his head. Already, the prominences of his skull were becoming visible again. "I cannot say. All I know is that you're strong together, all of you; stronger than your enemy. As long as you work together… as long as you fight as one… take this, Weylyn!" He held out his sword. "Take it! Use it for the prince's sake, and no matter what happens, don't…"

Whatever else he was going to say was lost as Captain Khesza's corpse slowly toppled over onto the ground. Weylyn stepped forward too late to stop his former teacher from falling, and he stared at the body with tears in his eyes.

Weylyn's breath shook. For all his bluster and bravado, grief hollowed him out with quiet precision.

"Well?" Eldrin asked after a moment. "Are you going to take the sword or not?"

Weylyn looked at the sword. The sword was a short, thick blade made of welded dragon scales. The razor-sharp point of the weapon made it the perfect choice to cut through the hardest of foliage or the wielder's enemies. The blade had a broad, curved cross guard that made sure the blade was both balanced and capable of protecting the owner's hands when clashing swords. The cross guard had an ornamented dragon head on each side, probably symbolizing the owner's status as leader of the Dragon Guild. A small pommel was marked in an unrecognizable language. The blade itself seemed simple with no distinguishing decorations or engraved patterns, but it did seem to have a light, fiery glow emitting from it. The weapon was decorated in battle, having been used in countless wars and training sessions under the tutelage of the master swordsman and guild leader, Khesza.

"I have a sword," Weylyn replied dully.

"As if that would stop a man like you from wanting more."

Kaden stepped forward and put a hand on Weylyn's shoulder. "It was his final wish," he said.

Weylyn exhaled heavily. "Fine. *Fine.* But I think it's sentimental nonsense." Nevertheless, his hands moved with reverence as he took the short sword from the ground.

The night was still; no more Fallen were moving to attack. *Thank you, Orealus.* "We should go help Ada and Petey," Kaden said. They moved in the direction of the prisoners, but Kaden hung back with Weylyn for a moment.

"Do you remember my siblings?" he asked.

"I never knew them well," Weylyn confessed. "Your oldest brother and your sister had over a decade on me, and your next brother was just a few years older than you."

Ezrah, his next brother. "What happened to Ezrah?

"I suppose he died, the same as the others."

But the others died in battle. If he was too young to fight, why didn't Bhalla send him away with me? What happened to him? Kaden wanted to ask, but only Bhalla would be able to say for sure.

"Kaden!" Ada's jubilant cry distracted him from his musings, and he ran toward her and her mother, putting questions about his own family aside. It didn't matter anymore. Blood or no blood, the people beside him were his family now, and he would face whatever waited in Karnergrien with them.

CHAPTER 12

Long ago, when Orealus cast Lucient from the heavens, he fell into a wasteland of hidden fire and ancient ash. The force of his impact reshaped the land, and in the centuries that followed, he bent that broken world to his will. From the scorched stone, he carved his stronghold, raising walls and forging a domain as cruel and unforgiving as he was becoming.

Against the largest volcano in this ancient mountain range, a hundred-foot wall of obsidian jutted out from the side of the crag. This wall enclosed a courtyard at the very base of the mountain; a place filled with red mist that prevented anyone whom Lucient didn't approve of from entering the grounds.

In the center of the courtyard was a massive forge that ran on lava siphoned from deep within the ground, where a phalanx of blacksmiths worked night and day creating weapons for Lucient's forces. Hundreds of feet above it, at the very top of the wall, was Lucient's castle, a creation of onyx stalagmites that shrouded the entire area with darkness.

The land of Lucient was a place where few living creatures could venture for long. Not simply because of its vileness, which was extreme, the air was sulfurous and choked with smog that would lay the strongest mortal creature low. Neither because of its terrible coldness, nor the layers of misty dunntaika—the dark spiritual energy from which all mortal magic is derived—that leaked from Lucient's own power and covered his realm so thickly that even a fairy queen would have trouble seeing through it.

No, the land of Lucient the Deceiver, Lord of Darkness and Shadows, was unassailable for the sheer distance it stood from anywhere that could provide humanity with the things it needed to live: arable land, clean water, and warm sunshine.

That didn't mean that Lucient was uninformed of the acts of mankind, however. Far from it. And with the help of his dunntaika, jealously hoarded apart from what he needed to strengthen and monitor his many spies, Lucient almost always knew what was happening before any of his generals did.

Every now and then, however, he was surprised by something. It was an experience he loathed.

"I am ready for this to end," he proclaimed to his generals as he paced the central chamber of his castle. It reeked of sulfur, the smoke settling into every inch of the room. Lucient was a being of dark energy more than flesh at this point—the chill didn't touch him, and the foulness didn't phase him. The castle clanged with the sounds of the frantically busy smithy at the base of the mountain, and the occasional screams of an unlucky minion.

Those who associated with Lucient regularly had learned, through painful trial and error, that the sound Lucient found most satisfying was his own voice. "This boy has wandered my world freely for far too long. It was amusing to watch him, for a while, but he's gone from a diversion to a distraction." He turned to Vicitious, who ducked his head with a submissive hiss beneath his master's gaze. "Your spy is nearly here. I trust they'll have good news."

"They are nearly here," Vicitious replied, not lifting his eyes. Normally, he loved to gaze on his master, so close in appearance to the beauty they both used to possess before falling to darkness, but right now... no. Vicitious's dual tongues danced nervously behind his sharpened teeth, and the lizard-like general bowed his head a bit lower. No, he had the feeling that what was coming wasn't anything he wanted to witness.

"Finally." The voice, beautiful and refined as it was, sounded like it couldn't possibly be coming out of the beastly creature that spoke it.

Six blazing fire-orange eyes sat three-and-three above a short, stumpy nose and the slit-like mouth below it, filled with sharp teeth flanked by two huge, retractable fangs and acid breath. Baal, another of Lucient's generals, could swallow a man whole with that jaw if he was close enough. "We've wasted enough time worrying about the child of our last great enemy. Even without the goblins, our ranks are fully recovered. It's time to finish what we started."

"It's *because* of what happened to the goblins that we must be cautious," Ozul murmured. Tall and gaunt and covered in a long, black robe, the Soul Reaper was the most cautious of Lucient's generals apart from Vicitious. "They were strong and growing stronger, and a force of fewer than ten beings destroyed them. They did so *without* Bhalla's aid. To ignore that would be foolhardy."

"Frightened little spirit." Defyle, the fourth general laughed, making Ozul turn and face him, full of menace. Defyle didn't blink. Once the pinnacle of purity, Defyle had fallen far in his loyalty to Lucient. His once-beautiful body was now a cesspool in humanoid form, as bloated as the wriggling maggots it dropped regularly. His features were barely visible inside his swollen, rotted face, but he had no difficulty making himself heard. "You've always been a coward, Ozul. Let me help you rediscover your spine, eh? We'll go out there together and break that little boy's neck, then we'll—"

"Silence." A raised hand from Lucient killed all conversation. A moment later, a raven flew in through the only window this deep, dark cavern had. A moment later, it morphed into an Orphidian.

A trembling Orphidian. Vicitious felt his blackened heart sink low.

"Well?" Lucient demanded, striding over to the messenger. Lucient was still lovely to look upon—everything his generals were not. His back was unbowed, leaving him a head taller than anyone else in the room. He was slender and strong, and in his black-and-red armor, he looked truly mighty. Only the eyes gave away that he wasn't still pure and beautiful beneath his helm—the eyes that burned behind the metal mask had the same dull flare as banked coals. "What news have you brought?"

"I… great lord, I…" The messenger shot his general a panicked look, but Vicitious didn't meet his eyes.

"It had *better* be word that the boy is dead and this charade of acting against me is over." Lucient's voice didn't change, but the air around him seemed to darken, sucking what faint light there was into his shadow.

"Great lord, I regret to inform you that Captain Khesza was… was defeated by the prince and his companions." The messenger prostrated himself on the ground, mumbling out the next part so quietly it almost couldn't be heard. "They are close to discovering another piece of the Armor of Orealuh-luh—" He stopped speaking, unable to get another word out as Lucient placed his armored foot on the back of the creature's neck.

"Pure incompetence," Lucient hissed and stomped down like he was crushing a bug. The messenger's neck was pulverized against the stone floor, and after a few moments of quivering, the Orphidian died. The tip of his tail continued to twitch, however. Vicitious couldn't make himself look away from it—not until Lucient grabbed his chin and lifted his head to look at him directly.

"This grand idea of yours," Lucient said, digging the tips of his fingers into Vicitious's flesh. Vicitious felt it when they penetrated his skin, a sharp sting that was followed by the incongruous warmth of blood trickling down his scales. "Baiting Kaden by making slaves of that village, drawing him out to the ruins of Karnergrien to feed him to the murderous impulses of the Fallen… and you thought that would *work*."

"My lord," Vicitious muttered, "between Captain Khesza and his legion of undead, I thought it was a sure thing. I—"

"You *thought*. You thought, you little *fool*." Vicitious waited for Lucient to kill him, trembling but willing to face his fate—as must all who failed their master—but a moment later Lucient flung him to the side instead. He crashed into a wall and lay on the ground for a moment, stunned, staring at the mangled neck of his dead messenger as he recovered the ability to move.

"Do any of the rest of you have brilliant *thoughts* to share?" Lucient addressed his remaining generals. "If so, speak them now."

"My lord," Baal murmured, his voice slipping into something smooth and inviting, "let me tempt the boy into destroying himself."

His monstrous form rippled like heat over stone. Scales melted into skin, jagged bone smoothing beneath a veil of illusion. A moment later, a young woman stood where the beast had been, with red hair spilling over her shoulders and a smile designed to disarm the unwary.

"Send me, my lord," Defyle got out from between his swollen, pallid lips. His heavy body jiggled with eagerness, knocking several more maggots loose. "I will consume him and all whom he holds dear. It's been too long since I've tasted royal blood."

"Why content yourself with breaking their bodies," Ozul whispered, "when I can unmake what lies within them?" His shadowed eyes glimmered. "A soul consumed by me leaves no echo for Orealus to call back. No memory. No trace. Only silence."

A tiny shudder passed through Lucient. "Never speak that name to me," he said to Ozul, who shrank in on himself as he realized his mistake. The name of his former god was one of the few things that genuinely pained Lucient.

"My idea, my lord, is—"

"I'll rip their flesh from—"

"*Silence!*" Lucient boomed, looking with disgust at his generals. "None of you has the strength to guarantee me victory against someone who is little more than a *child*. No." No, he wouldn't risk letting Kaden escape again. He wasn't ready to leave this place yet, but there was someone else, someone almost as powerful as him, who could handle a task like this. "This is a task for Morvar."

Yes. Morvar, the bringer of death, Lord of the Skies. He was the proper choice for this task now. The boy had evaded every previous attempt—he should have died when those goblins killed his foster father, but no. He'd survived, and in doing so, he'd shown a streak of luck that was severe enough to be… disconcerting. But there was no surviving a creature of pure power and flame like Morvar.

"That flying vermin can't be trusted," Baal snapped, crossing his arms over his very well-endowed human chest. "Morvar has his own ambitions, my lord. Are you sure you wouldn't rather—"

A second later, Baal was off the ground, with Lucient's hand wrapped around the entirety of his smooth, slender neck. Lucient squeezed until Baal was forced to give up his feminine form, once again becoming the thick-necked, six-eyed monstrosity that he normally was. "Are you telling me what to do, worm?" Lucient asked casually, as though he weren't choking the life out of his hapless general.

"I would never do such a thing, my lord!" Baal managed to squeak from between his sharpened teeth. "Never! I spoke without thinking, please! *Please! Mercy!*"

"You dare to beg me for mercy?" Lucient laughed caustically. "You don't know me at all." He threw Baal to the other side of the chamber, across from where Vicitious still cowered. "All of you,"—he turned to look at each of his generals in turn—"are no more than my beasts of burden. Useful, to a degree. Powerful, so far as I *let* you be. Obedient to a fault… and if not, you will feel the full weight of my displeasure.

"Beasts like you are only worth leaving alive as long as you are more helpful than otherwise. If you drift too far the other way…" None of them could see it, but it somehow *sounded* as though Lucient was smiling. That was more terrifying than anything else he'd yet done today. "Then you will be disposed of. Is that clear to you?"

It was as clear as a shard of obsidian lodged in a heart, ready to leave behind a bloody, broken path as it cut itself free.

"Yes, my lord," they all murmured. "Yes."

"Oh, and lastly, these vermin are getting help from someone. It must be Bhalla," said Lucient. "Reach out to his dear old friend in Lumhagen. If Bhalla moves, so must we. The game changes now."

CHAPTER 13

Eventually, celebration gave way to the fact that none of them wanted to stay in this cursed place any longer than they had to. Before they could leave, however, Kaden had to take on the other half of the task that came from being in this place.

"We still have to look for Aspis," he said, the words heavier than his own armor. His eyelids burned with fatigue, and the ache behind his temples warned that if he stopped moving, he might not start again.

He was exhausted from fighting—it seemed never-ending of late—and with that on top of the quick trek to get here and the fact that he'd been awake for far too long, if he stood in one place much longer, he might just collapse.

"The king's shield?" Ada's mother asked. "Aspis, the divine shield from the Armor of Orealus. You'll have your best luck in the castle itself. None of the beasts who took us liked to go there; they said it had the wrong sort of smell." She scoffed and swept her braids back from her face. "Anything those foul creatures disliked was usually a blessing to the rest of us. If they avoid the castle, that is where you will find the shield. Even if not, that is where the king lived. That is what all these poor people died protecting."

She looked at the corpses scattered around them with a grief that hollowed her voice, and Ada tightened her arms around her mother.

"As for us," K'Lani went on, "I think we should move beyond the walls and wait for you there. It isn't good to be around so many of the dead."

K'Lani was already sorting supplies as she spoke. Glass vials wrapped in cloth, packets of powdered bark, and resin-stiffened bandages bore the sigil of the Alchemists Guild. There was no ceremony to the work and no prayers spoken aloud. Only method, measure, and care. Alchemy was not faith, but it served it. Where prayer waited, science acted, binding wounds, easing shock, and keeping the living from joining the dead too soon.

"I'll come and protect you," Ada immediately said.

K'Lani shook her head. "We'll take the blades we need and post a guard, but we can protect ourselves now that you all have lifted the curse on these lost souls." She grimaced. "The worst we ever saw out here were the Fallen. Who can say what might lurk in the castle, though? It's better if all of you stay together until you've done what you came for."

"A wise woman," Bardicus said, sounding impressed. "Rare thing among most folk I meet, but she carries it well."

"If I had a mug of grog, I'd break it against your head," K'Lani said levelly, and Bardicus laughed so hard he had to bend over, slapping his knees in glee. Thalgrem rolled his eyes and prodded at his monarch with one massive gauntlet until the king finally straightened up again.

"Go on," K'Lani said firmly, picking up one of the undead guard's swords and holding it competently. "We'll be waiting for you all." The other people of Whaldalf's Landing murmured their assent, and Ada finally let her mother go.

"We'll be back as soon as we can," Kaden promised before turning toward the castle in the distance. It looked inexpressibly gloomy, half falling down. The town was no better.

Eldrin, surprisingly, was the one to lift the mood as they headed out. "Karnergrien had the best market in the whole continent," he said. "Dwarven axes that could split granite, elven cloth that could bend light, wizard constructs that were more personality than tool. Every stall had a wonder.

"Even we elves had a permanent booth in the largest of the markets, right here in this square." He pointed toward a ramshackle section of broken wood and stone to their right. "My aunt ran the shop. She sold the simplest versions of our bows and arrows, as well as some of our fine cloth. I remember visiting her here, and her telling me about how she had sold a special bolt of our softest material to the queen herself, to use for baby clothes." Eldrin glanced at Kaden and smiled. "You were likely swaddled in the fabric of my people."

"They probably made your nappies from it too," Weylyn said jokingly. Kaden was a little relieved—it was the first time the man had spoken since Captain Khesza had passed his sword on to him. Eldrin was clearly more relieved than offended as well, because instead of shouting at him, he just walked in close and bumped Weylyn's hip hard enough to make him skip a step.

"He should be so lucky as to have nappies made from such incredible fabric," Eldrin said.

"Elven fabric is quite lovely," Pepper put in. She sounded wan; Millicent was actually flying right beside her, holding on to one of her arms, while Redfern patrolled above. Kaden wondered whether he should have asked her to stay with K'Lani and the others... but no. It was her choice to continue with them, and he would respect that.

Hopefully, they'd be done with this stage of their quest soon. They all needed a few days to recover.

"My wedding dress was woven of elven cloth," Pepper said softly. "Pale green with threads of violet. My husband told me I shone brighter than the lanterns." She exhaled, wistful. "I used it for bandages during the war, but its beauty has never left me."

"My cousin ran our stall here," Bardicus said before Kaden could give in to the urge to ask Pepper whether she was all right. "Lucky dwarf that he was, too. Our people were always respected in this town, even though some human villages would sooner spit on you than let you sell them the best wares they've ever seen."

"It was a very fair and equitable place," Pepper agreed. "The king carried that tradition on from his own father, and he did a wonderful job of it." She sighed and looked around wistfully. "The world lost more than just the people who lived here the day this place was destroyed by Lucient. They lost an example of what a world could look like where all our peoples are treated equally, where everyone is welcome, and no one has to fear being isolated for their origin or appearance. I even saw goblins and dark elves here a time or two, always under guard but still allowed to shop or sell if that was their wish."

"Aye. The king was generous, but he wasn't stupid," Bardicus said. "He knew better than to leave those folk alone to make mischief."

"There are goblin artisans," Petey offered, looking a bit offended. Bug rubbed against the tip of one droopy ear affectionately. "Some of my people make amazing things. Our gemstone maps are legendary!"

"Gemstones maps?" Bardicus made a face. "Like maps to a cache of gemstones?"

"No, a carved map within the gemstone itself, only visible under the right light or with the correct sort of loupe. Much of our lore is locked inside gemstones like that." Petey sighed. "It lasts longer than writing down where we live. The dark and damp is no place for paper and parchment."

"Speaking of dark and damp…" Getting to the castle had gone faster than Kaden thought it would. He stared into the darkness of the semicollapsed ruin ahead of him and felt his adrenaline rise a bit. Duke pressed closer to Kaden's leg, hackles faintly raised, his armored paws careful against the broken stone.

* * *

From a shadowed balcony on the ruined second story, the watcher held his breath, the pale moonlight brushing his face in fleeting silver as the group passed beneath him. His fingers curled against the crumbling stone, knuckles white as he took in the sight of Kaden—older, sharper, carrying himself with the instinctive command of a true heir. So different from the boy he remembered. So achingly familiar. He dared not reveal himself… but he could not look away.

"We need to make a light," said Kaden.

"I could—" Pepper began, but Kaden immediately shook his head.

"Save your strength for an emergency," he said. "We have other ways of making light."

"We do?" Petey said.

"Torches, you dolt," Chum grumbled as he rummaged in his pack. "Spend five minutes with someone who can wield light, and suddenly no one remembers fire. He leveled a finger at Weylyn even as he dug into his own pack and pulled out three wooden torches. "Honestly, I thought you had better sense than the rest of this lot, but all it takes to distract you is a new sword and some pretty words. Where's the bastard I knew back in Westramore, huh?"

"Give me those," Weylyn groused. Chum tossed them over and followed it up with flint and steel. Once the torches were alight and distributed, Kaden had to admit—at least to himself—that while magic was delightful and wondrous, there was nothing quite so comforting as the sight of a little fire to light the way.

"Let's go," he said and stepped into the ruins. Bug clung tighter to Petey's shoulder, his faint glow dimming as the stale air closed in around them.

Kaden's pulse quickened the deeper they went. Every fallen beam, every dusty tapestry, felt like a half-forgotten whisper tugging at the edges of his memory. He kept expecting a scent or sound to trigger something real, but nothing came. The emptiness hurt more than he expected.

Really, it wasn't as ruined as it could have been. Sure, there were thick cobwebs everywhere he looked, and you had to keep looking back down at the floor not to trip over something, but the roof had mostly held up, which meant the place hadn't been flooded with rain or snow. There were even tapestries still hanging on the walls in places.

One in particular caught his eye. Kaden lifted his torch and stepped a little closer. It seemed to glitter, as though tiny sparks of light had been woven right into the cloth.

Was this some sort of special elven cloth, or—

Eldrin's eyes softened. For a moment, he wasn't a warrior in a cursed ruin, but a child again, threading ribbons through elven cloth at his aunt's stall. Seeing it here hollowed something inside him.

Bardicus coughed, and suddenly all the sparkling points of light *grew legs* and crawled behind the tapestry. Kaden flinched back right into Ada, who had also backed up as soon as she realized what she was looking at.

"I hate spiders," she said with a delicate shudder.

"Some of the ones in Kugdor grew as big as your hand. Blasted things give me the jitters," Bardicus agreed.

"I think they're delicious," Petey said brightly as he stepped up, plucked a handful of little spiders off the tapestry, and stuffed them into his mouth.

"Ugh!" Ada looked repulsed. "How can you eat those? That's disgusting!"

"What?" A single leg squirmed in the corner of Petey's mouth, tickling his lip before he finally noticed and licked it up. "They're good!"

"No," Kaden said, shaking his head. "Just… no."

"They really are!"

"We need to get to the keep," Eldrin said, keeping them on target. "It was the residence of the royal family within the castle. That's a good place to start looking for the shield."

Kaden nodded, more than ready to move on from crunching up spiders like they were pine nuts. "Lead the way."

"Let's see if I can remember…" For all that he said he was uncertain, Eldrin led them at a steady pace, only pausing now and then to check and make sure there were no traps ahead of them. There weren't… how odd.

"Not too odd," Pepper said when Kaden mentioned he was surprised. "Each piece of your father's armor has its own special attribute. Aspis is a symbol of protection first and foremost. It stands to reason that although this castle could be destroyed and abandoned, if the shield is still here, it makes those who intend harm uncomfortable."

"A good trait in a—" There was a rumbling sound from somewhere above them.

Chum immediately stepped in close to Petey, who had one of the torches. "What was that?" he asked.

"Nothing as long as we get out of here soon," Eldrin said unconcernedly. "We're almost there… one more hallway, and then I think we go right, and—ah!" He looked at Kaden with bright eyes as he pointed toward a pair of carved double doors, still bearing a bit of the gold they'd once been covered with. "That's the entrance to your first home." He stepped back. "Would you care to open it?"

"I… yes." Yes, he would, even though his hand trembled at the thought of what he might find behind those doors. Kaden knew he had been too young to remember the battle fought here, but still… would a scent remain? A single object that might spark something inside of him, give him the connection to his parents and siblings that he desperately wanted but had never been able to envision? He pushed open the doors, which creaked gently. There was a stir of air, and then…

"No. Wait." Weylyn grabbed Kaden's shoulder from behind to hold him in place. "There's something in there."

"Of *course* there's something in there!" Chum said, falling against the wall in full-on histrionics. "Because nothing can ever be easy! Nothing can ever be nice! This is the *worst* quest ever, and I want you to know that—"

Whatever he wanted them to know was lost to a scream as an enormous spider came bursting out of the darkness toward them. It was as big as two dwarves put together, and glittered in the light the same way the little ones had. In another context, it might have been pretty— but not when it was charging forward, mandibles clacking and spiny limbs reaching for them.

"Get the legs!" Kaden shouted as he pulled Vrangar free in one quick motion. He managed to get a slash in, but the spider's leg was resilient, almost bouncy, and instead of the blade's edge biting through it, it rebounded instead.

The leg shuddered like taut wire beneath his blade, the impact traveling up his arms as if the creature were made of coiled steel instead of flesh. The thing wasn't just large; it was constructed to endure.

"Damn the legs!" Eldrin said as his second arrow missed. "Go for the body!" He shot his third arrow into the spider's head, taking out one of its massive eyes. It made an angry rattling noise, drew itself up, and—

"Take cover!" Weylyn moved to the front of the group, spreading his arms as wide as possible. The razor-sharp hairs the spider fired from its legs mostly struck Weylyn's armor, skittering away in sparks. Duke surged forward from Kaden's side, bracing himself in front of Petey as several barbs glanced off his consecrated plating. One still slipped through, catching Petey's ear, and Redfern cried out as others punched clean through her wings. Duke was protected, thankfully, but Petey took one to the ear, and Redfern was downed when several of them shot clean through her wings.

Redfern crashed to the ground, her wings trembling as they folded unevenly beneath her. Millicent darted to her side at once, fury sparking in her eyes. Kaden's stomach tightened; seeing one of their fairies injured always struck harder than he expected. They were small, but their courage was fierce.

"Out of the way!" Bardicus shouldered past them, his hammer at the ready. He brought it down right where the spider's head was—or should have been, but it jerked it out of the way just in time.

Unfortunately for the spider, it jerked toward Thalgrem's flashing gauntlets. He smashed his fist into the spider's body... actually *into* it. The noise was indescribable, and the spider's clacks and thrashes as it tried to get away were even worse. Weylyn finally put it out of its misery by stepping in and cutting off its head.

For a long moment, all Kaden could think was *Gross, so gross!* "Um... Redfern, will you be all right?" he asked once his brain was able to focus again.

"I'll be fine," he said tersely. "But we'd better get this done before the queen shows up."

Kaden frowned. "Queen?"

"That's a male mordant spider," Millicent said from where she was bandaging Redfern's left wing. "A soldier. The worker breed is much smaller, about the size of hounds, and they hide in the walls, weaving the tunnels and tending eggs. Soldiers like this one defend the brood, and the venom is strong enough to paralyze a grown man."

A faint tremor shivered through the floor. It might have been settling stone... but it repeated, slow and rhythmic, like something vast shifting somewhere deeper in the ruin.

Millicent's wings stiffened. "The brood answers to a matriarch named Threlka. If she is still alive, she will know we are here."

"And she dwarfs even the soldiers," Millicent added.

Another tremor rolled through the stone, slow and deliberate. The castle seemed to hold its breath. Even Duke's growl died in his throat.

Deep within the stone, something stirred.

The webs stretched through the ruin quivered, carrying vibration and warmth along their threads. Trespass. Living blood. The signal passed through the brood-lines, pulsing outward like a heartbeat.

Threlka felt it and waited.

The web was not yet ready. Prey was best taken when it believed itself unobserved.

The air felt faintly resistant here, as though something unseen resisted their passage.

Another strand of thick, gleaming silk hung across the ceiling, thicker than a rope and taut as steel. Eldrin ran his fingers along it and immediately snatched his hand back.

"That is queen-web," he murmured. "Fresh."

Five times larger... and somewhere ahead of them.

"Yeah, let's get this done." Kaden picked his torch up from where he'd dropped it and stepped into the gloom of the inner keep. It was so thickly webbed he could barely make out the furnishings beneath the thick, musty spider silk. It wasn't until he got to the bedroom that he finally figured out what one of the objects in there was.

A cradle.

His cradle, most likely. The webs draped over it like burial cloths, making his chest tighten. For a heartbeat, he almost reached for it, almost brushed the silk aside just to feel something of his past. But there was no time.

Kaden wished he could get closer, that he could take the time to pull the webs off and examine it, see if it had any elven cloth in it or perhaps the sort of toy a baby might like... but none of them were in good enough shape to handle another spider right now, especially not one that was five times larger than the last. They needed to find the shield and leave. The shield, the shield...

When Kaden finally laid eyes on it, he blanched. It was gripped tight in the arms of a skeletal, kneeling corpse, mummified and wound tight with white webbing. Whoever this was, they must have served his parents very faithfully to defend the shield Aspis to the last like this.

"Thank you," Kaden said, making the sign of Orealus between him and the corpse. "Thank you for everything. You can rest now, friend." He reached out to take the shield, but the second before he touched it, it fell free of the corpse's grasp right into his hands.

"That's eerie," Petey said nervously, scratching hard at his spider-hit ear. "That's not natural."

The weight settled against his arm with surprising warmth, as if recognizing him. Not trickery, not illusion, simply legacy. A reminder that the royal line had not ended here, not completely.

"Natural isn't the watchword to apply to a place like this," Eldrin replied.

Kaden listened to them talk with half an ear, too entranced by the sight of Aspis to pay better attention. It was a perfectly circular steel shield with a raised lion figure in the center of it, while the edge had a bright and silvery glint that reminded Kaden of Eldrin's blades. The back had two leather straps for him to grab onto. When Kaden touched them, they felt strong and unbreakable, not like they'd been moldering in a castle for over a decade.

"Lovely," Chum said from somewhere behind him, "delightful, how nice, you've got a fancy shield and it's very pretty, and can we *go now?* I would really, really like it if we could just—ow!" The last part was shouted at Petey, who'd probably hit him; Kaden couldn't see it from his angle. It didn't matter. He stood up, the shield on his arm, and looked around the dimly lit, spider-infested room that had once been a place of joy and family. Had he really hoped he'd find anything left of that here?

I can't look back. There's no reversing time, no telling what might have been if things had been different. This family is gone, but I have a different family now. A family that, for all its quirks and strangeness, he cared for very much.

"Let's go," Kaden said.

They left.

It wasn't until they were almost outside of the fallen city once more that, after counting the months he'd been assembling this new family in his head, Kaden realized—"Oh. I think that today is my birthday."

Ada's eyes widened. "Your birthday? Really? How old are you?"

"Um… seventeen."

"Oh, aye?" Bardicus clapped him on the mid-back, making him stagger a bit. "Well, a fine gift you've found yourself for the occasion then! Excellent craftsmanship on that shield of yours, even if some of it is regrettably elven."

"Regrettably?" Eldrin exclaimed. "*Regrettably?* He should be so lucky as to have a shield made by my people!"

"Everyone knows the best smiths in the world are *dwarven*, of course."

"Goblins have some very good smiths," Petey put in.

"Men aren't so bad ourselves," Weylyn said, freeing his own newest addition and staring hungrily at the blade.

"Enough about weapons, it's his birthday!" Ada said, rolling her eyes. "Mama!" Catching sight of the people of Whaldalf's Landing's fires, she ran ahead to them. "Mama, it's Kaden's birthday."

K'Lani straightened up from her crouch by the fireside. All around her, most of her fellow refugees were sound asleep, unperturbed after their time as Orphidian captives, but she had several skinned rabbits roasting over the open flame, and handed one immediately to Kaden. "Congratulations then, my prince. I'll give you what most young men seem to want for their birthdays—more to eat. Here, the first rabbit is yours."

"Thank you," Kaden said appreciatively, accepting the skewer. The meat was hot, unseasoned, and a bit greasy, but delicious.

"Good woman, you are," Bardicus said. "Managing to find food at this time of night, right outside a city of corpses. We could use someone with your skills in Kugdor."

"I'll have to pass, Your Majesty," she said dryly as she passed the next rabbit to Ada. "Don't worry," she said, taking in the dismayed faces of the ones unfed even as she made space for Pepper next to the fire. "We caught a whole warren of them; there's enough to go around. I didn't want to make more than one fire, though. It feels like cheating death to be here, doing this."

"We'll keep watch over you," Weylyn promised. "We'll keep you safe until you're back home." It went unsaid that "home" would never be considered truly safe again, but that wasn't what Kaden wanted to focus on right now. He took another bite, then handed some of his rabbit down to Duke, who crunched it up merrily.

Ada touched his elbow. "Happy birthday," she said quietly. "You might have gotten the shield, but I feel like I'm the one who received the real gift. You gave me my mother back, and I'll never forget that."

"I'm glad we found her in time," Kaden replied. He finished the rest of his meal surrounded by good company and an air of merriment that would have seemed impossible just a few hours ago. Honestly, he couldn't have asked for a better birthday.

And if he wished in his deepest heart that the people who used to live in the castle's keep could have been there with him… well, that was no one's business but his own.

* * *

Several thousand feet distant, a young man watched the warriors emerge from the castle, grimy but triumphant. He knelt behind the prickerthorn bush and used his punishing grip on one of its sharp branches as a reminder that, despite what he wanted, he couldn't make himself known. Not yet. He could only watch and help from a distance for now, but soon…

"Happy birthday, brother," he whispered. "I'll see you soon."

CHAPTER 14

You had to keep a fire small for an elf not to see it, especially in a place so devoid of other sources of light as this blasted place. Ezrah managed it, though. The stealth techniques he'd learned at the hands of the Shadowblades never stopped being useful.

Even here, with no enemies in sight, he kept expecting shadows to move at the edges of his vision. Silence was never safety. He had learned that too young.

He reached under the low canopy, shielding the fire from view, and turned the bird he'd started roasting an hour ago. His mouth was watering—this catch had been a lucky one, way more food than he was used to. It was a waterbird, with white feathers and a bright blue beak, clearly confused to have come so far inland and drawn in by his lure. He'd strangled it before its cries could alert anyone to his presence, then plucked and gutted it in short order.

Survival had become so familiar that comfort now felt foreign. A warm meal should have been a blessing. Instead, it reminded him how long it had been since he felt like a person rather than a weapon being sharpened.

Another person might have felt sympathy for the animal, so separated from its normal way of life, alone and just waiting to die. Not Ezrah. He knew better than to sympathize with something that could mean the difference between life and death to him.

He twisted the spit a little further, then sat back and pulled out his brace of throwing knives. He'd sharpened them yesterday, but he might as well do it again. As he reached for his whetstone, the uncanny paleness of the scars that crisscrossed his dark skin drew his eye. He felt a twinge in his wrist, the one that hadn't healed right ever since it was broken when he was ten, and grimaced.

He hated how the scars caught the firelight. They made him look like the creature the dungeons had tried to turn him into.

Ezrah hated to look at himself, but he also wasn't a fool. He knew that everything he'd gone through had been necessary. What was the alternative? To have died with his parents and older siblings at Karnergrien? For Bhalla to have mystically induced where Ezrah was hiding when he came to spirit away Kaden, who'd been in his crib where he was supposed to be? Ezrah was meant to wait with him there, but the sounds of battle had frightened him, and the lure of finding a dark, secret place to hide had proven too strong to resist. In that moment, he hadn't even thought about Kaden—he'd just thought about saving himself.

The fact that you're alive is more than you deserve. Yes, Ezrah knew he had only been a child of five years, but he still should have been brave enough to stay by his baby brother's side or at least to have taken Kaden with him. Then Bhalla would have had to search for them both, and maybe he would have brought Ezrah along, even though he was not destined to be a legendary savior of Empyrea. Maybe he would have kept them together and given Ezrah the chance to be the big brother Kaden deserved.

He dragged his fingers across one of the old burns, grounding himself in the truth he had repeated for years: Pain meant he was still here. Still capable. Still useful.

Ezrah clung to that belief on his worst days, repeating it to himself to keep the darkness from swallowing him whole.

What good did looking back do, though? None at all. There was no room for regrets. Tears only brought more pain, and begging for mercy only made enemies laugh louder as they broke you. Ezrah had spent ten long years in the hellish dungeons of Talaifotia, tortured for sport and kept in constant agony. He had eaten scraps and raw meat and insects, whatever he could manage to stay alive. He had been set against other prisoners, against animals, and against his own mind. He had been cut and broken, had bled and screamed and prayed to Orealus… even for death.

Sometimes he wondered if those prayers had ever been heard. Or if Orealus had simply waited to see whether Ezrah would break.

But he hadn't died.

The escape had been a random chance, the sort of thing Ezrah knew he had to take advantage of the second it appeared. It had still been hard to force himself to move—to slit the drunk guard's throat and steal his keys, to glide through the shadows without anyone seeing him, and finally to crawl through the refuse tunnel out of the darkness and into the light for the first time in a decade.

The brightness had stabbed into his eyes like knives. Freedom hurt in ways captivity never had.

The sun had terrified him. Moving water had seemed like a mirage. It had been so, so cold, and Ezrah's clothes were insufficient to keep him warm. He'd hardly moved beyond the shadow of the Dark Lord's castle before he could move no more, starving and frozen and a wreck, mind and soul.

Ezrah tried to clear his mind as he began to run the whetstone over the edge of his largest throwing knife. *Why bother reliving all this? What good will it do to dredge it all up again? No one cares. Just forget it and move on. Think about your brother. Focus on Kaden.*

Kaden was the one thread he held onto in the dark. The only thing that kept him from becoming what Talaifotia wanted him to be.

But Kaden had enough people focusing on him for tonight. His birthday. Ezrah dearly wished he could be part of the impromptu celebration—he'd never celebrated a birthday with his younger brother. The war had taken them all before Kaden even turned one. Ezrah couldn't even *remember* when his own birthday was. He hoped it was in the summer, when everything was bright and hot, and he didn't have to worry about the cold seeping into his wounded bones.

No, Kaden didn't need his worry or concern tonight. Let his younger brother celebrate while Ezrah's mind tried, for the thousandth time, to exorcise some of its own demons. Who knew? Maybe tonight it would be successful.

And maybe satyrs will fly someday.

That was one of Ta'la's sayings. She was a Shadowblade, Ezrah's savior, and had taken it upon herself to look after him regardless of the closeness of their ages. Despite her youth, she was bold enough to haunt the edges of that terrible place, looking for minions of Lucient to kill. When she'd first seen Ezrah, lying there covered in filth and undoubtedly looking like a demon himself, she'd nearly stabbed him through the heart. He hadn't even bothered to defend himself—what was the point?

If she had struck then, he wouldn't have flinched. He would have accepted it as the final, predictable ending of a life carved out of suffering.

His lack of will was what had stayed her hand. "You're just a boy," she said, leaning in and looking at him with wide eyes. "Where did you come from? Not..." She glanced toward Talaifotia with venom in her face. "Did you escape?"

"Did I?" Ezrah asked. They were the first words he'd uttered of his own free will in longer than he could remember. His voice had been ruined by screaming, but he could at least still make recognizable sounds. "Is this an escape? Are you going to kill me?"

"Not if you're not one of them." She looked at him and shook her head. "But you can't stay here. Come on."

That part of Ezrah's past, unlike his fog-shrouded earliest years, was crystal clear in his mind. Ta'la's introduction to Jedrek, the leader of the Shadows Rift Guild of assassins, was Ezrah's best shot at making something of himself. He'd been afraid at first that his years of torment had ruined him for anything else, but Ta'la had believed in him.

Jedrek... well, he'd definitely tried to run Ezrah off at first. "What's this used-up cellar rat on your arm?" he'd demanded when Ta'la had taken Ezrah to meet him the first time. Even after a bath—several baths—and in clothes that covered most of his scars, Jedrek had seen Ezrah's damage. He'd walked over deliberately slow, then darted in fast. Ezrah had flinched, but he didn't look away. It was worse to wonder what pain was coming next than to see it and brace yourself.

Ezrah had grown used to men looming over him. What Jedrek never expected was that Ezrah was done being small.

"He's a boy, not a rat! His name is Ezrah," Ta'la had replied proudly. "I found him outside Talaifotia. I think he could be very useful to us."

"You think wrong."

"I don't—"

"Look at him! He's as skinny as a stick." Whereas Jedrek was strong and well-muscled, a healthy specimen of a human except for a long scar marring his face. "He's clearly been beaten to the point of uselessness. Keep him as a servant, or I'll make him a drudge here, but he's not Rift material."

"I can be." Ezrah was still surprised by the sound of his own voice back then. Jedrek had looked at him in surprise, then contempt.

"You can't even face me without flinching."

"Maybe not," Ezrah allowed, "but I can handle anything you throw at me and learn to be better. You think I survived a decade in the dungeons of Talaifotia because I'm weak?"

A new expression lit upon Jedrek's face. It looked something like… guilt? It was gone quickly, but Ezrah knew now was the time to press. "I might be damaged, and I know I'm young, but I can learn. I swear I can. I can be better, I can do more—do *anything*—with my life. Orealus guided Ta'la to me, I'm sure of it." Apart from surviving at all, that was the best proof he had that Orealus was still working in his life. "How else could she have found me in such a terrible place?"

"A good question," Jedrek said, glaring at the young woman beside Ezrah until she looked like she wanted to sink into the floor. "How did you know you weren't picking up a spy, hmm? What a chance for those bastards to sneak someone into our guild under the guise of a bruised-but-not-broken survivor like this young man?" He reached out a hand toward Ezrah's face like he was preparing to slap him. "How do we know this is truly you at all?"

Ezrah caught the hand right before it impacted his face. In that moment, he didn't care who Jedrek was or what he might do for him. All he knew was that he wasn't going to be a victim any longer. "Don't," he snapped, his arm trembling with weakness. His recently broken wrist twinged painfully. "Don't do that to me." He finally let go, heaving a breath in, then out. Fear and pride warred in his veins, making him feel like he ought to be running or fighting. Ezrah did neither. "I want to learn from you, but I won't let you treat me like I'm nothing but a training dummy."

It was the first line he had drawn for himself in years, and he felt the tremor of it in his bones.

"Give him a chance," Ta'la urged, getting her confidence back. "I'll take responsibility for him. Let me show him the ropes, and if he doesn't work out after a few months, we can make a new plan."

"Who are you to make these decisions for me?" Jedrek asked, but Ezrah could see he was considering it. "Opinionated little miss…" He looked back at Ezrah. "Fine. You get three months' probation in our guild. If I catch you contacting anyone on the outside, if I catch you working against us, if I catch you bringing harm to anyone in here, it'll be a fate worse than death that awaits you, boy."

"I won't betray you," Ezrah promised.

I've still got so much to do.

Healing came first. "We can't push you the way we need to if you're about to keel over from old wounds," Jedrek announced. The use of yah'zaval to heal him was intense, taking days to complete, but at the end of it, Ezrah was healed of all but his deepest, most grievous wounds.

The warmth of yah'zaval lingering in his veins felt almost unbearable. Mercy had become something foreign to him, yet his body remembered it even when his mind did not.

"I'm sorry about the scars," the healer apologized. "The power of Orealus can work many wonders, but it doesn't erase the past."

"It's all right," Ezrah replied honestly. "I don't care about them." All he cared about was being the best trainee he could be. Ta'la had the skills to sneak around one of the most dangerous places in the world and carry him out of there without being seen. Ezrah wanted to be able to do that. He needed to be strong. He needed to be deadly.

He needed to be good enough to find the baby brother he knew had survived.

Oddly enough, Ezrah's early lessons with Khalon, the High Sentinel of the Crown and top guard of his father, King Karatheas, came back to him as he trained to become a Shadowblade. There was so much more to it than being good at hand-to-hand combat and being able to survive the worst life could throw at you. You had to learn to move through the darkness as silently as a shadow; to follow a target through a crowd without losing them or giving yourself away; to live off the land, no matter how remote or inhospitable it was. The one quality all of those things had in common: You needed great patience, something Ezrah had once been very bad at.

Patience had been his older brother's gift. Ezrah had only learned it through suffering.

"You've just got to slow down, little colt," his older brother had teased him after Ezrah complained to him one day. "Slow down just enough to see what you need to see."

Like the wizard taking your baby brother away to safety while you cower in the closet. You could have screamed, kicked, made a racket... but he was already vanishing by the time you saw him.

The memory stabbed sharper than any blade. Every day since has been shaped by that moment of fear.

Kaden was constantly on Ezrah's mind. He was the goal, always, the constellation that Ezrah used to guide his life. He had to survive to help Kaden. He had to find his little brother, protect him, and give him the chances that Ezrah himself would never have now.

He wanted to sit Kaden down and share what he remembered of their family. The strength of their father's arms when he hugged you, the sweet smell of roses that surrounded their mother, their brother's laughter, and their sister's strength. He wanted to be of use, to love and serve, and be a part of Kaden's life. And now, after so much searching, after years of working and striving and hoping... he'd found him.

But Kaden didn't need his help.

The realization hollowed him. He had shaped his entire existence around reaching someone who no longer needed rescuing.

How can anything I can do compare with the people who've already joined him? I can't summon yah'zaval or take down an ogre. I haven't been on this quest with him from the beginning, and I can't tempt him with companionship when he already has so much. I'm nothing but a stranger to him, a remnant of a past he doesn't remember.

Should I even bother…

It wasn't a true question. Ezrah knew he would follow his brother to the ends of the earth and back if he had to. Just… it might be best if he kept to himself. For now.

Maybe forever. That was something he would decide later.

Ezrah's stomach growled. He retrieved his meal, one small piece at a time, careful to keep the scent contained under the canopy he'd built. He shivered in the night breeze, colder than usual. Maybe it was seeing the distant glow of the fire that Kaden and his companions were celebrating around that made him feel the wind so acutely.

Ezrah sighed.

Maybe next year I'll celebrate your birthday with you.

He let the hope linger only a moment. Hope was dangerous. But tonight, he allowed himself to hold it anyway.

CHAPTER 15

The next morning looked the same as the others since leaving Whaldalf's Landing—gray and cool, misty and insubstantial, and yet without the air of menace that even the sunlit hours had held before. After an evening of celebration, cheer, companionship, and a good night's sleep, Kaden was feeling downright optimistic as he got ready for the day.

The optimism felt fragile, like a thin shell over something heavier. Part of him was still waiting for the next disaster to fall out of the sky. It always seemed to, lately.

He walked Duke out to the edge of their slowly waking group and signaled for him to go do his business. A moment later, Petey joined him.

Kaden smiled at his friend. It felt like he'd known him for years when in reality it had been less than one. Other than Duke, Petey was the very first person to join him on his journey, and now…

"It's different from how we started, isn't it?" Petey ventured.

"So different," Kaden agreed, wondering if his friend had somehow read his mind. *Probably just my face.* "It's strange to think about just *how* different it was in the beginning when it was just us."

He hadn't realized until now how much he missed the simplicity of those days, even with their dangers. Back then, the world felt enormous and terrifying, but his choices felt smaller, clearer.

"I'm honestly impressed that we made it as far as we did on our own."

"Yeah. That was fun," Petey said wistfully. "Traveling through the forest together, sneaking into the city of Lumhagen…"

"Fighting off the goblins who wanted to kill me, holding the grawlers back until Pepper could take them out…"

"Getting caught in the magic of Lumhagen and marched to Bhalla like prisoners," Petey finished. "Yeah, all right, there were some parts that could definitely have gone better."

"True, but… I think you're right, too. It *was* fun when it was just you and me."

"And Duke and Bug."

"Right." Kaden looked around. "Where is Bug, by the way?"

"Oh, ew." Petey wrinkled his nose and grabbed the ends of his ears in dismay. "He fell asleep in the crusty cookpot last night and ended up absorbing the leftovers into himself. He got as swollen as a whole colony of ticks. I'm letting him eject it all in private right now."

"Eject it… You mean—actually, never mind, I don't want to know."

"It smells so much worse coming out than it did going down, let me tell you," Petey muttered.

"Thanks, don't want to know."

"Suit yourself. But if he leaks into my pack again, I'm mailing him to Bhalla," Petey said. "And the *color*, Orealus save me, you don't want to know about the—"

"No, I don't! I don't want to know, stop telling me." Kaden laughed. Petey didn't push, and they stood in comfortable silence a bit longer before Duke came back tail wagging.

"So," Petey said after fending off Duke's slobbery and enthusiastic greeting, "what's next for us?"

"We've got to get K'Lani and the others back to Whaldalf's Landing," Kaden said. "They have a lot of work to do rebuilding, and there are plenty of families who need to be reunited."

"And after that?"

After that… Kaden had been giving that a lot of thought, and so far, he hadn't come up with a concrete plan. Now that he had the Aspis, what piece of the armor should they go after next? "I'll figure it out soon," he said.

"You'd better," a new voice remarked from behind them.

Petey jumped, and Kaden almost followed suit from the surprise, but it was just a particularly grumpy-sounding Chum, rubbing his eyes with one hand and scratching his furry rear with the other. Kaden braced himself. No one could derail a morning faster than Chum.

"Because if you think," Chum went on around a yawn, "that I'm going to march around for no good reason while you try to figure out east from west, you've got some more thinking to do. And for what my opinion is worth," he added, "I think we should go *that* way to get back." He pointed not toward the plain to the north of them, but to the forest to the east that was just beginning to be visible through the fog.

"Oh yeah," Petey said, nodding sagely. "That dark, ominous forest looks like a great place to go for a walk with a bunch of unarmed villagers. Brilliant."

"Forests offer hiding places!" Chum retorted. "There aren't a lot of those out *here*, and given how many awful creatures of evil and wickedness have tried to attack us lately, having a hiding place sounds like a pretty good idea to me!"

"There are plenty of dark creatures who could track you through a forest," Eldrin scoffed as he joined them, his long, pale hair pulled back into a tight set of braids today. "Besides, that's the Forgotten Forest."

"So? And? Therefore?" Chum asked impatiently.

"It's not a safe place," Queen Pepper put in as she flew over. "Like so much of this part of the world, it carries terrible memories, and the creatures to match them. Before the war, it was a beautiful place. I haven't visited it since then, but when the binicorns were driven away, so too were the original inhabitants of the forest. It's rumored to be very unsafe these days."

Pepper's wings dimmed slightly as she spoke. Even saying the forest's name seemed to draw old memories to the surface.

She still looked a little pale, Kaden thought. He hoped that whichever way they went, Pepper would be able to rest and recover.

The other side of the plain was a craggy, bare-boned mountainside that would slow them down even more than fumbling through a forest would. "Then we'll go back the way we came," Kaden said. "Now that we've taken care of the Fallen, it should be pretty safe."

"Famous last words," muttered Chum, but he got to work packing his things up without any further dissent. After half an hour, everyone was ready to go. Luckily, none of the villagers had been injured badly enough that they couldn't walk, so they headed north at a brisk pace, leaving Karnergrien behind, letting the ruins sleep until a day when it was safe to reclaim them once more.

Kaden looked back only once. The fallen city lay quiet, its shadows no longer hostile but still heavy. He felt the weight of every life lost there settle somewhere deep in his chest.

They had walked for less than a mile when Petey's ears began to twitch. He slapped at the tips of them for a second, looking around like he expected a fly buzzing above his head, or a spray of spores to be settling on him, but Bug was resting in his sack, and there were no insects here.

"You okay?" Kaden asked.

"Fine," Petey said slowly. "Fine, just… yes, I'm… hmm." He took two more steps, then stopped and whirled around. "No, I'm not fine! I hear something!"

Petey's ears vibrated sharply. Whatever he heard, it wasn't small.

"So do I," Eldrin said dryly as he walked past Petey. "Your voice is *very* noticeable."

"No, it's not one of us, it's something different!"

Kaden focused on listening as closely as he could, but he didn't hear anything unusual. "Are you positive?"

"Yes, of course I am," Petey said, the tips of his ears twitching so fast they appeared as a blur to Kaden. "Goblins have better hearing than every other race! It's a thrum, and a beat, and a… a…"

"I hear it now, too," Weylyn said, turning and looking in the same direction as Petey.

"So do I," Queen Pepper said, her skin going more translucent than Kaden had ever seen. "I've heard it before, during the war. Look above the ruins of Karnergrien."

Kaden looked. At first, all he saw were faint wisps of fog clinging to the sky despite the sun's efforts to burn them away, but then he saw a dot appear.

His stomach tightened. Nothing that big should move that fast.

It moved in and out of his vision, vanishing behind clouds and reappearing, and only once it had almost reached the ruins did he recognize it for what it really was.

"Is that… a dragon?" Kaden asked. It had to be—nothing else could be so large. The creature's hide shone a deep obsidian black even from a distance, and it had to be over a hundred feet long, perhaps even two, once you measured the tail, and its *wings* shadowed a huge swath of the plain beneath it. Everyone could hear them as they *swoosh, swoosh, swooshed* closer.

"That's not any dragon," Weylyn said grimly, closing the faceplate of his helm and reaching for his massive sword. "That's Morvar! Ready your weapons," he shouted. "K'Lani, lead the rest of the villagers to the forest! We need to distract Morvar, or he'll kill all of them before they get there," he added to Kaden.

"Get that big bastard on the ground," Bardicus said with a fierce grin, spinning his massive hammer like it was no heavier than a blade of grass. "Then we'll see who kills who." Beside him, Thalgrem banged his gauntlets together, throwing sparks.

At least someone is ready for a fight. Kaden certainly wasn't. He reached for Vrangar, but even as he took his sword in hand, he felt a surge of despair. How could they possibly take on a creature that was so powerful? Besides, didn't dragons breathe fire?

"They can," Pepper said, and Kaden was startled as he realized that he'd said his last thought out loud. "But it takes a lot of energy and time to build up to it. They prefer to take out their opponents using the advantage of their size and strength if possible. Which means he'll likely settle on the ground before long."

"Good," Weylyn said. His voice sounded hollow from within the helmet. "Then he can have the pleasure of paying for his crimes against my family even sooner than I'd hoped."

"But we don't have a weapon that will kill him," Kaden said. Didn't they need something made from his own scales to strike a killing blow?

"That doesn't mean we can't make him regret the day he was spawned," Bardicus said. "Either get ready for the fight or run Petey an' Chum off to the forest as well, lad, but either way, Morvar is coming!"

Glancing behind him, Kaden saw that Chum and Petey were clutching each other a few feet away. Chum was wailing, but Petey just looked scared stiff. "Go with K'Lani!" Kaden called out, and that got the two of them moving. The villagers were already halfway to the forest.

Kaden would help make sure they made it all the way there.

This is part of my role as the future king of Empyrea. It's my destiny to face this foe. And he would face Morvar bravely. He readied his sword and his new shield, his resolve firm. The metal of his weapons seemed to glow in the sunlight, and Kaden couldn't help but grin as he looked at them.

"That's the spirit, lad!" Bardicus shouted encouragingly. "That's it!"

His words sent a surge of confidence through Kaden, and a moment later, a shaft of light rose from his sword. It nearly struck Morvar, and the immense beast twisted ungracefully in the air as it struggled to get back on track to confronting them.

"Aye! Do it again!"

"I don't know how to," Kaden confessed.

"Then let us take it from here with more traditional weapons," Eldrin suggested as he nocked two arrows on his bow. "Care for a shooting contest, Ada? First one to wound the flying snake buys the other the finest meal in Whaldalf's Landing."

"You're on," she said, her voice barely shaking as she nocked an arrow of her own. She glanced after her mother, who had nearly gotten the rest of the villagers to the forest, and her shoulders straightened. "Let's do this."

"I'm here!"

Kaden was surprised to see Petey running back at full speed, Loyal Dwingent out and in his hand. "I'm here, I'm back, I'm here!" He reached for Duke and mounted up like the big dog was a horse. Duke, to his credit, didn't try to throw Petey off either. "I'm going to do this with you," Petey said with determination. "Even if it's the *last* thing I do."

"It won't be the last," Kaden said, touched by his friend's courage.

"He's about in range now," Eldrin said. He drew, aimed, and fired two arrows at once. They soared up to strike Morvar's belly, where they immediately broke into pieces.

"Bad aim," Ada said. "You should have gone for the head." She fired next, just as Morvar began to glide closer to the ground in preparation for landing. Her arrow went straight toward his face—and was bitten in half.

Then it was too late for more arrows, because Morvar swooped down to the ground, dust billowing over all of them from the backdraft caused by his wings. When the grime and grit cleared, all Kaden could see was the dragon in front of them. He seemed to fill both the earth and the sky, as grand as he was menacing. His scales were a shining black, and the ones around his throat emitted steam with every exhale. His eyes were the color of ivory, enormous, and set high into his rounded skull. He had long, thick horns that curved up and out at the back of his head, and his long snout held rows of razor-sharp teeth. Spikes traced the path of his spine all the way down to the tip of his tail, and his scythe-like claws dug furrows in the ground with every ponderous step.

Morvar looked over them all, slowly and deliberately, until he finally focused on Kaden. "Lah ah oom tii paak grazat mu kip na bokt," the dragon said.

"What's the great brute sayin', eh?" Bardicus grumbled.

"I can tell it's Draakonlor," Queen Pepper said, her hair swirling as she gathered her yah'zaval in defense, "but I don't speak it myself."

"He said, 'So you're whom my lord speaks of, tasty little swine,'" Kaden said.

Weylyn turned his helmeted head toward Kaden. "How could you understand him?"

He was just as confused as Weylyn was. "I… I don't know."

The words had slipped into his mind like they belonged there, familiar and unwelcome at the same time.

"A sign of your lineage through your father," Pepper said. "He was also blessed by Orealus to understand many different tongues."

"Oh? Is it goin' to help us at all for Kaden to talk the dragon to death?" Bardicus asked impatiently. "Let's get on to the beheading!"

The dragon hissed something that sounded like a laugh, followed by, "Gwaw Gwaw fengash mu kip domaas baaga dwerzno."

Bardicus stabbed a finger toward Morvar. "What did that brute just say, eh?"

"Um…" Kaden shook his head. "I don't think you want me to repeat it."

"Tell me now!"

"He… he laughed at you and called you a foolish, bearded, brainless little dwarf," Kaden said.

"*What?* No one talks about me that way!" Before anyone could stop him, Bardicus raised his hammer and began running full speed at Morvar, who was still chortling to himself. Ten feet away, he leaped into the air, swinging his hammer through a massive arc and bringing it down against the dragon's right front shoulder with a crash.

The sound was devastating, the effect of the impact even more so. Bardicus sailed backward, losing his grip on his hammer when he finally smashed to the ground twenty feet away. Morvar, Kaden was surprised to see, wasn't unaffected by the strike either. The dragon retracted his arm and bellowed in anger and pain.

Kaden's heart lurched. If Bardicus died because of a single insult, he'd never forgive himself.

"Thalgrem, get Bardicus!" Kaden shouted. "Everyone else, get ready for an attack!" He raised Vrangar and hoped against hope that it would be able to cause at least as much damage as Bardicus's hammer had.

Morvar didn't come any closer, though. Instead, he opened his mouth wide, showing off row upon row of blackened teeth. A gout of smoke emerged from his throat, and a dull red glow began to build at the back of it.

"Kneel down!" Pepper cried out as she suddenly raised a wall of rock in front of them. A second later, fire hit it, seeping around the corners and over the top with the force of the dragon's deadly breath. Kaden crouched next to Ada and pulled Duke in close. The dog was panting fiercely, already far too hot.

"I won't be able to hold for long," Pepper cried out.

Her hands trembled violently, flecks of light slipping from her fingers like sparks.

"We need a distraction," Weylyn said.

"I'll go." Redfern hoisted her spear. "He can chase me with his fire while you flee!"

"Are you an idiot? He'll just lift his flame and roast you the second you leave the safety of the rock!" Eldrin snapped.

"Better for me to roast than my queen!" Redfern yelled back. "I'm going!" She began to fly up, but all of a sudden, the flame stopped. The stone wall in front of them crackled with heat, but the attack had moved on.

Kaden felt his boots growing hot. Even the air tasted scorched.

But to what? Kaden chanced crawling over and looking around the edge of the stone.

An arrow three times larger than any he'd ever seen before sailed through the air and hit Morvar at the base of his wing. It didn't just hit—it *exploded*.

Kaden flinched at the force of it. Whoever this stranger was, he wielded enough firepower to take on a dragon alone.

The core of the projectile shimmered with an iridescent, hardened surface that Kaden recognized even from a distance. Dragon scale. Not newly forged, because only the Great Forge of Kugdor had the heat to shape a fresh scale. These must have been relics from the old Empyrean armories, reforged centuries ago by the Dragon Guild and later scavenged or preserved by Seward's people. They could attach new shafts or explosive heads to them, but no one outside of Kugdor could make new ones.

Morvar roared and tucked his wings in close—clearly, that was a sensitive spot for the dragon.

"Hey! You there!" A burly man Kaden had never seen before waved at him as he wound the crank on an enormous crossbow. "Run, you fools, run!" A second later, he fired again, this time hitting Morvar's face. The dragon shrieked as the explosion momentarily blinded him.

"Come on, we have to go now!" Kaden pushed to his feet and led the charge for the forest, streaming right past the stranger who'd saved their lives, only looking back to make sure everyone was following.

He didn't look back again. Leaders moved forward. Leaders kept people alive.

He watched as arrow after arrow struck Morvar. The attack was a distraction enough to keep the dragon from being able to focus on his own fire—every time he opened his mouth, an arrow hit him in the jaw or snout. One even came perilously close to his eyes, and left the dragon reeling from both anger *and* more annoyance than actual pain.

As soon as Weylyn, who was bringing up the rear, passed the boundary of the forest, Kaden followed him in. Half of him was expecting Morvar to set the entire forest on fire in his pursuit of them, but either there was something in here he didn't want to disturb, or he was simply uninterested in the inconvenience of it. The sound of beating wings filled the air again, and a moment later, the dragon was aloft, flying back in the same direction it had come from.

Even retreating, Morvar looked powerful enough to level kingdoms.

Oh, thank Orealus. Kaden almost slumped to the ground from relief, but he had to thank the people who'd come to their rescue. The three of them, motley in appearance but all well armed, had gathered beside them.

Kaden opened his mouth to speak, but it was Weylyn who broke the silence first as he said in an incredulous tone, "Seward? What in the blazes are *you* doing here?"

Kaden blinked, thrown by the familiarity in Weylyn's voice. Whoever this man was, he wasn't a stranger to all of them.

CHAPTER 16

The man at the head of the party of three blinked. "Weylyn?"
Weylyn pulled off his helm and beamed, the guarded weight he usually carried slipping away for just a moment.

Kaden blinked. He had never seen Weylyn look like this. Not guarded. Not burdened. Just human.

"Seward, you old son of a centaur. What's happened to you of late, eh? You used to be such a gilded face, and now you could be something an ogre scratched out of his rear."

That was a little—okay, a lot—harsh, but Kaden could see some truth to it. Seward was fair-skinned with broad shoulders, dark eyes, and a long, pointed nose. He reminded Kaden of the mayor back home, a man who had once worked hard and then stopped. There was strength there still, buried beneath a sagging stance and a scar over his left brow that looked more earned than ornamental.

Men like that survived wars not through glory, but through stubborn refusal to die.

"You're one to talk, you brute," Seward replied in good humor. "You're as thick as a slab of peat these days—and you smell just as bad. What, do your companions make you run at enemies with your arms over your head to stink them out before engaging?"

"Glib as ever," Weylyn said.

"Perhaps too glib," the shortest of their three saviors chimed in. It took Kaden a moment to realize why the voice was pitched so high—she was a woman! The armor hadn't hidden her presence so much as sharpened it. She stood like someone who expected to be disappointed and was ready to punish anyone who proved her right. There was something coiled and furious about her, like a blade waiting for a reason.

A second later, she opened the faceplate on her helmet, and—yes, now Kaden could see it. Her skin was the color of cream, and she had surprisingly delicate features. Wisps of blond hair marked her forehead, but none escaped from the bottom of her helmet. *She must keep it short.* "Seward might like your banter, but I prefer to get to the heart of things. What's the man who left us for dead doing here, on the outskirts of the Forgotten Forest?"

Weylyn looked wounded. "I didn't leave you for dead, Anika. I wouldn't do that."

Kaden felt the air tighten. Whatever this history was, it wasn't settled. Not even close.

"Easy to say, and yet one moment we're fighting for our lives against that wyvern, and the next, I'm waking up in a healer's tent with these two louts and no sign of you."

"Who do you think carried you to that tent?" Weylyn demanded. "Who do you think paid the healer to treat you? Who do you think finished off the wyvern before it could make all attempts at healing futile?"

"Who abandoned us there without even leaving a note as to his intentions?" she shot back.

The third man among the newcomers raised his hands. "All right, all right." He spoke like a man used to standing between worse tempers than these.

He was only wearing partial armor, probably because taking on the job of supporting the massive crossbow was hard enough without being weighed down with plate. His face was lean and expressive, and his left eye was covered by an eyepatch. He had thin black hair slicked back against his head, and his expression was somewhere between welcoming and wary as he looked at Weylyn. "No need for a fight out here when we've just gotten through a bad one. We found your little lambs, wolf cub." He nodded his head to the left. "Sent them ahead to our home base. I assume you want to be reunited with them."

Kaden exhaled without realizing he'd been holding his breath.

"Rowden." Weylyn nodded with respect. "That would be ideal, yes."

"Good. Then come with us."

"Aye, and then you can explain how you came to this part of the world, of all places!" Seward exclaimed, clapping Weylyn on the shoulder as they began to walk.

Kaden glanced at Petey, who shrugged, then at Pepper. She smiled, flew over to him, and murmured, "I don't think there's any harm in going with them, especially after they came to our aid. We can always leave later if we need to."

That was a good point. Kaden knew his reluctance to trust these people wasn't unreasonable, but if they really were old friends of Weylyn… or in Anika's case, perhaps old enemies? Then it ought to be safe.

He hoped it was safe.

"I believe them to be Empyrean Knights," Pepper went on quietly as they walked. "Or at least, knights in training before the war. They would be young to have fought at that time themselves, much like Weylyn."

The word *knights* settled heavily in Kaden's chest, carrying memories he'd never lived and expectations he wasn't sure he was ready to meet. That title had once meant loyalty, honor, and sacrifice. He wondered how much of that still survived.

"So why are *they* living in the middle of a forest with a bad reputation like this one?" Eldrin asked.

"Precisely *because* of that reputation," Anika called over her shoulder. Her gaze was harsh. "You of all people ought to know the benefits that can come from hiding away in the middle of a great wood, elf."

The words landed with deliberate cruelty. Old wounds spoke louder than reason here.

Eldrin bristled. "What do you mean by that?"

"Only that if you had bothered to be more active in the war instead of secreting yourselves away at the end, we might not *need* to hide away now! We could have—"

"Ah-ah." Rowden laid a hand on Anika's shoulder. "No picking fights with the guests, please. We haven't even shown them our hospitality yet."

"Perhaps they don't deserve it," she said, shrugging off his grip. "Given that their judgment is bad enough to lead them to ally themselves with *Weylyn*, of all people." She stalked off ahead, and Weylyn turned around with a sigh.

"It's not about you all," he explained. "It's… Anika and I… well, let's just say that we were close, once upon a time. Very close. And that came to a rather abrupt end when I… decided to move on."

Kaden suspected the truth was messier than Weylyn let on. It usually was.

"Dumped her cold in that healer's tent and didn't even look back," Seward said jovially. At least one person was able to get some entertainment from the situation. "We all knew it was coming, of course—the Dragon Guild wasn't as expansive as our dear wolf cub would like, didn't go after the targets he craved. It was inevitable that Weylyn would leave."

"You didn't have to break her heart, though," Rowden rebuked him, shifting the massive crossbow to his other shoulder.

"I… didn't think breaking her heart was possible." Weylyn sounded baffled.

Ada sniffed. "Just like a man," she muttered. Kaden was tempted to ask what she meant by that, but… maybe later. It wasn't long before they were led into a clearing, and there…

Well, it was actually a very cozy little community. Half a dozen huts on the edges of the trees made up the outskirts of it, each one small but neat, and in the center was a communal firepit edged with boulders big enough to sit on if you were inclined. There were no chickens—perhaps the people here thought they were too noisy to be part of a secret village like this one—but two cows were staked to graze nearby, and they were chewing grass and fallen leaves contentedly.

It didn't look forgotten at all. It looked careful.

This place *was* called the Forgotten Forest, wasn't it? Kaden wondered how long that name had ceased to apply.

More importantly, the villagers of Whaldalf's Landing were all there, sitting near the firepit in various states of alertness. Some were napping, a few were whittling or stitching, and K'Lani had already taken over the task of cooking and was holding a spoon out to none other than Chum with something for him to taste.

"Mmm," he said as he swallowed. "Delicious. Could use more salt, but since we don't have any, it's about as perfect as possible."

Kaden wondered if Chum had ever tasted anything he didn't believe could be improved.

"Wait until we get home," K'Lani promised him. "I've got a version of this that will knock you off your hooves." She looked over at Kaden and Ada and smiled, her expression full of relief. "One of these noble knights told me you all were all right, but it's good to see it for myself," she said.

Ada went to her mother. Kaden was about to follow suit, but Weylyn's hand on his arm stopped him. "We should tell them who you are," he said quietly.

Kaden's pulse quickened. Once spoken, there would be no taking it back.

"Why?" Kaden asked.

"These are former knights of Empyrea, just as I was meant to be. They were some of your father's most loyal subjects," Weylyn explained. "If some of them chose to pledge their fealty to you, we'd be fortunate to have them."

"I…"

Seward came over and put his arms over their shoulders, breaking the moment. "What're you two whispering about, eh?" he asked in a tone both friendly and wary. "Wolf cub, is this lad your benefactor right now?" He leaned back a bit and looked Kaden up and down. "You don't have the look of a spoiled young lord, but I can't think of anyone else who could afford this bastard's fees."

"What fees?" Chum moaned, momentarily distracted from the meal K'Lani was dishing out. "He hasn't charged a decent fee in months!"

"Oh? Sounds like there's a story there."

It looked like Kaden was going to have to tell the truth, whether he was confident about these people or not. He looked at Weylyn and nodded.

"You could say he's my benefactor," Weylyn said, taking over the conversation. "This is Kaden, the last living descendant of King Karatheas. I'm sworn to follow him and help him recover the throne of Empyrea."

Seward stared at Weylyn as his hair had just changed from black to white. "What?"

"You heard me."

Now that intense stare was on Kaden again, picking every feature apart. "I see it," Seward muttered as he let go of them and stepped back. His fear wasn't for himself. It was the kind born of knowing exactly what monsters followed royal blood. "I see it, damn these eyes of mine. Why would you bring this boy *here*?" he demanded of Weylyn, his tone verging on hysterical. "He'll be the ruin of all of us!"

Kaden saw fear there, not malice. The kind that came from surviving horrors no one should have endured.

"Morvar, that great old beast—he was after this boy, wasn't he?"

"I don't mean to put you in any danger," Kaden said quickly, holding his hands up in a gesture of peace.

It was lost on Seward, who was quickly flanked by both Anika and Rowden, their hands on their swords. At the same time, Kaden was aware of Eldrin, Bardicus, and Thalgrem moving up behind them. No one had drawn steel yet, but he was starting to get worried.

"Didn't *mean* to—boy, do you have any idea the horrors that Lucient and his army wrought on us during the Great War?" Seward snapped. "Did Weylyn neglect to tell you? Then let me do so! He slaughtered *thousands* of us, then took our leaders and skinned them alive before our very eyes. Those who were taken by his army, if they were killed quickly, they were lucky. The unlucky were stripped of their bodies and fed to the war engines of Lucient's army, or taken to be slaves at Craig Diávolos Castle." Seward's hands were shaking, but his voice was firm.

These weren't stories meant to frighten a boy. They were memories that still hadn't loosened their grip.

"You need to leave. *All* of you need to leave. We can't have you here."

"Please." Kaden took a short step forward. "I swear, I'm not here to cause you any harm, and we'll leave very soon, but the townspeople we rescued are exhausted. A few hours of rest would—"

"Did you not hear me, *boy*?" Seward abruptly drew his sword. Everyone else around Kaden did the same, even Pepper hovering in a protective stance over Kaden's head. "I said, get out!"

"Ridiculous!"

Her voice cut through the tension cleaner than any blade.

Everyone in the melee turned to look at K'Lani, who was standing now, the long spoon she'd been using to stir the pot held in her hand like a field marshal's baton. The other villagers were standing as well, even those who'd been asleep moments ago. "You." She pointed the spoon at Seward. "If you've even a shred of decency, you're bound by hospitality to give us time to rest and recover a bit before kicking us out. It would be different if this place were under attack, but it's not. You and your people just took on one of the fiercest beasts out there and *won*, so don't pretend to be afraid of shadows now."

"We're Dragon Guild now," Seward said, a little bit of sheepishness seeping in under the belligerence in his voice. "Dragon Guild hunts dragons."

K'Lani raised an eyebrow. "And that disqualifies you from hunting any other kind of evil creature because…"

"Um."

She shook her head. "Try not to let your fear run away with your good sense, is all I ask." She lowered her spoon and sat down again, which rather effectively took the wind out of everyone else's sails.

"She's right," Weylyn said, sheathing his sword very deliberately. "There's no need for conflict between us, especially since you three and I are old friends."

Imagine Weylyn being the voice of reason, Kaden thought to himself.

"We have a common goal," Weylyn went on. "The three of you clearly aren't satisfied with lives as simple farmers if you've joined up with the Dragon Guild. Only the boldest and bravest are willing to commit to fight a creature as fabled as Morvar."

"How could we be satisfied with a simple life?" Anika asked, pain clear on her face. "You can't tell me the pain of the past has lessened for you, Weylyn. Not after everything we saw, after what happened to our families and everyone we loved. How is it not the same for you?"

"It is the same for me," Weylyn replied. "I just didn't let myself realize it for a long time. Too long." He set a hand on Kaden's shoulder. "That's why I'm following Kaden now. For the first time since my father's murder, I've got the hope of revenge—not just against random creatures of Lucient here and there, but against Lucient himself.

"No one since Karatheas has been able to bring so many different factions together under one banner. Look at us," Weylyn continued, gesturing to their motley company. "I'll be the first to admit that I didn't truly believe in him at first. He's still getting his full growth, tramps through the forest like an ox, and has all the fighting skills of a drunk city guard—"

"Hey!" Kaden protested. He thought he was getting pretty good!

"But he pulls through when it counts the most," Weylyn insisted, and Kaden stopped protesting then. "He's absolutely determined to do what's right, whether that means standing tall against a goblin commander or cutting down dozens of Fallen in an effort to achieve his goal. He's gone up against ogres, dark elves, and even faced down a beast of the deeps in his quest, and both his promise and courage only grow with each day." Weylyn squeezed Kaden's shoulder, gently for him, but it was nearly enough to make Kaden wince.

"When he says he's going to do everything in his power to defeat Lucient, I believe him," Weylyn said, finally letting go. "And I trust him with my life. If you really want to strike at Lucient, if you really want to get revenge for our beloved dead, then you should consider doing the same." He nodded his head toward the fire. "And that's enough out of me. I'm starving." He headed toward K'Lani, and after enduring another moment of intense scrutiny by the three Dragon Guild warriors, Kaden followed him.

There was little speaking among their group as K'Lani distributed food. There didn't need to be—Weylyn had said all that needed to be said, apparently. Kaden sat next to Ada and ate slowly, appreciating her presence at his side and the gentle press of her shoulder against his. The people of Whaldalf's Landing surrounded them like a physical barrier, as fierce in defense of him as they could be.

For the first time in his life, Kaden felt what it meant to be guarded instead of hunted.

It was a pleasant way to spend an hour, but Kaden knew it couldn't last. The day was wearing on, and if they weren't going to be seen as friends to Seward and his crew, then they shouldn't stay here any longer.

He finally stood up, and his people stood up with him. Now, where were they... ah. Firming his shoulders, Kaden walked over to where the three Dragon Guild members were huddled together, speaking in furious whispers. Seward turned to face him as he got close, and the look of affability on the man's face momentarily took Kaden's voice away. Pleasantness was... not what he'd been anticipating.

"We'll be taking our leave," Kaden said. "We should make as much progress to Whaldalf's Landing as we can while the light is with us. Thank you for your assistance against Morvar. I don't think we would have survived him without you."

"Is that it for you and Morvar, then?" Seward asked, trying to act casual, but Kaden could tell how important this was to him. "One and done? You've survived to tell the tale, now you'll happily ignore him?"

"Not at all," Kaden said firmly. "I don't intend to let any of Lucient's generals get away with their evil. I've got a long way to go before I'm ready for a confrontation, but Morvar won't escape. I promise you that."

Seward sighed, but a smile was starting to creep across his face. "Me and mine, we've been on our own for a long time now, doing what we can, when we can. We call ourselves Dragon Guild, but... truth is, dragons are few and far between here." He shrugged. "We've talked it over, and we think it's time that we expand our scope to include more of

Lucient's vile servants. You're not my king, lad. Not yet. But you might be, in time." He inclined his head. "And I'm content to let you lead me for now if it means striking out against the evils that plague this land."

The words landed harder than any oath. Possibility carried its own burden.

Kaden froze. "Really?"

"Just take the win," Weylyn murmured at his side. When had he gotten here? "And the rest of you?" Weylyn asked, his gaze catching for a moment on Anika.

Anika and Rowden inclined their heads as they laid their fists against their breastplates. "We will follow you as well," Anika said formally, then grinned. "Let's kick some baddie butt."

"Those are the knights I remember!" Weylyn shouted while clapping each of them on the shoulder. "We can move on in the morning, right, Kaden?"

"Right," Kaden said quickly. A decent rest could only help the villagers, after all. As he spoke, he became aware of movement around them, familiar presences drawing closer, conversations falling quiet as the weight of the decision settled.

"Then let's drink to our new alliance!"

"*Now* you're talkin' my language," Bardicus bellowed, putting his hammer away. "Where's the ale, eh?"

"No ale," Seward said. He forestalled Bardicus's complaints with a raised hand. "I've got mixed berry rotgut brewed in a boot, though."

"An old boot?"

"Ancient," he promised.

"Lots of berries in there, eh?"

"So many, and yet flies still drop dead whenever they fly over our homemade still," he said.

"Oho, now *that's* a brew worth sampling!"

"Perhaps not for *all* of us," Rowden added, looking at Kaden and Ada doubtfully. "It might, ah… not sit well in your stomachs."

"More for me," Bardicus said gleefully.

"Oh, I'll drink you under the table," Chum said.

"You're on, goat man!"

"It's *satyr*, not goat man. There's no need to be insulting, after all. Nothing manly about us!"

People finally began to relax, and Kaden let Ada take his hand and lead him back toward the fire and K'Lani. Everyone was dispersing... except Weylyn and Anika, who appeared to be talking very intently.

But that wasn't his business. Kaden was sure that, no matter what was between them, they wouldn't let it affect the group... which was growing larger and larger by the day, it seemed.

Kaden actually had people to *lead* now. He just hoped he didn't mess it up.

If he faltered, it would not be his fall alone.

CHAPTER 17

Waking up was hard, which wasn't surprising after a day spent keeping Morvar from burning them alive, but it was made easier by the company Kaden woke to. The suspicion and sharp edges that had marked yesterday's interactions were gone. Weylyn's former colleagues were, if not warm, at least welcoming, and they were downright enthusiastic that someone else was cooking for them, if the way they hovered around K'Lani asking if she needed anything else for the scramble she was making was any indicator.

"Dillysage? I know it goes well with eggs."

"What about Preuwen's capers? They grow wild around here, might give it a nice herbal flavor."

"Rock salt," another voice added eagerly. "Pink and purple varieties. There's a quarry nearby that used to be famous for it."

"Yes to the purple salt, yes to the dillysage, and if you can get me some fairy-tear petals, you're in for a real treat," K'Lani said, then frowned apologetically at Pepper. "It's just the folk name of the flower, Your Majesty, but I'm afraid I don't remember the proper name."

"I'm not offended by the name of a simple flower," Pepper assured her. "We call the same plants 'skygems' for their radiance in the sunshine, but the name is only known within my community, I'm sure."

"Very pretty, though," K'Lani said. "What would you add to the mix here?"

"Oh!" Pepper looked pleased to be asked and flew over to K'Lani with a smile.

"She's looking better today," Ada murmured to Kaden, relief softening her voice. Kaden nodded, pulling steadily on the rope as the water-filled bucket rose from the well between them.

"She is," Kaden agreed. "I still think we should be careful of asking much of her abilities for now." The last thing he wanted was to exhaust Pepper to the point where she was injured from it.

"Probably." They carried the immense bucket over to the fire, where the water was promptly divided among a dozen different needs, then were sent back for more. It was the fifth time this morning—apparently, Seward wasn't about to go without his morning tea, and he'd offered up the same to everyone else. That meant the kettle was being refilled constantly.

"And then another after that for me bath!" Bardicus called out after them. "Got to freshen up, I do!"

"Not in public!" Eldrin immediately snapped.

"What, afraid you'll go blind from my dwarvish radiance, boy?"

"No! Afraid I'll go blind from the glare on your bare dwarvish a—"

"Gentlemen!" K'Lani banged the side of the skillet she was cooking in with a wooden spoon. "That's enough bickering for one morning, if you please."

"Aye, shut it, you pointy-eared princeling!"

"I'll shut your *mouth* with my—"

Kaden and Ada retreated to the well, where they leaned against each other, laughing as the argument got more and more lurid until finally Pepper herself had to intervene by asking them, firmly but politely, to both shut up.

"I'm surprised to hear them argue," Ada said, wiping her eyes on the edge of her sleeve a moment later. "I thought it would be Petey and Chum, or Weylyn and Chum, or well… anyone and Chum. Bardicus and Eldrin have gotten along pretty well so far."

"I don't think it's serious, just… everyone needs to let off steam at some point," Kaden said.

"What about you?" Ada lowered her eyes slightly, looking up at Kaden from beneath her lashes. "Do you need to fight with someone to let off steam?"

"I…" Was this flirting? "I don't… think so?" Wait, was that the right answer? Or—

"Because I'd understand if you're a little bit upset with me. I was a nightmare about going after my mom."

Oh. Serious topic. It probably wasn't flirting, then. Kaden ignored his disappointment and said, "I was never upset by that. I'd be a nightmare if I were in your shoes, too."

"Do you miss your mother?" Now Ada was looking straight at him, no longer shy. "Even though you never met her?"

Kaden sighed. "A part of me does, but it's… removed. I wish I knew her, I wish we'd had the chance to be a real family, but the truth is that I *did* grow up with a mother." And she'd been alone for a year now, no husband or son to help her on the farm, no guard dog for their flock of sheep, no one to spoil with bonberry buns… "I miss Lydia," he said. "She's the only mother I've ever really known, and the day we were separated, I didn't know it was my last time to see her for… however long this quest takes." The rest of his life, probably, judging from how swiftly it had moved so far. For every step forward he took, it felt like he was driven two back.

"I think she would like you," he added, forcing himself away from the maudlin thoughts that were threatening to take over. "And your mom. They're the same sort of woman, very no-nonsense. Although she was always a softer touch with me than my dad was."

"I'd like to meet her someday," Ada said.

"I hope you do."

"Oi! Bath water, Kaden!"

He and Ada looked at each other and started laughing again. "Coming," he called back.

Baths aside, the morning passed quickly. Kaden decided to take the opportunity to ask Seward about fighting dragons—Morvar in particular.

"Well," Seward said, scratching at his head with one hand while he held a cup of water in the other, "you have to remember, it's bloody hard to off a dragon if you don't have the right weapon. You might say we're better at holding them back than we are at killing them—we've got good weapons for that, and decent tactics. Good enough that we've been able to live here for years now, keeping this place safe."

"The real trouble is tracking down their lairs," Rowland put in. "They're all secreted away in the mountains somewhere, and the big lizards can fly. That makes it hard to match their pace. They prefer to fight in wide-open spaces and don't like being cornered, so that makes them extra paranoid about being followed."

"I suppose that's understandable."

"There's nothing quite like cornering a dragon, though," Anika said, and there was a vicious edge to her voice that had everyone looking at her. "Backing them up someplace small, where they can't use their wings or crush you with their bodies. Sure, their heads are dangerous, and they've got those awful claws, but fire enough of our arrows into one, and it doesn't take long for you to make a hole *somewhere*, and once you breach them, it becomes easier to keep pressing the wound."

"You're talking about Falstar the Red," Weylyn murmured. "I remember hearing of that beast's death a few years ago."

"The Dragon Guild's greatest victory to date," Rowland said proudly, keeping his eyes on Anika. "We managed to force him into the quarry after injuring one of his wings. He couldn't fly out, and we kept the high ground and fired down at him from beyond where he could reach us. It took all day to kill that beast, but we did it."

"We used his scales to tip our arrows," Anika added. "It makes them dangerous to other dragons even if they're not fatal."

"I'd like to look at some of those," Bardicus said, and Seward nodded his approval.

"Of course. We've even got some scales leftover if you've ideas for how to use them." He got up and led the dwarf king over toward one of the huts, with Thalgrem trailing them.

"You look a bit green."

It took Kaden a moment to realize that Anika was speaking to him. She was cleaning beneath her nails with a dagger as she eyed him. "Does the thought of killing disgust you?" she asked.

Several of his companions inhaled, ready to defend him. Kaden held up a hand. "Of course it does," he said honestly. "I hate the thought of killing another living being, no matter who they are or what they've done. But I also know that sometimes it's necessary."

"Done much of it, have you?"

"Enough," Kaden replied. "Enough to know that I don't want to do any more of it until I have to. I'll never invent a fight for the sake of spilling blood, and I would never ask that of anyone allied with me either."

"That's not the way of kings," Anika said flatly, like someone reciting a lesson learned the hard way. "Kings have always existed to give orders for others to carry out, and that includes killing. Your father broke that mold, and look at what happened to him. He left his people without a leader, and the land fell prey to even more darkness. Don't you think it would be safer for you to hide yourself away somewhere and let others fight your battles?"

"I'm not a king," Kaden pointed out. "And if I don't stand up and fight for what I believe in, I'll *never* be a king, no matter who my father was or what my birthright could be."

"But look at your company." Her gaze swung toward Eldrin. "It's not his *father* on your quest."

Eldrin, remarkably, didn't rise to the bait. "Did you not see, hear, or *smell* the dwarf king who just went off with your colleague?" he asked dryly before turning to Kaden and ignoring Anika completely. "We probably ought to get K'Lani and the other villagers back to Whaldalf's Landing as soon as possible, don't you think?"

Kaden took the out. "Absolutely. We should pack and—" A second later, he flinched as a bird dove out of the sky and landed on the ground right in front of him.

The thing clicked softly as it settled, metal wings folding with unsettling precision.

"What the devil?!" Rowland shouted, already going for the knife at his belt.

"No, stop!" Kaden held up an arm. "This isn't a real bird." No, it was a *mechanical* bird, the kind he'd only seen in one place before. "I think it's from Lumhagen." That must mean that it was from Bhalla! But how could he have known where to send it? *Does he have a way of tracking my necklace?* Kaden clasped the crystal even as he held out his free hand to the construct, which hopped over, opened its mouth, and a moment later deposited a tiny scroll into his palm.

He ignored the murmurs around him and unrolled it, squinting to read the tiny writing:

> *I see you encountered Morvar and survived. Congratulations! That's quite a feat, although I had the utmost faith in you and your companions. I also sense that you've found a couple of the pieces of the armor of Orealus. You've taken many steps on your journey, Kaden, and it's time for me to assist you in the next one. I look forward to your return to Lumhagen at your earliest opportunity. Oh, and could you grab some soothsage while you're still encamped with the Dragon Guild members? It's quite useful and only native to their particular stretch of forest. Sincerely, Bhalla*

"What does he want?" Ada asked.

"Um… for us to come back to Lumhagen." He passed the note to her, prepared to answer more questions from his companions.

He wasn't prepared for Seward to step up and start questioning things. "Wait, how do you know this isn't some sort of trick?" the older man demanded, his hair scrunching as he ran his hand through it over and over. "Hells, I'm not convinced Bhalla is even alive anymore—he was a cowardly bastard during the Great War, couldn't be bothered to help the king and his men defeat Lucient. Perhaps he was already dead by then."

"I know this is from Bhalla because I've met him before," Kaden said. "Multiple times. And so have my friends."

"That's a crock of Agwhin manure," Seward snapped, fear bleeding through his anger.

"No, it's true," Weylyn said, looking a little pained.

All three of the guild members seemed stunned. "You can't be serious," Anika said. "You, of all people, can't think that any good can come from associating with a wizard, especially one like Bhalla."

"I didn't for a long time," Weylyn admitted. "But that's a story for another day. We need to leave before the sun gets away from us." He turned to Kaden, ignoring his friends' astonished looks.

"Don't think you can get out of talking about this just because you're leaving," Anika said.

"We'll be coming back," Kaden pointed out. "We have to if we plan to take down Morvar." Which they did. There was no ignoring the dragon now that he'd found his team once, and the sooner, the better, so that they could focus the rest of their energies on Lucient.

Besides, if they couldn't handle a dragon, they'd never be able to take on the Lord of Lies.

"Then we'll wait here for your return," Seward said, sounding relieved that he wasn't going to have to go anywhere yet. Especially not Lumhagen.

"We'll stay too," Bardicus said, thumping Thalgrem on the shoulder with one massive hand.

"Oh." That was unexpected, but Kaden wasn't about to force people to come with him, even though it would feel very strange not having Bardicus along.

"Got to get a handle on using those scales of theirs, after all. Might be able to combine them with some dwarvish weaponry to make something that can at least put a dent in ol' Morvar."

The decision made sense, even if it felt wrong to leave part of their strength behind. "All right, then we can—"

"I'm staying too!" Chum said, slurring his *s*'s slightly from behind a tankard. How early had he started drinking? "I need a break from all this toing and froing and hither and yonning and fighting and—it's just all too much!" He put a hand against his forehead and mimed fainting. "I'm overcome, I tell you. Overcome!"

"Over*indulged*, more like," Weylyn muttered, but he seemed amused. "Fine. We'll take these people back to their village, then move on to Lumhagen. Hopefully Bhalla will offer us a portal back," he added to Kaden, "or this will be a very long detour."

"I'm sure he will." At least, Kaden hoped that, but he didn't quite know how to read Bhalla.

"Don't come back as a corpse," Anika called over to Weylyn. Her tone was insulting, but there was something serious in her eyes.

"Don't worry," he said, meeting her gaze. "I won't."

CHAPTER 18

It felt strange to travel without Bardicus, Thalgrem, and Chum. Quieter, which was a relief in some ways, but unsettling all the same. Bardicus was a force of nature, as brash as he was brave, always talking about getting into a fight or reminiscing about a fight he'd been in. He talked enough for two people, which, given that Thalgrem never spoke, seemed to even things out, and yet even Thalgrem had made noise. The sound of his armor creaking as he walked with inexorable steadiness in his king's footsteps, the crackle of his gauntlets as they impacted each other, all that was gone now. And Chum…

Well, actually, not having to listen to Chum's complaints was something of a relief. Not that there weren't complaints—the villagers whom they were escorting were of tough stock, but days of work and fatigue had taken their toll. Men complained of aching backs, women of sore feet, everyone of the tragedy that had befallen them. They were looking forward to getting back to Whaldalf's Landing, and yet even that was something to complain about.

"We have so much rebuilding to do!"

"Aye, not a moment's peace for us, I fear."

"And the dead… will we even have a chance to mourn them?"

"Who's been keeping my children safe since I was taken? That's what I want to know."

Fortunately, with K'Lani along for the march, her fellow villagers didn't complain for long. "We should reflect," she said, raising her voice halfway through the day's march, "on our good fortune for surviving. Things could have gone very differently for all of us, and as bad as things might seem, they could be much worse."

"You could be in the belly of a dragon, for example," Ada said, then winced as her mother gave her a *look*.

"That's enough 'help' from you, young lady."

Luckily for Kaden, his own people were handling their situation with equanimity, even pleasure. He got it—after all, walking through a forest or along the edge of the same blasted plain they'd followed to get to Karnergrien was easy compared to so much of what they'd suffered making it this far. Eldrin and Redfern actually relaxed enough to make a game of it, with him firing arrows into the sky while Redfern darted after them, testing both his strength and her speed.

"Children," Millicent murmured with an eye roll as she flew alongside her queen.

"You can't blame them for wanting to take a bit of time to enjoy themselves," Pepper said gently, a smile on her face as she watched Redfern's antics.

"Yes, Your Highness," Millicent said in a tone that meant she was humoring her monarch.

"You could join them. I'm perfectly safe."

"Of course she is!" Petey chimed in. "She's with us!" He reached up and patted Bug on the head, who sprayed a little cloud of pink spores in pleasure. Duke butted his head under Petey's hand a moment later, demanding his own share of affection, and Petey grinned and scratched behind the big dog's ears. "You, see? We're all very fierce. Ready to guard Pepper with our lives."

"*So* fierce," Weylyn said while sounding like he was saying the exact opposite. He and Millicent exchanged nods. Kaden hadn't realized they'd become friends, but he could see it. They had a similar sense of duty.

"We're only five miles out from the village," Eldrin drawled as he caught the arrow that Redfern dropped to him.

His tone was relaxed, but his eyes never stopped scanning the tree line.

"I daresay we'll be all right." He fired the arrow again, and the fairy took off into the sky so fast her wings buzzed.

"The village was attacked in broad daylight via portal not a week ago," Kaden reminded him. He didn't want to be a dark cloud, raining on his friends' pleasure, but he reminded himself that the safety of these people was *his* responsibility. And with two of their best fighters temporarily displaced, he needed to be even more vigilant than before. "I think being careful is warranted."

"Not to mention what happened the first time we came to Whaldalf's Landing," Petey added.

"Oh, right." Ada frowned as she glanced at Kaden. "You were shot."

Kaden had nearly forgotten that. So much had happened since then...

"Where is Redfern?" Eldrin said, very quietly.

"You just shot the arrow ten seconds ago," Weylyn pointed out.

"And she hasn't taken this long to bring one back to me since the game began," he replied, then froze. "Stop."

Kaden held up his hand in a fist, and everyone came to a stop. At the same time, Pepper marshaled her yah'zaval and sent it into the very ground beneath the villagers. A second later, youthful roots thrust up out of the soil, combining with each other as they climbed, thickening and strengthening until eventually they formed a shield over the most vulnerable in the party. It wouldn't stop a strong attack, but it would give Kaden and the others time to respond to one without people dying. "What is it?" he asked Eldrin quietly.

"Listen," Eldrin murmured. Kaden did, but he heard nothing other than the wind in the trees, pine needles rustling, the crack of a branch breaking as something stepped on it—

"Attack incoming!" he shouted just as the first arrow flew out of the trees. Petey squealed and ducked, and a moment later the arrow split the space where his head would have been and lodged in a tree behind him.

"Dunnissé!" Eldrin called out. "Protect yourselves at all costs!"

"Who are the dunnissé?" Kaden asked before he was forced to cut another arrow out of the air in front of him. Eldrin dodged two more, then fired into the trees with a look of concentration. In the distance, Kaden heard a guttural voice swear.

"Dark elves," Eldrin said. "A cursed form of my own people, the same kind that tried to kill you last time. It appears that one failure wasn't enough for them." He peered into the trees. "I don't think there are more than a single squadron, perhaps six at best. We should be able to fight them off fairly—"

"*In the name of Garth, attaaaack!*"

What the…

Petey turned in a rush, ears perking up until they stood nearly a foot over his head. "Goblins!"

"What in the hells are dark elves doing working with goblins?" Weylyn asked as he pulled his sword free. "I thought they hated each other."

"The enemy of my enemy is my friend, perhaps," Queen Pepper said. She was maintaining the root shield around the villagers, but her wings were beating off tempo, and her face showed signs of strain. "We need to handle them quickly."

Right. Kaden knew that. He brought his shield up in front of himself just in time to deflect an arrow. "Eldrin, hunt down the dunnissé," he said firmly. "The rest of us will handle the gob—"

Before he could even finish his order, a goblin came flying out of the trees at them. Not in an intent and bloodthirsty manner, though. This one was flying because something, or someone, had apparently hit it hard enough to send it airborne. It collapsed into a heap five feet in front of Kaden, half its helmet stove in.

Another goblin ran out of the trees like its rear was on fire, only to be taken out by Weylyn before it even noticed him. Kaden stared. Whoever was in there was doing a fantastic job with one of their enemies. *Don't leave the hard work to someone else.* "Go!" Kaden shouted and charged forward to meet the next goblin that came at them, dodging a blow from its wicked war hammer before cleaving the weapon—and the arm holding it—in two with his sword. The goblin screamed, blood spilling from the wound, and Kaden couldn't help wincing even as he finished the creature off.

"Sounds right nice, that does!" a voice called from the woods. A short, sturdy dwarf walked out, pickaxe resting easily on her shoulder.

Kaden recognized her immediately. She had served him grog in Kugdor during their first visit, and he had seen her again in the chaos when the city burned.

"Malacheen," he said.

"Aye, that is me," she replied with a broad smile. "Didja miss Miss Malacheen?" she asked before spinning around and burying her pickaxe in the middle of a goblin who'd been trying to sneak up on her.

Malacheen! That's it! She had malachite gemstones woven through her thick, braided brown hair, and none of the usual heavy armor that most dwarf warriors wore. Perhaps she wasn't a warrior? But she was handling these goblins like they were made of paper...

"Duck, lad!"

Kaden ducked just as an arrow went overhead. Right, there were still the dark elves to consider, although given that Eldrin had vanished into the forest with a murderous expression on his face, Kaden didn't think they'd be a problem for much longer.

Malacheen turned to watch Ada send an arrow through the throat of a lunging goblin, who collapsed soundlessly. "Ooh, nice!" she complimented her. "It's lovely to see another lady showing these evil blighters what for, lass."

"What are you doing here?" Kaden asked. The first part of Malacheen's answer was lost as Duke suddenly howled and ran full tilt into the woods. Had he scented something?

"—soon as we heard the Landing was attacked, I knew 'twas time for me to come and join the bodyguard for my king. Thalgrem's good, but he's a one-trick pony as the saying goes, and our Bardicus can be a bit hot-headed, I'm sure ye've noticed." Malacheen glanced up and raised her shield over her head just as an arrow came shooting straight down at her. "You cheeky little shite!" she called out merrily before throwing her pickaxe up into the overhanging branches of a nearby tree. A second later, Kaden heard a scream, and then a dark elf fell out of the branches thirty feet up.

Ada hit the creature with an arrow on its way down.

"Nice targeting!" Malacheen complimented her.

"Same to you," Ada said with a smile. "We're fortunate to have your help here."

"Och, weel." Malacheen seemed to blush a bit as she shook some greenish blood off her pickaxe. "My Lucky Friend here deserves most of the credit. A dwarf is only as good as her weapon, y'ken."

Another goblin, this one taller than any other Kaden had seen so far, came barreling into the party, waving a spike-studded mace and screaming a guttural war cry. Weylyn and Kaden both stepped forward, but Malacheen got there first. She swung upward, disrupting the arc of the goblin's weapon, before spinning around and sending the sharp, shovel-like back end of the pickaxe straight into the goblin's leg. It was wearing armor, but Malacheen's blow still managed to shatter the goblin's shin at a ninety-degree angle. The goblin fell to the ground, shrieking and clutching its wound for all of two seconds before another blow to the head finished it off.

For a moment, the entire clearing was silent. Then Eldrin reappeared with Duke at his heels and Redfern riding on Duke's back, a sour look on her face as she cradled one shoulder.

"There you are!" Pepper exclaimed. "I was so worried!"

"A dunnissé got the drop on me," Redfern grumbled. "But I'm perfectly fine."

"You're not fine, you're bleeding, and for all I know, you might be poisoned. Come here."

"No more dark elves," Eldrin announced, sounding much more cheerful than his fairy companion. "One or two might have slunk off into the trees, but there's no one left to attack. It was a fun little hunt," he added. "Not many are as quick in the woods as my people."

"Odd to find dark elves and goblins working together, though," Weylyn said as he glanced at the motley corpses strewn around them. "It makes you wonder what else might come hunting us on our way to Lumhagen."

"Lumhagen?" Malacheen beamed. "Is that where we're off to? I've always wanted to see the wizards' den!"

Eldrin stared at her like he was just noticing her. "And you're coming with us… Why?"

"To guard my king, o' course." She looked around, checking the group of villagers as well, before frowning. "Why isn't he here?" This time, when she turned to Kaden, her genial grin had been replaced by a glare. "Has something happened to my king?"

"No, no," Kaden assured her. "Bardicus is fine, he just decided to stay with the Dragon Guild to try and make us a weapon better suited to fighting Morvar."

Malacheen blinked. "Excuse me?"

Kaden explained the situation to her while Pepper tended to Redfern, and Millicent ensured the villagers were all right. They were so close to the Landing, it would be awful to lose one of them to an attack like this when they were nearly home. By the time Kaden finished, Malacheen had a look of glum acceptance on her face.

"I s'pose I'd better go to these people meself, then… not that it sounds like he needs my help. I'm a good miner, but not as good at crafting as my da." She rolled her eyes. "As he continually likes to remind me."

"Where is your father?" Eldrin asked, still suspicious. "I'm surprised he'd let someone your age on a quest like this without supervision."

"Weeeeeell," Malacheen drawled, "I might not have exactly asked him before leavin' Kugdor. I'm of age to travel on my own, though!" she insisted. "Just…" She sighed. "I'm not ready for my adventure to end, y'know? And it sounds like my king isn't so much adventurin' as he is smithing right now, and that means he'll probably set me to work chopping wood or hauling ash, which is *fine*, just fine, but…"

"You should join us."

Kaden, Eldrin, and everyone else in hearing distance turned slightly incredulous eyes on Ada, who shrugged defensively. "What? She should! She's amazing with that pickaxe, and she wants to be useful. She'll be far more useful with us on the road than she would be stuck in a tiny village in the middle of nowhere. Besides,"—she smiled a little—"don't tell me it doesn't feel more right having a dwarf along to charge into battle."

"Aye, we're great chargers, we are!" Malacheen said, picking up Ada's thread and running with it like they'd planned this. "And my da always said I was worth two boys, because I always try twice as hard. That takes care of your dwarf deficit quite nicely, doesn't it?"

"Just when I thought I'd be able to get through a night without being woken up by a dwarf's snoring," Eldrin muttered.

"Oh, poor prince." Malacheen smiled and hefted her pickaxe. "Keep talkin' like that, and I'll break your pretty little nose for you, and then y'can offer up the snoring yerself."

"No fighting amongst ourselves," Kaden said quickly. He glanced at Pepper, who nodded back. *She thinks it's a good idea too.* With Pepper and Ada all for adding another member to the party, Kaden didn't see how he could resist. "All right," he said, and Malacheen whooped for joy, startling a flock of grackles right out of a nearby tree. "You can join us." He inclined his head. "Welcome to the crew, Malacheen."

She curtsied with surprising grace. "Thanking you so much for the invitation, Yer Highness. You won't regret it."

Kaden really, really hoped not, but hope had become part of the job.

CHAPTER 19

It was a surprisingly merry party that finally made it back to Whaldalf's Landing just as the sun set, a week since they had first started. *Only a week, and yet so much has happened since then,* Kaden reflected as he stood back and let the villagers have their joyous, and sometimes tearful, reunions. The atmosphere was festive, and casks of ale had been broken out, mugs filled, and toasts drunk in gratitude for the living and remembrance of the dead.

In that single week, Kaden had crossed a dead plain, fought monsters, infiltrated a castle, gained another piece of the armor, faced down a dragon, found new allies, and been ambushed by a group of goblins and dark elves—again—just before arriving here. It was so much, so *incredibly* much, and on top of it all, he'd turned seventeen.

Seventeen. If you were back home, you'd be celebrating with sugar-crusted bonberry buns and a day's reprieve from the farm work. Everything would be simple, easy—just another year, like all the others before this quest.

There was a part of him—a small part, but a stubborn one—that regretted it. Not so much leaving his old life behind, but the loss of innocence that came along with it, the knowledge that there was so much more out there in the world, that it was so much bigger than he was qualified to take on. Yet that was what he had to do now—take on the world, rally light to fight darkness, and hope that in the end his side would be strong enough to overcome a dark power that not even his famous, powerful father had been able to handle.

Kaden shut his eyes for a moment and traced the circle of Orealus over the center of his chest. "Be with me," he murmured, "guide my footsteps and help keep me on the path you've laid out for me. I have the feeling I've got an awful lot to get through before I can do more than hope that the future I dream of becomes a reality."

Duke whuffed gently beside Kaden, nosing him with his muzzle, and Kaden smiled and petted his dog. "You overgrown dust mop," he said affectionately. "I can always count on you, can't I? You never lose hope."

"Easy to do when all he has to be hopeful about is his next meal," Petey said, coming up next to Kaden with a shy smile. Bug was perched placidly on his shoulder. "It's weird, isn't it?"

"What?"

"Coming back to places you've been before and seeing how they've changed," Petey said wistfully. "The first time we came here, this place was like any other seaside town. Then it was in shambles, and now it's full of rebuilding and renewal. It makes you wonder what kind of effect you've had, doesn't it?"

"Yeah," Kaden agreed. "It does." He glanced at Petey. "I hope we're leaving places better than we found them, but…"

"It's hard to know for sure," Petey agreed. "But in the end, I hope that too. Even if there are some stumbling steps and growing pains along the way."

"Wheest, lookit tha pair o' ya!" Malacheen was surprisingly quiet for such a boisterous dwarf. Before Kaden could turn around to look at her, she'd clapped him and Petey between the shoulders so hard they both almost lost their balance. "Such long faces, and a' such a happy time! 'Tis a period of celebration, ya ought to be doin' what the rest of us are!" She hoisted a simple wooden mug that some reveler had pressed on her. "Drinkin'!"

"Oh, I'm not—"

"I don't care to—"

"No, ah won't have it," she said firmly, pushing them over toward where the knot of villagers was thickest. The rest of their party was there as well, and all of them were drinking something, even Pepper. "Ye've got to join in, or ye'll make the rest of us look bad, ye ken." She shoved some flagons into their hands—apparently the mugs were in short supply—then sauntered off with a pleased look on her face.

"Um." Kaden stared at his drink for a second. He really wasn't that fond of alcohol, and this smelled rather... strong. He'd learned early that dulled senses had a cost.

Well. He would just have to find a good spot to get rid of it without anyone seeing him. Kaden began to move, sharing smiles and congratulations with everyone who crossed his path, always toasting but never drinking. He made it to the outskirts of the group and into an area where there were heaps of burnt timber and broken tiles, all remnants of the attack that still needed to be removed. Somewhere over here, there had to be a nice spot where he could just pour this out and...

"Ada! Come here, darling. I need to speak with you."

Kaden froze. That was K'Lani's voice... had he wandered close to her house? He'd only visited it once before, and he'd spent most of his time then unconscious. It sounded like they were going to have a private conversation, so he'd just go back the way he came and—

And nope, because a knot of drunken revelers had sprawled nearby, loud and unsteady, blocking the quickest path back without making a spectacle of him.

Kaden hesitated. He could push through them easily enough, but it would mean laughter, questions, and someone slapping him on the shoulder and insisting on another toast. He wasn't in the mood to explain himself or why he hadn't taken a single sip.

He shifted his weight, intending to wait only a moment, just until the noise moved on, when he heard K'Lani's voice nearby.

He stopped without meaning to.

"What is it, Mom?"

"Oh, Ada..." Kaden heard the sound of a warm hum, and he envisioned the two of them hugging.

"What's that for?" Ada laughed.

Ha, got it right.

"I just want you to know how incredibly proud I am of you," K'Lani said, her voice thick with emotion. "And... and I know your father would be too."

"Mom." Ada's voice quivered a bit.

"He would be, believe that. Adena, you'll always be my daughter, my little girl, but you're also a grown woman now. More than that, you're a fighter, just like your father, and it's time I treated you like one. I got these things for you…" There was the sound of cloth unraveling, or perhaps unwrapping? Either way, Kaden heard Ada gasp a moment later.

He risked peeking his head around the corner to see what had Ada so interested. Her mother was holding a recurve bow and quiver out to her. "This is Arcinde," she said, her voice filled with pride. "It was your father's bow. The range isn't quite as far as a longbow, but you'll never find better for speed."

"It's beautiful," Ada said, running her fingers over the blue waves painted on the bow before touching the fine embroidery on the leather quiver. "Did he decorate these himself?"

"He did. He was always an artist in his soul, though the times turned him into a warrior as well." K'Lani was quiet for a moment, then leaned the bow and quiver carefully against the side of the house before lifting a sword out of the rough canvas sack by her feet. "This is yours now as well. Its name is Acantha." The scabbard was a bright blue reminiscent of fish scales and matched the hilt perfectly. When Ada drew the short, narrow blade, it emerged without a sound.

"The metal is folded steel," K'Lani continued. "The pattern can be almost anything, but the smith who made this favored a wave pattern, so that all who carried his weapons into faraway lands would be reminded of their home."

"Mom… I don't know what to say." Ada looked from the bright blade to her mother, and her face crumpled as a few tears rolled down her cheeks. "Thank you… I don't know what I would do without you." She sheathed the blade and stepped into her mother's embrace.

"Oh, darling." K'Lani held her close and squeezed, then pulled back with a grin on her face. "I'm grateful we have more time together, but I'm satisfied to know that no matter what happens to me, you won't be alone in the world. Not with those friends of yours." She nudged Ada with her hip. "Especially your young man, Kaden, hmm?"

"Mom!" Ada wiped her tears away, grinning and shaking her head. "It's not like that!"

"No? Because I remember a young man looking at me like that once, and I ended up married to him."

"Mom, honestly, it's *nothing*. I don't like Kaden like that."

That... actually hurt a bit. Kaden knew he shouldn't be here, knew it wasn't right for him to be listening in on a mother and daughter's private conversation. That he ended up hearing something that hurt his feelings was his own fault, but still.

He turned to look at the other side of the stack of burned wood and was gratified to see that the drinking party had moved on. *Time to get out of here.* He quietly emerged from the piles of rubble and headed toward the wharf. He needed some space for a while.

Kaden didn't get it. He hadn't gone more than ten feet before he was hailed by a familiar voice. "Kaden, lad! Is that you, then?"

Kaden stopped. "Captain Herrington?"

"Ha!" The older man looked just as Kaden remembered—rich clothes slightly disheveled by the wind, long hair ruffled from the spray of the sea, moustache elegantly curled. He swaggered over and slapped Kaden on the back. "Well, look at you, still alive! Have to say, I didn't hold out much hope after what happened last time."

Last time... right, last time Kaden and his friends had been trying to evade a terrible leviathan while rowing a lifeboat toward a swirling vortex of water that looked certain to drown them all. It had actually been the entrance to Nethopolis, the underwater kingdom of the merfolk, but Captain Herrington hadn't been happy that he'd dragged Ada along with him.

"And Ada?" he pressed. "How is she?"

"Fine," Kaden assured him. "She's with her mother right now. Whaldalf's Landing was attacked by Ophidians last week, and K'Lani was kidnapped—"

"*What?*" Captain Herrington's grip on Kaden's shirt tightened, and Kaden remembered—too late to be careful about his delivery—that the captain had been courting K'Lani for years.

"She's fine too!" he said quickly. "We rescued her! We just got back here, actually."

"Did you know? Well." The captain looked at Kaden grimly. "It seems you carry an ill wind with you, Young Master Kaden."

The sound of clanking footsteps announced Weylyn's arrival. He was followed by Queen Pepper and her bodyguards. "Not an ill wind," he said lightly, "just a focus for it. You cannot blame the sun for needing to burn away the fog, after all."

"Well, you son of a gun," Captain Herrington said with a grin. "I'm glad to see this lad hasn't gotten *you* killed yet either."

"I wouldn't say no to him improving his sword work, but at least I'm still alive to complain," Weylyn replied. Herrington laughed.

"Come! Let's get to the tavern, and I'll stand you some drinks!" he said. "Since the place is still standing, it's the least I can do." He waved his second over to lead the way, then turned back to Kaden and murmured, not quite as quietly as Kaden would have liked, "Do my lady love a favor and stay away from her daughter from here on out, mmm? Let the lass settle back into the life she ought to be living here, in her own village." Then he walked away to catch up with Weylyn, leaving Kaden stewing in anger and feeling called out for no good reason.

"Who does he think he is?" he muttered.

"The captain is letting his concerns get the better of his sense," Pepper counseled him, because of course she overheard it. "Don't listen to him, Kaden."

"Yeah," Redfern said, glaring at the man as he walked away. "Or Weylyn. Who does he think he is, poking fun at *you* for sword work after the way you handled Garth? And you've improved so much since then!"

"I'd be happy to slap the smug looks off both their faces for you," Millicent offered with a cheeky grin.

"Ladies." Pepper flew in between them. "Let's not encourage such things, hm? We have plenty to do without giving in to anger and violence. Kaden." She reached out and took his hand. "The captain seems to be in a talkative mood. You could go and join the meeting, or you can get the information afterward from Weylyn and help us with clearing rubble and getting temporary shelters up."

Kaden thought it over. On the one hand, he was the leader of their party—he *ought* to hear any intelligence Captain Herrington had brought himself. On the other hand, he wasn't too pleased with either the captain or Weylyn himself right now, and there was plenty more work to be done that would be of use to the people of Whaldalf's Landing.

"I'll help," he decided. "Weylyn can fill me in later."

Pepper smiled so brightly her face seemed to shine. "Wonderful. Come with me." She led him to where temporary homes were being erected for those who had lost theirs, and Kaden quickly found a rhythm preparing thatching for roofs. The houses normally used slate, but so much of it had been shattered by the Ophidians that they would have to make do with grass ceilings for now. It was work he had helped Daneyel with every spring back in Ashland, and it felt good to be of immediate use.

He worked until dinner was called, then worked some more until the light went down. Captain Herrington and his people pitched in a bit, but they returned to their ship for the night. Once they were gone, Weylyn approached Kaden and said, "Can we talk?"

Kaden straightened up from where he was stacking sheaves of dry stalks. "I think we'd better," he said, wiping his forehead.

They found a spot near one of the fires in the central square that was unoccupied, and Weylyn said, "Look…" To Kaden's surprise, he seemed uncertain. Weylyn, Son of the Wolf, was *never* uncertain.

"It's come to my attention," he continued stiffly after a moment, "that I might have been kind of a bit… undiplomatic in my description of you earlier."

"Huh," Kaden said, not giving Weylyn an inch of assistance.

"Yes. And that… hmm… it was rude of me to walk off with Captain Herrington without inviting you along."

"I see."

"And…" Weylyn sighed. "All right, here—I'm sorry. You are not a poor swordsman, and I should have stuck up for you to Herrington, especially since I keep pushing you to put yourself into leadership positions. It doesn't do for me to shove you forward with one hand while cutting you down with the other. It's just, he doesn't seem to care for you, and I thought a moment of commiseration would put him at ease."

"Ah."

Weylyn made a face. "Will you say more than that, please?"

Kaden let his friend stew for another few seconds before he said, "I understand why you did it, but don't do it again. All right? I can deal with people who don't like me, especially with your support, but not without it."

"I won't do it again," Weylyn promised. "He *did* have some interesting things to say. Apparently, the serpent Thálassa is becoming a real nuisance in the sea lanes, sinking a lot of boats and making the traders afraid to use ships for getting their goods to and from Wildepointe. Overland routes take a lot more time, but they're safer—for now." He shook his head. "Trade with places like Wildepointe is how this village, and a lot of others like it, survive. There's a bit of additional trade with the merfolk, which is good, but it's no substitute yet."

"That's good to know," Kaden said. "Anything else?"

"Yes, actually." Weylyn's eyes glittered mischievously. "Why *does* he dislike you so much? Is it anything to do with his 'little girl' and how you might be leading her into ruin?"

"All right, we're done, thanks!" Kaden headed for one of the larger fires, where Bug was spitting out spores that made the flames flare in different colors, leaving Weylyn's knowing chuckles behind.

CHAPTER 20

The trip to Lumhagen seemed faster to Kaden this time around. Whether it was because he was visiting for the second time, because someone was expecting him now, or simply because he had grown since his last visit here and his strides were longer, it felt good to return to the mystical city.

Once they got inside it, at least.

"Tell me we don't have to go through the waterfall again," Petey murmured to Kaden as they got close to where they'd entered the city before.

"No, I don't think we'll have to do that," Kaden assured him. His amulet had been glowing for several miles now. He held it loosely in his hand, holding it up into the dappled light of the forest and staring into the glow. Surely it was trying to tell him something. Surely it was trying to help him enter Lumhagen.

"Hard to get into a place that doesn't really exist," Weylyn said, but Kaden ignored his friend's doubts and looked more closely at the amulet. It was bright, but translucent, and if he held it close enough and stared right through…

"Ha!" A gate! He could see a gate, two tall doors limned in white light that looked like nothing but a bramble thicket ahead of him. "I can see the way!" He stepped forward and laid his hand on what looked to the naked eye like thorny rose canes, but felt like smooth metal beneath his fingers.

"Well done," Pepper said, flying up next to him.

"I'm not sure what comes next, though," he confessed. There were several sigils on the door he didn't understand, and he worried that touching the wrong one, in the wrong order, would result in them being locked out completely.

"I think you can leave that to me." She reached out and touched three symbols in quick order, finishing on one that looked like a stylized heart. The doors opened smoothly, eliciting gasps from the rest of the party. Kaden dropped the amulet against his chest and stared at her.

"You can see it too?" he demanded.

"Of course." Queen Pepper outright grinned. "I *have* been here before, you know. I would be a poor ruler if I didn't know the way into my neighbor's kingdom." She gestured Eldrin forward. "Step where Eldrin steps for the next twenty paces or so," she said to everyone else. "Just for caution's sake."

Lumhagen was just as delightful as Kaden remembered, filled with complicated, tempting scents and sounds, welcoming people—now that he wasn't being arrested by the city's guard—and mechanical marvels in all sorts of shapes.

It was also rather gratifying to see Ada's reaction to the place. She stopped dead at the edge of the city, staring with wide eyes all around. "I've never... I've never even imagined a place like this!" she marveled. "Is that—is that a snake? But it's got wings..."

"And it's made of clockwork, keep up," Eldrin said.

Petey shot him a frown. "There's no need to be rude."

Eldrin, to Kaden's surprise, grimaced and apologized. Kaden took advantage of their momentary break to approach him and ask, "Is something wrong?"

"Not exactly," Eldrin said. "Just... we're fairly close to my home now. Part of me feels like I should go and check in with my father, and see how he's doing."

"Well, that seems reasonable. It probably wouldn't take too long," Kaden said. Eldrin didn't look cheered by the prospect, though.

Did he not want to see his father? Kaden was under the impression that they got along well, but perhaps Eldrin was enjoying being independent for a while. Kaden could definitely understand that. "Actually, we have no idea what Bhalla is going to say to us. He might ask us to stay for a week, or he might send us off on another quest before the sun sets. I think it's best if you stay with the group for now."

Eldrin smiled at Kaden. "I think so as well." He looked toward the heart of the city. "Shall I lead the way to the Truthoriam?"

"Please do." Eldrin moved ahead, and the rest of them fell in behind them, Ada and Petey bringing up the rear as he told her the story of how he and Kaden had gotten in here last time.

"That was kind of you," Pepper said softly as she fluttered near Kaden's head.

"It was nothing," he said.

"No," she insisted. "It was insightful and generous. You've learned a great deal about leadership since we first met, Kaden. I'm more and more impressed with you as time goes on."

Was he blushing? Kaden had to be blushing. He hoped she couldn't see it. "I think I still have a long way to go. My ability with yah'zaval could be a lot better, for starters."

"Oh, I think you've done fairly well with that," Pepper said. As they began to walk the main street that led to the Truthoriam, the residents of Lumhagen began to whisper, recognizing them—at least, recognizing Queen Pepper, and probably Eldrin as well. Weylyn seemed disturbed by the chatter.

"These are the least discreet people I've ever met," he grumbled. "Don't they know how to mind their own business?"

Kaden knew that Weylyn, with his distaste for religion, wouldn't be at ease in a city that revolved around the worship of Orealus. "I'm sure they're just not used to strangers," he said.

"Some of them seem to know *you*."

"Not me! Pepper and Eldrin—both their realms are neighbors to this one."

That placated Weylyn enough to relax his grip on his sword, and it wasn't long before they arrived at the steps to the Truthoriam.

They were stopped before they could go farther than the first one by a regrettably familiar face. Kaden groaned inwardly. *Do I have to deal with this guy again? Wasn't once enough?* "Evias," he said, hoping that his antipathy didn't show on his face. "How nice to see you again."

Evias, the captain of the guards who had enthusiastically arrested Kaden and Petey the last time they came to Lumhagen, had exchanged his guard's leathers for more imperious-looking red robes. He still carried a spear-like staff, though, and had several guards stationed at his heels.

"I'm afraid I can't say the same," he said with a sneer. "I thought your business in our city was concluded."

"It was."

"Then why are—"

"We got a message from Bhalla," Kaden said, knowing it was rude to interrupt but not quite having the patience to deal with Evias's posturing right now. "He asked us to meet him here. If you'd let him know we've arrived, that would be very helpful."

The sneer deepened. "I'm not your messenger," Evias snapped. "However, in this case, I'm happy to inform you that Bhalla is unavailable."

Wait… what? "What do you mean?"

"Exactly what I said." Evias's guards came a bit closer. "He's been called out of the city on urgent business. It would be very unwise to interrupt him, so I'm afraid that no contact should be attempted. He'll come back in due course, and until then, *I* can see to whatever it is that's brought you here."

It figured. Kaden opened his mouth to tell Evias about the next step in their quest, but before he could speak a word, Pepper took over. "I'm very sorry," she said, kind yet unmovable all at once. "But we are unable to speak of our purpose here to anyone other than Bhalla himself."

"How distressingly secretive of you," Evias said, his eyes narrowing. "I'm afraid I can't, in good conscience, allow such secrets to persist. I am a representative of the Truthoriam and Bhalla's right-hand man. If you won't share your purpose here with me, then you need to leave."

"So be it," Pepper replied. "We will leave the Truthoriam directly. Rest assured, you won't have to deal with us again, sir." With that, she turned and flew away from the steps of the imposing building. Kaden, who was as confused as anything right now but knew he needed to support whatever Pepper was doing this for, nodded politely and followed her. As a group, they walked for five blocks before Millicent suddenly flew down to hover in front of Pepper.

"They've stopped following," she said, and Pepper suddenly relaxed.

Well, if that meant it was safe to talk… "What was that about?" Kaden asked.

"Not here," she said, and led them to a nearby restaurant full of customers and teeming with delicious smells. They were able to get a table in the corner, but the noise made it hard to hear.

Which, Kaden was realizing now, was entirely the point.

"There was something about that man," Pepper said, her voice serious as she stared at Kaden, as though willing him to understand. "Something that struck me as… off. Terribly so. A shadow within his eyes that should not have been there. His peremptory manner of requesting information from us without so much as inviting us inside, and his readiness to threaten… none of it was proper." She gestured to herself, then to Eldrin. "It isn't possible that he didn't recognize the two of us. As neighbors *and* royalty, we should have been afforded a more courteous greeting as a matter of duty. All of it together left me feeling… unsettled."

"Evias has never been the most friendly person here in Lumhagen," Kaden said, glancing at Petey. Petey nodded so emphatically that the tips of his ears flopped. "But I trust your judgment. We'll find someplace to stay in the city and try again tomorrow." He set his jaw. "We're here to see Bhalla, on his own invitation. It's going to take more than some threats by Evias to get me to back down."

"As long as we're cautious and keep our faith in Orealus, we should be fine," Pepper said.

"I'll keep my faith in the strength of my limbs and the sharpness of my steel, thank you," Weylyn scoffed.

"Whatever brings you joy."

"You're impossible to argue with," he muttered. "I never thought I'd say it, but I actually miss Chum."

"Liar, there's nothing to miss," Petey immediately said, and the rest of dinner passed more lightheartedly.

Not everyone was lighthearted.

Asitra stepped forward from the entrance to the Truthoriam as Kaden and his company moved away. Her face remained serene, though unease stirred beneath it.

"What was it they wanted?" she asked Evias, who didn't even stop long enough to meet her eyes as he replied, "None of your affairs. Go back to sorting books."

Asitra was accustomed to poor treatment from Evias—they all were, except Bhalla, who, for some reason, had always gotten along well with him. Perhaps it was because Bhalla was the one person Evias bothered to perform niceties for. The man was impatient and had a temper to match, and constantly pushed for more than he had earned in every facet of life. But he performed his duties adequately, and the Truthoriam was not in the habit of dismissing its officials, and so he persisted… like a boil.

Asitra should have gone back to her duties, and yet… her curiosity was piqued. Instead, she found herself following Evias at a distance as he motioned his guards away and began a quick stride down one of the side halls of the Truthoriam. It was an internal hall that ended at the central courtyard, so Asitra was surprised when Evias stopped in front of a bare, inconspicuous wall halfway along the corridor. She shrank back into a recessed alcove, using the narrow plinth within it for cover, and watched to see what he intended to do.

What she saw astonished her. She would later wish she had turned away.

Evias raised the staff in both hands and, in a low voice, began to chant in a language that Asitra had never heard before. A few seconds later, she heard a faint noise like the sound of stones sliding on sand, and before her eyes, the wall retracted, leaving a dark hole in the wall that Evias immediately stepped through.

Asitra was stunned. She had read every history of the Truthoriam that existed, and *none* of them mentioned secret passageways. Beyond that, this place was steeped in the power of yah'zaval, but the power Evias had used to open the door was nothing like what she knew.

Is he using dunntaika? How is such a thing possible right here, in the heart of Lumhagen?

She knew she ought to leave now, to find someone to report this to, and yet she was struck with the urge to go after Evias. How could she bring any kind of accusation against him before she really knew what he was doing? She crept down the hall, ready to slip in through the door—

Only for it to close just as she reached it, coming within an inch of hitting her nose. Asitra scowled at the wall, now as innocuous as it ever was. Should she try to open it with her own power? Or should she find Bhalla and tell him what was going on?

Would he even believe her?

It never seemed to matter how often he descended into the depths beneath the Truthoriam. Cobwebs always returned. He batted several of them away from his face as he finally came to the bottom of the stairs, then used his staff to light the lanterns on the walls. The light glowed a sickly green color, making the entire place look as though it suffered from a mold infestation. Perhaps it did anyhow—this room was the lowest in the entire Truthoriam, level with groundwater that seeped in through the rock walls during the rainy season. It was bad for the books, or would have been if they weren't protected by dunntaika, preserved against rot so that their vile spells and curses were always fresh at hand.

The bones didn't fare so well, but Evias didn't care about those. He was no simple conjurer, needing finger bones and teeth to make little guesses about the future. He was a great wizard, the strongest in the entire Truthoriam… after Bhalla, but that wouldn't be true for long. Bhalla would soon fall, and Evias would take his place and turn Lumhagen to the worship of its rightful master.

Speaking of which…

He sat down on a creaky chair and moved a shred of torn tapestry from the table in front of him. Beneath it gleamed a black obsidian mirror, perfectly round and extensively polished. Evias stared into it for a moment, admiring the fineness of his likeness, before saying, "Great Lord, I beseech thee, come to me. Lord Lucient, hear me."

Black smoke poured out of the mirror and billowed onto the floor. It was freezing cold, and Evias winced as it washed over his hands and legs on the way down. He schooled his expression to perfect calm when Lucient's haggard yet powerful visage appeared a moment later.

"My lord, thank you for—"

"What did you learn from the boy who would be king?" Lucient demanded, cutting right through the pleasantries.

It's fine, Evias assured himself. *You've done nothing wrong. Nothing particularly* right, *either, but Lucient won't take it out on you.*

Probably.

"My lord," he began, keeping his tone respectful—some might even call it obsequious. "A thousand apologies, but I was unable to extract any information from the boy before his escort squirreled him away. But do not lose hope! It's possible that I could—"

"'Possible' is rarely something to count on with you," Lucient said mercilessly. "You had one task, and you failed. Are you so incompetent at gaining the confidence of others? How will you lead Lumhagen in my name if you have no ability to hold the attention of others?"

Evias wilted. "My lord, I—I—"

"Enough. Initiate the plan." Lucient's head tilted slightly, as though he were listening to something. "And get rid of the little mouse that's nibbling at your door."

Little mouse? He—what, had he been *followed*? "I'll take care of it at once," Evias assured him.

"Do so. For your own sake." Lucient's face vanished, and the smoke began to dissipate. Evias was left staring at his own face once more, and he was displeased to see that most of the confidence in his expression had vanished.

Well. He would begin to recover it by seeing who was following him, and put an *end* to them.

CHAPTER 21

Kaden was roused from his dreams by what felt like the sun shining just an inch or two away from his face. The light stabbed his eyes even through the lids, and he groaned and rolled over in the small inn bed to hide his face. The light carried no warmth with it.

Even half asleep, Kaden felt the wrongness of that. Light touched by Orealus always came with a sense of presence, a quiet reassurance that he was seen. This felt hollow, like brightness without breath.

He heard Petey, his roommate, make a similar sound of discontent, followed by "Wait… Bhalla? Is that you?"

"*Bhalla*?" Kaden was suddenly wide awake. He sat up, barely avoiding knocking his head on the curved slope of the roof above him—he and Petey had gotten the last room the inn had, way up in the point of it—and blinked as the light slowly died out, leaving behind the figure of an elderly man with a white, shaggy beard propping himself up with a wooden staff as he smiled at them.

Warmth returned to the room at once, gentle and familiar, settling over Kaden's chest like a hand laid there in blessing.

"Rise and shine, young friends," the wizard said merrily. "Forgive my rude method of entering your room, but stairs are a bit hard on these old bones of mine, and Queen Pepper told me that you wouldn't be too offended by my presence."

"Not offended at all," Kaden said. He was pleased beyond words that Bhalla had found them, especially after yesterday. "I thought you weren't available to meet with us!" Kaden continued as he kicked off the blanket and reached for his tunic.

Bhalla frowned. "Now, why would you think that? I was in my study all day, awaiting your arrival. I came down here to find you because I thought *you* had been held up in some way."

"That's what Evias said," Petey put in as he lifted Bug off his resting place on Petey's pillow and placed him on the floor. The little creature spritzed a small, glittering cloud of spores into the air in thanks. "He said you weren't available."

"How odd." Bhalla shook his head. "I'm afraid my old friend tends to let his mouth run away with him at times. He's a man who treasures the quest for knowledge, but he isn't always good at discerning when that quest should be interrupted for other things. He must have thought I was engaged in some serious work with yah'zaval at the time, and took it upon himself to keep anything from distracting me."

"Huh." It didn't seem like that had been Evias's intent to Kaden *at all*. It was possible he'd misread the situation, but… no. Pepper had confirmed it. She wasn't the type to get carried away by emotion or overwhelmed with inexperience. Evias had left her concerned as well.

Kaden was tempted not to make anything of it. The politics of Lumhagen and the people who ran it weren't his business, and he didn't have the standing to tell Bhalla how to deal with his subordinates, much less his friends, and yet…

"Queen Pepper thought he was lying." Once the words were out of his mouth, Kaden felt better, even though they prompted a frown from Bhalla.

"That comes as a surprise," he admitted over the noise of Petey tugging his boots on. The three of them began to head down the steep stairs, Bhalla taking Kaden's arm to lean on as soon as he offered it. "Evias has never shown any inclination toward deceit with me. Is it possible that you're missing some sort of context?"

Bhalla hesitated, then added more quietly, "Evias has always been… intense. Intensity can look like ambition, or arrogance, or even cruelty, depending on the eye judging it."

Kaden shrugged. "I mean, I suppose it's possible, but he definitely told us you weren't in. And…" Should he say the rest of what Pepper had told him?

He didn't end up having to. Pepper met them on the landing, flying over and inclining her head to Bhalla. "Greetings and good morning," she said. "I've arranged for breakfast to be delivered to my room, as it's large enough to fit all our party. This way we'll have some privacy as well."

"Greetings, my friend," Bhalla said, inclining his own head to her with a smile. "It's very good to see you once more. I trust you've been well?"

"Quite well," she said, and they passed the time getting back to the room she'd shared with her bodyguards with pleasantries. "The others will be in shortly, but we might as well get started," she said as they settled in, gesturing toward the massive spread of food and drink laid out on two tables against one wall.

It wasn't until the six of them were seated and had started on their breakfasts that Pepper, after sipping from a tiny, delicate teacup, said to Bhalla, "You should know that I discerned great deceit and darkness within Evias yesterday."

Bhalla set his own cup aside and folded his hands in his lap. "I don't mean to discredit your knowledge and understanding in any way, but are you certain? I've known Evias a long time, and while he is certainly very prideful, he's never been less than honest in my hearing."

Pepper nodded. "I'm quite certain my perceptions are accurate. I've learned many tells over the years that indicate a person is lying to me, and to be blunt, Evias wasn't even *trying* to hide the fact that he was dissembling. More troubling than the lies is the sense of darkness that seems to shroud him, though." She gestured at Bhalla. "You carry a light within you, my friend, no matter what your surroundings are. Evias, however, is inhabited by shadows so deep I can't penetrate them."

Now Bhalla looked troubled. "This is a very concerning accusation, and one that I take seriously. I'll need to consult with Asitra about it… If I can find her. She wasn't at her post this morning, *or* last night, in fact.

"She never leaves without notice," Bhalla continued, his brow creasing. "Not even to rest."

"Is that unusual?" Redfern asked.

"Very. Asitra is an incredibly reliable member of the Truthoriam, but I assumed she needed a break from her forward-facing duties." He sighed. "I have to admit: I've been so deep in my own studies and prayers of late that it doesn't surprise me there are things afoot in the Truthoriam that I haven't noticed. I've given over the training of all our cadet wizards to Evias, ever since he became the guild master…" Bhalla paused, then shook his head. "Avoid him for now, so that he isn't alerted to any of your suspicions, and I shall speak with him on these matters myself. I—"

His words were interrupted by a sharp bark from Duke, who pushed the door open with his nose and bounded across the floor to Bhalla, wagging his tail so hard he nearly knocked himself over. "Ah, the bold hound appears at last!" Bhalla said, petting the hound behind the ears. "I was wondering where you'd gone. I thought he would be with you, Kaden."

"He didn't fit in our room," Kaden said a bit sheepishly. "Weylyn and Eldrin were kind enough to let him stay in theirs."

"Ah." Bhalla held out his hand to Duke, who shook it politely. "How is that armor treating you, then?"

Duke barked again, and Bhalla laughed. "I see."

"This is why you can't trust wizards," Kaden heard Weylyn say to Malacheen as she entered with Ada just behind them. "They're all completely mad."

If he heard that rather harsh judgment, Bhalla ignored it as he turned his focus to Ada. "Adena Davenrich," he said with a smile. "How this is our first formal meeting, I don't know, but I'm pleased to make your acquaintance at last. You look so much like your father."

Ada blushed, her cheeks darkening charmingly as she inclined her head to Bhalla. "Thank you for saying so," she said. "I—I really don't know much about him; he died when I was very young."

"Aye, so many of your fathers did," Bhalla said mournfully. Kaden watched Weylyn shift on his feet, like he was thinking of speaking out before deciding not to. "But Enan Davenrich was one of the greatest men I ever had the pleasure of knowing. He was honest in a way that few can be, and did his duty with honor. More than that, though, he stood up for his fellows with no thought for himself." Bhalla set his free hand on Ada's shoulder and squeezed gently. "And I know that he loved you very much, Adena."

Tears sprang up in her eyes, trickling down her face like tiny jewels. It made Kaden uncomfortable, seeing her cry like this, but he couldn't bring himself to look away either. "I wish he were here," she said at last.

"So, do I. But tell me, how is dear K'Lani?"

The change in subject seemed to help Ada regain control of herself. She straightened her back and wiped her face clean as she said, "My mother is doing well, thank you for asking. Ever since we rescued her from the Ophidians, she's thrown herself into the work of rebuilding the Landing with vigor."

"The act of renewing our homes can be a powerful motivator," Bhalla agreed, then turned his attention to Weylyn, who was alone by the door now that the others had pushed through to the tables bearing breakfast. "Weylyn, Son of the Wolf, I see that you're doing a fine job following in the footsteps of your father in protecting Orealus's chosen king."

Had there ever been a sentence more designed to provoke? Kaden groaned inside as he pressed to his feet—he was probably going to have to intervene to keep Weylyn from starting an enormous fight with the wizard. But then Weylyn… didn't attack.

"It was challenging at first, given how it seemed like Kaden was always trying to get himself killed," Weylyn said casually, and ouch, that stung. "But he's turned out to be braver than I thought possible, and has become someone I would gladly lay down my life for."

Kaden searched for something worthy to say and found nothing. Gratitude felt too small. Doubt felt too loud. All he could do was meet Weylyn's eyes and nod, hoping it was enough.

That paused Kaden in his tracks. It *was* enough to make his jaw drop, but then Weylyn looked at him with a clearly amused expression, and Kaden snapped his mouth shut again.

Did he really mean that? Kaden knew they were friends now, but he wouldn't have said before this that Weylyn was doing any more than what he thought was his duty. Was he really someone Weylyn thought so much of?

What did I do to deserve that kind of consideration? Well, apart from the dragon, and the fight with Omak, and the battle against the Ophidians, and… okay, so he'd done a few brave things. But he'd only ever accomplished anything with help! Kaden wouldn't have been able to do any of those things on his own.

Thankfully, the conversation had moved on without his intervention. "Is that Dragon's Fury?" Bhalla asked, pointing to the enormous sword strapped across Weylyn's back.

"It is," he said, curiosity in his face. "What do you know of the blade?"

"Not as much as I would wish," Bhalla replied. "But now that it's with you, as was foreseen, I've more faith that things will turn out as they should. That sword may well be one of the only weapons in the world with the ability to pierce Morvar's armored hide, you know."

Weylyn smiled slowly, baring his teeth in a hungry smile. "Is that so?" Kaden knew his friend would love to be the one to take the great dragon down.

"It is indeed," Bhalla confirmed, then brought the mood down by continuing, "But without the proper poison on the blade, the beast will not die even if you *do* get past his protections. His ability to retain his strength even when wounded is extreme."

"Where would I find the appropriate poison to deal with that?" Weylyn asked, as easy as if he were shopping for food in a marketplace.

"Oh, it has to be brewed fresh for it to work properly, and it contains some rather hard-to-find ingredients. Not impossible, though," Bhalla allowed. "Hmm… I've got a list of them somewhere…" He patted his robes for a moment, then reached inside and pulled out—

A book. Not a pamphlet, something thin and light that one might expect could be carried without complaint, but a genuine *tome* bound in dark blue leather with a smear of dust along the top binding. How… what… Weylyn was staring in surprise as well, which made Kaden feel a bit better about his own wide eyes.

"Here we are," Bhalla said as if nothing out of the ordinary had just happened. He blew the patina of dust off the top, then opened the front cover and began to turn the thick, ragged-edged pages. "Yes, just as I thought! *Orealus's Wrath*—I don't think much of the name myself, mind you, but it's said to poison one so completely that not even the power of prayer or yah'zaval can save you. All you need is a liberal scoop of troll mucus as the base, a tot of ground briskly tooth, the contents of a mature venom sac from a virulent thornbloom bush, and one white binicorn hair follicle."

"Ha!" Weylyn shook his head. "You lost me at the binicorn hair, old man. Those creatures don't exist. They're nothing but a tall tale old men mumble about when they're deep in their cups." The expression on his face clearly said that he thought Bhalla was one of those old men. "Let's talk again when you've got something *useful* for me."

"Mm, perhaps you're right," Bhalla mused. "We'll see what I can cook up." He turned to the rest of the party and greeted them, from congratulating Petey on his continued survival, saying, "What a marvel!"; to letting Eldrin know he'd received a letter from King Valymr "asking after you, but of course I told him I knew nothing because, at the time, that was true"; to Malacheen, commenting, "By Orealus, that's a large hammer." Even Bug got a pat on his little cap before Bhalla finally turned back to Kaden.

"You've done well so far," he said, and the serious intonation in his voice quieted the rest of the room down. "You've found Liasti and Aspis already."

The belt and the shield. Kaden's hand automatically went to his waist, where he was wearing the belt beneath his outer layer.

"But there remain many pieces of your father's armor and weaponry to be recovered. The boots, known as Paz, can be found in the Labyrinth of Heham near the city of Nula."

"The what in the where near the huh?" Malacheen shout-whispered to Ada, who shrugged.

"Those are guarded by a minotaur by the name of Gunsag," Bhalla went on. "The helmet Sozonos lies in the Sunken Creek near Trolling Bridge, and is very appropriately guarded by a troll named Bagul. The gauntlets, the Deimanus, are buried in the sizzling sands of the desert just outside the slave town of Elderpass Way. Lots of giants around there," he said reflectively.

Kaden felt his heart sink a little with every new piece of armor Bhalla mentioned, and the wizard wasn't done yet.

"Then there's Justicia, the ornate chest piece engraved with your family's crest," he said. "Many believed Morvar kept it after the war, but new reports suggest otherwise. I believe it's residing in the belly of the leviathan Thálassa. The Megalos, the greaves that fit the Paz perfectly, are in the Barren Badlands, kept under the watchful eyes of the scorchcrawlers. And of course," he added gently, "you know that Morvar guards your father's sword, Ruach, in Wyvernpeake."

Kaden realized his jaw had locked tight. He forced it to loosen before his teeth cracked.

Hearing it all listed out like that, Kaden felt an odd mixture of anger and sickness in his gut. That his father's precious armor had been doled out after the war as prizes to the worst beings imaginable, a symbol of the fall of his house and the death of his entire family… it was disgusting.

"Given that binicorn follicles are rather hard to find right now," Bhalla went on with a sly glance at Weylyn, "I believe that Ruach should be the last piece you attempt to regain. Megalos, on the other hand, isn't far from familiar territory to you, near the Barren Badlands. That might be a good piece to continue your efforts with."

Malacheen made a sound somewhere between a scoff and a grunt. "Aye, s'all well an' good for a wizard to talk about hi'ing off across the land, innit? Yet we're the ones who actually have to do the walkin'! Wi' that many pieces left to gather up, it'll take us ten bloody years to get it all done!"

Weylyn pointed at her. "Exactly."

"Oh, I thought of that," Bhalla said brightly, reaching into his robe again. Kaden wasn't sure what he expected him to come out with—another map or book, perhaps? But no… instead, he withdrew a small, flat golden circle that fit perfectly into the palm of his hand. Bhalla pressed on one edge of it, and it popped open to reveal… "A compass," Bhalla said, tilting the device toward Kaden so that he could see it. It *did* look like a compass, but the needle hung limp, not pointing in any particular direction.

"Great," Weylyn drawled. "Now we can find north." Eldrin chuckled in agreement.

"Oh, you can find much more than that, my boy," Bhalla chided, then addressed Kaden again.

"This is, of course, no mere compass," Bhalla said, then turned fully to Kaden. "It does not create paths of its own. It reveals only those Orealus already permits. The destination must be somewhere you have already walked, somewhere you can clearly picture in your mind—but even then, the way will open only if Orealus allows it."

He tapped the side of his head lightly. "Memory guides it. Faith powers it."

"Wow," Kaden breathed, his fingers itching to reach out. "That's... that's amazing."

"Isn't it neat?" Bhalla agreed.

No one spoke. Even Weylyn stood still, his hand hovering near the hilt of his sword as if unsure whether to draw it or kneel.

"Of course, whoever is using it must have complete faith in Orealus and offer up a brief prayer to him before it will work. Absolute faith, my boy," he emphasized. "Ab-sol-ute faith. That's the key ingredient. Now..." He handed it over to Kaden. "Why don't you test it out? I'd recommend using somewhere relatively close to start."

It felt like a lot of pressure, to suddenly have to make a portal fueled by the power of his own faith, but as Kaden held the compass and focused on the shape of it—an O, of course—he realized that he believed. He *had* that faith in Orealus, and he'd had it for a long time now. This was a gift beyond measure, one that would help him serve Orealus and do his will, and he was blessed to be able to use it.

Kaden smiled as he opened the compass and made the symbol of *O* over his heart with his free hand. "Orealus," he murmured, "I place my trust in you and hold faith for you in my heart. Please, show us the path to your creation."

A light similar to the one that beamed forth from Kaden's crystal pendant sprang out of the compass, illuminating the space between him and Bhalla. It spiraled into a golden circle, and once the circle was complete, Kaden realized that the scene in the center of it wasn't the room they were in at all. It was darker, forested, and he could smell the scent of wet loam and hear the sound of a blackbird shrilling in the distance. There was another sound as well… a welcome one, that of a familiar, booming voice somewhere close.

"What the…" Weylyn stared like he couldn't believe it.

"Oh, that's right handy!" Malacheen piped up.

"Beautiful," Queen Pepper said with a smile on her face. She looked at Kaden. "Shall we test it?"

"But…" All their things were still here; no one had packed.

"Just a test," she promised. "We'll come back in a moment." She held out her hand, and Kaden took it.

"Let's go," he said, and together they stepped through the portal and emerged, seconds later and many miles away, in the Forgotten Forest.

Kaden exhaled slowly. Whatever lay ahead, the world had just become much smaller—and far more dangerous.

CHAPTER 22

A moment after they stepped through, the brilliant shimmer of the portal dimmed, and a split second later it vanished entirely, as though it had never existed at all. The sudden stillness felt heavy, pressing against Kaden's ears, and his stomach lurched as if the world had taken an extra heartbeat to remember where he belonged.

They reappeared hip deep in juniper bushes beside the path rather than upon it.

"Interesting visualization technique you have there," Eldrin noted, but he didn't sound all that bothered by it. Probably because he was so lightweight that he could step on *top* of the bushes to get out, instead of hacking his way through like the rest of them, except for Pepper and her bodyguards. "Is there any reason you have a particular fondness for the side of this path?"

"I didn't mean to do it," Kaden said sheepishly. "I was thinking of the path and imagining it in my head, but… apparently I was imagining it from the side." He broke through the edge of the prickly bush, then turned back to offer his hand to Ada.

"We're lucky you weren't picturing a spot next to a cliff," Weylyn noted sourly as he smashed his way out of the bush as well, "or we could all have been in for a very nasty surprise."

Pepper shook her head. "The compass doesn't work like that," she said. "It won't allow you to place yourself somewhere that will immediately harm you, like reappearing in the middle of a wall or deep underwater, for example. Even here, with the bushes, you'll note that you each appeared in a hollow spot."

Kaden nodded slowly. The compass wasn't obeying him so much as judging him, weighing his intent against something greater than his own will. It would take him only where Orealus permitted, and nowhere else.

"Oh, that's handy," Kaden said. Using the compass made him feel euphoric, like he was surrounded by the spirit of Orealus himself, but if he couldn't use it safely, then he wasn't sure he would trust himself to do it.

"It's all part of having faith in Orealus," Pepper said beatifically. Weylyn made a face. "It is! Trust in Orealus to put you on the right path, and he shall."

"Or right next to the path," Petey added, and Eldrin laughed.

"You're all hilarious," Kaden said, but in truth, he wasn't upset. It was good that Petey, especially, had found his place with them, given his retiring nature. "All right, hang on…" Which way was the hidden village that sheltered the last of the Empyrean Knights?

"Ha!"

The voice carried authority without effort, ringing down the path with the confidence of someone who belonged here and expected others to know it.

Kaden, Ada, Petey, and Weylyn all just about jumped out of their skin at the sudden shout. Eldrin, Pepper, Redfern, and Millicent didn't, probably because they'd heard the newcomer's approach, and neither did Malacheen. Maybe it was because she was genuinely unsurprised… which couldn't be said of the person who'd greeted them once he realized who she was.

"Back so soon, eh?" Bardicus called as he strode down the path toward them. If you didn't know him well, he would seem the picture of unconcern, but Kaden could see the crinkle around his eyes that meant he was relieved. "Naturally, nowhere so close to a bunch of elves could hold your attention for long. Better that you're back, we've got loads to show you that we've been working on in the forge, and…" He paused, then stopped moving altogether as his eyes took in the new person traveling with them. "Bless my hammered soul, is that… Malacheen?"

"Ho there, sire," she said, bobbing in a little curtsy. "I—"

"By the bloody horns of Eldor, what are you doing here?" Bardicus bellowed as he stepped forward, holding his hammer out in front of him like he wished it were a paddle he could spank her with. "Ye're meant to be helpin' yer father in Kugdor!"

"What, Uncle?" she asked, widening her eyes mischievously. "Ye didn't miss me, then?"

Kaden held up a hand before the noise of their greeting—or confrontation, he wasn't sure what it was yet—got even louder. "Wait, King Bardicus is your uncle?" he asked Malacheen.

"Oh, aye!" she said. "The elder brother of my father Haltro, who's been beating Kugdor into shape ever since our liege abandoned it to go questing with ye."

"Abandoned?" Bardicus roared. "Abandoned! I never abandoned my home—not like you've apparently done, miss! Ye were meant to stay behind and help put our sacred mountain back together, not gallivant around the countryside looking for adventures that don't concern ye."

"Uncle!" Malacheen sounded hurt. "I did my duty! I stayed with my father and helped every step o' the way until all of us heard about the tumult in Whaldalf's Landing. Father was concerned for ye, but he knew better than to pull more of us from our tasks at home, so he sent me to do the lookin' instead. And here I've found ye, safe an' sound." She grinned. "Won't Father be pleased now?"

Bardicus looked at his niece grimly. "Pleased he may be, but I'm not. I not only gave him an order, but I gave *you* one as well, and here ye've gone and disobeyed it without a second thought."

"That's not true," Malacheen said firmly. "I gave it plenty o' thought. I honored my duty at home until the work there was steady again. But when word reached us of Whaldalf's Landing, I chose to act. Not out of rebellion—but because I believed it was right."

"Nevertheless, ye shouldn't be here."

Malacheen put her hands on her hips. "I'm no' a child anymore, Uncle! I know what I'm doin' and I'm doin' it well, as any of these fine folk would tell ye."

Kaden felt like that was an ideal moment for him to step in, but Ada beat him to it. "She's right," Ada insisted, stepping forward. "King Bardicus, Malacheen has been a wonderful addition to our forces. We'd never have completely retaken my village if it wasn't for her efforts."

"She's tough," Weylyn put in. Kaden wasn't surprised that physical prowess was the most important part to him.

"And she has the best woodcraft of any dwarf I've ever met," Eldrin added.

"She's excellent at intimidation," Redfern said. "You can never have too many intimidating women around, that's what I say."

"She's a great fighter," Kaden said, "and more importantly, she stands with us by my decision." That was the real crux of it, as far as he was concerned. Malacheen might have gotten here by disobeying an order from her king, but she'd done it for a good reason.

"A king must rule with both strength *and* compassion, I've found," Pepper said, subtly reminding everyone that she, too, was a ruler. If anyone could judge Bardicus over his reaction now, it was her. "Malacheen's valor is unquestionable. She's exactly the sort of ally I hoped that Kaden would find on this journey."

Malacheen looked away from her uncle and smiled at all of them, beaming like the sun rising over the horizon. "I'm right fortunate to have met such as ye on my travels," she said. "I'd thought only of helping my uncle, but I feel like finding ye was fate."

The will of Orealus, perhaps. Kaden was learning, slowly but steadily, that putting his faith in the workings of Orealus was always the right thing to do. Orealus had never failed him, and he wasn't going to let his faith falter for any reason.

"Ach, *fine!*" Bardicus snapped at last, his opinion roundly conquered. "Ye can stay, but don' go complainin' to me when Thalgrem puts you to work fanning the forge for yer insolence, Mal." He came forward and clapped her hard on the shoulders in what Kaden recognized as the dwarven equivalent of a hug. "An' don't let yerself get killed, y'hear me? I'd never hear the end of it from yer father."

Malacheen laughed, her eyes a bit wet as she clapped her hands on Bardicus's shoulders in turn. "The same to you, Uncle. Father has no desire to handle all this kingin' forever, y'know."

"Do I ever," Bardicus muttered, and a murmur of laughter passed through the group. Kaden felt a warmth inside his chest, a contentedness he could remember feeling with his family back in Ashland. So much had changed since then—*he* had changed—and he was grateful to be able to get that feeling of family once more.

Weylyn coughed into his fist. "Right, enough of the emotional reunions. What have you been working on since we left, Bardicus—other than drinking, that is?"

"Ha!" Bardicus released his niece and shook his head as he led the way back into the village. "The only one's been working on drinkin' is yer old friend Chum, I'll have you know. The rest of us have been at serious business."

Chum was the first person they saw as they traded the trail for the village itself, sitting on a chair carved from a stump in the center of town with a flagon in one hand. Duke barked and ran ahead to him, and Kaden was a bit startled to see Bug *and* Petey sitting on his back. "Oh, here you all are, how ni—*oof*," Chum said just as he was knocked right off the stump with the force of Duke's enthusiastic greeting.

To the left of the bustling plaza was the forge, and Seward, Anika, and Rowland were gathered on benches watching Thalgrem put the finishing touches on something that Kaden couldn't quite see from so far away.

"Oi, 'Grem! Hold up yer masterpiece and let them see what ye've wrought, eh?" Bardicus called out. Thalgrem, silent as ever, removed his metal and glass goggles and held up the thing he'd been working on. It was a heavy crossbow—obviously not as big as the one their friends had wielded in their defense against Morvar, but the limit of what one person could probably handle on their own.

The body of it was made of a wood covered in brown-and-black whorls, reminiscent of whirling winds and roaring fires, and the fittings shone so brightly that for a moment Kaden wondered whether or not they'd been crafted in silver instead of steel.

The weapon seemed purposeful in a way Kaden had learned to recognize, like something that had been made not just to exist, but to be used at exactly the right moment.

"Ironwood," Bardicus said proudly. "Thalgrem's specialty. Not many out there can craft with it without blunting every tool they own. But it's the mechanical bits that are the real tricky component, y'see." He pointed at the mechanism that stood out on the side and over the top of the wooden body. "The gears operate a pulley that goes right through the heart o' the wood, perfectly blended. Ye use the crank on the side there to pull the string back—s'made of boar sinew and vynthium, an' that stuff's hard to get during the best of times. Let the flanges fly out to the side to help stabilize, and whoever's shooting will have the best balance an' accuracy possible."

"This is it?" Eldrin demanded, spoiling the air of awe a moment later. "This is what you've been spending all your time on since we left? A bow so heavy only a dwarf or a giant could wield it by themselves, and yet not as useful as the bow these three here used on Morvar? And"—he peered around the forge—"I see no arrows. A crossbow without any ammunition, how very utilitarian. An elf *child* could craft a better bow than this."

"Oh, could they?" Bardicus shouted, his volume rising effortlessly as Eldrin goaded him into an argument. "The same sort of weakling elves who couldn't handle a crossbow that even a slender thing like Ada could manage?"

"Please don't drag me into this," Ada said.

"Indeed, there's no need to bring in a third party to try and prove your ridiculous point," Eldrin agreed. "When we all know that the fact of the matter is, a dwarf needs every bit of assistance they can get when it comes to their shooting, as they have the visual acuity of a mole and the—"

"*What* did you just call me?"

The argument devolved into bickering. Kaden might have been tempted to step in if he couldn't see how Eldrin and Bardicus actually seemed to be enjoying the argument. He'd met people like that before—people who liked the back and forth, the banter, the charge of disagreement as a touchstone for a discussion. He wasn't one of those people himself, but it didn't bother him.

It *did* seem to bother Ada, though, who looked over at Malacheen with a worried expression on her face. "Aren't you offended too?" she asked.

"Ach, no, darlin'." Malacheen shook her head, making her long hair swish back and forth. "Dwarves an' elves have to have somethin' to argue about if we're to get along proper, ye know. Otherwise, it just ain't natural. Too much tension builds up, and the next thing ye see is us takin' great big swings at each other. Besides," she added a bit more loudly for effect, "the prince made a good point, even if he is too stick thin to wield a crossbow like ours properly!"

Bardicus turned a glare on his niece. "Who's side are ye on, turncoat?" he demanded.

"Stick thin?" Eldrin snapped. "I'm not stick thin!"

"Seems like a good description to me, eh?"

They began arguing again to the sound of Malacheen chuckling as she turned back to Ada. "Dwarves craft for power over accuracy when it comes to our bows. That's why we've got to include all the extra bits an' bobs to help us hit the broad side of a barn, see? But that extra oomph is important when yer up against a creature like Morvar. Ye need every bit of punching-through power ye can get.

"An' the proper bolts probably can't even be crafted here," she added. "Ye need a forge capable of melting down dragon scale, an' yer not going to find that outside o' Kugdor. My father is the best when it comes to using the Big Burner."

Kaden nodded. "That's something to consider once we actually have dragon scales to use," he said. "But the first thing we need to do is decide which piece of the armor to go after next." Raising his voice over the sound of the fight, he called his friends in close.

It was time to choose their next target, and whatever they chose next would shape everything that followed.

CHAPTER 23

The greatest challenge to ruling Nethopolis did not come from the sea itself. The depths held enemies enough, traitors like Agalus whose betrayal led to the death of the former king, and beasts like the Leviathan, once bound to serve Nethopolis but twisted into a weapon against it. No, the true challenge was remembering that Nethopolis was only part of a greater whole.

It was easy, in the depths, to think that there was nothing more to the world than those who swam within the seas. Whoever ruled Nethopolis had plenty to contend with in his sphere; what did it matter what they did in the harsh, inconstant air up above them? How could it affect them? Why should they care who lived and died? It had taken Lucient's influence on Agalus and the subsequent near destruction of their kingdom for Varun to truly believe differently. It wasn't until his uncle was finally, if only temporarily, defeated that Varun turned to the wisdom of Orealus and, it had to be said, the wisdom of his wife, Dinereus, and ventured into the deepest room in his palace to look closer at the surface.

Long before Dinereus had taken that place beside him, Varun had been shaped by another presence whose influence never truly left the Deep. His mother, Aelunara, had taught him that faith was not a weapon to be wielded, but a responsibility to be borne. She believed in balance over dominion, in restraint over force, and in sacrifice undertaken without expectation of reward. Her final act was meant to shield the innocent and contain the corruption spreading through the depths, not to claim her life. Yet the cost proved greater than any living vessel could endure. In the years since, Varun had come to understand that her passing was not absence, but weight, quiet and constant, guiding his hand when fury would have been easier.

The greatest gift Orealus ever gave to the rulers of Nethopolis—those who kept their faith with him, at least—was a crystal the size of a whale set into the structure of the sea floor itself. When Varun made the proper prayers to Orealus, the crystal would glow with the great god's light and show Varun scenes from the world above. It didn't always show what he asked for or what he expected, but he'd never known it to show him a falsehood either.

He was just beginning his prayers to Orealus in preparation for igniting the crystal when Dinereus joined him, her long tail fanning elegantly behind her. Dinereus had a presence that rivaled Varun at his most majestic without even trying. Her eyes were the deepest shade of emerald, reminiscent of the most protected coves in the ocean. Her long, flowing hair shimmered with streaks of aquamarine and turquoise even in the poor light available in this part of the palace. Her tail was a mesmerizing blend of indigo and violet, with hints of gold at the edges, and adorning her neck was a necklace made of rare opalescent gems, a betrothal gift from Varun that she seldom took off.

He smiled at her despite the seriousness of the ritual he was about to undertake. "Our children freed you from their captivity, I see."

"Our tiny overlords are fierce but benevolent," she agreed, stopping beside him. She brushed her tail against his, an intimate caress that made Varun's heart beat more quickly, no matter the many years they'd been married. "I was able to bargain my way out of their presence for a time, but I'm afraid the price is a high one. They demand to see their father once your business here is done."

"I'd like that," he confessed, turning to stare at the crystal. Inert and uncharged by prayer, it lay as black as a sinkhole, the kind of pit in the bottom of the sea that even merfolk knew not to trespass in, lest they never find their way out. "As long as I learn nothing that requires immediate action."

"What could possibly do so?" Dinereus asked. "You've checked regularly since the boy king and his people left, and they continue their quest largely unscathed."

Varun closed his eyes for a moment, feeling the rhythm of the water move ever so slowly around them. They were too deep for the tides to pull them the way they did on the surface, but the effect of the rest of the world on his realm was still ever present. "I feel as though things are verging on a change," he confessed. "Like something is building bigger and bigger, and we're nearly at the tipping point now. There might not be anything I can do to directly influence the outcome on the surface, but the more I know, the better I can prepare our people if something is indeed heading our way." Lucient's shadow no longer crept. It pressed.

Dinereus laid a hand on his arm. "And if they are sending some great evil toward us?" she said quietly. "What will you do? Think carefully, my husband. I know the lives of Kaden and his people concern you, and that you would never foreswear yourself once you've given an oath, but more people are living in the depths of our great city than warriors. We are a last bastion against the depredations of Agalus and those who follow him; we spill blood every day for the safety of our city and the people who come to us for protection.

"*Our* people. Our elders, our children… they depend on your strength and presence here, in Nethopolis. Not weighed down with the cares of every leader in the world."

Varun was a bit surprised to hear this from his wife. "You yourself encouraged me to look in on Kaden and ensure his safety."

"I know, and I stand by that," she said, "but I've seen the effect that looking upon his company has on you. They are a mighty group, and Kaden himself is only growing stronger in the love and light of Orealus. I can feel how you yearn to be more involved, to use our people to strengthen his claim. I just ask for you to wait until it's necessary to do so." Her eyes were sad. "Let our children have the peace of this place a little longer. Let them have their father before he swims away to do battle for the sake of a world they know nothing about yet." Her voice did not waver, but the plea beneath it did.

Varun nodded immediately. "I would never rush to war," he assured Dinereus. "Not for anyone's sake. That's why I feel it is important to learn as much as I can about what's happening, so that we can be informed before our choice is taken from us." He took her hand. "Will you pray with me? Stay and see what I do?"

"Of course." She traced the sacred *O* of Orealus in front of her. "Lead the prayer, husband."

There was never just one way to pray to Orealus. Every culture, even within the merfolk, had its own traditions for reaching out to their holy creator. Varun often modified his words depending on the moment—how he felt, what he was searching for, how he hoped Orealus would help him. This time, the prayer came to him easily.

"Holy Orealus," he intoned, circling his hand in an *O* shape but not stopping after a single rotation. "Your servants beseech you to give us your insight into the world above. Bless us with your vision and imbue this holy talisman with your power that we may learn and be guided to honor you and your plans for peace." The water swirled and swirled, powering up from a simple susurration to a full-on whirlpool in front of him. "Let us search for the truth in your power and presence, Mighty Orealus. All honor and love to thee."

"All honor and love to thee," Dinereus repeated, and then Varun brought his hand to a stop. The swirling cone of water moved outward like a wave, washing over the enormous crystal, and everywhere it touched, the crystal went from pitch-black to as light as day.

The visions given by the crystal only lasted as long as the water was stirred, so Varun knew he had no time to waste. He looked into the light and saw Kaden in the center of a group of his companions. Some of them were familiar to Varun, while others were completely new, including the female dwarf who seemed quite jolly, given the rather dire circumstances they were in. They stood around a massive weapon of war, their attention fixed upon it with a mix of awe and urgency. Nevertheless, he got a chill looking at the enormous crossbow. Weapons forged in desperation often demanded a terrible price.

He looked more carefully at Kaden, taking in the sight of his shining shield and belt, pieces of his father's armor he'd collected along the way so far. He was making progress… but was it coming fast enough? Was he going *too* fast? Could he truly trust the people he was questing with? Queen Pepper was beyond reproach, of course, but some of the others…

Dinereus squeezed his hand. "I know that look," she murmured. "You're concerning yourself too deeply with things you cannot change."

"Perhaps, but—"

"No. It does no good to dwell on that which is beyond our control." As they watched, Kaden threw his head back and laughed at something one of his companions said. The vision faded just as he turned toward a new voice, giving Varun a clear look at the boy's face.

No, not a boy. A man. A man with the potential to lead all of them to a more peaceful future, if he could survive long enough to build a coalition capable of fighting against Lucient. Then again… what one man could build, another could break. And it was so much easier to break things than it was to raise them.

"I fear for him," Varun said heavily. "I fear that he's not taking enough time to grow into his own adulthood. He's had his fair share of pain, I know, but… he's going to be expected to carry not just *his* pain, but the pain of others. He's going to be responsible for not just *his* acts, but the acts of those in his company." Dinereus went still, and Varun knew she was thinking about the same things he was: Agalus's defection and the murder of Varun's father, and all the terrible consequences that had come with it.

"I could not be a good king to my people if I didn't grapple with the consequences of my family's actions toward them every single day," Varun said. "Ours is a legacy of blood and pain and fear, and only now are we beginning to recover some of the beauty that our civilization lost to the war. Kaden is so young. So very young. It makes me wonder how he'll handle himself when something happens that he can't move on from or look away from. Something where no amount of guidance from his friends is enough to silence his own sense of responsibility."

"He'll have to learn," Dinereus agreed. "As do we all."

"I learned in a time of peace. He's learning in a time of war and conflict."

"Then," she said firmly, "we must all pray that he learns in time to bring peace, rather than falling to that conflict."

"Well said, my wife." Varun drew her in for a kiss, then turned them from the chamber. It was time to swim in the light for a while, to visit and play with their children so he might renew his own sense of hope.

Varun was right to be hopeful.

He was also right to be afraid.

Far below the surface world, the Leviathan turned its vast body toward Nethopolis, and the darkness followed in its wake.

CHAPTER 24

They returned to Bhalla's chambers in Lumhagen only moments after testing the portal in the Forgotten Forest, the air still faintly warm where the light had folded in on itself.

For the first time in a long time, when Kaden looked at the map spread out before them of the vast expanse of Empyrea, he didn't feel overwhelmed. "We can go anywhere," he said confidently, one hand against the center of his chest. That was where he felt the prayer Bhalla had taught him taking root, steady and directional, like an inner compass waiting to be aligned.

"It isn't quite that simple," Queen Pepper said with an air of caution. "Remember, Kaden, that your new power is most effective when you use it to take us somewhere you've already been. It can take us somewhere new as well, but that will require a much greater use of your power, and we'll have to be very careful about describing the correct location to you or risk ending up stranded somewhere we don't know."

"Oh." She was right, and Kaden felt his cheer diminish with the knowledge that he'd gained a gift that *might* be a great help, but wasn't as limitless as he'd thought. And yet… "What if there's some way for me to share the power to do this with you?" he asked, warming to the thought. "You've traveled far more widely than I, haven't you?"

She smiled but shook her head. "Apart from the travels I underwent as part of the war effort, I've scarcely ever been away from my home. It isn't the place of a queen to be away from her people the way I have been lately, and I'm glad of it." She sighed and laid a hand against her chest. "I'm afraid I don't have the heart for a life of adventure. I miss my trees, my lights, and the songs and laughter of my people. I miss looking after them and being there to help them in whatever way they have need of."

Saying it aloud seemed to cost her something. Kaden realized then that leaving her people again was not a small sacrifice, even when doing so for him.

"That's a long way of saying she can't do it, kid," Weylyn said, and Redfern glared at him. "I'm probably the best-traveled of the entire group," he went on, "but I'm no believer, so don't even think about asking me to help. I'm not going to mess around with some weird, wizard-given ability that might just as easily send me to the bottom of the sea as the place I mean to go."

"We weren't in danger of ending up on the bottom of the sea," Kaden said.

"Maybe not," Weylyn replied, "but I meant it when I said we were lucky you only landed us off the path." His eyes were apologetic, but his voice was firm. "If that's the worst that ever happens while using that thing, we'll be lucky."

Kaden wanted to argue the point, but given that he was the one who'd tumbled them into a section of prickly juniper bushes, there wasn't much he could say. "Then what do we do?" he asked.

Eldrin shrugged. "The same thing we were doing before, just a bit faster, I suppose."

"We need to prioritize whatever pieces of the armor will give us the greatest edge over Morvar," Weylyn said. "The dragon knows we're looking for it now. We want to be the hunter, not the hunted, so the sooner we get what we need to go after it, the better. I'm thinking the gauntlets are a good next target." He pointed at a barren section of the map. "They're right outside Elderpass Way, so we'd have a base of operations to work from there."

"Elderpass Way is a slave town," Ada objected. "We can't work out of a slave town! We'd be taking advantage of the people there."

"We do what we have to do."

"It's immoral."

"So's Lucient! Which do you think is *more* immoral, huh?"

The silence that followed was heavy. Kaden felt the weight of leadership press against him again. Winning mattered, but how they won mattered too.

Ada decided to try a different tactic. "It's too slow," she said. "The gauntlets are the most isolated of all the pieces of armor. In the time it takes to go get them, we could find two or three other pieces. Not that *any* of them are going to be easy," she added with a frown. "They're all guarded by horrors."

Eldrin spoke up unexpectedly. "Kaden's new ability is a gift from Orealus," he said, catching Kaden's eyes. "He might have learned it from Bhalla, but the power only works for a person who has great faith in Orealus. I don't think something like this would lead us so dangerously astray."

"An admirable idea," Pepper said judiciously, "but one that I think should remain academic for the time being." She pointed at the map. "The Barren Badlands, where the greaves Megalos are hidden, are only a short distance away from Westramore. You've at least laid eyes on the land close to that city from afar, Kaden, and I can help you with details if you need something more to go on. It's a good spot to branch out from."

That made... a lot of sense, actually. Kaden started to agree, but Chum spoke up over him before he could get out a full word.

"Ah, y'know," Chum said as he rubbed his stubby fingers together nervously, "Westramore, it… It might not be the best place for Weylyn and me to go right now. Given that we, y'know, left in such a lather last time."

"What exactly does that mean?" Petey asked suspiciously, one clawed hand stroking Bug's glowing cap like the motion soothed him.

"Oh, it's just… ah… well." Chum spread his hands and smiled winningly. "I *might* have left my former appointment with the Thieves Guild there without paying the, ah, the yearly *dues* that they decided were necessary—and quite unfairly, I might add!

"He owes them a lot of money," Weylyn translated with a grin. "Nearly got his head taken off for it, too. But I managed to get him out of there."

"You're even worse than me!" Chum screeched. "You showed up the Sword Brothers syndicate!"

Kaden resisted the urge to shake his head to try to settle some of the names bouncing around in there now. "Wait. What's that?"

"'Tis a mercenary guild," Bardicus put in from where he was polishing up a bit of his hammer with the tail of his shirt. They have a reputation for producing fierce fighters. Said to stand by their word no matter the coin on offer, but that was before their current boss came around. Now they're a little better than a band of ruffians allayin' good folk for coin."

Eldrin stared aghast at Weylyn. "You were a bandit?"

"Not me," Weylyn protested. "Why do you think I left? I wasn't happy with the new management. I beat their leader fairly badly before I took off, too. I doubt he'll want to come up against me a second time."

"We don't actually have to land inside the city itself, either," Ada pointed out. "We've all heard tales of how bad it is in Westramore, but the lands around it are said to be sparsely populated."

"Aye, because of all the scorchcrawlers," Malacheen added helpfully.

"That doesn't make me feel better!" Petey said, petting Bug so hard that the frolicking mushroom was starting to bow down under the weight of Petey's hand.

It was clear to Kaden that this was the sort of discussion that would last all day—or longer if he let it. "Unless anyone has a really firm objection," he said, looking at Chum, "we'll go for the greaves next. Bhalla suggested that path as well, and they're one of the closest pieces to where we are now. And if we get into trouble,"—he tapped his chest with a small smile—"I can get us out of it again."

Chum looked a bit more cheerful at that. "Good point. I suppose, ah… I suppose it's all right, then. But… how will you know if we're in the right place?"

"I'll just…" Kaden thought about how he'd done it before—praying to Orealus, visualizing where he wished to go, and then seeing the portal open up before him as clear as day. He hadn't been able to make the last one something he could see in detail on the other side through, but perhaps this time. "Give me a moment."

Kaden considered what he knew of Westramore from both memory and story. He had skirted its outskirts once before during his early travels, and the tales Weylyn and Chum had shared over the fire only filled in what he hadn't seen himself.

The city lay near the largest coal mines on the land mass, populated with underfed workers who stretched their poor incomes as far as they could. They came home each evening coated in black dust, and when that mixed with the red grit blowing in from the Barren Badlands, it left the entire city covered in a grimy brown patina that was nearly impossible to wash away.

Even from memory alone, the place tasted bitter in his thoughts.

Kaden could visualize the wall of the city, surrounded by the cut-off, ossified stumps of a forest long-since burnt for fuel. There was one road in, and he picked a spot for them a little ways down it, thought hard about where he wanted them to be, then made the sacred symbol of Orealus in front of his chest as he held the compass up. Golden light blossomed in front of them all, swirling into a circle with a clear center, and through that—

"Och, blow me down, eh," Bardicus muttered, then nudged Thalgrem with one heavy elbow as everyone stared at the distant walls of Westramore. "Good thing we stopped back in Lumhagen to pack before heading out. Would've been a right mess showing up here with naught but the clothes on our backs."

"Well done, Kaden," Queen Pepper said with a knowing smile. "Very impressive."

"Yes, yes, so impressive," Chum muttered, looking at the portal like he was staring at a noose. "You know, I really think it's better if I stay here. I can, ah, help with the—you know, with the things and the stuff and all of the—"

"If I'm going, you're going," Weylyn said firmly, and grabbed Chum by the scruff of his neck as he strode forward. He was the first to go through the portal—rather impressive, all things considered.

Kaden watched them step through, then motioned for Eldrin and Queen Pepper, Redfern, and Millicent to follow. "We should hurry." If the other side was being watched, the less time anyone had to stare at people stepping out of nothing, the better. Holding the portal open pulled at him now, not painfully, but insistently, as a muscle pushed too far without rest.

Next went the dwarves, Bardicus pushing a protesting Malacheen ahead of him like a recalcitrant child. "Stay where I can keep an eye on ye!" Petey and Bug followed them, but only once Duke pressed in tight to his side, like a living piece of armor. Then there was only Ada left with Kaden, and before she stepped through, she looked at him for a long moment, her mouth opening as though she was going to say something before she closed it abruptly.

"What?" Kaden asked. Sweat rolled down his forehead, and his arms were beginning to shake, but he wanted to hear what she had to say. He wondered… he *hoped*…

"Later," Ada said and stepped through after the others.

Kaden's heart felt lighter even as it raced from the strain. "All praise and blessings to thee, Orealus," he murmured, and the burden of maintaining the portal seemed to lighten for a moment. Then he stepped through himself, finally releasing the holy symbol. His yah'zaval flickered out, and the portal went away with it.

They were indeed left on the outskirts of Westramore, surrounded by the broken skeletons of dead trees and beaten upon by the persistent wind coming off the Barren Badlands. Bardicus looked around with a frown on his broad face. "Not much to recommend the place, eh?"

"Oh, I don't know, sire," Malacheen said with a smile, putting her hands on her ample hips as she stared all around. "Not a bad view, all told. The wind is bracing. The sun's quite nice, in a stark kind o' way. Plus, there's all that—" The shrill cry of a hawk echoed overhead, and Kaden could just make out the silhouette of the raptor against the sun before the light dazzled his eyes too much. "That lovely birdsong," Malacheen finished.

The sound did not belong to the wild. It was measured. Commanded.

Thalgrem, for his part, smashed his gauntlets together once, sending up a brief spray of sparks. "Right ye are," Bardicus said. "We shouldn't linger here. We've all got our packs, plenty of provisions an' the like, and Kaden's got his compass. No need for us to head into town. So." He turned a full circle. "Which way are these greaves, then?"

"We're going to need to head east, I think," Weylyn said. "That's where all the local legends speak of treasure, in the low hills. Plenty of thrill seekers have gone up against the nearest scorchcrawler nests thanks to those rumors, but few of them ever came back."

"Do we have to do this?" Chum whined. He was wringing his hands together so hard that his fingertips were blanched and pale. "Just seeing this rotten place is enough to dredge up some of my most *painful* memories."

"Oh, please," Weylyn said. "I got you out of the guild's clutches before they could do more than pry the top layer of your hooves off."

"Exactly! It was one of the worst days of my life!"

"We shouldn't debate this on the road," Queen Pepper said. She was fighting against the pull of the wind, and after a moment, she gave in and landed on the ground. "Come down," she called to her bodyguards, and Millicent and Redfern joined them a moment later, looking decidedly disheveled. "I'm afraid we won't be able to fly in this," she said apologetically. "It's simply too strong."

"It's fine," Kaden said. It wasn't like he'd be able to do much more than manage a slow walk for now himself; he felt exhausted from the yah'zaval he's expended on the portal. "Hmm." He looked around and saw a group of stumps in the distance that were taller than the rest, tall enough for them to get a bit of shelter from them while they figured out their next move. "Let's head over there to get our bearings and prepare for what comes next."

It occurred to Kaden that he might have been a bit hasty in bringing everyone through a portal without having a firm plan for once they got here, but then again, if he'd learned anything on this quest so far, it was how to adapt quickly. They'd be all right.

They moved fast, Weylyn leading the way and Eldrin bringing up the rear. The hawk's cry sounded twice more in the time it took them to get to the minimal protection offered by the taller tree stumps, and on the third cry, Duke raised his head and barked up at it.

"No!" Kaden chided his hound as they came to a stop within the stumps. "Stop that. *Still.*" That was one of the commands Kaden and his father had taught Duke when he was just a puppy, useful for when they took him hunting. It meant he was to be completely silent and unmoving until they made the signal that meant he could relax. Duke knew this command like the back of his paw, and yet—

Duke, to Kaden's astonishment, didn't heed his command. Instead, he barked, louder and louder, ignoring every attempt to shush him.

"Shut the animal up!" Chum hissed. "Or you'll bring the city guard down on us!"

"He's never acted like this before," Kaden protested. "He wouldn't be doing this unless something was very wrong. I'm not sure what it is, but—"

A second later, close enough that Kaden could see that the tips of its tailfeathers had been dyed blood red, a hawk flew overhead. In its talons was a small, metal contraption, which it released right in the center of their party.

"Smother it!" Weylyn shouted just as the object hit the ground, but—it was too late. It made a sound like a series of tiny explosions as it bounced along the dirt, and with each bounce, a cloud of gray dust rose into the air. The dust stank like sulfur, and worse than that, it made Kaden feel slightly dizzy.

Queen Pepper was the first to realize what was happening. "Dunntaika," she exclaimed. She waved her hands, clearly trying to summon her yah'zaval to aid them. Nothing happened, and her expression became grim. Yah'zaval answered, with resolve, not desperation.

"Everyone, protect Kaden from the dust! It will sap his powers!"

Dunntaika… Kaden had never felt the corruption tied to Lucient so clearly before. It was not power meant to be wielded, but decay pressing inward, heavy and suffocating, as if it sought to hollow him out rather than empower him.

"Make another portal!" That was Ada, standing in front of him, trying to shield him as best she could with her own slender body. "Kaden, we need a portal out of here."

He tried. He tried as hard as he could, drawing the circle of Orealus and praying with every ounce of faith he had in him, but it was so hard to concentrate with the evil, crawling sensation of dunntaika surrounding him, surrounding them all. Kaden couldn't push it back, couldn't make space for his yah'zaval to awaken within him and emerge. He was still so tired from the last portal, and now this?

"Kaden, you need to—"

Whatever Weylyn had been going to say was cut off by the impact of an arrow straight into his upper back. It didn't penetrate his armor, luckily, but the hideous sound of metal scraping against metal was a rude awakening.

"We're under attack!" Bardicus hefted his hammer and glared out into the wasteland around them. "Ah, see there—crawling forward on their bellies like the serpents they are!" It was an entire group of men, low to the ground, just like Bardicus said. Both Eldrin and Ada went for their bows, but three more arrows fired just over their heads as warning shots stopped their hands.

"All the better to avoid your notice until it was too late for you fools to do anything," a new voice said. One man stood tall among the creeping ambush party. As he stepped forward, a familiar hawk flew down and perched on his right forearm, which had a thick leather vambrace that looked made for just such a thing.

The newcomer looked to Kaden like the classic picture of a pirate, from his leather tunic and high black boots to the patch he wore over his left eye. The other eye was as black as a starless night, and his long dreadlocks chimed against each other as they swayed in the wind, full of gleaming golden charms. He wasn't a tall man, but he had an undeniable presence.

"Mad-Eyed Malech," Weylyn said, disgust clear in his voice. The name carried weight, like a blade set gently on a throat.

"Weylyn, Son of the Wolf," the man replied, his satisfaction clear. "I always said I'd get my hands on you again someday. Thought I'd have to hunt you down, but fate—and our benevolent Lord Lucient—have delivered you to me instead." He laughed as the rest of the ambushers closed in, finally standing up tall. There were over twenty people, and half of them had arrows nocked and ready to fire.

"Welcome," Mad-Eyed Malech said softly. "To Westramore."

CHAPTER 25

Kaden had thought nothing would ever be harder to bear than their descent into the goblin city of Shroudscar, where danger pressed in from every side, and failure meant death. He still dreamed of the moment he had believed Petey was dead, of the crushing certainty that he had lost him forever. That Petey had survived felt less like luck and more like a mercy Kaden did not dare expect again. On sleepless nights, he had prayed that he would never again be forced to stand helpless while someone he loved suffered beyond his reach.

He should have known better.

The second they laid down their arms, Mad-Eyed Malech's goons came forward and clapped them all in manacles. Not just any manacles; the second they closed around his wrists, Kaden's already-faltering connection to yah'zaval collapsed inward, smothered as if wrapped in cold ash. "What…"

"Oh, is this your little wizard, then?" Mad-Eyed Malech had sauntered over to him, a feral grin on his face. "Seems young to have that sort of power… but I saw the portal you made with my own eyes. You know what a lad like you has the potential to be, m'boy?" Malech winked his one eye at Kaden. "Useful."

"I'll never work for you," Kaden snapped.

"Not with those on you won't," Malech agreed. "The metal's infused with pure dunntaika. They shut down your connection to your god so tight that not even a peep of light gets through. All the better for me."

He reached out and gave Kaden's bound wrists a little shake. "Can't have wizardlings like you thinking they can do whatever they want as long as they *believe*, can I? That's the sort of thing that gives people ideas." He narrowed his look into a glare. "And I don't like ideas."

"Oh, leave him be," Weylyn drawled from where he was standing, casual, as though he hadn't just had his armor and sword stripped from him. Even without his armor, he looked big and intimidating. Kaden wished he had half the natural presence of Weylyn. "Are you really so weak that you torment someone who hasn't even reached their majority yet? Pathetic." He spat derisively onto the ground, and that was enough to make Malech forget about Kaden.

The self-proclaimed "Lord of Westramore" strode over to Weylyn and hit him hard across the face with the back of his hand. Weylyn's head swung with the blow, and a second later, Malech had a nasty, jagged-edged dagger pressed to the side of Weylyn's neck.

Kaden shouted and tried to lunge forward, but the chain attached to his manacles was held fast by a bruiser of a man almost twice his size. He was nearly jerked off his feet as his captor hauled him back, then kicked him sharply in the back of the leg to make Kaden fall to his knees. There were other tousles going on as well, but they all ended the same way—with Kaden's company subdued.

"What a loyal group you've found," Mad-Eyed Malech murmured as he pressed the blade deeper. A thin trail of blood began to trickle down Weylyn's neck, but he didn't move, just stared stonily at his assailant. "Far more loyal than scum like you deserve. I think…" Malech grinned nastily. "I think such loyalty should be rewarded. I always planned to use you as the main event in the Coliseum when I found you, and now I'm going to do you one better and give all your little 'friends' front-row seats to your demise."

He looked around at his people. "We're going to have a hell of a show tonight!" he shouted, and a ragged cheer went up from the men. He finally put his knife away, pausing to gather the blood on the blade with his fingertips and flick it straight at Weylyn's face. "Let's get these scum to the Coliseum."

Malech paused, then pointed a finger at something Kaden couldn't see. There was a shrill cry, and then—"Get this bird offa me!"

Chum! Kaden watched as the little satyr was dragged forward by his manacles—actually, just one manacle. The other one was dangling free from his wrist. Perched on one of his horns and attacking his head with its razor-sharp beak was the hawk from earlier, and Chum was beating fruitlessly at it with his free hand as he yelled.

Mad-Eyed Malech whistled, and the hawk released its grip on Chum, gliding over to land neatly on his shoulder. Only now did Kaden realize what he was actually looking at. He'd noticed that thick leather pad earlier when the bird first descended and had assumed it was a reinforced pauldron. But the way the hawk settled onto it made the truth unmistakable—it was a crafted perch designed specifically for the raptor.

"Chum, my old friend," Malech said with a leer. "My goodness, have you grown?"

"Big enough to kick you in the—" A sudden tug jolted Chum into silence, and the brute in charge of his manacles clapped the open one back on him with a scowl.

"And as slippery as ever," Malech went on before looking at his lackey. "You were supposed to search him."

"He had the wire in his mouth," the man said with a grunt.

"Sounds like an excuse to me." Malech was almost half a foot shorter than the bruiser holding Chum's lead, but the big man seemed to shrink as his boss stopped in front of him. "He's your charge until we turn him over to the Thieves. If he escapes, I'll put you into the Coliseum next. Understand me?"

The man nodded. "Yes, sir."

"Good." Mad-Eyed Malech turned around to look at the rest of them for a moment, then clapped his hands. "Well, there's no time to waste! Let's get this rabble to the arena while the sun's still burning! Joust, Goram, go spread the word that fresh meat is coming to play." He grinned again. "I want the whole city to see Weylyn, Son of the Wolf, brought low."

If there was one thing Kaden could say about Mad-Eyed Malech, it was that the man knew how to put on a spectacle. The city of Westramore was a dirty, dusty place, and even though he'd been inside its walls for less than an hour today, Kaden could already feel the deep sense of hopelessness that permeated it. No one seemed to be here because they truly wanted to be. This was a place for folks at the end of their ropes, readying themselves for the next day of hardship because it was all they knew how to do. The only break from the glum monotony of their lives, the only chance for something other than depression to take over, lay with the arena. The arena was not an escape from despair, but its loudest expression.

He tried to remember that they were suffering too, as he and his friends were shoved into cages by Malech's crew on the side of the arena, just far enough from the stands that the filth people hurled didn't quite hit them.

But not everyone was there.

Weylyn's cage sat empty, the chains inside untouched. Kaden's stomach tightened. Wherever the Westramore thugs had taken him, it wasn't here with the rest of them. Malech clearly had *other* plans for him.

He tried to remember his sense of compassion as all their equipment, including his precious pieces of armor, was heaved into a pile like a treasure hoard for the crowd to gawk at. Kaden fought to keep his anger focused on Malech, but it was hard. "Nothing but lads, lasses, and little people in there!" someone brayed obnoxiously.

"And an elf! Think he can walk on water?"

"If we had some other than the well, we could try it, but can't risk him fouling it if he drowns."

"Look at those wings! How hard do you think it would be to pluck 'em?"

"Hell with the wings, look at the curves on *that* lass."

Kaden whirled around to look for the speaker, but Ada firmly pulled him back to face into the arena beside her. "Don't bother," she said. "It's not worth it."

"They shouldn't speak that way about you."

"No," Ada agreed. "They shouldn't, but we can't stop them. The only thing we can do is not give them the satisfaction of knowing that we care what they have to say about us, so I'm not going to look at them."

Everyone else in the group was doing a good job of ignoring the taunts and catcalls, so Kaden resolved to do the same. Well… almost everyone.

"You like little lasses, eh?" Malacheen shouted at one particularly loathsome man who was spouting off about all the things he'd like to do to her. "Why don't you come down here where my little hands can reach you, hmm? We'll see just what you like about me when I'm squeezing your bits so tight they pop right off your filthy body, eh?" She turned to Thalgrem, whose gauntlets must have seemed innocuous enough to Malech that he let him keep them. "Give me those, I've got a pair of bollocks to handle."

"Calm yerself," Bardicus snapped in a low voice.

"I'll not! Can't you hear what they're saying? It's *vile!*"

Bardicus shrugged. "When are other beings not vile to dwarves? Too short for elves, too strong for humans, too earth-bound for fairies… none of them care for us, niece. That's one reason we stick to our own kind, and why you ought to have done just that."

Kaden frowned. "When have humans been mean to you? Why?"

Bardicus shook his head. "It's an old state of being, lad, going back for centuries. Yer father tried to change it, tried to truly bring us all together in the fight against Lucient, but old enmities are hard to change. If we'd fought more cohesively, if he'd had time to really gather us under his banner… well, things might have gone differently. As it is?" He gave Kaden a serious look. "We've got to hope you'll do better."

"Oh sure, he'll get right on that," Eldrin said, keeping the moment from getting too dark. "Right after he miraculously delivers us from these shackles, this cage, and the entire city. Maybe start a bit smaller, is all I'm saying."

Kaden tugged fruitlessly at his shackles. The dunntaika he had inhaled earlier no longer pressed so heavily on him. His yah'zaval stirred again within his chest, present but locked away. But he couldn't access it. It was there, welling up in his chest, but with these shackles on, he could do no more than feel it.

Even Duke, lashed to Kaden's waist with a chain, had a dunntaika collar around his neck. Mad-Eyed Malech was taking no chances with their group. He wanted them to be unable to interfere with what was going to happen next. Which—

A trumpet sounded. The horn, faulty and cracked, blared across the sand, an assault on the ears. Everyone went quiet, and a moment later, the Lord of Westramore himself stepped into the center of the arena.

"My good people!" he bellowed, spreading his hands wide as he turned in a circle. "Cutthroats and thieves, bastards and brigands, laborers and ladies of the night! You who toil for my pleasure, allow me to assure you that today, it is *I* who toiled for *you*!"

"Typical," Bardicus muttered. "He gets lucky and trots it out like a gift for his audience."

"Tonight, I bring you a rare entertainment!" Malech went on. "The return of one of our own, home from distant lands. I suppose it's just because he missed this place so much." The stands rumbled with laughter. "Those who are lucky enough to escape this hell would do well to never return. Weylyn, Son of the Wolf, doesn't seem to understand that. He returned and brought with him a whole passel of fresh meat." He waved at the cages where they watched from. "Travelers of all kinds, a feast for the eyes, especially once we set *them* to fight." There was another surge of cheers, and Kaden wrenched at his shackles even though he knew it did no good.

"But first... It's time for our old friend Weylyn to see how he stacks up against the great beasts of the Waste." Malech took a sword from his belt—not his own, and likely not a good one given what Kaden knew of him—and tossed it into the sand. "He might stand a chance if he gets to this blade first." The Lord of Westramore left the arena, and a moment later doors on either side opened.

From the door on the right, his hands still bound, Weylyn emerged. That entrance was closer to the cages, and Kaden could clearly make out the fresh cuts and bruises on Weylyn's bare arms and face. Still, he moved like lightning toward where the sword lay in the center of the arena, and a second later, Kaden knew why.

The creature that came in through the other entrance had also been abused; that was clear. The second its silhouette crossed the threshold, Kaden's stomach dropped. He knew that shape. He knew the sloping shoulders, the elongated snout, the way the claws dragged in uneven patterns across the sand.

A scorchcrawler!

Memory slammed into him—the nest he'd fallen into, the heat, the screaming, the way the beasts hunted in packs, the terror of fighting them in tight quarters. He'd sworn he never wanted to see one again. And this one had been mangled into something even worse.

The size of a large horse, it was skeletal and underfed, and its leathery hide bore evidence of plenty of wounds, some healed and others so fresh they were still bleeding. It was limping from damage done to one of its front legs, and it looked as though it had been blinded. Kaden's breath caught. He knew this shape. He had fought its kind before. A scorchcrawler. A broken, brutalized one.

That didn't keep it from looking absolutely terrifying. So many of the monsters they'd fought so far had been humanoid enough that the terror of them was lessened, but this one—this was a predator through and through. Its nostrils flared sharply, and a moment later, a shrill scream of hunger emerged from its fanged maw. It charged forward at a breakneck pace even as Mad-Eyed Malech called out, "Weylyn, Son of the Wolf against the dread hunter of the Waste, a scorchcrawler!"

Kaden watched in horror as the two ran forward, seeming set on colliding. At the last moment, Weylyn dove forward and smoothly caught up the blade in his bound hands. As he rose back up, he darted to the side, but not before he scored a long line on the scorchcrawler's side with the blade.

"First blood to the Wolfson!" Malech shouted, and the crowd went wild. The scorchcrawler tried a few more direct charges, but Weylyn was dangerous enough with the blade that the peril seemed to get through even that creature's thick skull. After a few minutes of darting attacks that left Weylyn none the worse for wear, the creature stopped moving completely, and then—

It vanished.

"Oh, damn," Bardicus growled. "Who knew those cursed beasts could become invisible?"

"It's got yah'zaval?" Kaden asked.

"No. It's a form of natural camouflage," Queen Pepper said tensely, her eyes on the place where the scorchcrawler had disappeared. "Similar to how a mirage can distort things in a desert. Watch, you'll see it when it—there!" It was moving again, and Kaden *could* see it now... sort of. The scorchcrawler's outline was blurred, and as he watched, it was able to sneak around the side of Weylyn, then dart in. Weylyn barely got the sword up in time to keep from being bitten, but it *did* manage to knock him off his feet.

"We've got to help him!"

"Thalgrem," Bardicus said, "punch us out of here." The other dwarf moved up, leveling his gauntlet at the lock before smashing his fist into it. There was no electric crackle, not with dunntaika shackles on, but the gauntlet was strong enough that it *did* dent the front of the lock.

"The guards will shoot us the moment we step out of here!" Eldrin said, pointing at the men in the stands, crossbows in hand. "Without magic to protect us, we'll be taken out before Weylyn is!"

"Can't stand here and let the lad get eaten alive," Bardicus snapped back.

Ada turned to Kaden as the others began to argue. "There must be something you can do," she said fervently. "Orealus loves you. Ask him for help!"

Kaden was gratified by Ada's faith in him, but right now, he didn't feel equal to it. He'd done a terrible job of keeping his people safe from the moment they stepped through the portal—how could he protect them now? And yet... he had to try.

Kaden closed his eyes and made the symbol of Orealus in front of his chest. *Holy Orealus, I need you. I don't know what else to do...* What could he say that was honest? Was that true to his heart? Not that he deserved to lead his people to victory. Perhaps... *I pray for your forgiveness for my faults, for not living up to your expectations of me. I pray for your aid for Weylyn, who deserves to live and find his way back to faith in you. I pray for anything at all that will help him to live through this challenge. Please, I beg of you...* He heard the crowd begin to jeer and knew it meant that Weylyn was hurting. *I beg of you, save your son so that he might learn your love and do your will.*

Kaden felt his power surge out of him. There was a faint whoosh in the air, a clatter, and then—

"Duke!" Ada exclaimed.

What? Kaden opened his eyes and looked in astonishment at Duke, who was not only outside the cage but also missing the collar that had been forced on him. He barked once, and his armor appeared. Then he raced toward where Weylyn was wavering on his feet, turning this way and that in an effort to track the nearly invisible scorchcrawler.

Duke didn't have to rely on his eyes. With a massive growl, he threw himself just past Weylyn and clamped down on something in midair. A moment later, the scorchcrawler reappeared, pain forcing it out of its camouflaged state as it shrieked and tried to bite at Duke, who was biting its injured foreleg. Its sharp teeth slid right off the big dog's armor, though, and Duke snarled and savaged it for all he was worth.

"Shoot the mutt!" Mad-Eyed Malech shouted, and every guard in the stands let fly. Weylyn threw himself to the sand to avoid the shots, and Kaden feared the worst, but every one that hit Duke was turned aside by his armor.

The scorchcrawler wasn't so lucky, and the incoming missiles maddened it even worse. It turned away from Weylyn and began to run back toward where it had entered the arena, dragging Duke along.

Weylyn, meanwhile, ran straight over to their cage. He raised his sword and brought it down hard on the lock, and despite how poor the blade was, the blow was enough to shatter its target. "Get your things!" he shouted, pointing at the pile.

"Get these off us first!" Kaden replied, holding out his hands.

Weylyn frowned. "You're still shackled? Then how did you—" He and Kaden both flinched at the sudden sound of metal striking metal, and a second later, Thalgrem tossed the arrow aimed at Weylyn he'd caught in his gauntlets to the side. He raised an eyebrow as if to say "Get on with it, lads," and Weylyn nodded to him gratefully before bringing his blade down on Kaden's dunntaika shackles.

It was like stepping into the sun after being pummeled by rain. Kaden took a deep breath, his yah'zaval flourishing in his chest, then ran for his sword. He needed to help Duke.

The scorchcrawler wasn't being let back out the way it had come in. Out of sheer necessity, it had turned back to fight Duke, but the big hound wasn't giving it any quarter. No more arrows were flying—Kaden wasn't sure why, given that he could hear Mad-Eyed Malech barking orders, but it made it easier to come to Duke's aid. He pulled up next to his dog and raised Vrangar menacingly. The scorchcrawler, swaying on its three good legs, snapped its massive jaws at him. It was no longer invisible and bleeding from several bad wounds.

Kaden felt a surge of compassion for the creature. *We need to make this fast.* Duke seemed attuned to him, and as he darted to the left, his dog went right. The scorchcrawler, unable to track both of them at once, opted to keep its jaws between it and Duke, the known threat.

Kaden's blade cut into its neck a moment later. The cut was deep, and blood gushed onto the sand as the scorchcrawler screamed in pained defiance. It turned to snap at Kaden, but it had already lost too much blood to be effective. It wobbled down onto its knees, then fell to its side. A few moments later, it took its last breath.

Kaden stared at the beast for a long moment before Duke's nudges and whimpers brought him out of it. "Good boy," he said, then again, louder, "Such a good boy. Come on, we need to—"

Only the chaos he expected to find when he turned around was nonexistent. Every man of Malech's in the stands had been overcome, some of them by Kaden's party, but most by the citizens themselves. Mad-Eyed Malech was nowhere to be seen, and in the center of it all was Weylyn, looking disheveled but pleased.

"Are you all entertained?" he roared at the crowd, and every one of them roared back.

It wasn't how Kaden had envisioned their trial in Westramore ending, but as long as everyone was all right, he was pleased with the results.

Praise and blessings to you, Orealus. Thank you for seeing us through this day.

CHAPTER 26

All across the Wildepointe plains, jewelgrass bloomed. Each slender stalk glittered in the golden hour, the hazy moment when the low sun set the world alight. On the day of his son's passage into adulthood, Chieftain Cimetes looked upon his homeland and knew that more would change today than the fate of their children alone.

"You wear a dark look for such a glorious day," a familiar voice said from behind Cimetes. He turned his head to look at his second in command, Muk Muk, join him on the edge of their tribe's territory. "What could spoil a view like this?"

For a moment, Cimetes was tempted to keep his thoughts to himself. After all, Muk Muk had no reason to remember their visitors fondly, not after his very thorough defeat at the hands of the Son of the Wolf. And yet... "I sense a change coming upon our tribe, whether we wish it or not."

Muk Muk shrugged. "Of course you do. Our boys must grow up sometime. After a—oh..." He grimaced. "You mean a mystical sort of change."

"Spiritual, perhaps."

"Ugh." Muk Muk shook his head. "Better you than me for thinking such thoughts. What sort of change?"

Cimetes squared his massive shoulders. "I think it's time that we chose a side in the coming conflict."

Muk Muk went still for a moment. Finally, he said, "I should have known better than to think you'd simply forget about that boy."

"Kaden is well on his way to becoming a man, much as our own sons are," Cimetes reminded his old friend. "And he is the man destined to be the face of opposition to Lucient the Deceiver."

"Lucient stayed away from us last time."

Cimetes shook his head. "Lucient *ignored* us last time," Cimetes said. "That is not mercy. It is a calculation. I'm not willing to risk our people on the hope that he might ignore us a second time, not when things are becoming so unsettled. Our lands aren't as remote as we might wish they were, and many forces might find value in being able to cross our territory unmolested. The question is…" He paused to gather his thoughts. "Who will support us and acknowledge our claim while still seeking that use? I defy you to tell me it's Lucient."

"Obviously not, but—we're a sovereign nation!" Muk Muk burst out, sidling sideways on all four legs in a fit of pique. "We bow our heads to no overlord!"

Cimetes waited for his friend to finish his thought.

"… and I suppose that's why we should ally ourselves with that whelp of a lad and his muscle."

"Mm. That, and the fact that Lucient is drawing all manner of vileness to him. Those are people I have no wish to be associated with," Cimetes said firmly. "I won't leave my son a legacy of shame when he becomes chieftain someday."

Muk Muk laughed. "Wait a few more decades before you go writing yourself off as lame, eh? Your legs are still strong enough to carry you, and your arms can still fire a bow or wield a spear." He sobered a bit as he continued, "And our sons will need us to be examples for them if we are to fight. None of them has lived through a great conflict before."

If Cimetes had things his way, their sons would never need to know great conflict. They would be secure in their homes and families, great leaders of their tribe who stood for peace and prosperity, not blood and death. *There is no telling the future.* But only a fool wouldn't prepare for the storm they saw on the horizon.

Two more sets of hoofsteps cantered up to them. Cimetes knew the moment he detected the measured sound that his wife was one of them. He fully turned to face her, matching her joyous smile. Ah, it had been a bright day when he made Elara his wife. She bore the same tribal tattoos that Cimetes did, black, speckled bands on her arms, torso, and across her cheeks, but his gaze was always drawn first to the marriage tattoos she sported on the backs of her hands—blossoming jewelgrass, just like what he saw all around them now. Elara was his everything.

Zalindra was with her. Muk Muk's wife was taller than Elara and broader through the shoulders. She needed to be, in order to toss her husband around the way she sometimes did. Muk Muk was one of the best warriors of the Woo'apma tribe, but part of what kept him sharp was continual sparring with his wife. Even now, on this peaceful day, she carried a spear in her right hand and frowned with disapproval when she saw her husband without his.

"What's this?" she demanded as she came to a stop in front of him. "My bold husband, now apparently such a great warrior that he doesn't feel the need to carry his spear for protection? What have you gained some ability with yah'zaval? Can you kill your enemies without even needing to touch them?"

"Zalindraaa…"

"Are you going to arrive at your own son's rite in the Woo'apma without so much as a blade on you? Are you going to shame Toran into thinking he's not good enough to fight his own father?"

"All right, all right!" Muk Muk raised his hands in surrender. "You've convinced me, I'll go get my spear. Or…" He smirked at her and reached out. "Perhaps you'd let me borrow yours…"

"Ha!" she snapped, pulling her weapon out of reach. "Get your own."

Cimetes ignored the bickering as he said to Elara, "Are they ready?"

"They are," she confirmed. "They're nervous, of course, but that's to be expected." She laid a hand on his arm. "Are you ready to welcome our new warriors?"

Cimetes grinned. "More than ready." His son Galen, Muk Muk, and Zalindra's Toran, and half a dozen other of their youths were even now waiting in the traditional fighting circle for their elders to arrive. They would fight to claim their places in the tribe, to prove that they were worthy of being Woo'apma. It could get bloody, but no one had been killed during one of these rituals since Cimetes was a foal.

It was time to bring his son into adulthood.

Elara nodded her head, long braids waving. "Then let's do so. The fires are lit, and the drums are ready." They ran together back toward their village, Cimetes waving his massive spear, Wind Piercer, over his head. As he reached the edge of the Woo'apma, the females overseeing the drums began to pound out a battle rhythm.

Eight boys—soon to be adults—turned toward Cimetes, their faces eager, hooves churning nervously at the dirt. Cimetes made eye contact with Galen and delighted in the fierce light he saw there, the willingness to put himself on the line for what was right for their people. Toran was so excited he let out a whoop of glee, causing some of the elders to laugh.

This was the flush of their youth, the culmination of years of work and hard lessons. As he looked out at the next generation of their tribe, Cimetes felt nothing but intense pride. Once the battle rhythm ended, he stepped forward. "This," he announced, his voice resonating in the twilight, "was your last day as children. No more will you be protected behind the spears of your elders, held back from conflict and trial. No more will you stay behind as others run into the fight. No more will you play at combat." He paused to let cheers and hollers from his tribe wash over him, to watch the nerves of these young ones battle their pride—and see the pride he felt for them mirrored in their own bodies, winning out over fear.

"Tonight—"

Thwack. Out of nowhere, an arrow fell into the center of the Woo'apma. It was so dark that it had blended in with the night sky. A second later, Toran raised his spear and knocked another out of the air—one that had been heading straight for Galen. "We're under attack!" he shouted.

The others in the circle hesitated, perhaps wondering if this was some aspect of the ceremony to surprise them. But Cimetes was already turning and shouting, "Shield the women and children! Run our foe into the ground!"

A moment later, the ambush was fully upon them.

Cimetes cursed himself even as he brought his spear to bear on the figures hanging back in the tall grass. Several arrows flew his way, and one even impacted his skin, but centaurs of his age had skin tougher than any leather armor. The arrow bounced right off, but left a sticky residue behind. He sniffed the residue and roared, "Poison. Guard yourselves!" before rearing up and crushing his first opponent into the dust.

A dark elf fell beneath his spear. Silent. Even in death, they denied him the release of a scream.

I'll make you scream yet.

It was chaos, but Cimetes took faith in how the discipline of his people pulled together. He knew Elara and Zalindra would do everything to protect the young ones, that they were nestled in the center of the village with a full guard and inside sturdy tents. In the meantime…

He stabbed again and again, laying into his enemies with all the pent-up fury of a father driven to fear for his child, his son, who didn't deserve this disruption to his ceremony. The smartest of the dark elves fled the moment they saw Cimetes bearing down on them, while the bold overestimated the damage their little blades could do—to their detriment. He killed a dozen of them himself and heard Muk Muk yelling with fervor nearby.

Still, the fight seemed to go on for a long time—too long. Once the survivors had finally melted away into the darkness, leaving the corpses of their fellows behind like the cowards they were, Cimetes finally lowered his spear. He heard the shouts of battle rage turn into screams of pain and loss, and what he saw when he turned back to his people took his breath away.

So many were down, wounded, or slain. The poison that did not affect him had taken too many, and Cimetes cursed his short-sightedness even as Muk Muk ran over to him.

"Why an attack?" he demanded. From anyone else, Cimetes wouldn't have accepted such a confrontational tone, but he knew his second didn't mean it. "We haven't provoked the dark elves! We've had nothing to do with them at all!"

"This was a probe," Cimetes replied grimly. "A test of our readiness against Lucient's forces, and one we failed. They chose their time of attack wisely; we were distracted by the ceremony."

Muk Muk opened his mouth to speak, but then a scream so loud it tore through their hearts resounded in the air. "Zalindra," he whispered, then ran at a full gallop back to the Woo'apma. Cimetes followed him, his heart in his throat, holding out hope that he was wrong even though he knew that nothing but the deepest pain could make Zalindra cry out in such a way.

His hopes weren't rewarded. In the center of the Woo'apma, Toran lay splayed on the ground, two arrows in his chest. The arrows alone had not slain him. The foam at his mouth told the rest of the story. His mother had gone down on all four knees beside him and pulled him into her arms, screaming her agony to the sky.

"My son." Muk Muk fell beside them, and the sight of their fiercest warrior brought so low, shattered Cimetes's heart. "My *son*!"

Cimetes looked around desperately for his own son and felt a bubble of relief when Galen trotted over to him. That relief faded when he saw the devastation on his son's face.

"He saved me, Father," Galen choked out before throwing his arms around Cimetes's neck. "Toran saved me, and it cost him his life!" He wept, and all Cimetes could do was hold him through it. *A storm indeed.* And they'd been unprepared. This was his fault, not his son's. "I don't deserve it," Galen cried. "Why should I live when he died?"

Cimetes pulled back and shook his head firmly. "No," he said. "Toran died a grown warrior of our tribe—he knew his role, and he did it, magnificently. He is worth no less because he died, just as you are worth no less because you lived. And now you must be a warrior for our tribe," he went on a bit more gently, "by fighting with this sacrifice forever in your heart.

"And the time to fight has come." There was no doubt left in Cimetes's mind. "We will not fall victim to the forces of Lucient again. It's time to ready ourselves for battle and bring the fight to them."

But first, they had to mourn.

In the end, twelve of their warriors had died, including another of the young ones whose ceremony had been so brutally interrupted. They burned their bodies, drums echoing all through the day and night as the pyres flared. Once the flames finally went out and the ashes cooled, Muk Muk walked forward to the blasted earth where the bodies had once lain. He bent over, picked up a handful of ash, and let it fall over the top of his head, coating his hair and face in specks of gray. Then he wiped his hand across the center of his face, leaving behind a ghostly print. When he turned to face the tribe, everyone went quiet.

"My son," he said, his voice wavering for a moment, "my Toran, gave his life for our people." He looked at Galen and nodded respectfully. "For our future. For his best friend." He straightened to his full, imposing height. "I will not let his sacrifice be in vain." Cimetes read the challenge in his oldest friend's eyes.

Will you answer the call?

Cimetes had already had a long, painful conversation with Elara about the future of the tribe. She didn't want to encourage them to fight before Kaden came back, looking for help; she wanted to shore up their defenses and make their home more secure.

"It cannot be, Wife," Cimetes had told her. "This act must be answered with more than intent."

"Spilling more blood will not bring back our lost loved ones!" she'd protested.

"And hiding in our village will not make our son any safer," he'd replied shrewdly, and watched his wife's shoulders begin to shake with tears.

Nothing would bring Toran or their losses back, but the best anodyne for fear was action. Cimetes hadn't lived as long as he had without knowing the hearts of his people, and right now they had hearts of war.

"Nor shall I," he said to Muk Muk, and his second nodded with satisfaction. "That these worms got so deep into our territory is shameful. Our first act shall be to cleanse them of any intruders we find." He held up his spear and shook it. "This land of hope is ours, and we reclaim it!"

"Aye!"

"This spirit of fire is ours, and we reclaim it!"

"*Aye!*"

"This heart of war is ours, and we reclaim it!"

"*AYE!*"

Every member of the war party picked up a handful of ashes and covered their hair and faces. Galen put an extra handprint on top of his heart—a testament to Toran's loss, and his determination to fight in his memory. Elara and the other female elders collected the rest of the ashes, some to be used in dyes and paintings, and some to be saved for more war marks.

The only stumbling point was Zalindra, who was ferocious in her declaration to join the hunt. "What am I to live for, if not to see my son's killers brought low?" she demanded of Muk Muk and Cimetes. "What am I to do with myself if I'm not avenging his loss?"

"Wife—"

"Don't you 'Wife' me, not when you get to do everything and leave me with scraps! What am I to do with my own heart of war if I can't *go* to war?"

It was Elara who kept a fight from breaking out. "War will find us here," she said, a note of prophecy in her voice. Cimetes looked at her uneasily—often she predicted with accuracy. The last time had been foreseeing the birth of their son. "We will need our strongest warriors to protect our most vulnerable." She laid a hand on Zalindra's arm. "Please, stay with us." Zalindra bowed her head and fell into Elara's arms.

Muk Muk kissed the top of her head before he turned to Cimetes. "And now, Chieftain?"

Cimetes smiled grimly. "Now, we hunt."

CHAPTER 27

As much as Kaden wanted to move on to the Barren Badlands as quickly as possible, some things could not be rushed. Westramore had lived under Mad-Eyed Malech's rule for a long time, and without him, its people were left floundering. As soon as the arena was cleared and Kaden and the others emerged into the town proper, a delegation of the town's business owners—almost all of them running disreputable taverns—came to them and, with great fanfare, loudly pronounced Weylyn their new lord.

"Not on this side of hell," Weylyn said quickly, holding both his hands up and physically backing away from the group. "I'm no leader of men outside of a battle."

"Don't be hasty," one of the men said eagerly. "Your skills couldn't be a better fit for a place like this, if fighting is your calling! And Westramore has plenty to recommend it beyond that. Reliable weather—"

"Hideous heat, you mean."

"Interesting sights to see—"

"Yes, all the rocks! Rocks in every direction!"

"And let's not forget the magnificent wildlife, milord!"

Weylyn had burst out laughing. "That's the least accurate description of a scorchcrawler I've ever heard."

"There are also many beautiful venomous snakes," the man said placidly. "And lizards. Even the occasional griffin, but they tend not to stay for long."

"How can I possibly refuse?" Weylyn asked, his voice full of sarcasm. "Oh, wait, it's actually really easy. *No.*"

"And the position comes with a salary of five hundred gold per annum, your percentage of the taxes and local… um… donations."

Everyone there understood what *donations* meant in Westramore. A coin that never passed through the ledgers. Debts that could not be challenged. Promises enforced not by law, but by fear of what might happen if they were broken. Malech had ruled the city without banners or titles, and his absence left behind habits that did not vanish simply because he was gone.

"Doesn't matter if Malech's dead," someone muttered nearby. "The Exchange never closes."

Which even Kaden knew was code for "what we manage to steal from travelers." These people were utterly shameless.

Chum's long ears perked up immediately. "Is that so? Well, let's not be too hasty then, hmm?" He nudged Weylyn with his elbow. "I think it's worth considering. There might be more to Westramore than meets the eye."

There was, but most of it revolved around corruption. Kaden and his crew, persuaded by the silver-tongued owner of the largest tavern and inn in the city, took rooms with him and set up something like a court. Kaden hesitated to name it as such, having never seen a true court himself. But he was determined not to let the city fall back under the thumb of someone as bad as Malech the second they left, and that meant talking to a lot of people, building consensus, and in the end, instituting a council of the most influential people in the city to run it. It was the only way to keep Westramore from sliding back into rule by shadow and coin the moment they turned their backs. Orders were still being carried out, contracts still honored, as if no one had bothered to tell the city its master was gone.

As the council dispersed, Kaden noticed a silver coin left behind on the table. It bore no crest he recognized, only a faint fanged serpent pressed across its surface. When he reached for it, a chill crept into his fingers. Someone had taken it before he could ask who it belonged to.

"And we'll check in on our way back," Bardicus warned the obsequious businesspeople as they headed out into the Badlands a full week later. "So you'd best prove ye're more capable than ye look, or we'll have to do this all over again!"

"Ach, noooo," Malacheen groaned. "I can't stand another stretch of *talkin'* when we should be *doin'*. I'm more than ready for some action."

"The Badlands will certainly test your survival skills," Queen Pepper said as she wrapped her head and face in a thin, gauzy length of cloth that would keep the sun and sand from stinging her skin while letting her see and breathe easily enough. "I brought enough for all of us," she added, holding the thin scarves out toward the rest of the group.

Ada took one, as did Redfern and Millicent. After a moment, Kaden took one as well—he had no experience in deserts, and if Pepper thought something was a good idea, then he would follow suit. He was gratified to see Eldrin do the same, and Petey actually asked for two, "because my ears are hard to cover and I hate digging sand out of them," he explained.

The dwarves were the holdouts. Half a day into their march into the hostile Badlands—red dust swirling around them in the hot breeze and sharp rocks impeding every path they had been directed along—the heat was getting to them. It was worse for Bardicus and Thalgrem, in fact, because they insisted on wearing their full armor.

"Ye'll be glad," Bardicus said, sopping the sweat off his face with a thick woolen handkerchief that was far better suited to his mountainous home than this place. "Next time we get attacked by a scorchcrawler or a griffin or, who in these blighted hells even knows, a sphinx or ogre or—"

"There won't be any ogres out here," Pepper informed him with a little smile. "They are actually quite bad at cooling themselves down. We fought one battle against them in the last war where the sun was absolutely blazing for most of the day, and about halfway through it, the ogres just began to collapse." She tilted her hand from straight upright to a bent position. "Although," she added, "I daresay they didn't help themselves by keeping on their helmets."

Bardicus glared at her. "I'm no' givin' up my helm."

"Perhaps just the breastplate, then."

To the astonishment of everyone, but mostly Malacheen, Bardicus did, in fact, take his massive metal breastplate off. There was a layer of chainmail beneath it that he kept on, but it was easy to see that he was far more comfortable without it. Even Thalgrem unbent long enough to do the same, although he smashed his gauntlets together a few times to indicate how annoyed he was by it.

"Is yer queen an enchantress?" Malacheen murmured to Redfern as they set off once more. "Because I've never seen our king come 'round on a point so quickly!"

Redfern rolled her eyes. "She's *obviously* an enchantress, haven't you been paying attention?"

"More than that," Millicent put in with a warm look forward toward Pepper, who was sitting daintily on Duke's back as she chatted with Petey, "she's a good leader. Some people, like that wretched Malech, force others to listen to them by acts of violence. Queen Pepper has never started a fight in her entire life to get her way; she speaks her piece and talks people around to her way of thinking."

"She certainly can end a fight, though," Eldrin said with a little smile on his face. "And her powers of persuasion have worked even on my father, when no amount of my pleading or arguing could. She's a rare one." He glanced at Kaden. "You'd do well to follow in her footsteps as best you can."

"Nonsense." Chum shook his horned head vigorously. "It's different for men. Of course, Queen Pepper has had to learn diplomacy; talking is what women are *for*. Whereas men only understand the language of fighting and plunder and—" He stopped with a gulp as Malacheen, knife in hand, suddenly appeared right beside him, and far too close for Chum's comfort.

"Oh, ye think ladies are only good at talkin', eh?"

"I—no, that's not what I meant."

"I'm not much of a talker," she went on with a broad, cheerful grin on her face. "I daresay if I was to try an' talk meself out of, say, putting a hole in a little satyr who was speaking foulness, I wouldn't be able to bring meself around. But lucky for me, I've got actual *brains* as well as brawn, and I know not to pick a fight where your big friend might step in for you." Not that Weylyn looked anything other than amused at the moment. "But I think it's safer for us all if you *don't* test me, eh?"

"Yes!" Chum squeaked, and Malacheen nodded her head and withdrew her blade.

Huh. Sometimes, a simple action really could be worth a thousand words.

They stopped in the evening on the lee side of a tumbled pile of stones dotted here and there with withered, twisted trees. There was almost no vegetation to speak of in the Badlands, and what Kaden could see was small and spindly, with none of the tall, strong trees he'd grown so used to seeing in their travels. He could not be surprised. If he had to grow in such heat and constant wind, he would likely stay small and low to the ground as well.

"Why can't we use your yah'zaval to take us right to where the Greaves of Megalos are?" Ada asked as she sat down next to him and handed over a cup of tea. With Weylyn on watch, after dinner, the other members of their party had settled down to try and get some sleep. Kaden found himself restless, though, and lingered by the fire. Apparently, Ada felt the same.

Or maybe she just wanted to keep him company. He was glad she couldn't make out his blush.

"It's too dangerous," he replied, blowing on the hot tea to cool it a bit before sipping. He hadn't thought he'd be interested in a hot drink tonight, but the temperature had dropped precipitously from its heights earlier in the day. "I don't know enough about where they're kept to get us there without potentially killing us. We might land in the middle of a nest of scorchcrawlers, for example."

Ada sighed and looked away. "I just—this is the worst place we've been so far. Why not open a portal somewhere comfortable for the night, then bring us back here in the morning?"

Kaden thought carefully about how to phrase his feelings on this. "I think... I'm not meant to use this power from Orealus lightly," he said after a moment. "I'm not saying I wouldn't portal us out of here if we were in danger, of course, but to do so just because we're uncomfortable… it feels frivolous."

Ada was silent, staring down into her tea.

"And it's very tiring," Kaden added, not wanting her to think he was criticizing her. "It uses most of the yah'zaval that I carry each time I make a portal, and it can take quite a while to replenish itself. It's just not practical."

"I see." Ada tossed her head back and drank her tea quickly, then got to her feet. "I'm going to sleep now."

"Maybe you—" But she was already walking away, leaving Kaden wondering what he'd done wrong. He stared into the fire moodily, slowly sipping his tea and thinking—more like berating—himself.

What kind of leader are you when you can't even have a conversation without upsetting one of your people? You need to get better, you need to be better. The flames seemed to agree with him, sputtering with purple and green sparks that rose high into the sky.

There was no doubt that Kaden still had much to learn. He closed his eyes against the firelight and made the symbol of Orealus over the center of his chest. *Guide my feet, Orealus, and keep me on the path that best serves your will.* He was under no illusions that the road ahead would be easy.

The next day was even worse than the one before in terms of heat and wind. All of them wrapped their faces and the tops of their necks to keep sand from getting down into their clothes, and Petey bundled Bug up and placed him at the top of his pack to keep him from blowing away altogether.

"Where's this place we're headed again?" Eldrin asked peevishly as he restrung his bow during the first break of the day. They were simply huddled up facing each other—there was no shade to be had as far as any of them could see.

"The ruins are so old they don't even bear a name," Weylyn said, turning his head to squint at the horizon. "They're the only place of note within a week's travel of Westramore, though, and the likeliest place for us to find Megalos."

"Why, though?" Chum grumped between sips from his canteen. "Most of the pieces of armor are held by terrible monsters fighting for Lucient, aren't they? So why are these greaves in the middle of an Orealus-forsaken desert?"

"Ask your wizard," Weylyn said easily. "He's the one who told us where to find all these things."

"I presume they were put there with the intent of being returned for," Queen Pepper put in, her voice a bit muffled by the scarves she wore. "It seems likely that the person who left them was subsequently killed and unable to return for them."

"I—" Kaden began, then paused. He shook his head for a moment, wondering if he had some sand in his ears.

"What?" Petey asked.

"Did you hear that?" Something had changed, somehow. He wasn't sure how to articulate it, but—

"The wind," Eldrin murmured.

"It's lower," Millicent said with a glance at Redfern. "Fiercer, somehow."

"Sounds the same as it always does to me," Bardicus said as he bit into a dry piece of meat, his massive molars making quick work of it. "Irritatin'."

"No, they're right." Queen Pepper looked straight up. "Hmm." Then she whispered something and wove her hands together in a spiral, and a moment later, a glowing rope made of pure yah'zaval appeared. She affixed one end to her ankle, then handed the other end to Malacheen. "I'm going to fly high and see if I can detect anything," she told them. "The wind might be worse up there, and my wings are delicate. If I get into trouble, the rope will go taut. Please pull me down if it does."

"O' course!" Malacheen looked pleased to have been given that particular responsibility. "I'm well-grounded, no worries about that!"

"Thank you," Queen Pepper said politely. Then, working her wings so fast they blurred, she launched up into the sky. The rope unraveled at a rapid pace as she was blown backward, but it didn't stiffen up. She got higher and higher until Kaden couldn't even see her anymore against the glare of the sun.

"What's she doing?" he asked Eldrin, who he knew had the best eyesight of the group.

"Circling," he replied. "It's hard to see up there—not due to the distance, so much as there's something in the air obscuring my vision of her. She—"

All of a sudden, the rope went taut. More than that, it *pulled*, jerking Malacheen right off her feet.

"Uncle!" she cried out as she was dragged along the ground. Bardicus and Thalgrem, moving quickly, ran after her and, as one, threw themselves down on top of her. There was a clatter of armor on chainmail, but Malacheen was made of stern stuff and shouted, "The rope, grab the rope!"

By the time the rest of them reached her, she and the other dwarves all had their hands on the rope, which was at a sharp angle compared to where it had started. "Help us haul the lass in!" Bardicus roared, and everyone grabbed hold and began to pull. Little by little, they reeled Pepper back in until, all of a sudden, the rope went slack.

She didn't fly down to them, though; she was falling instead.

Redfern and Millicent took off immediately and managed to catch their queen before she hit the ground. They flew her, unconscious in their arms, back to the group, worry clear on both their faces.

Ada was the first to grab her canteen. "Water," she said. "Try patting her face with water, see if the coolness will wake her." Her voice went a bit wry. "No need to waste yah'zaval if we don't have to, after all."

So she's still sore about that. It bothered Kaden, but there was nothing he could do about it at the moment. He watched as Millicent wet the end of one of the scarves and gently wiped Pepper's red-coated face with it. Her own scarves were missing, blown away in whatever wind she'd encountered up there.

They didn't have long to wait; a few seconds later, she was opening her eyes. They wandered until she found Kaden.

"What's happening?" he asked. "What affected you so badly?"

Pepper coughed. Her voice was hoarse as she said, "The change in the wind is driving a sandstorm toward us."

"Oh, hell," Weylyn muttered.

"There's a wall of sand and dust coming this way," she went on, and that explained the red dust coating her face. "We need to get to shelter as quickly as possible, or we'll be trapped in the storm.

"Luckily,"—she gave them a small smile—"I saw the ruins. They're only a few miles away." She sat up slowly with Millicent's help, then pointed her finger to the west. "That way."

"Then we'd better run," Weylyn said grimly. "Or that sandstorm might strip the flesh from our bones before it passes."

"I won't let that happen," Kaden said.

"Save your magic," Pepper advised as she stood up. "I have a feeling we'll need it. Weylyn is right." She took the scarf Redfern handed her and wrapped it firmly around her head. "We need to run."

CHAPTER 28

The way the sky darkened in the space of just ten minutes was uncanny. With the wind whistling at high speed and battering them with increasingly painful sheets of sand, it became a race against time to see if they could make it to the ruins before the heart of the sandstorm made it to them.

Eldrin, with his sharp eyes, took the point position, guiding them unerringly toward their goal even as the light began to fade. Right behind him were the dwarves and Weylyn, the heavy-armor bearers and sturdiest on their feet. They made a barrier out of their bodies for the smallest members of the party: Queen Pepper and her bodyguards; Chum, who complained nonstop even though it was letting sand into his mouth; and Petey, who'd bundled Bug securely in the top of his pack to keep him from blowing away altogether. Bringing up the rear were Kaden, Ada, and Duke.

"Keep a sharp eye," Weylyn had warned Kaden before they began their forced march. "This is nasty weather, but that doesn't mean there aren't beasts out there who're ready to take advantage of it. Scorchcrawlers can ride sandstorms out by burying themselves; if they catch our scent and think we're a worthwhile target, they'll go for a quick kill."

"Men can be worse," Weylyn added. "And they do not need storms to hide in."

His words struck a note of fear into Kaden that had him spending half of the run looking back, sword at the ready. That, in turn, left him tripping over his own feet more often than not until Ada finally reached out and took his free hand. "I'll guide you," she shouted over the wind. Her face was invisible beneath the fine cloth scarf she'd tied over it, but her grip was strong enough to hurt. Was she worried about him?

"Thank you," Kaden shouted back, but she'd already turned away. Maybe she wasn't helping out of concern so much as wanting to be as efficient as possible. Either way, Kaden didn't have time to wonder about it now. He looked down at Duke and said, "Alert!" and Duke, good hunting dog that he was, immediately pricked his ears up beneath the cloth Kaden had tied over them to protect them and hunkered down low, nose twitching.

It was the best they could do, and Kaden was worried it wouldn't be enough, but as the full might of the sandstorm thundered toward them across the desert sands, he found his mind going curiously blank. The noise, the tumult, the continuous pricking pain of the sand as it was whipped against his body—it had the strange effect of hyperfocusing him on one thing and one thing only: movement. He held onto his sword and kept his readiness as best he could, but something in Kaden knew that the greatest threat to them right now had nothing to do with beasts or Lucient and everything to do with a force of nature that was as inescapable as the whirlpool that had dragged them down into Nethopolis.

He didn't even realize that they'd reached the ruins until Weylyn's hands bodily pulled him up against a surprisingly cold stone wall. It was so dark out that he could barely see. "I can't find the way in," he shouted. "If it's a trapdoor, it could be covered over with sand already!"

Kaden nodded. "Let me see what I can do."

"Whatever you do, do it quickly!" Bardicus added from a bit farther down. "The little ones are fading fast!" Kaden could just make out the nodding, exhausted form of Queen Pepper in the center of a tight embrace from Millicent and Redfern, her bodyguards literally using themselves as shields for her, but none of them would last long if they stayed out here.

Kaden reached for the crystal beneath his tunic and overcoat. He hoped this worked; he'd have to try to use his yah'zaval, and he was so sore and scattered he could barely feel it right now. "Gift of Bhalla, spirit of Orealus," he murmured as he closed his fingers around the long, slender gem, "help me find the way. Show me the path to safety so that my friends don't have to suffer any longer, I beg you."

It took so long that Kaden almost lost hope, but then a light emerged from his tightly clasped hand and shot a beam that traveled along the stone pillar for almost twenty feet before stopping. He followed it and found himself in front of a… well, a slab of stone. Where was the door, though? He ran his hands along the wall, as high as he could reach and then lower, lower, until his fingers brushed something hollow.

"Ha!" Kaden felt the top of an open arch beneath his fingertips. The sand had nearly covered it, but not completely. "I think I've got it!" he called out. "But the sand is in the way. We'll have to shovel it out."

"No time!" Bardicus said, pushing Thalgrem forward. The burly dwarf smashed his gauntlets together a few times, making sparks fly. "Thunderfist will take care of it!"

Kaden had just enough time to scramble back when Thalgrem reared up, then hammered his doubled fists down onto the sand as hard as he could. Sand flew *everywhere*, practically erupting from the ground, and Kaden had to look away as Thalgrem struck five more times, each time moving huge amounts of sand. Then the arch was clear, and beyond it the door was visible. One more hearty smash and the door was broken in two.

"In, in!" All of them hurried into the antechamber, and as soon as the last of them cleared the door, Bardicus and Malacheen pushed the broken stone slab that had been the door back into position. A little sand still seeped in through the cracks, but the constant sting was gone, and the howling thunder of the wind dulled to a low, distant roar.

Malacheen quickly used her flint to strike a light on one of the torches she'd kept in her pack, illuminating the small space. It was an oval chamber with various passageways leading out from it, all of them pitch black. "Water," she said as she pulled away the cloth wrapping her head up. "Pepper must need water, poor thing; they all look parched."

They *did*—even their wings looked dry and shriveled where they'd been tucked under their shirts—but Redfern managed to free herself from her own wrappings and take the full skin Ada offered up in her own hands. "We're hardier than we look," she snapped—or tried to, but broke into a cough halfway through the last word and ended up doubled over. Millicent took the skin from her and used a bit of it to wipe the rime of sandy crust from Queen Pepper's eyes, nostrils, and lips before coaxing her to drink. For a second, the water just trickled over her lips and down her face without going in, and everyone tensed. Then, finally, she began to sip, and a few moments later managed to open her eyes.

"Ah," she said blearily when she'd drunk her fill. "We made it. Wonderful."

"Rest yerself," Bardicus advised gruffly. "We're not going to be going anywhere for quite some time."

"We can't leave before we find the greaves anyway," Weylyn said from where he was taking off his own armor, piece by piece, and shaking the sand out of it before wiping it down with the cloth he'd used for his own face. "I'm going to be feeling this for days," he muttered, rubbing his hand tenderly over the back of his neck.

He was right, Kaden realized. Even now that they were out of the storm, his skin still stung like he'd been bitten by a thousand ants. He wanted to scratch it, but he knew that would make a bad situation worse, so he settled for a quick wipe down with a wet cloth before turning to Duke and doing the same for him. Duke, not surprisingly, had handled the storm like a champ; his fur was caked with sand, but other than that, he'd weathered it well.

"I'll have to brush you out," Kaden murmured as his dog slurped at the bowl of water he'd laid out.

"I can do it," Ada said from where she was working on her own hair. "I have a spare brush."

"I don't—"

"Let her," Petey whispered from Kaden's elbow. "It's good to feel useful," he added a bit morosely.

Kaden stared at Petey for a long moment before saying, "All right, thank you," to Ada. He then pulled Petey a little way aside. "Is something wrong?"

Petey cracked a weak smile, his ears drooping at the tips. "Oh no, not… not really. Just…" He wrung his hands together. "I haven't done much for the quest lately, have I? Not like before."

"You *died* once," Kaden reminded him with a shudder. "I'd be happy to never see you repeat that level of service to the quest, thank you."

"Yes, that's kind of you, but—"

"Petey." Kaden knelt down so he could look the goblin in his large, lamp-like eyes. Petey had been his first companion after Duke—the first person to believe in him, to follow him for no other reason than he thought it was the right thing to do. He'd stood by Kaden through so many adventures and perils and given his *life* to save Kaden. "You don't have to lead every charge or solve every problem to be a useful member of our company. You don't have to do anything other than your best, and I know that you do that every day. I value you whether you're fighting off scorchcrawlers or taking care of Bug or foraging for food, okay?"

"Okay," Petey said, his smile turning a bit more genuine. "But I wish I could do more…"

An elegant hand landed on Petey's shoulder, surprising him so much he yelped. "Then do I have the task for you?" Eldrin said with a grin. Of all of them, the elven prince seemed to have recovered the fastest. "I've checked this room for traps, and it looks clear, but we can't stay here forever. We'll have to pick a tunnel, and I can't see in the dark as you can, nor do I have hearing quite as keen as yours. We should scout them together."

"Oh. Oh!" Petey looked pleased at the prospect. "I'd be happy to do so!"

"Excellent!" Eldrin gave him a little squeeze. "Bring your dagger and some extra bandages, will you? There's no telling what sort of traps we might run into, so it's best to be prepared."

"B-bandages?" Petey asked a bit faintly.

"Just in case," Eldrin said soothingly. "I'm sure we'll be fine, and we won't go so far that Kaden can't save us if he needs to." He looked at Kaden and winked, and Kaden smiled back.

"Well… all right." Petey and Eldrin equipped themselves, then vanished down the tunnel to the left. Kaden strained his ears to listen to their progress, but the storm was still too fierce and drowned out the sound of their footsteps before they'd gone ten paces.

"Good advice," Weylyn said from where he was emptying his boots. "Better than I'd expect from someone your age."

Kaden went over to him and sat down to do the same. "I feel a little weird giving advice at all," he confessed. "I'm almost the youngest person here."

"Yet the most important."

Kaden shook his head.

"No, you are. You weren't raised to rule like you would have been if your father had lived, and you're naturally deferent to elders. But you're learning," he added, clapping Kaden on the back. "You're already leagues beyond the boy I first met. As long as you find your confidence, you'll do well enough."

Well enough was not good enough. Kaden wanted to do better than that. He wanted to be a great leader, as great as his father had been. Better even, because as brave as his father had been, he'd been overwhelmed in the end. His family had been murdered, and Kaden... Kaden was all that was left. When he let himself dwell on it, the loneliness pressed in hard.

The only one. You're the only surviving child of King Karatheas; you have to challenge Lucient. You have to bring all the tribes together and send people into a fight against the greatest evil this world has ever known. You have to do it, and you'll have to watch people who believe in you die on your say-so.

But how can you?

Orealus was with him, of course, he was, and Kaden had all of his loyal friends. They were fighting with him, helping him reassemble the armor that would give Kaden a fighting chance against Lucient, and yet... for all that he'd craved adventure and knew he was doing the right thing, sometimes he missed the boy he used to be. He missed the simple life of a farmer's son, the guiding hands of his parents, and their easy, ever-present care and love for him.

"Do you ever miss your father?" he asked suddenly, then felt embarrassed about it. Weylyn was a grown man and had been for years, surely he didn't—

"Every day," Weylyn said immediately. "Why do you think I carry him with me in my title, hmm? I'm the Son of the Wolf, and I always will be." He smiled slightly. "I think most of us, no matter how old we get, hold a loving parent close in our hearts. I was fortunate to have him as a boy, and now? I'm fortunate to have the chance to avenge him."

Kaden nodded in understanding. A moment later, Eldrin and Petey reappeared. Both of them were grinning. "Time to pack up," Eldrin said, clapping his hands together and jerking those who had been dozing awake. "We've found a better place to rest, and you're not even going to need torches to get there."

"What do you mean?" Ada asked.

Petey's ears were almost pointing straight up; he was so excited. "You have to come and see! It's beautiful!"

"And quiet," Eldrin added, and that was what really got people moving. It was *loud,* so close to the storm.

Kaden felt a bit of apprehension stepping into the dark corridor, but the floor was at least level. Petey led them around two turns along perhaps two hundred feet, and then— the darkness softened.

Faint points of light began to glimmer along the walls, at first no brighter than distant stars. As they moved closer, Kaden saw that the stone itself was threaded with thin veins of crystal, pale and steady, glowing just enough to outline the curve of the passage. The air felt cooler here, quieter too, as if the storm's fury could not quite reach this far beneath the ground.

Queen Pepper drew her scarf back from her face, eyes still glinting with starlight and sand.

Though the crystals gave off plenty of pale, steady light, they'd built a small campfire in the center of the chamber. After the storm's fury and the cold stone of the tunnels, its warmth was a comfort none of them was willing to forgo.

"Fire," she said softly, staring into the flickering flames, "is not just destruction. It is also the forge. The seedbed of rebirth. I have long believed this journey we are on is not merely a path to reclaim armor, but to forge something far greater."

Kaden turned to her, curiosity rising through the dust and fatigue. "Forge what?"

She glanced at him with a faint smile, the kind that danced on the edge of foresight.

"A king. A people. A journey. A future. All cast in fire."

She let the words settle in the silence that followed. "Sometimes, only fire can temper the soul strong enough to carry the hopes of a broken world."

"Wow." The tunnel walls curved inward like the ribs of some ancient beast, lined with crystal veins that glowed softly in shades of blue, violet, and green. The light pulsed faintly, as if stirred by the presence of living souls. "Are they reacting to yah'zaval energy?" he asked.

Petey shook his head. "I think it's a natural phenomenon," he said. "Like the bioluminescent mold that we used for light in Shroudscar."

"Ah." Right, he'd forgotten about that. "It's lovely," he said, and it was… although there was something decidedly eerie about the colors as well. Perhaps it was the grayish tinge the mixed light gave everyone's faces, making them look like walking corpses instead of living beings.

"It gets even better," Petey promised. They kept going, and soon the tunnel let out into a chamber that was much larger than the one by the entrance. Kaden wrinkled his nose—it stank of scorchcrawler in here, despite the fact that he couldn't see any of them. But now, in addition to the crystals, the walls seemed to be covered with glowing tiles.

He set his pack down and moved over to the nearest one. Kaden used the edge of his cloak to brush away generations of cobwebs, and what he found beneath was more than just light…

It was a picture. The wall was covered with a mural of some sort. "Look at this," he said as he stared at it. "I think it's… doesn't that look like the Leviathan from the old legends to you?"

Queen Pepper, finally steady on her feet again, stepped beside him. "It does," she murmured. "Although… look, this one has legs. I did not know such creatures ever walked upon the earth."

She swept more dust from the mural, and her bodyguards joined her. Bit by bit, the stone revealed the shapes beneath, as if waking from a long-forgotten age.

The creatures carved there were vast. Their bodies were serpentine yet heavy with ancient strength, thick as river pillars and coiled with sinew that spoke of ages spent shaping the world. Each bore four immense limbs ending in claws like carved obsidian. Their necks rose in sweeping arcs, crowned by horned heads that resembled the earliest depictions of dragons found in Empyrean ruins. Some had ridged crests that looked like hardened flames. Others wore layered scales that resembled the armor of kings long buried.

As more of the mural emerged, the full scene took form. It showed an ancient people standing beside these land-wyrms, struggling against a spreading darkness that poured from a central figure whose shape was lost in shadow. It felt less like a battle and more like a memory carved into stone to keep a warning alive.

Soon, they uncovered a huge picture that seemed to depict an ancient civilization; Kaden thought it had to be ancient, for so many of these colossal land-wyrms to stride across the earth, fighting against a dark-hearted evil of some kind. All of the creatures were shown with reflective shards of obsidian set into their chests, and at the top of the mural waited a being made entirely of those same shards, its long tendrils reaching across the wall and spreading darkness wherever they touched.

"How fascinating," Queen Pepper said, briefly touching a line of what looked like a script of some kind. "I've seen this style of writing before, carved deep into some of our oldest stones. I never could translate it, though. As far as I know, that knowledge has been lost to time."

There were pockets of light as well, where precious opals had been set into the stone. Those seemed to be guarded by massive stone-beasts with many legs—creatures shaped like armored centipedes or squat, broad-shelled guardians, their bodies fused from opal plates that glowed like living embers. But the dark tentacles were already winding through the joints of their limbs, corrupting them one segment at a time. There was something about it that struck a familiar chord in Kaden's heart.

Light warriors fighting against a powerful darkness, while monsters roam the lands trying to destroy what they hold dear. Yes, it felt almost too familiar.

As Kaden stepped back from the glowing mural, the images burned into his vision like flame-branded omens. Yet it was not just the battle scenes that lingered in his mind; it was the creatures.

At the mural's edge, barely visible in the fading light, were forms carved not with reverence but with warning. A great horned beast, towering and furred, stood against a white wind, its tusks twisted like frozen thunder, its sorrowful gaze cast toward an unseen horizon. Kaden did not know the name, but he felt its grief.

Another shape surged upward from beneath crashing waves, a sea leviathan whose eyes shimmered with both starlight and sulfur. Coils of scaled muscle threatened to crush entire ships, while smaller beasts clung to its flanks like barnacles. Bound in a silver chain, its agony bled through the stone.

And high above them all, wings spread like eclipses, loomed a hunched colossus, man-shaped but burdened, as if shackled by invisible chains. The sorrow in its carved eyes was unmistakable.

"These aren't just monsters," Kaden whispered. "They're prisoners."

Pepper's wings flickered beside him. "Or weapons waiting to be claimed by the wrong hands."

He finally looked away. "Let's build a proper fire and eat," he said. "We'll look deeper into the ruins once we've all gotten some rest."

CHAPTER 29

The city of Lumhagen, for all that it buzzed with activity, whether it was night or day, was widely regarded as an oasis of calm and peace for those who lived within its borders. The youngest of them, those who only knew life after the Great War, might not recognize their situation as special, but everyone older did. They knew the price of a presence in the wider world; they knew the smell of burning buildings and broken bodies, and how yah'zaval could be both a shield *and* a sword. They knew what yah'zaval could not mend, and so they set their hearts and minds ever more fervently on Orealus, whose will endured beyond power alone.

That wasn't to say that there weren't moments of chaos and discord. Anywhere you got powerful people together to learn the aetheric gifts, there would of necessity also be competitiveness, jealousy, and accidental eruptions that led to unforeseen consequences. It was not unusual for an inexperienced wizard to misjudge their reach. Some transported themselves far beyond their intent. Others singed stone and timber where discipline failed. In one memorable instance, a portal briefly linked the sea floor to the lower halls of the Truthoriam, flooding corridors and nearly destroying irreplaceable texts before it was sealed.

Even the hard moments were more used as learning experiences than to foment fear and worry. At the end of the day, children and teachers left the ancient academies of faith and science where they honed their spiritual abilities and went home to be welcomed by their families and asked about what they learned that day over a communal meal, cooked by many and shared by all.

Parents were asked to keep an eye out for children who showed particular interest or affinity for the Keepers of the Light guild, which, next to the high-powered wizards of the Truthoriam, were the most difficult positions to fill. Guild members had to be completely committed to the protection of Lumhagen and the artifacts they oversaw, including the sacred scrolls of Orealus. Only the most faithful could lay eyes on those without breaking down, and only a true adept could glean great wisdom from them. They were not adventurers, nor judges, nor conquerors, but custodians of truth entrusted to endure beyond kings and wars alike.

After the evening meal came the devotional, with the brilliance of Lumhagen's faith-powered lights creating a soft, tranquil atmosphere. The noise of the day abated as most people settled in to sleep, while the most faithful practitioners among them used the time to pray their devotion and seek enlightenment from Orealus himself. Bells rang out in praise and entreaty, yet through all the constant murmur of humanity, there was always an underlying sense of tranquility, one that had endured in Lumhagen for a thousand years and, despite the scars of the Great War, had begun to settle over her people once again. Lumhagen, as a living city, was unflappable.

That didn't mean her inhabitants couldn't be rocked out of their own tranquility, no matter how hard they tried to hold onto it.

"Wizard Bhalla," one of the scribes from the lower level called out respectfully as she entered his observatory, "there are two members of the guild of the Keepers of the Light here to see you."

Bhalla raised an eyebrow. "Why should they want to see me?" he asked. "The next in line to speak to them is Asitra." Her presence within the Truthoriam was so constant that many apprentices used her movements as an unspoken measure of time.

"That's the problem, sir," the scribe said apologetically. "They can't find Wizard Asitra."

Can't find her? What in the name of... she's right here in the Truthoriam, isn't she? She almost never left, not just because she was dedicated to her oversight duties but because she enjoyed working with promising children as well. Asitra had a way of phrasing complex ideas so that a child wasn't intimidated by them, and her enduring faith in Orealus made her an excellent role model for the children she guided. For her to be missing…

"Bring them to me, if you please," Bhalla said, already sinking into a light trance and casting his conscious self across the Truthoriam, hoping to find out that the guild members were mistaken, and Asitra was simply too deep into her personal research to have remembered a meeting. Or, at the worst, that she was ill and needed assistance, but not entirely missing.

Bhalla's faint hope faded as he searched level by level with no sign of Asitra's guiding signature to be found.

He opened his eyes and turned to look into the faces of the guild members that the scribe had led to him. One man and one woman, they were both dressed in the yellow-and-white robes typical of the Keepers of the Light guild, but while the woman's braids marked her as a scholar, the man had shaved his head completely, a symbol of his warrior status. Their colors marked them as sworn not to power, but to preservation, a quiet oath older than Lumhagen itself. He wasn't carrying his weapon—it was considered rude within the Truthoriam if you weren't an outsider who didn't understand such things—but the empty scabbard at his hip made it plain that he didn't trust the circumstances that had led him here.

"Be welcome," Bhalla said, both with warmth and warning. "I am Bhalla Bristlekamp, Protector of the Light. What brings the Keepers to the Truthoriam at this hour?"

"Thank you for your welcome, Honored Bhalla. I am Keeper Lavinia," the woman said with a bow.

"And I am Keeper Roum," the man continued, bowing as well.

They exchanged a worried glance before Lavinia stepped forward. "Honored Bhalla," she began, her fingers twisting at the edges of her long, voluminous sleeves. "We were wondering if you could tell us what's become of the Wizard Asitra."

Bhalla was surprised and didn't bother to hide it. "As far as I know, nothing has become of her. While I can't detect her presence in the Truthoriam currently, I expect her to arrive soon and attend to her duties as she normally does." He looked between them for a long moment, then said, "I take it that's not what's happening."

"I'm afraid so, sir," Lavinia said solemnly. "Wizard Asitra has missed two meetings, two days in a row, with members of the Keepers of the Light. Even if she were sick, I know she would have sent a messenger to inform us of that. She's not the sort of person who would simply forget her obligations."

"I've been working with Wizard Asitra in my role as the head of the Keepers of the Light for the past five years," Roum added. "No matter what was going on here in the Truthoriam, she always made time to meet with me or sent another wizard in her stead."

"We made our own inquiries," Lavinia continued, "with other members of the Truthoriam, but they told us we were concerned for nothing and that Asitra would get back to us when she had the time." She pressed her lips together firmly. "But, Honored Bhalla, my instincts tell me that she *doesn't* have the time, that something must have happened for her not to reach out to us. And so, we wanted to ask you, as you are the highest authority among the wizards of the Truthoriam, where Wizard Asitra is."

Bhalla resisted the urge to get up and pace at this unsettling news. They were right; Asitra would never be so callous as to abandon a contact without a word. And had Kaden not warned him only days ago that something within the Truthoriam felt wrong? He had told Bhalla he should look into it, into Evias, into the unease settling over the Truthoriam. Bhalla had brushed it aside, telling himself the boy was simply overwhelmed, choosing to trust Evias's assurances instead. Now, with Asitra missing, that choice gnawed at him, and the echo of Kaden's concern felt like a cold hand closing around his heart. He should have acted sooner.

"How long has it been since you saw her in person?" he asked.

"Five days ago, I observed her in prayer in the hilltop temple," Roum said. "She seemed to wish for solitude, so I didn't speak with her then, but she seemed well enough."

"While I haven't personally seen her for several weeks," Lavinia added, "I did ask around, and it seems like the last person to verifiably see her was one of your apprentices, who witnessed a rather lively discussion between her and the wizard Evias."

Evias… that was odd. The two of them had very little to do with each other under normal circumstances. Evias was a warrior wizard who focused his energies on the defense of Lumhagen; Asitra was a teacher and a researcher.

Bhalla stood and inclined his head to the Keepers of the Light. "I thank you for bringing this to my attention," he said. "Rest assured, Asitra is a dear colleague of mine, and I will not allow another day to go by without discovering the truth of her absence."

He schooled his expression, hiding the unease twisting beneath his ribs. No need to alarm the Keepers until he understood the full shape of this calamity. Out loud, he offered the most reasonable explanation he could manage.

But doubt pressed on him. Evias had dismissed Bhalla's concerns so quickly the day he'd sent Kaden away. In hindsight, too quickly.

"It could be," he added carefully, "that she has withdrawn for extended fasting and prayer, and simply did not think to inform anyone. When the will of Orealus works upon you, all a wise person can do is accede to it."

The pair exchanged another glance. "It just doesn't seem like her," Lavinia said at last, "but I suppose it is a possibility. Will you let us know, please?"

"I will," he said again. "I promise." They bowed once more and left the observatory. Bhalla waited for the echo of their footsteps to die off, then closed his eyes and extended his senses throughout the Truthoriam once more, this time with painstaking care. He had been a wizard here for a long, long time, and there wasn't a nook or cranny of this place that he hadn't chanced upon at one point or another.

Stretching his yah'zaval so finely did not weaken him, but it demanded focus and restraint. It felt protective, like laying a careful hand over the place he loved most and everyone in it, guarding rather than probing, steady rather than reckless. Yet the one presence he sought, whose familiar guiding light was normally simple for him to find, was nowhere to be seen.

"Asitra," Bhalla thought worriedly as he slowly drew his senses back into himself. "Where have you gone?"

The bell announcing final prayers at the temple began to ring. It was later than Bhalla had realized.

"Tomorrow," he said to himself as he pushed to his feet, knees creaking and back aching. He'd been sitting for longer than he'd intended. "I'll find her tomorrow."

It was hard to fall asleep that night, and when he did finally sleep, Bhalla's dreams were far from restful. He found himself wandering through the dark, calling out to people who never responded. It wasn't until he called out to Orealus himself that the darkness parted, and Bhalla found himself on his knees before a glowing circle of light. From within the circle, the voice of Orealus spoke to him.

"THERE IS A BETRAYER IN THE HEART OF THIS HOME."

Bhalla's joy at the presence of Orealus melted into fear and resignation—resignation because in his heart, he felt the truth of this. In fact, if he were honest with himself, he'd been feeling it for some time.

"Evias?" Bhalla asked, the name weighing heavily in his chest.

"YOU MUST DISCOVER THAT FOR YOURSELF," Orealus replied. "AND DISCOVER IT, YOU MUST."

He was right. There was no more avoiding this uncomfortable conversation. No more looking the other way and hoping that he was wrong. If Evias had something to do with Asitra's absence, Bhalla had to know. Not just for Asitra herself, but for the safety and well-being of everyone in Lumhagen.

"I will act," he promised Orealus, bowing his head as he traced a circle in the air before his heart. "I will discover the truth." A warm sensation of faith and love washed over him, and when Bhalla woke up, he was no longer dismayed but felt determined instead.

It was early in the morning, the sky somewhere between steel gray and midnight blue, with the last of the stars still lingering on the edges of the horizon. But Bhalla knew he would sleep no more this morning. He was filled with purpose and guided by the will of Orealus himself. There was no sense in delaying the inevitable.

Moreover, he knew that Evias would already be awake, bent over the training schedule he'd prepared for the day, making notes and tending to his duties. Bhalla had thought him so diligent for so long. Now he wondered what dark thoughts were going through Evias's head when he bent his will to tasks that should have benefited them all.

Bhalla flexed his fingers, feeling the crickle and crackle of arthritis that made holding his staff so early in the morning uncomfortable. Should he go and get more guards? Seek support before this confrontation?

No. Bhalla wasn't the chief wizard of the Truthoriam for nothing. He had more raw power and sincere faith than Evias ever would. He could handle this.

Pressing to his feet, he gathered himself and his staff and went in search of confirmation of his worst fears. He found Evias in his office just like he'd expected. The younger man turned to look at Bhalla as he entered, his severe expression lightening a bit.

"Bhalla," he exclaimed, getting to his feet. "I didn't expect to see you so early."

Bhalla looked at Evias for a long time, for a long, silent moment, extending his enhanced senses directly toward the other man. Now that he was looking for it, he could see the concentration of darkness around Evias's head and heart, not flowing, but rooted. He had been touched by the power of Lucient. Bowing his head in sadness, Bhalla said, "Where is Asitra?"

Evias affected a look of concern. "I don't know anything about Asitra's absence. Has she gone somewhere?"

"You know everything about her absence," Bhalla replied. "I had hoped that you would allow yourself to be honest with me. I've never wanted anything more than to help you be the best and most faithful follower of Orealus that you could be. Yet, I find my hopes were all for naught." He watched as the look of concern slid off of Evias's face, replaced by the expression of a man who felt hunted.

"I don't know what you're talking about," he reiterated. "Are you sick? You look tired. Maybe your fatigue is making you confused. Let me call one of the healers for you. I'll—"

"Sit down," Bhalla ordered. Evias's legs gave out from under him, and he sat back heavily in his chair. "I can see his dark influence in you," Bhalla said more gently. "I see it in the deepest parts of your soul, yet it's not too late to turn back, my friend. It's not too late to let Orealus back into your heart, to let him comfort your spirit. Where is Asitra?"

"I don't—"

"Where is Asitra?"

"I'm telling you, I don't—"

"What have you done to Asitra?"

"Nothing she did not deserve," Evias snapped, and then froze.

Bhalla held up a hand. "It's too late for regrets," he said sadly but sternly. "You can explain yourself in front of all your brethren, and have judgment laid upon you. But first, you will tell me where Asitra is." Bhalla raised a hand, but before he could call forth the power of Orealus to bind his former friend, Evias snarled and brought both his hands up, fingers clawed like they wanted to rip Bhalla's heart out.

A second later, an immense surge of power shot forth from his hands, driving Bhalla to his knees. He maintained his grip on his staff, though, letting decades of the power that had poured through it over time act as an ingrained sort of shield. The fierce surge of dunntaika flowed around him and out into the hall, and moments later, a group of four guards appeared. Bhalla didn't even need to look at them to know that they were deep in the influence of Lucient.

"Get rid of this old fool," Evias said hoarsely, his hands shaking from the effort of maintaining the flow of dunntaika.

The guards surged forward, and Bhalla sighed. This was what he'd hoped to avoid, but since he couldn't... he closed his eyes and clapped his hands together.

A moment later, a sphere of golden light surged outward from Bhalla, driven not by force alone, but by unwavering will. It suffused the room, burning away the influence of dunntaika wherever it touched. It poured through the men behind him, and like the scouring force of a flame, it burned out the darkness in their bodies. The change was a wrenching one, and the guards collapsed where they stood, several of them convulsing from the dramatic changes that had been wrought in their bodies and spirits in such a short amount of time.

It was a massive act of power and faith, but to Bhalla's surprise, his light did not touch Evias. In fact, the darkness between the other wizard's hands seemed to grow deeper and more powerful. It changed from a flowing river into a swirling maelstrom that flashed into a portal, and from that portal stepped—

Bhalla gasped as the Dark King emerged, the Deceiver given form, his eyes burning like coals in a dying hearth. There ought to be alarms and alerts going off to alert the other wizards to the presence of the very font of dunntaika itself, and yet... of course, Lucient could get around such things. He had turned Evias to his will, and it was Evias who was responsible for the security of Lumhagen.

"Now you see," Lucient said, in a silky, wicked voice, a voice that spoke of both power and decay. "You see that nowhere is safe. You see how outmatched you truly are, and you will see more." He smiled cruelly. "Much, much more before your end, Bhalla." Dunntaika surged around him, swallowing the last remnants of golden light. It seized the old wizard, jerking him upright, and as Lucient stepped back through the portal, he dragged Bhalla through with him.

CHAPTER 30

The language of dragons was a complex thing. To a dragon, past, present, and future blurred together, layered rather than separate. Their long lives made memory a weapon as sharp as a claw or flame.

It also made it hard for them to put a defeat behind them, because a part of them was always reliving that defeat. If vengeance had yet to be accomplished, the dragon would stew on it, sometimes for months, and often for years. They would neglect those around them, the small number of things they cared for beside themselves, as they focused on the imbalance they felt—wronged, and not righted. Damaged and not repaid tenfold.

Morvar the Dark, Lord of the Skies, obsidian ruler of all dragonkind, was strong enough that even the Great Deceiver could not command him. Stalking from one side to the other of his vast, cavernous home near the top of Wyvernpeake, tallest of the mountains of Empyrea, he relived the moment when that insolent insect called Kaden had escaped him. Nearby, his latest mate panted with exhaustion as she blew a constant flame over their clutch of eggs. The eggs were close to hatching, and the only way for the young of their kind to penetrate the tough shells—so tough that some species sought them out as armor—was to heat them to a more malleable temperature with fire.

The heating lasted for days and was usually shared by both sires. She didn't dare ask him for help, either; interruptions were as good as attacks when Morvar was in such a dark frame of mind. So she blew, draining her reserves to the point of no return, and waited desperately for the dragonets to hatch.

Morvar didn't even notice her exertions. "Insolent," he rumbled with all the depth of a volcano nearing eruption. "To defy me—to commit violence against *me*, greatest of all beings in the land, bringer of death and destruction to all who stand in my way. To *stand upon* me, and then hide like the cowards they are when my righteous vengeance is due." That was the worst part—that he had sought them out and failed to find them. No one should be able to hide from Morvar! He had the keenest senses, the sharpest sight, the greatest knowledge of both land and sky. There was nowhere that little imp and his ilk could hide, and yet...

"I will feast on their flesh," he went on, claws gouging lines into the floor as he twined his massive bulk in circles, revisiting his defeat over and over in his too-sharp memory. "Burn them until even their bones are gone, and grind the ashes to powder beneath my feet. Or—or, let them live, bring them here and turn them to ribbons bit by bit as they bleed and scream before giving them the bliss of a fiery oblivion."

His movements were so heavy they caused his hoard to shift, gold and gemstones tumbling against each other as a shower of them spilled out across the floor. Morvar looked dismissively at the pieces. It was the wanting that mattered more than the keeping. The satisfaction lay in conquest, not possession. The only exception to that was Ruach, the greatest piece of the panoply that once belonged to the dead King of Empyrea. As Morvar was the greatest of beings who had helped make that triumph possible, it was only right that he was given the best of the treasure as promised by Lucient after the war.

I deserve all of it. He ground his foreleg into the stone, turning an untold wealth of finely cast gold into nothing more than a smear. "I deserve all of it," he repeated aloud, warming to the thought. Morvar, greatest of the greats, deserved *all* of the armor of Orealus. And he would take it, he would pry it right off the corpse of that awful little ant of a human, he would—

"Oh, my friend," a new voice suddenly said. "What a state you've worked yourself into."

Morvar swiveled his head and blasted the newcomer with a jet of fire so hot it melted the wall behind him to slag, dripping down onto the floor where it sizzled as it began to slowly, painstakingly cool. Such a blast should have killed anyone else, even another dragon.

Lucient, however reluctant Morvar was to admit it, was something different from others. Not an ally, far from that, but not an enemy either. Still, his presence was far from welcome right now.

"Get you gone," Morvar said stiffly, turning away from the strangely alluring light that Lucient radiated. He knew trickery when he saw it, but he was too old and canny a dragon to fall for such things. Lucient wasn't really here; he was only projecting himself to look it. Dark energy that created an illusion of light—that was the essence of Lucient. He was known as a deceiver for a reason. *Save your little magics for fools and the weak.*

"I sensed your rage," Lucient said in a tone of unwelcome compassion. "And it made me wonder, what could possibly drive the most powerful dragon the world has ever seen into such a frenzy? Do you really feel so strongly about the little tussle you had with the boy and his companions?"

Little tussle? The indignity of such a description! "If you have a mote of wit left in your body, you'll stop spying on my affairs," Morvar snarled, wrapping his tail around a mound of treasure and hurling it in Lucient's direction. It didn't hit him, of course, but the impact was pleasing. At least, it was until his mate whined as one of the swords he'd sent flying cut a line along her flank.

"Weak!" he bellowed. "Pathetic!"

Her fire faltered, and she coughed several times before she managed to spit out, "My lord, I only feared for our offspring. If an egg is cracked before the hatchling is ready, they will die."

"Then," he hissed at her, lowering his head and leaning in so he could watch her recoil from him, "they die. Only the strongest live— that is the way of our people. Now do your duty and warm them, or I'll know who to blame when the eggs fail to hatch."

"Morvar, Morvar." Lucient sounded disparaging, and it took all Morvar's control not to launch another attack on his image. It wasn't the futility of it that dissuaded him so much as his sneaking suspicion that if he did, Lucient would only laugh at him. "Why do you waste so much of your anger, your *power*, on such silly things? The boy and his companions may have evaded you so far, but there are ways of drawing them out."

"What ways?" Morvar huffed. "The dwarves live so deep in the mountain they cannot be burned out; the elves and fairies hide themselves in forests that would take too long to burn, and the land where the humans live is contested and would lead to a fight among my own kind." Which he would win, of course, but he didn't care to ruin other dragons unless it meant he got access to their hoards, and those were tucked away in caverns too small for him to access. Perhaps with his mate's help…

"The boy has a parent left," Lucient said. "In a village that's not shielded by the forest's canopy."

"Useless," Morvar replied. "He has left her; therefore, she has no more hold over him."

"That is the practical path, and one that smart beings believe in," Lucient agreed. "But it isn't the way of someone who still loves. Take his mother, and you take away one of the pillars of his heart and mind. Take his mother, his village, the place of his birth, and you strip away his identity and his sense of self. Kill her, and you will deal your enemy a blow he will not recover from, all without ever having to lay eyes on him or his troublesome friends."

There was… merit to that thought, Morvar decided. Indeed, the longer he considered it, the more merit it held. *Look at my own mate. She fades to nothing, firing our eggs, all in the hope of seeing them hatch. She could focus on just one or two and relieve the burden, yet she spreads herself thin.*

She is a fool, like Kaden. I shall not be. The strongest survive.

"I shall feast," Morvar hummed, his voice low but rising, layered with power and might. "Feast and burn. Feast and burn! *Feast and burn them all!*" By the last word, his mighty voice echoed so fiercely around the cavern that everything within it vibrated. Treasure rattled and rumbled, his mate whimpered and used her wings to block her ears, and their eggs—as one—began to crack.

Morvar watched with mild interest as the hatchlings began to push themselves free of their shells. Not all of them had survived—three of the eleven eggs were duds—but before long, eight of his offspring were crawling across the floor, peeping with displeasure as they experienced a dragon's ravenous hunger for the first time. They fell on the dead eggs, ripping them apart and consuming their innards, and when those were done, they turned insistently to their mother, who looked at them with pride... and a growing sense of fear.

"My lord," she called over to Morvar, "your children need meat. Will you not hunt for them?"

"Why should I hunt for them," he asked silkily, "when they can hunt just fine for themselves?"

His mate's tired eyes went wide. "My lord... surely you don't... I have been a good mate to you, and I will tend to them well once I have time to recover! My lord!" A hatchling began to gnaw on the tip of her tail, and she jerked it away, but two more followed. "*My lord!*"

"You must kill your prey before it has a chance to call attention to its plight," he told his children. Eight sets of burning eyes looked his way. "Otherwise, you might lose your chance to feast in peace. Now take her, consume her, and let her body strengthen yours for the battles that lie ahead of you."

His mate screamed and tried to flee, but the weight of their eight hatchlings was enough to keep her down. The one who'd tasted her flesh wriggled up her body until it reached her neck and dug in fiercely with tiny but sharp teeth that could naturally cut through a dragon's armored scales. Their mother lashed out with her claws, wounding several of them, but then shuddered and went limp as the fierce one finally severed the artery that carried her heart's blood. It gushed from her body, steaming in the cool air of the cavern and coating the hatchlings as they crowded in to feast.

As her heartbeats died, Morvar turned with satisfaction toward the exit. His mate would tend to their children one last time through her death, while he got satisfaction by killing another mother.

Love was only for the weak. If the boy wished to survive long enough to face Morvar again, he would learn that truth.

CHAPTER 31

While it was nice to be out of the sandstorm, and by nice, Kaden meant an absolute life-saving necessity, if there was one thing he could have passed on in this underground ruin, it was the smell. He hadn't really noticed it when they first entered the place, but the deeper they went into the tunnels, the thicker the haze around them seemed to become. It was almost like a mist or a fog, redolent with a stench that somehow reminded Kaden of both death and heat at the same time. It was spicy, clinging, and uncomfortable inside his nose, and he sneezed more than once in an effort to blow it out.

Beneath it all lingered something else, sharper and cleaner than rot or creature musk. The faint scent of scorched stone. It made the hairs on Kaden's arms rise, and he could not say why, only that it felt older than the tunnels themselves. As though a dragon had passed through the world somewhere beyond his sight.

Weylyn noticed his preoccupation and smiled grimly. "That's from the scorchcrawlers," he said.

"Scorchcrawlers?" Petey piped up. "There are scorchcrawlers in here?"

"Just because a scorchcrawler can survive outside in a sandstorm doesn't mean it *wants* to," Weylyn explained. "They prefer enclosed heat. Stone holds warmth better than sand." "They've got burrows all over the desert, but why bother digging your own hole when someone else has made this lovely shelter for you?" He stamped his foot on the stone, then shrugged. "It would be more surprising if there *wasn't* a nest of them living here, honestly."

"You know, ye could have told us this before we came barreling in here," Malacheen pointed out, her eyes narrowed.

"What difference would it have made?" Weylyn asked.

"No difference at all," Queen Pepper put in calmly. "Not if this is where we're going to find the greaves."

"We'd have to be here one way or another, right?" Millicent added with a sidelong glance at her fellow bodyguard, who didn't disappoint.

"We could have chosen a more opportune time," Redfern protested in a bitter tone of voice. "One which didn't leave our queen imperiled and exhausted."

"Oh, I'm sorry. Do you know a way to predict sandstorms?" Weylyn demanded. "Because I don't, and I know far more about places like this than you do, I reckon."

"And apparently, you're far more comfortable than the rest of us when it comes to living in filth," Redfern retorted.

Things were getting heated enough that Kaden felt he should intervene. Before he could, though, Queen Pepper gently clapped her hands. "I think that's enough," she said, gentle but firm. "We're here now, we're safe, and we're together. If it makes you feel better, dear Redfern, feel free to set some traps along the entrances to this corridor. For my part, I'll create a protective barrier so we can rest without enduring the scorchcrawlers' stench. Is that acceptable to everyone?"

The guilt hit Kaden hard. There was no need for Pepper to be the one to expend her yah'zaval, especially not after she had been so battered by the storm. "I can help," he said, sitting down next to her.

Pepper patted his hand and smiled at him, her eyes twinkling. "That's very kind of you, Kaden," she said. "But this is only a small expenditure of my power. I can handle it without hurting myself, I promise you."

"So you say," Redfern muttered, then looked down when Queen Pepper cast her a remonstrating glance. "Sorry, milady."

"It's all right," Pepper said, "but don't let your protectiveness turn into anger, my dear. We all must do our part if we're to defeat Lucient. And right now, let me do mine." She closed her eyes, rubbed her hands together, and then slowly spread them apart. A bubble of golden light appeared between her palms and, with a gentle push, began to extend outward, first over her entire body and then past Kaden's.

On and on it went until all of them had been enveloped in the golden light, which swept the stench and the worst of the darkness away with it. "There. That means making sure that all of us get the best rest possible."

"Ah, Majesty, you're too kind," Bardicus said with a relieved grin. "Don't know if you've noticed, but we dwarves have larger than average sniffers. Good thing to have underground." He tapped the side of his bulbous, hooklike nose. "Keeps you keen, helps you scent things that might give you trouble before that trouble comes at you with a fist to the face. Nevertheless, it does make certain things a wee bit challenging." Both Thalgrem and Malacheen nodded in agreement.

"I'm grateful to be able to help," Pepper said. "I think everyone should take the opportunity to get some sleep if they can. We've all been through quite a lot lately, and we should endeavor to be rested before we go after the Megalos."

Kaden could admit to himself that he was, in fact, pretty tired. He walked back over to where he'd laid his pack down and propped it up behind his neck to use as a makeshift pillow. Then he put his hands behind his head and stared up at the ceiling, where more bits of colored crystal and brilliant opalescence shone down on him.

At least the ceiling held no images demanding interpretation. He could stare at it and just relax, instead of trying to interpret the image that he was looking at.

Eldrin wasn't so easily satisfied. He was still moving down the hall to the very edges of Queen Pepper's light, peering closely at the pictures and murmuring to himself in a voice so low Kaden couldn't hear it.

Well, at least he was content. Kaden smiled slightly, then turned his head to look at Ada, who'd come up to stand about five feet away from him. "You look comfortable," she said lightly.

"I can't complain," he said. "It's pretty soft if you avoid the parts with the weapons and cooking gear."

"Is it really?" Ada asked.

"Find out for yourself," Kaden said and, feeling a bit bold, scooted a little further down to make room for her. Would she accept his invitation or leave again, still sore from their argument earlier? He breathed a sigh of relief as Ada shrugged and then lay down next to him.

It was silent for a long moment before Ada finally said, "So, I'm sorry about that. What I said out there, I mean."

"It's okay," Kaden said quickly.

She shook her head. "You're always so quick to forgive," Ada replied. "I don't understand it. I don't understand why you're not *angrier*." She glanced at him. "You're our leader, after all. I shouldn't be questioning you."

"No, you should be," Kaden said, a little surprised. "Of course you should be. It's *because* I'm the leader that you should be questioning me. I mean, I appreciate your support, of course, and I want to do things right by you, but how am I going to do that if you don't feel like you can be honest with me when things are good *or* bad?"

"Don't you think that'll lead to paralysis?" Ada asked. "Not knowing what to do at all?"

Kaden shrugged. "It's possible," he admitted. "I'm still not very confident in a lot of my decisions. I know I have a long way to go when it comes to being a good leader, but I'm trying, and I know now that part of being a good leader means knowing when to listen. I don't want you to feel like you can't depend on me to listen to you. It doesn't mean I'm going to take what you say, though," he added with a little smile.

"Oh, of course not," Ada replied, equally blithe. "That would be ridiculous."

"Ludicrous," Kaden agreed.

"Absurd."

"Entirely unprecedented."

"Uncalled for," she finished, and they both laughed. "Still," she said after a moment, "it wasn't right, and I know that. I think I tend to be a bit..." She pursed her lips for a moment. "Sensitive, I suppose, about how young I am. This is my first quest, after all. I'm basically untested apart from this, and I'm just not sure I'm contributing the way that I should be. The way that the *others* are. I can't win against a scorchcrawler in single combat, I can't summon yah'zaval to protect us from sand or…"

"Or smells," Kaden said.

"Or smells," Ada agreed. "Now that's a good use of power."

Kaden thought about that for a moment. "You know," he said, "I might not have thought so just a few hours ago, actually."

"What do you mean?" Ada asked, rolling on her side so she could look at him better.

"I mean that if you had asked me, oh, half an hour ago, if I thought a worthy use of yah'zaval was to basically put up a *stink* barrier, I might have said no. I probably would have, in fact. I'd have said it's just something we need to deal with. But now that it's gone?" He sighed with relief and closed his eyes. "I honestly don't know how I could have relaxed without it." That realization unsettled him more than he expected.

"It was incredibly foul," Ada said.

"And Queen Pepper is far more experienced in the use of her powers than I am," Kaden went on. "So if she feels that it's right, well, I certainly wouldn't accuse her of being spendthrift with her power."

Ada nodded thoughtfully. "I can see that," she agreed. "It must be hard to strike that balance, though."

Kaden sighed. "It is. I'm always worried that I'm going to make a mistake. Orealus has blessed me with a great amount of power, but it's also a huge responsibility, and I don't know what I would do if harm came to someone I cared for because I made the wrong decision. You know?"

"I do," Ada said. "So you'd act, then," she went on, "in order to prevent harm?"

"Yeah," Kaden said. "Absolutely."

"But not discomfort. Like, say…" Ada scooted a little bit closer. "Say I'm getting a crick in my neck on your oh-so-lovely pillow here. But I can't leave. How would you help me? Would you use your power to ease my pain?"

Oh, boy. Kaden felt like he was on the precipice of something larger than himself. A thrill of excitement surged through him. "Maybe not my power," he said, and Ada's lips began to transform into a pout. "But, I might, um, offer something else as a pillow."

"Oh?" she asked archly. "Like what?"

"Well." He extended his arm between them and patted his bicep. "What about this?"

"Hmm." Ada smiled. "I guess I'll give it a try."

What could have happened next, Kaden would always wonder about. Just as he leaned over, Eldrin's voice rose in the distance. "Kaden, you need to come and look at this," he called out.

Kaden sighed, and he and Ada exchanged a wry glance as he got to his feet. "What did you find?" he asked as he came up next to the elven prince.

When Eldrin looked at him, there was so much excitement in his face that Kaden was genuinely surprised. His friend was normally so composed—or, if he was feeling something at all, he was more likely to show anger or annoyance. But excitement?

"Kaden," Eldrin said eagerly. "Look, it's *us*. This is us, you and I. It's our first meeting." He stepped to the side even as he pointed at a section of the wall. Kaden moved in closer to take a look, ready to humor his friend, and yet…

He peered closer. The figures in the drawing were only vaguely sketched out, little more than lines, but they were clearly denoting a human, a goblin, a dog, and flying fairies, all of them being rowed across a lake toward an enormous tree, when he saw the figure of an elf with a bow.

Kaden was stunned. "It's, this can't be—"

"It seems impossible, I know," Eldrin said, "but look at it. Who else could this be? And look a little further down." He tugged Kaden another few feet along. "It's us meeting Bardicus for the first time."

"What are you talking about?" King Bardicus, roused by the mention of his name, unfolded himself from where he'd been bent over the small fire he and Thalgrem had gotten started and came over to look. He leaned in toward the wall and pushed up onto his toes a bit—the picture was higher than eye level for him.

"I'll be damned," he said. His voice wasn't as wondering as Eldrin's had been, though. If anything, it sounded concerned. "What sort of dark power is this, then?"

"Dark power?" Eldrin protested. "How could it be dark? These must have been made thousands of years ago, and yet look—they show the steps of our journey with complete accuracy, as far as I can tell. Here's the fight against that awful ogre, and here, this shows when we were dragged down into Nethopolis. And then here, that's where we fought the tree golem on Cimetes's lands."

"Incredible," Kaden murmured. His heart began to race as he considered the implications of this. "Do you think it could show us our future?"

"Nothing can accurately predict the future," Queen Pepper said as she flew over to them, her face somber. "But some truths echo forward," she added quietly." "It might be tempting to believe so, but Orealus invested in his people's free will."

"Well, then, he must have invested in someone the ability to see the outcome of that free will," Eldrin said in exasperation. "And then put it up here on a wall. Look, it just keeps going, look." He pulled them further, and Kaden's eyes widened as he saw more of their journey.

Here was when he was poisoned and almost died, and here was their first fight against Morvar. Kaden shivered as he saw the depiction of the great black dragon in flight. Then here was them being taken captive by Mad-Eyed Malech, and then…

"That's us in the ruins," Kaden said. "That's us right now. But what's this?" There was a line of tiny triangles pointing down like arrows. Kaden's eyes followed the glowing indicators, and when he got to where they were pointing, his breath caught in his throat. That was Morvar, and he was flying over…

"Ashland," Kaden breathed in horror. "That's Ashland," Kaden said, his voice breaking.

"It doesn't say it's Ashland," Queen Pepper was quick to point out, her tiny finger tracing the inscriptions that accompanied the image. "This text only indicates Morvar's attack on a village dear to the hearts of those he hates."

"Then it's Ashland," Kaden almost shouted. "What other village is so dear? If it were Whaldalf's Landing, it would be indicated with water around it, not all of these trees. It's my home. It's where my mother is.

And it's on *fire*." He took a step away from the wall, hands shaking. "I need to check on my mother."

Every voice around him rose in immediate disagreement. "There's no indication that this is happening right now." Eldrin, who had been the most excited about this find, was now protesting it the loudest. "We need to stay together. We need to treat this as a sign that—"

"I need to go and protect my mother," Kaden snapped. "You don't understand. I haven't seen her in so long." His heart ached as he realized it had been over a year since he'd laid eyes on his last surviving parent.

Lydia might not be his birth mother, but she had done everything she could for him. She had raised him, loved him, and he hadn't so much as sent her a letter letting her know he was all right. Regret and guilt churned in his stomach so strongly he was almost nauseous from it. "I have to go to her now."

"It's not safe," Queen Pepper argued. "The best way to defeat your enemies, including Morvar, is by fulfilling Orealus's prophecy and gathering all the pieces of the armor together. To do that, you have to be here, Kaden."

A swell of unexpected anger rose up in him. Kaden couldn't remember the last time he'd been angry at Queen Pepper, if he ever had before. But now? "Are you saying my mother doesn't matter?" he demanded. "Are you saying saving her is less important than what? Then adding one more piece to a set of armor? My mother is one of the people we're trying to save this land for. What good is it going to be if she's not alive to see it?"

Pepper raised her hands in a gesture of comfort. "I didn't mean it that way. I know you love your mother, but—"

"If she needs him," Ada suddenly put in, "he should go to her."

"Just what I'd expect from an undisciplined, untested young maid," Bardicus snapped. "You need to stay here." Weylyn was silent, and Kaden couldn't judge the look in his eyes, but he didn't speak out against the idea. Malacheen looked uncomfortable, glancing between her king and Kaden like she didn't quite know what to say.

"How hard would it be," Ada went on, "for Kaden to create a portal, check on his mother, and return directly?"

"He should be saving his power for an emergency," Eldrin said.

"What's more important than family?" Ada protested.

All of a sudden, Thalgrem, who had wandered to the edge of Queen Pepper's protective light, held up a hand. His nostrils quivered as he sniffed deeply. A second later, Bardicus said, "Ah, bloody hells. Perhaps there's nothing more important, but there's definitely somethin' more pressing." He reached for his enormous axe with a grim expression.

"There's scorchcrawlers coming this way."

CHAPTER 32

"We can't engage with them here, it's too tight!"
"A larger chamber will only make it easier for them to come at us, we need to—"

"This sounds like a good reason to run to me! How about that portal, Ka—*ow*!"

"Shut up, Chum."

Kaden placed his hands around his mouth and shouted, "Quiet!" The noise faltered, then broke apart entirely. One by one, the others turned toward him. It took a few seconds, but eventually everyone complied. "Everyone, armor up and get ready for a fight," he said. "We knew we'd have some sort of battle ahead of us to get the Megalos—no piece of the armor has ever come easily. At least we know how to fight scorchcrawlers."

"Aye, by gettin' lucky," Bardicus muttered even as he drew his second axe.

"Are you saying you're incapable of fighting off a scorchcrawler?" Eldrin asked, the target of his argument changing effortlessly from Kaden to the dwarven king as he picked up his bow. "How sad."

"I said nothin' of the sort! I simply—"

Kaden got into his armor as quickly as he could, then made sure Duke was ready as well. "Stay close to Petey," he whispered to his faithful dog, then drew Vrangar. He could hear the clamor of the scorchcrawlers down the hallway heading toward them, and stepped forward to be the first one to face the enemy. He was the leader. If someone was going to face the danger first, it had to be him.

Ten steps in, the stone beneath Kaden's feet gave way without warning. He shouted as he fell into darkness, none of the eerie blue-and-green light following him down. He didn't fall for long, but the impact still jarred his body painfully, especially his right ankle, and he collapsed onto his side with a grimace.

Ada screamed, "*Kaden!*" and a glance upward showed him a host of faces on the edges of the hole he'd fallen through —Petey clutching Duke's collar as the dog strained toward him.

"I'm here," he called up with a grimace. "I'm… all right, but—"

"Behind you!" Weylyn shouted, and there was a sudden hiss and a clash above Kaden. All the faces vanished except for Redfern, who tossed down the torch she carried. It clattered to the floor a few feet away from Kaden.

"Get up here when you can!" she yelled, then charged into the fight.

A fight that was happening *without* Kaden. A fight that he'd just thrown into disarray by falling through a hole in the floor.

My father would be ashamed to see this. For once, it did not matter which father he meant. He needed to get up, to use his power to help him rejoin the fight instead of counting on others to do the hard work for him.

And yet… Kaden's head spun, the air thick with a miasma of dust and death. He grabbed the torch and held it aloft as he slowly sat up. His head still rang, but his back was fine at least. His landing had been partially cushioned by what looked like a pile of rags, but what were rags doing in a place like this? Kaden peered closer, and…

He jerked back with a start as he realized he was looking at a cloak. Given the embroidery around the edges of it, it had once belonged to a member of the Empyrean Royal Army. Beneath the cloak was a pile of rusted chainmail, and under that… Kaden closed his eyes as he made out the scattered bones that had been strewn across the floor with his awkward landing. "May Orealus keep your soul," he murmured, then raised his eyes once more.

This was more than just a hole. The fighting above him seemed to fade away as Kaden took in more of his surroundings. This was an entire floor, a manmade cavern with thick pillars supporting the hallways above it. It extended out for several hundred feet, and in the distance, Kaden could just make out a double gleam, something that picked up the light from his torch in an uncanny way. What…

He closed his eyes for a moment. "Holy Orealus, give me clarity that I might see your will." Kaden felt a surge of his yah'zaval go through his head, and the store of it within him dipped lower. When he opened his eyes, though, he could see the objects in the distance clearly.

Greaves. Golden greaves, laid at the top of a heap of bodies that were no more now than bones. *Megalos!* His fall hadn't been futile after all, then! But his new vision showed him more than the greaves… it allowed him to look into the opaque darkness and see things he hadn't been able to distinguish before.

He wasn't all that happy about being able to distinguish them now, either.

That is the biggest scorchcrawler I have ever seen. And something about the way she moved told him she was not alone down here.

The last scorchcrawler Kaden had gotten a good look at had been the size of a horse, perhaps a bit larger. This one… it was easily twice as long as the last, but more than that, it was *thick*, so round through the middle that as it slowly pressed to its clawed feet, its belly still scraped the floor. Its mouth was long and filled with a double row of curving teeth, and dust rose from its hide as it puffed air through its skinny nostrils.

It took Kaden a moment to realize that this scorchcrawler was different in another way, too. It only had three legs—one of its rear limbs was a stump that ended well above where the foot landed. Perhaps that was why it was hibernating down here, or perhaps it was watching over the greaves.

Whatever the reason, Kaden knew where his path lay. He shouted out, "I found the armor! It's down here!"

"Get it then, lad!" Bardicus yelled down to him. "An' hurry up, will you? We've got two beasties up here and could use your help with 'em."

Kaden groaned. "I was about to ask *you* to come to *me*."

After a moment, Redfern flew down to join him. "What is it?" Kaden pointed, and the fairy blanched, hands tightening on her spear.

"The queen," she whispered. "Once she has your scent, she will not lose it!"

"I think she's already done that," Kaden said a bit unsteadily as the scorchcrawler began to hobble toward him. "What does it mean?"

"It means she's going to be able to find you no matter how fast or how far you run. Curse it!" Redfern turned and flew back toward the hole. "I'll get you backup!"

Backup. Great. But what would Kaden do *until* then?

You fight. If you want the greaves, you'll do whatever you need to for them. Kaden wasn't going to give up just because things were hard. As the queen lurched his way, opening her mouth even wider to bare her fearsome teeth, Kaden called upon his yah'zaval. He clenched his free hand, then opened his fingers wide.

A brilliant ball of white light illuminated the room around him. With a shout, Kaden flung it at the scorchcrawler, which shrieked and shut its eyes against the gleam. Kaden immediately followed up the attack with his sword.

This beast, for all she was wounded, was truly ferocious. If he hadn't blinded her with the light, Kaden had the feeling he'd be dead already. As it was, he was barely able to block the massive back-and-forth shakes of the scorchcrawler's head as she flung her body toward him, following her nose now that her eyes couldn't be counted on. Even Vrangar barely made a dent in her thick hide, especially when Kaden had to be so careful where he stepped, or risk a piece of bone or loose armor sending him tumbling.

"How about that backup?" he shouted behind him as he blocked another of the queen's heavy strikes. He was being forced to give way to her now, to fall back instead of pressing forward like he needed to. Every step took him further and further from the greaves.

"Coming!" A heartbeat later, something small and fast dropped through the hole, bounced once, and landed not five feet from Kaden.

It was Bug, hurled with surprising accuracy from above through the opening. Kaden, panting with exertion and fear, couldn't quite believe his eyes. "Are you *serious*?" he yelled. Wonderful, now he was going to have to protect Bug from being stomped on as well as himself, all while losing ground, and—

Bug seemed to draw himself up for a moment. His mushroom cap began to glow a sickly green color, then—*whoosh!* A jet of spores shot straight at the queen, striking her in the center of her long, bony face. She sneezed, then almost immediately clamped her nostrils shut before scraping her face across the floor like she was trying to wipe away the spores. The glowing stuff clung to her tenaciously, though.

Kaden turned to Bug with a huge grin on his face. "Well done!" he beamed. It was going to be so much easier to press his attack now. He took a step forward, then another. Then—

The queen screamed, a shrill and haunting sound. Her cry echoed through the chamber, and a moment later, a dozen smaller cries answered her. A second after that, dark shapes began to emerge from the corners of the room, all of them heading toward Kaden and Bug.

More scorchcrawlers… but these were different from the others as well. These were shorter, with fewer claws and smaller jaws. Even their teeth looked blunter, but that didn't mean they weren't dangerous.

Kaden glanced at Bug. "I don't suppose you can…" The hopping toadstool shivered once, then jumped up so that it was sitting on his shoulder. *All right, then.* That was fine. Bug had done his part. Now, Kaden needed to do his in return.

The smaller scorchcrawlers weren't as heavily armored as their queen. Their skin was particularly thin around the neck, and Kaden was able to find purchase there with Vrangar's edge and give every one of the little beasts a quick end, if not a painless one. They were dogged, though, throwing themselves toward him until they bled out or he decapitated them completely. He had never seen a creature drive itself so ferociously before.

The queen, in the meantime, was drawing back into the shadows. Much farther, and she might vanish completely. That would be fine, except for the fact that she was backing up right against the greaves themselves, diminishing their golden light with her bulk as she fled. If she took them with her deeper into the tunnels, tracking them down would be so much worse than fighting in the relatively open space they had now.

Kaden needed help. "Bug," he shouted, then pointed at the greaves. "Can you shoot that far?"

Bug seemed to understand. He moved from Kaden's shoulder to his head, suctioning his lower half on with an uncomfortably wet-sounding *squelch*. Kaden did what he could to fight his way closer, wary of the greaves vanishing completely. Bug suddenly squeezed him tight, and Kaden froze.

A sticky ball of spores flew and struck home, and a moment later, the queen screeched with rage as she was denied her exit *and* her prize. She snorted viciously and turned back toward them, her discomfort forgotten in the wake of her sheer anger. She trampled over the fallen corpses of the smaller scorchcrawlers as she came, and Kaden braced himself for an attack that he worried he might not be able to weather on his own.

Thankfully, he didn't have to.

An arrow punched through the still-flickering light and struck the queen square in one of her eyes. It was a perfect shot, and Kaden turned to congratulate Eldrin, then froze in surprise as he saw Ada come up behind him instead, her bow in hand. "Pay attention!" she shouted, shooting one of the smaller ones straight in its gaping maw. It fell over with a bloody sigh.

Right, right.

Weylyn was there a moment later, and he and Kaden were able to flank the queen on either side as Ada used her arrows to keep her from charging straight forward and down the corridor behind her. They attacked in unison, and despite her massive head shakes and snaps with her jaws, the queen was too bulky to turn and face one of them in an effort to finish them off. That gave them time to break off and handle the smaller scorchcrawlers as they came in, as well as back up Ada whenever one got into striking range of her.

The queen took blow after blow, blood streaming from her blind eye to pool beneath her claws and causing her to slip at times. Gradually, she began to shrink in on herself, and that was when the rest of the party finally joined them in the underground lair.

"Ha! She's a right big 'un, isn't she?" Bardicus roared, swinging his hammer with delight as he charged in. He smashed it against the queen's side with such force that he actually dented her body there, and her next scream was tainted with agony.

"Watch out for the workers," Weylyn called, and—ah, that made sense to Kaden. Workers, soldiers, a queen… they were like big killer versions of the bees that their neighbor in Ashland had kept.

Ashland…

The scorchcrawler queen was faltering now, her legs slowly going out from under her. The workers were still attacking, but they were down to fewer than a dozen in number. The greaves glimmered in the distance, still here.

If he left now, he could reach his mother. He could see her with his own eyes. Now that the rest of the party was here, success against the queen was assured. Kaden knew he ought to stay, but the thought of his family home burning and his mother in danger was too strong to ignore.

He retreated, lowered his sword, and grabbed the amulet around his neck to help him focus.

"Kaden?"

Orealus, hear my prayer… I must go to my mother. Grant me a portal to Ashland.

"Kaden, what are you doing?"

A portal opened in front of him, just wide enough for one and already closing.

"Kaden, wait!"

He ran through it without looking back.

CHAPTER 33

As the two Shadowblades stared out into the churning sands of the Barren Badlands, the remnants of the recent sandstorm still hanging in the air, a lean, masked warrior muttered, "This is a waste of time."

"Shut up." His companion didn't look like a woman at first glance, bundled as she was in layers of cloth and cloak that muted every curve, but her voice gave her away. It was light, feminine, and right now fiercely focused. "I think I see his perch."

Khalkjon thought so too, which meant his chances to dissuade his sister from her goal were almost nil, but he had to try anyway. "Ta'la… he might not even want to come with us right now."

"Ezrah will come back. He'll come home."

He'll come back to me, Khalkjon heard beneath the certainty in her voice, a certainty he did not share.

If Ezrah had been content staying with the Shadow Rift Guild, if he'd been happy to be part of their Sundaki tribe, then he wouldn't have started wandering the moment Jedrek certified him as a full-fledged member of the guild. He would have stuck to the shadows, taking contracts and building a fortune like the rest of them, instead of isolating himself by hunting down a boy he had nothing to do with.

It wasn't that Khalkjon found nothing admirable about Ezrah. He was a great warrior, easily one of the deadliest among them after his time in Lucient's dungeons. He was capable of feats that few of them could match, and he'd managed to capture Ta'la's heart—even though she was older and supposedly wiser—without even trying. If only he could be content with that…

Khalkjon had even considered killing the boy Ezrah was tracking to help his sister secure his devotion, but one long look at his company had killed that goal. Weylyn, Son of the Wolf? An elven prince? A fairy *queen*? He didn't have a chance in hell of pulling off an assassination, and he knew it.

Ta'la started moving, and Khalkjon heaved a sigh and set off beside her. This wasn't going to be pretty, but if his sister wanted to punish herself by hanging all her hopes on a man who would never put her first, then that heartbreak was hers to manage.

Khalkjon knew the moment Ezrah spotted them, because the shadows in the rocky outcropping near the ruins shifted, a deliberate invitation. No Shadow Rift warrior would be seen if they didn't want to be seen, not once they'd settled into their chosen bit of gloom. The fact that he was making himself obvious was a good sign, actually, and Ta'la's steps lightened as they reached Ezrah's perch.

He was deep in the shadow of the rocks, staring out toward a particular section of ruins with a single-mindedness that was typical of the man. There was a reason Ezrah was said to never lose sight of his target. He was as bundled up as they were, with his hood pulled low over his shaggy dreads and a mask covering the bottom half of his face. His hand idly stroked the hilt of the throwing knife attached to his thigh, like a child seeking comfort from a doll, only—well. Not quite like that. He'd unbound his twin short swords from his back and laid them beside him, but they were still in grabbing reach.

His voice was flat and controlled as he asked, "What are you doing here?"

Oof. Not the best start, though. Khalkjon opened his mouth to reply, but Ta'la beat him to it. "Ezrah, don't you think it's time to come back to the guild?"

"No." *Obviously*, his demeanor seemed to say, all stiff shoulders and defiantly lifted chin.

"You were just named the next leader once Jedrek retires," Ta'la said. "You have a responsibility to the tribe, and you need to come home and—"

"I have a responsibility to my brother." That stopped Khalkjon cold.

Wait, his brother? Khalkjon didn't know the kid Ezrah was chasing around was his brother. Yish, that made this… rather more complicated.

Ta'la put her hands on her hips, exasperated. "You already told me that he doesn't even know you're out here! He has no clue that you even exist, and it doesn't seem like you're in a hurry to tell him either." She shifted from a posture of condemnation to one of appeal, stretching a hand out to Ezrah. "He has people of his own now, doesn't he? Friends and guardians to help him on whatever quest he's embarked on. *You* have a new family as well, Ezrah."

Khalkjon's eyes narrowed as he saw his sister's hand waver, swaying back toward her midsection before reaching out once more. Was she… did she…

Ezrah didn't seem to notice. "Kaden will always be my brother, whether he knows it or not," he said staunchly.

"And what am I?" Ta'la demanded. "I saved your life, I gave you training and purpose, I gave you my *heart,* and now you just don't care?"

Ezrah's eyes softened a bit. "You know I care about you," he said. "I care about the guild, I care about our tribe, but…" He shook his head. "You don't understand."

"So help us understand," Khalkjon snapped, tired of listening to Ezrah make excuses. "Tell us exactly why you won't prioritize the people who've been there for you from the beginning, huh?"

"Because I wasn't there for *him* from the beginning," Ezrah said with the edge of a snarl on his face. "Because the reason I needed saving at all is that I was a coward. Is that what you want to hear?" He pushed to his feet and stood toe-to-toe with Khalkjon, who couldn't look away from those ferocious eyes even as Ta'la tried to push between them and intervene. "You want to hear about how I hid away when our home was attacked? About how I left my baby brother alone, helpless? About how I could have been saved right along with him, only I was too afraid to step into the light?"

"You were a child!" Ta'la insisted. "You didn't know any better!"

"I knew my duty," Ezrah said, the fire inside of him giving way to an icy coldness that crept over his face like frost. He looked back toward the ruins. "And I failed. I will not fail him again. Not now."

"But—"

"Fine," Khalkjon said, tired of pushing against an unfeeling block of stone. "Stay here and waste your time babysitting a person who doesn't even need your help, who you won't even reveal yourself to! But don't think that our tribe will forget this choice."

"Khalkjon, stop it," Ta'la pleaded.

"I wouldn't expect them to," Ezrah replied. He looked at Ta'la again, but this time there was no hint of softness. "Go, then."

Khalkjon took his sister by the arm and pulled her away from Ezrah, even as she protested. He could hear her longing in her voice, see it in her eyes, and the way she laid her hands on her belly... in the end, he could only restrain his curiosity for a mile before he turned to her and blurted, "Are you pregnant?"

Ta'la stiffened. "What?"

"Are you carrying Ezrah's child?"

She lifted her chin defiantly. "And what if I am?"

"What if you—*Ta'la*!" How could she be so foolish? "He's already given away his heart," Khalkjon said, his voice heavy as he stared at his sister in consternation. "You knew that from the beginning. Ezrah was never going to give us, our people, his full loyalty, not after what he lived through."

"We saved him!"

"We saved him for someone else!"

"I *love* him!" she cried, her voice crumbling, and Khalkjon took his sister into his arms and held her as she shook through a storm of emotions. "He does love me," she whispered, "he does, I know he does. He'll come back to us."

"We don't need him to."

"He's the guild's best warrior and tactician, *and* our next leader. We do need him."

Not if he makes you feel this way. Khalkjon sighed. There was no arguing with Ta'la sometimes; what she believed in, she believed in wholeheartedly. And if she believed in Ezrah… "Why didn't you tell him about the baby? He might have come back with us if he knew you were expecting his child."

She sniffed. "Because I know Ezrah better than you do, brother. And I do want him to come back, but not if it means tying him down to a life he's not ready to fully commit to. That would break his spirit faster than anything. And if I am to have him, then I will have him whole."

Well. That sounded like a load of crap to Khalkjon, but it wasn't his business. Still. "If Jedrek removes him from the lists, I won't fight it," he warned her. "The leader must be present to lead. Ezrah has shown he doesn't prioritize the guild despite his position as heir apparent."

"He'll be back before Jedrek is ready to step down," Ta'la insisted. "I know it. We just have to wait for him."

Ta'la might be right about Ezrah, but when it came to waiting, Khalkjon certainly wasn't going to be holding his breath.

Ezrah watched Ta'la and Khalkjon vanish into the dust and, for a moment, his heart panged in longing. It would have been so easy to go with them, back to a place where he was wanted. He knew he was upsetting Ta'la and the others, and he regretted it, and yet…

He couldn't leave Kaden. Not again. Not after everything he had learned and how far he had come. There might be a day when his brother didn't need someone to watch after him, but today wasn't that day, and Ezrah didn't trust the people who traveled with Kaden to keep his best interests at heart. Why would they? To them, Kaden was a symbol first and a person second. They needed him, but that didn't mean they cared for him the way they should.

Ezrah told himself as he waited for them to emerge that he was willing to be proven wrong. If they could care for Kaden as well as he did, if they loved him, truly loved him, then he might be able to return to the Shadow Rift Guild with an unburdened heart. It wouldn't be the first time he'd been wrong after all, he thought more than a touch bitterly. And yet…

The distant sound of stone grating against stone captured his attention. Sand shifted, and a moment later, the first of Kaden's companions stepped out into the open air. It was one of the dwarves, the one with the sparking gauntlets. He was followed by the other two, then Weylyn, then the useless satyr and the nearly useless goblin. More people emerged, and the knot of tension in Ezrah's chest tightened with every face that wasn't his brother's.

Kaden wasn't with them. He wasn't there.

What had happened to him?

Ezrah immediately pulled his hood down low and crept out of his rocky shelter. Crouching down so that his body hovered less than an inch above the ground, he began to crawl toward them. It was dangerous exposing himself out in the open like this, but it was nearly twilight, and the shadows were growing longer by the minute. They'd have to be looking for him in order to see him, and Ezrah had no intention of giving himself away. He needed to know, though. He needed to know what had happened to his brother, and the only way to learn that was from these people.

Soon, he was close enough to make out their conversation.

"—believe he just left like that!" one of the fairies was saying in an irate tone of voice.

"He needed to make sure his mother was all right," the young woman with long braids replied.

Kaden's mother? Not *their* mother, of course, but Kaden's… the woman from Ashland, who'd raised him. What was her name again…

"He could have waited to get the damn greaves first!"

"Kaden fought long enough for us to handle the end of the fight by ourselves," Weylyn said, although he sounded a bit put out. "I agree that he shouldn't have left without talking to us about it first, but—"

"You would have told him not to go," the goblin said, his voice unexpectedly strong. "You already told him not to go, in fact!"

"With good reason!" the elven prince exclaimed. "It's ridiculous to let pictures on a wall dictate your actions, even if they look to be true. There are half a dozen explanations that are just as likely as the one Kaden decided to settle on."

"So, you wanted him to risk his mother's life for no reason?" the girl asked.

"I wanted him to prioritize actually laying hands on the Armor of Orealus, the armor that *he* is meant to wear to defeat the forces of Lucient, over creating a portal that he didn't even bother to leave open for the rest of us."

Wait, what? Kaden had used some sort of portal to leave this place behind, and these fools hadn't even managed to go with him?

The fairy queen sighed. "I think he likely didn't have the yah'zaval left for a large portal," she said. "Kaden's store of energy has to be at least as diminished as mine. Indeed, I'd be surprised if he manages to make one back to us until tomorrow morning."

"At least we have the greaves," the useless little satyr pointed out. "Now we can go rest and relax and wait for Kaden to finish whatever it is he's off doing."

The girl made a sound of pure discontent. "Why are none of you willing to believe that what he saw in there might be genuine?" she demanded. "What if, right now, Kaden hasn't gone back to his village and found his mother safe and sound? What if Ashland really *is* on fire right now?"

On fire? *What?*

"What if Morvar really *is* taking his vengeance on Kaden by destroying his childhood home?" the girl went on, unaware of the blows she was delivering to Ezrah with every word. "Imagine if that's what he's returned to! Never mind him possibly confronting Morvar as a result; he's going to be devastated if his mother is injured, or worse. We ought to be going to him right now!"

"He chose his path," one of the dwarves put in, "an' if it leads away from the object of our quest right now, then I say we leave the lad to it while we move on to searchin' for the next piece of armor. Let him handle himself for a time while we stay vigilant."

"You're missing the entire point!"

"*Kaden* is missing the entire point if he thinks gallivantin' off to satisfy his curiosity is more important than gatherin' the pieces of the Armor of Orealus!"

The company dissolved into more arguments, but Ezrah was done listening. As fast as he could, he moved away from them, his mind working at a thousand leagues a minute as his heart quivered in his chest.

Fools. *Fools.* There wasn't even any contest—they ought to be going to Ashland to help Kaden. And if these people, the ones who purported to follow his brother through thick and thin, wouldn't do it?

Then Ezrah would.

CHAPTER 34

When Kaden stepped through the portal, barely making it through before it collapsed behind him, he expected to find a place he remembered. It would be different, of course. How could it not be? More than a year had passed since he'd lived in Ashland. The seasons had turned, and Kaden himself had changed.

He imagined small differences. A new barn raised by neighbors. Extra rains keeping the benthilea flowers clinging to cottage eaves in swoops of blue and purple. Lydia, with her curls braided differently, had a new kerchief tied at her brow. She might be angry to see him. Or sad. Kaden thought he was prepared for all of that. He was ready to make amends, to reach out and assure her of his love, to convince her and the others that they needed to leave Ashland. It was time to hide, to be quiet and safe, and let him lead them to safety. He was ready to grovel if he needed to, if that was what it took to convince his mother of his sincerity.

He wasn't prepared for what awaited him.

Heat struck him like a physical blow, leaving him gasping as the portal flickered out. Everywhere he looked, there was fire—cottages aflame, trees crackling and breaking apart as they burned, even the ground itself flaring up wherever there was grass poking through the dirt. And beneath the crackle of those flames, Kaden heard screams.

"No!" he shouted, drawing his sword and running deeper into the village. He refused to believe it, refused to let this be the way Ashland ended. This was his *home*. He was going to save it.

Through the smoke all around him, he could see people running. Some were screaming; others saved their breath for the run itself, coughing against the smoke and heat. One of the older men—it was Peyter, one of his father's oldest friends—was staggering, leaning on a cane that was burning at the tip as he struggled toward the deeper, wetter woods of Brightshire Forest. Kaden ran over and grabbed him around the waist to support him.

"Peyter," Kaden shouted over the sounds. The old man looked at him through streaming, teary eyes, blinded by ash and smoke. "Peyter, it's me! It's Kaden!"

"Kaden…"

"Yes," Kaden said urgently. "Daneyel and Lydia's son."

"*Kaden*." Recognition seemed to strike him all at once. "God above, get out of here," Peyter gasped, bringing his free hand up to Kaden's shoulder and shaking it for all he was worth. "You couldn't have picked a worse time to come back, lad—there's nothing left!"

Kaden wasn't going to hear it. "Where's my mother?"

"Listen to me!" Peyter insisted. "You've got to get out of here! There's a dragon up there, a massive one, black as night and dark as the depths of hell. He set fire to us, then he put his monsters down among us to consume everyone they can chase down. We're in a fight we can't win, son!"

Monsters? "What do you mean by monsters?" Kaden demanded.

"What does it matter? Quick, toothy beasts the size of horses, every color in the rainbow, and all of them as cruel as the day is long, and you must *flee*, Kaden, now!"

He shook his head. "I can't. I need to find my mother."

Peyter shook his head sadly. "Your home was the first one to go up in flames, my boy. It's too late to do anything for Lydia, but if you save yourself, you'll be saving her heart. She spoke of your return for so long… please," he begged, the beads capping his gray locks clattering against each other as he shook his head. "Please, you've got to go, now. While you still can!"

Kaden couldn't have been set for a more impossible challenge. "I can't. Not without knowing whether she's alive or dead," he said, then disengaged from Peyter and carefully pushed him in the direction of the forest. "Run, save yourself."

"Kaden—"

"Run!" He turned back onto the path and ran toward where he thought his home was in all this chaos. It was nearly impossible to tell, with every landmark on fire, but the plaza should be just up ahead, and then—

Jaws appeared through a wreathe of fire, snapping in his direction. Kaden dodged and brought Vrangar around, instinctually slashing out at the attack even as he moved into a defensive position. The beast roared, then stepped through the fire into the relative open.

It was a dragon.

A young one.

It had the appearance of a dragon, at least, with all its more fearsome attributes, but its wings seemed too small to lift it, and its teeth were more like needles than daggers. This… this was nothing like the Morvar Kaden had confronted before. What *was* this?

A roar from somewhere above shattered the impasse. To his surprise, the little dragon hissed balefully at Kaden, then turned and ran away as fast as its short, stubby legs could carry it. He followed it, ready to fight, but it climbed up to the top of the massive ash tree in the center of the plaza—a tree that had shaded Kaden's entire childhood, that now burned at half its original height and groaned from the weight of the dragon atop it—and raised its forelegs to the sky. A moment later, an enormous black talon descended from the smoke to snatch it out of the tree.

Fury tore from Kaden's chest as he recognized the massive black talon. Morvar. "Stop!" he shouted, staring fiercely into the sky for any sign of his adversary. "Come down and face me! *Come down to me!*"

There was nothing, though; no great bulk descending to the ground, no shudder of falling trees and broken buildings as Morvar made his presence known. There was only a hissing chuckle, and then a flurry of embers flew into Kaden's face, stinging him terribly as those immense wings beat hard enough to smother most of the fire as the dragon flew away.

Ashland was now true to its name, nothing but ash and burning embers in the wake of the vicious attack. Part of Kaden was screaming, screaming deep inside where he tried to push down all the fear and uncertainty he held about his place and the role he was meant to play. *Look at what happened. Look at your home. It's gone. And it's your fault!*

But that wasn't true, Kaden told himself as he began to stumble through the smoke for the place he'd called home. It wasn't true, and he was going to prove it. His mother... Lydia was still here. She was here; she wouldn't leave him like this, wondering about her. She was alive, and he was going to find her and tell her how sorry he was. He was going to beg her forgiveness and promise to make amends, and she would crush him to her chest and tell him she knew, and she forgave, and it was all right.

As long as he still had his mother, it would be all right.

The dead were everywhere. It was easy to get turned around in smoldering remnants of the town, and it felt like every direction Kaden turned, he found more bodies. More people he'd failed to save, more people he'd brought ruin on by standing up to Lucient and Morvar. Some of the bodies were charred beyond recognition, but others Kaden could still recognize.

There was Ma Shaye, the woman who'd been running the village school for the past fifty years. She'd taught Kaden his letters the same way she'd taught Daneyel, her back bent from so long bending over desks and guiding small hands across slate boards. He could tell she'd died in agony from her tortured expression.

There was Farmer Blake, who had the biggest fields in the whole village and generations of family to help care for them, everyone from his own mother to his grandchildren, still living in their immense house. That house was gone now. Kaden prayed to Orealus that some of them had escaped.

Leyton. Rubea. And Charlus, who used to race him up the ash tree in the plaza, daring each other to climb faster, higher. Charlus was slumped against a three-pronged pitchfork, each of its prongs dark with blood. He hadn't died of the fire; his throat had been ripped out, and his belly had too, everything inside of him eaten by a needle-toothed predator. *The baby dragons,* Kaden thought clearly, his eyes overflowing with tears now. They were just as bad as their sire. He wouldn't forget this, but he couldn't afford to focus on it right now; he had to find his mother, please, *Holy Orealus, hear me. Guide me to her. Let me find her before it's too late!*

Kaden wasn't sure if it was the result of his desperate prayer or just that he'd reached the outskirts of the village, but he finally recognized the telltale knots his mother used to tie a laundry line to a tree. The tree was charred, but the line was still attached. Kaden followed it into the smoke, and soon enough, he saw the ruins of his house. Two stories reduced to rubble, to nothing but tumbled mud brick, broken beams, and the tail ends of the thatch that had formed its roof.

"Mom!" he shouted, surging toward the ruin. "Mom!" *Please let me find her... No,* don't *let me find her, let her have run, let her find me this time—Mama, Mama—*

There was a cough nearby, just audible over his own shouting. Kaden went quiet and still, like he was tracking an animal, and Eldrin was judging to see how well he was doing. The cough sounded again, and Kaden followed it, ignoring the residual heat from the fire until he found—

"Mom!" He fell to his knees beside his mother's body, shoving aside the heavy wooden beam that had pinned her to the ground. "Oh, please, no," he whispered as he took in just how badly she was hurt. Her hair was burned away completely, leaving her scalp raw and red. Her chest looked concave in places, and her breathing was terribly rough. Red froth bubbled up in the corner of her mouth, and every one of her nails was broken from prying at the beam that had held her down. "Mama..."

"Kaden," Lydia whispered, her eyes widening as she realized who she was seeing. "*Kaden.*"

"It's me," he told her, his voice heavy with tears he couldn't let loose. Once he did, they might never stop, and he had work to do here. "It's me, I'm home. Mama, I'm sorry, I'm home now, I'm back."

"M' baby..."

"Yeah." He dashed his hand across his face; he would *not* cry right now. "It's me. Mama, it's going to be all right. I'm going to save you."

"T' late f'r me, baby."

Kaden laughed brokenly. "No, it's not! Mama, so much has happened since I left. I—I found out who I am. Who I *really* am, I mean, who my parents were before you and Daneyel. I'm blessed by Orealus, Mama, I have yah'zaval." He smiled. "And I'm going to use it to save you."

Lydia stared up at him, a little smile on her face. "Kaden," she gasped. "Kaden, baby, I love you."

"Don't speak right now," he said, closing his eyes and reaching inside of himself for his store of power. There wasn't as much as he'd like, but surely it would suffice for one person, one single rescue. *I pray to you, Orealus, God of Light, giver of hope and healing. Help me save my mother. She's your true servant, good and honorable, always generous and loving. She taught me everything I know about compassion and kindness. I pray to you, heal her. Save her life.*

Yah'zaval flowed through him and into his mother, and he heard her exclaim as her awful pain dwindled. Yes, yes, he was doing it! He was healing her! He could feel the worst of the damage in her chest slowly closing, and yet… yet it didn't seem to be enough. Even as he healed her, her life force seemed to slip away faster than he could replace it. "Mama, no," Kaden said, forcing more of his dwindling power into her.

"Kaden…"

"Mama, *no!*"

"Look at me, baby."

He cried out in pain as his own body began to weaken, the toll of the power he was taking too much. His heart began to race, and a headache like he'd never felt before began to sound through his head like a gong.

"My sweet boy. Look at me."

Reluctant but unwilling to disobey Lydia after he'd already left her alone for so long, Kaden looked down at her. The rawness across her scalp was healed, and some of the damage to her chest had been repaired, but her skin was going gray. She was dying right in front of him, and when Kaden reached inside himself for more, there was nothing left to draw upon.

"No," he whispered. "Please, Orealus, please. Please!"

Lydia lifted her hand like it weighed a hundred pounds, barely able to brush her fingertips across Kaden's cheek before she had to let it fall once more. "My darling son," she murmured. "I'm so blessed… to see you… one last time. I love… I love you." Her eyes closed, and her head began to tilt back to the ground.

"Mama?"

Her labored lungs slowed, and the blood that poured out of her wounds with each heartbeat went from a flood to a trickle.

"Ma?" Kaden's voice was almost inaudible. This couldn't be, it couldn't. He'd done everything right, hadn't he? He'd done what he was asked, he'd listened to the will of Orealus, he had fought *so hard* against *so many* awful beings, come so close to death himself, and now here he was, alive and well, and he couldn't save the last member of his family? His own mother?

"…" It started as a breath, just as labored in his healthy lungs as her final one was in her dying ones. As he watched, Lydia exhaled with a pained shudder and then…

She was gone. Gone, and Kaden couldn't do anything to bring her back. He couldn't track her to a distant castle or build a portal to her. Lydia, the only mother he'd ever known, was dead.

The scream that had been getting louder and louder in the back of Kaden's mind burst free from his lips. It overwhelmed everything, driving conscious thought from his mind as grief and guilt and *pain* took over, drowning out everything else. There was no quest, there was no Orealus; there was nothing to have faith in or pledge himself to.

His mother was dead, cruelly murdered. And with her, Kaden's faith broke.

CHAPTER 35

The devastation was painful to look at. The damage Thálassa had wrought in his latest attack, sudden and furious, unseen even by Varun's most distant spies, was impossible to overstate.

More than painful, it had the capacity to break him if King Varun allowed it. If he allowed himself to gaze upon the ruin of Nethopolis—the city he was born to rule, the city he had done his best by in the hundreds of years it had been under his protection—and let his emotions get the better of him? He would be ruined along with it, broken under the weight of his own regard for the place that was the heart of him. He had to keep working. If he stopped, he might not move again.

There was plenty of work to do. Too many of his people were caught in damage, swept up in the ruin that for a while had seemed like it would consume them all. Varun wasn't going to let it, though, not without a fight.

He went out into Nethopolis with his recovery teams, leaving the defense of the city to the head of his personal guard as he shifted rubble, tore apart broken buildings, and summoned every ounce of his strength to rescue merfolk who were trapped in the wreckage. For every one person he saved, he knew another passed, despite all the effort he and his workers were putting into it, but it was better than nothing. It was better than ruing fate or Orealus, better than staring into the void that threatened to overwhelm him. He was their king; they depended on him. Even if he couldn't offer them perfect protection, he could at least offer them his help when they needed it most.

"There you are," he crooned to a little girl whom he'd just uncovered, trapped beside her father's body for the past two days. Spotters had heard her whimpering, and even though the home seemed so collapsed that no one should have survived in it, Varun had put his will—and his considerable strength—into digging her out. And now he'd found her, and… "Oh, little one." Her tail was partially crushed, but he thought that with some proper healing, she could recover enough to swim again. He lifted her into his arms and brought her out, and a muted cheer rose up from the other rescuers.

Varun didn't chide them for it, even though part of him wanted to snap that this was hardly the moment to celebrate. Her father had died there alongside her; her mother might be anywhere, quite probably dead as well. The child was injured and traumatized and alone… but they needed any reason to keep going, to keep their spirits up. She was the first living person they'd found that day. It was the third day after Thálassa's attack.

Varun handed her off to the healers, then turned back to the rubble to free her father's body. By the time he found the third person in the rubble of another room, his heart was heavy enough that when word came that his queen was requesting his presence, Varun took the chance to go instead of pressing on. He needed a moment, just a moment, to look away from destruction.

He didn't expect Dinereus to pull him toward the crystal room the moment he arrived at the palace entrance. "There is something you have to see," she said somberly. A chill traveled down Varun's tail.

"What happened?" he demanded as they made their way to the seeing chamber. All around him, servants were working on shoring up the parts of the palace that had been damaged. Part of him wanted to tell them to go, to refocus their efforts on places that needed the help more, but he understood the optics of such work as well. If the palace stood strong, the people would be heartened. Leaving it a wreck wasn't an option. At least they'd turned some of the larger rooms into triage spaces for wounded merfolk. "Did something happen above us?" Surely Kaden couldn't be calling them to fight already. He didn't want to say no to the young man, but Nethopolis had to come first under the circumstances.

"I'm afraid so," she said, long hair waving as she nodded reluctantly.

A hundred different visions immediately began to vie for control in his mind. Some were worse than others, but the worst of all… "Has Orealus's champion fallen?" he murmured to Dinereus, hardly able to bring himself to ask the question. Her head shake heartened him a bit, but her next words trampled that moment of hope back into the seabed.

"His home was attacked as well," she said as they reached the private room where their viewing crystal stretched from wall to wall. "The damage done… well, look for yourself, Varun."

Despite his exhaustion, Varun reached into his yah'zaval and bent the crystal to his will. "Show me the home of Kaden Sheppard," he said, and the swirling potential of the crystal sharpened into a scene that was—*Oh, Orealus, say it isn't so.*

Everywhere he looked, there was fire, or rather, the effects of fire. Varun had little exposure to that element, but he understood its intense destructiveness. Fire was the riptide of the dry world, a surging, hungry force that ruined everything caught in its wake. And the damage that had been done to this place…

What were once tall trees now smoldered as little more than stumps, surrounded by their own riven pieces. The earth itself had been charred in places, long, sweeping arcs of blackness that put Varun in mind of something he hadn't seen for a very long time. Homes had been destroyed, fields reduced to ash, and the humans stumbling around seemed dazed, lost in the horror of what had happened to them. Varun understood that look very well; he'd seen it on the faces of his own people time and again.

But the people were in fairly clean clothes, some of them sporting bandages… so the fire hadn't just happened. "When was this?" he asked his wife.

"Several days ago, from what I can glean," she said. "It seems to have occurred at almost the same time as the attack here by Thálassa."

Varun's expression of concern twisted into a scowl. *Of course.* He sensed the hand of their mortal enemy guiding this. "And Kaden?" he said, his voice an octave lower than it had been a moment ago.

"See for yourself."

There was an undercurrent to his wife's voice that concerned him, but Varun was too intent on learning the truth to pursue it right now. "Show me Kaden Sheppard," he said, and the vision shifted. Now they were in the forest, a section unburnt and still green and vibrant. The focus of the vision was on a disturbed patch of earth, fresh soil recently tamped down into a rough hillock. The space next to it was also slightly rounded over, and then Varun saw the rough-hewn headstone at the top of what he now knew to be a grave.

"Daneyel Sheppard," read one side of the wooden marker in savagely scrawled letters. "Lydia Sheppard," read the other. There were no dates. No descriptions. Only their names. The last name told Varun enough; grimly, he pulled the vision back a bit until he could see the foot of the graves. And there…

"Oh," he whispered, the mild current momentarily taking his breath away. "Oh, Kaden."

The young man was hardly recognizable. It wasn't just the dirt smeared across his hands and arms, or the soot that dulled his face and turned his hair gray. It wasn't just the way his clothes were fraying around the edges, burnt here and there, stained with unmentionable substances. It wasn't even that his armor and sword were nowhere to be seen, which was dangerous given how important they were to the cause. Wasn't his quest to regain the Armor of Orealus? Didn't he need it to take on Lucient? So where was it?

All of that gave Varun a moment's pause, but that apprehension was nothing compared to what he felt when he finally got a good look at Kaden's face. The light that had been such a clear, fateful part of him, a lightness of spirit that reflected through his eyes and out for everyone to see, was gone. All of it dimmed, like a candle guttering into smoke… *or a village reduced to its very bones,* Varun reflected sadly.

Varun had seen this look before. He had seen it in Nethopolis, in those who survived when others did not. Survival without purpose hollowed the spirit faster than death ever could, and left even the strongest drifting in its wake.

Kaden's lips were moving, but no sound came forth. It took a moment for Varun to realize that he was chanting "I'm sorry, I'm sorry, I'm sorry," over and over again, staring at his parents' graves as if he'd personally put them there. The thought tormented him. Lucient's designs were too deep, too patient, for a boy with such an open heart to have anticipated. Not yet, not at such a young age. Evil for some people quickly became a way of life—one taste of the power that it could bring you, and they were hooked. Others had to learn the machinations of true evil by brutal experience to combat it.

Varun searched the vision instinctively for the quiet resonance of Orealus's will. It was there, distant and watchful, like a presence holding its breath. The will of Orealus did not reach the boy. It did not withdraw either. It simply waited.

Varun had gone through his own trials when it came to the nature of evil in his life—his own brother wanted him dead. His people had been driven to the brink, and his capital was falling around him. He understood better than most how hard it could be. But Kaden… "Where are his companions?" he asked Dinereus. "They should be with him right now. The death of a parent is a wound that no one should have to face on their own."

"I couldn't find them," she admitted, concern written across her face. "It's as though all yah'zaval itself is focusing on Kaden right now, unable to look away."

The crystal did not respond to distance or direction. It responded to the gravity of the soul. Grief bent yah'zaval toward itself, warping even sacred sight around the wound it left behind.

"My husband, I fear… I fear this may be the thing that breaks him."

"No," Varun said immediately. "He's stronger than that. Kaden is the chosen of Orealus; our god won't forsake him in his hour of need."

"Look at him," his wife urged. "Don't you think he already feels forsaken? His father died at the beginning of his quest, and now his mother has followed. I think it's safe to assume that both were violent deaths. How do you think a young man—a boy in some respects, not yet twenty—will handle that? Will he look at these events and see the vile hand of Lucient, and let that knowledge pull him closer to Orealus, or will he see only his own failure? That he must have been found wanting by Orealus, and that's why he wasn't able to save his mother?"

"That's not how Orealus is!"

"And Kaden is not a scholar of religion or philosophy," Dinereus said firmly. "He was raised a farmer, not a fighter. He isn't sanguine or understanding about death. He wants to save everyone, and now he's failed to save one of the most important people in his life. Worse yet, he has no one around to tell him that he's not to blame for losing her."

Where are his friends? Varun tried to use his own yah'zaval to change the vision to Kaden's companions, but Dinereus was right. The crystal was fixed on Kaden, on his agonizing loss and his fall from grace.

"They'll find him," he said out loud, half to his wife and half to convince himself. "Kaden's friends will find him. They'll help him recover, help him learn to deal with the loss. He'll be all right."

"I'm not so sure," Dinereus said, sadly contemplative as she looked into the crystal. "I think this might be a mortal blow, my love."

"He has a destiny he cannot escape."

"Grief makes a mockery of every plan, even those of fate. He—" She stopped speaking as the scene suddenly changed. A sheathed sword landed on top of the freshly turned earth. The weapon was elegant and deadly, and now discarded like a piece of broken crockery. A second later, Kaden got to his feet, staggered for a moment until he caught himself against a tree, then turned and shuffled deeper into the forest. The canopy was so thick that he was almost impossible to see, but it was clear that he carried nothing other than his ragged clothes and the weight of his mother's death on him.

"We must prepare ourselves to survive the coming battles without him," Dinereus said.

"He'll recover," Varun insisted, even though a part of him wondered if he was being truthful or simply stubborn. "Once his friends find him again, they'll bring him back to himself. They'll help him."

"*If* they find him," Dinereus said softly as the image faded.

A champion alone was not merely vulnerable. He was malleable.

CHAPTER 36

It was cold. Bhalla turned instinctively to reach for the thick wool blanket he kept close for nights like this, then groaned as pain surged down his back and settled into his hips. He was not in his bed. He was flat on his back on stone, and from the deep ache in his bones, he had been there for a long time.

Grit stuck to his cheek as he slowly turned his head and tried to look around. It was dark where he was, like a starless night in the depths of the forest, and yet there seemed to be something shimmering in that impenetrable darkness. Something flowed through the darkness like a narrow silver current. It was familiar. A glimmer he had seen before.

His memories crashed into him all at once. The warning about Evias. Their confrontation. His demand to know where Asitra had gone was answered with a portal and darkness.

Asitra! Now he knew why that glimmer was familiar. She had a silver thread worked into one of her braids, part of an ancient altar that had been repurposed generations ago. That silver, steeped in the long presence of Orealus, carried the faintest hint of his light along with it. That meant...

"Asitra," he tried to say, then began to cough uncontrollably. Curse his *lungs*, curse his dry *throat*, curse the way he felt undone by pain, and he'd only just woken up. To live long enough to see old age was a blessing, yet there were aspects of it he could certainly do without.

"Bhalla? You're awake?" There was a pause, then the light brightened a bit. A moment later, he could see Asitra's face, and his heart clenched harder than any pain in his body. One of her eyes was swollen shut, and several teeth were missing behind bleeding, cracked lips. Her nose was broken, her eyebrows had been burnt off… she'd been tortured most cruelly.

"I wasn't sure," she said—babbled, really, oh, his poor friend. "I thought I might just be imagining it, I've imagined so many wonderful things since I was brought here; I think it's all that's been keeping me sane." She swallowed hard. "Am I still sane?"

"You are," he assured her with his creaky voice. "You're still sane, my dear. I'm here. I'm real." He let out a bit of a groan. "Although I must say, part of me wishes I wasn't."

She didn't quite laugh, but quirked a tiny smile on her lips. "I understand. I… did Evias get you as well, then? He must have. Curse him, I should have been more careful of him," she snarled, anger coming to the fore where before there had only been resignation and fear. "I should have left a note, left some trail for you to follow, a hint of my suspicions. Instead, he took me by surprise. I've been here for… I don't even know how long."

Bhalla couldn't say how long it had been, either, entirely to his shame. "What matters now is that we're together," he said, sitting all the way up. He scooted over to her, pleased and a bit surprised to find that he was completely unshackled. "You'd think they'd have tied us up," he commented.

"Who, Lucient? No." She shook her head. "The only way into and out of this dungeon is a portal, and the stone itself is steeped in dunntaika, so dense that I cannot reach my yah'zaval abilities. It's like… like trying to light a fire in a windstorm. I can see the flame for a moment, I can almost feel its heat, but then it's smothered before it has a chance to grow."

"Ah." That was a clever, if rather passive trap for anyone in… "I assume we're in the dungeons of Talaifotia, then," he said, adjusting his worldview by rather a lot when Asitra nodded at him. To be in the lair of Lucient himself, to be so *feared* by a god that the only secure place they could be held was in a web of dunntaika… it was almost a compliment.

Far better that it was a sign of how deeply they were underestimated, however.

"My faith has failed us," Asitra said, her voice breaking. "I haven't given anything away to Lucient, I swear to you, but… neither have I been able to reach Orealus with my prayers. I live, but I fear I won't for much longer. Soon Lucient will get tired of toying with me and start in on you, and I don't have the strength to prevent him. I'm sorry, Bhalla. I'm so sorry!"

"My dear," Bhalla said gently, slowly rubbing life back into his chilled hands, "I do not doubt the depths of your devotion to Orealus. How could I? You *live*. You have survived foul torment, and even now your faith responds to the silver in your hair." Her hand, several fingers brutally twisted out of place, rose to touch her braid. "You speak of your power being smothered, and that is true. This is a dire place." He patted her shoulder. "But I think between the two of us, we might yet be able to break through the darkness that's swallowed us and see the light yet again. I—"

There was a deep rumble overhead, as if the mountain itself were moving… or screaming. "And I think we'd better do so as expeditiously as possible," Bhalla finished up. "Come, now. Sit with me, and let us find a path to Orealus together."

Far above the dungeons of Talaifotia, Lucient looked out on the chaos he had created and felt the fierce thrill that only bloodletting could bring. So much death. So much despair. All of creation lay open for him to bruise, batter, and destroy at will. And he did. He would burn it all down in the name of rebuilding, create a new and better society that understood its place was beneath him… but first, he would steal every part of it from Orealus.

He had already begun so well.

"An inspired use of that winged brute, my lord," Baal purred as he stepped up beside him, sharing in his vision of Ashland's annihilation. He draped an arm over his shoulder, and Lucient considered whether or not he should remove it for the other's impertinence. But his good mood was powerful enough that he let it go.

"Morvar is easy enough to control once one understands his vices."

Baal hummed in agreement. "That is true for almost everyone, I've found."

Naturally, the Lord of Chaos would see the wisdom in Lucient's methods. Baal might present himself as a beautiful woman, red-haired and fair-skinned and designed to tempt, but beneath it, he was a ravenous creature who thrived on the unexpected. He could tempt a saint to sin, or a city to fall.

"Perhaps even you, my lord."

Lucient's patience vanished, and he shoved Baal away even as he raked a hand down his general's face, leaving four bleeding scratch marks that went all the way to the bone. Baal stumbled, shrieking so loud it reverberated throughout the stone itself, and clutched at the wound, which was blackening already.

"Do not presume to know my weaknesses," Lucient snapped. "Or prepare for me to take advantage of your own."

Baal prostrated himself on the floor. "Forgive me, my lord. I spoke out of turn in my excitement for your impending victory."

"So you did." Lucient was still tempted to make this into a punishment Baal would never forget, but there was too much to do. His other generals had arrived during the altercation and waited in shifting silence on the other side of his throne room. He looked at them. "Approach," Lucient commanded.

They came, Vicitious stumping on all fours, Ozul gliding forward with an aura of flames extending behind him, and Defyle leaving a trail of writhing maggots in his wake, tiny mirrors of his own monstrous shape. The Lord of Lies, the Soul Reaper, and the Defiler—all fallen spirits like him, all eager to get the ultimate vengeance against Orealus for causing their fall in the first place. The Lord of Light had lost before, but this time... this time his worship would never rise from the ashes they left it in. Lucient would make sure of it.

He had already begun strongly by breaking the spirit of the last of King Karatheas's line. Breaking the boy's body would soon follow. Perhaps he would torture Bhalla in front of Kaden first... make him watch as his mentor screamed in agony while Lucient let his generals loose on the frail old man's body.

The mere thought of it made him shiver with anticipation.

"It's time to gather troops," he told his assembled generals. "The days of creeping in the shadows are over. I want preparations underway for assaults on all the major cities of the lands of Empyrea."

"All?" Ozul clarified, his voice a dry hiss.

"All." No metropolis would be spared, not even those belonging to his allies. Oh, Lucient would make sure to use them first, but where there were large groups of beings, there was the possibility for dissent, and that was something he wouldn't tolerate. First, he would use them to fight, then he would cleanse them as well, until all that was left was a perfect, barren land ripe for rebuilding.

The survivors would thank him someday.

"The forges are running day and night," he went on, "and soon there will be enough armor and weapons to equip ten thousand. Each of you will take a quarter of this and prepare a personal force to lead your larger battalions. Choose your lieutenants wisely; I want them to be utterly relentless. There can be no turning back, no surrender, no negotiation. They win, or they die. If they die, strip them of their armor and choose again."

"I will drive them before me." Defyle laughed, a choked, glutted sound. "To retreat would only mean to feed me better."

"What will our first target be?" Vicitious asked. Lucient stared at him until Vicitious bowed his head. "My lord," he added obsequiously.

Lucient smiled, his good mood finally returning at the thought of what was going to happen next. "Lumhagen," he said. "Of course. A little more time to work on the wizards in the dungeon, and we'll have the quickest ways into the city."

"The wizard Asitra has been uncommonly determined in the face of torture," Baal murmured. Lucient glared at him, but his general stared meekly at the floor.

"She will be less determined after we start removing her limbs. Let us—"

Lucient shuddered as a feeling of utter wrongness spread across him. It was like being dipped in acid, like burning alive in a holy fire. It was… *Orealus*. But—no, the Lord of Light couldn't affect Talaifotia, Lucient had made *sure* of that! Unless…

Ignoring his generals' cries of agony, Lucient transported himself to the dungeon. As he stepped through the layers of dunntaika securing the wizards' cell, the pain sharpened. Yah'zaval, the distillation of Orealus himself, *here*! He watched in dumbfounded awe as a golden, glowing portal erupted around his prisoners, whisking them out from under his nose in less than a second.

They were gone. His wizards had used their faith to summon his dire enemy into his own stronghold, and had faith that was so strong it penetrated *centuries* of his own layers of power. That… that should be impossible.

Lucient stared at the place where they had been and felt, for the first time in a long time, something close to foreboding.

A thousand miles away, Bhalla and Asitra tumbled onto the main floor of the Truthoriam. Even as a furor erupted around them, Bhalla let the power of Orealus spread across every level of their home until all within it could hear his voice and feel the truth he was about to speak.

"The Great Deceiver has penetrated our sacred home," he said, yah'zaval singing through every part of his body. "He lurks among us with the face of a friend, but we have finally seen past his lies. Today, we put an end to his meddling. Today, we will shift the tide in the war against Lucient.

"Today, we move Lumhagen beyond the reach of our enemy." The act of ensuring Lumhagen remained a sanctuary of light meant it would be cut off from the outer world, only penetrable by those who had yah'zaval, but it was worth it to save them from destruction.

I should tell Kaden. No. Afterward, Bhalla decided.

After all, the young man was no doubt busy with his own adventures. They had time.

CHAPTER 37

Everything felt heavy. The light filtering through the canopy pressed on him as much as the darkness had at nightfall, birdsong fading into the cautious movements of animals at dusk. Every step was an effort, his toes dragging through the loam as he pulled himself forward. Moving hurt, but the thought of stopping hurt more.

To stop and look at his failure again? To take the time to inspect it from all sides, pull it out from the depths of his mind, and examine it in all the detail he couldn't stand? That was worse than heavy; that would be death. And for all that he hated life right now, Kaden couldn't bring himself to seek death. Not deliberately, at any rate.

Not yet.

He moved for as long as he could, drifting through the shadowed forest like a wraith and keeping himself alive more out of habit than anything. Drinking water came from creeks, and once from a rainfall that soaked the last of the smoky scent of his ruined home off him and left him sobbing like a baby at the loss. Food was less interesting—a berry here, an edible root there when he happened to catch sight of one, but the painful pang in his stomach was more comforting than not.

Pain was what he deserved. He should suffer for every way he had failed them. His friends. His father. His mother.

Sometimes, they walked with him. Usually at night, when the light didn't poke holes through his illusions. Kaden would be ambling along, determinedly not thinking about anything, maybe cradling his middle as he did more and more now as it ached worse and worse, and then the next thing he knew, someone would be there, walking with him.

Often it was Petey or Duke, and they were the best companions because they didn't expect him to talk to them, just walked along in comforting silence. Sometimes it was Eldrin or Weylyn, more rarely one of the dwarves, and they were harder but still tolerable. They would berate him, tell Kaden he was a coward and a fool and a bad son and leader, but they never expected anything back. He could take their abuse in silence and let that be all of it.

The worst ones were the people who were able to be soft with him. Usually, it was Ada, reaching out for Kaden with an open expression and eager arms, but he couldn't bear for her to even want to touch him. He couldn't look at her, so he'd walk for hours in circles, always turning away from the side where she appeared until the mirage finally gave in and vanished. Worst of all was Pepper. Sometimes, when he looked at her, she became Lydia.

No. Kaden would sooner gouge out his own eyes than face his mother right now.

Hallucinations haunted him while he was awake, and nightmares haunted his sleep. Kaden never got more than an hour or two of rest at a time, always waking up gasping and shaking as the fire and screaming faded from behind his eyes. He was surprised he didn't dream of Morvar; for all that the dragon was the source of his wanderings and woes, he simply didn't appear in Kaden's visions. Instead, his sleep was filled with images he did not understand. Darkness and death. A wraith wrapped in shadow. Beauty tangled with blood. The serpentine tail of a familiar foe. One-on-one, they were intimidating. All together, they kept Kaden awake for literal days from fear of falling asleep again.

Finally, he stumbled and fell onto his hands and knees for what felt like the tenth time that day… night? Kaden couldn't really tell anymore; there was nothing to differentiate the states with a mind as stricken as his. He fell, and for the first time in a long while, he did not want to get back up again. He didn't want to move at all, actually. It was… good, to be still. Less heavy than moving, less heavy than breathing.

He rolled over onto his back and stared upward, watching wind shift distant leaves and change the chiaroscuro effect all around him. It was transfixing, almost relaxing. His heartbeat slowed, going from frantic to easy and slow, and Kaden's cracked lips stretched in an unfamiliar expression he finally identified as a smile.

He could stop. He could stop now, and nothing would ask anything of him again. For once, no one was pushing him. No one was yelling at him or frowning or, worse yet, saying that he'd be okay. He would never be okay again, and *that* was all right too, because he could just… stop. Finally, he could stop. All he had to do was close his eyes and let his weary heart rest.

It sounded so simple, and yet Kaden couldn't quite bring himself to look away from the mesmerizing play of light and dark. It was beautiful, and it both hurt and relieved him to know that he could still think of *something* as beautiful. Simple, natural beauty, nothing exceptional or emotional about it. It was perfect, and finally, Kaden felt true acceptance begin to filter through his mind and body. It was all right. He could stop. He *had* stopped, and now the only thing left to do was let go.

Close your eyes. Close your eyes. Close them…

But just before his lashes touched down on his cheek, the beauty above him was blocked by a shadow he didn't understand. It looked vaguely humanoid, but concealed by so many scarves that Kaden couldn't even begin to guess the nature of the person's species. Was this another vision? Had he been found by a goblin? Was he about to be murdered? *That would be all right too…*

But no, there was no death in the hands of his new keeper. Only a quiet oath, then a hard hand under the back of his head, right at the connection of neck and skull. It lifted him, and then there was a cold metal rim pressing against his mouth, followed by a trickle of water. The liquid tasted strange, as metallic as the vessel it came from, but as soon as the first droplets found their way down his throat, Kaden realized he was terribly thirsty. He gulped once, twice, then tried to sit up and get more, but the figure above him shook their head.

"No. Slowly. Or not at all. The last thing we need is for you to choke to death when I'm trying to bring you back to life."

"Who… who are you?" Kaden asked hoarsely. His body longed for water, but he didn't have the strength to demand it. All he could do was beg for respite, and he'd like to know the name of the person he was begging.

There was a long pause before the man finally said, "My name is Ezrah." His eyes, the only part of his face Kaden could really see, were intent, as if he was waiting for Kaden to react in some way.

"Ezrah." The name was sharp and unfamiliar on his tongue. "I don't know you."

His savior shook his head. "Not for a long time, no. But I know you, Kaden Sheppard. Or should I say Kaden Rosenhelm?"

Kaden shut his eyes. "That is not who I am."

"It is. You can't escape it, even though you might want to."

"Watch me."

Ezrah laughed. It wasn't a happy sound. "Oh, I did. I watched you almost succumb to despair and die right in front of me. Do you have any idea—no, of course you don't, if you did, you'd never have done something so stupid. Kaden, you're *important*."

"I'm defective."

"That's not true."

"It is." He was positive about it. "I've failed the most important people in my life. My family… I don't have one anymore."

There was that strange, intent look in the eyes again. "Yes, you do."

Now it was Kaden's turn to laugh. "Call them what you want, but my friends and my family aren't the same thing." They occupied two very different places in his heart, no matter how his mind tried to conflate the two. His friends were important to him, enormous parts of his life and what he used to think of as his future, but his family was the foundation on which everything about him had been built. Without them, he was crumbling.

"Kaden." With his free hand, the man undid the scarves covering his face. The visage he revealed was startlingly familiar. It took Kaden a long moment to realize that he might as well be looking into a mirror, except for the scar over the other man's right eye. "You do," Ezrah said firmly. "You do still have family. You have *me*."

Kaden stared at Ezrah for a long moment, and a sliver of the despair inside him gave way to a new emotion: curiosity. It was refreshing, reviving, and he groaned as he tried to sit up. Ezrah helped him—dragging him a way until his back was against a thick, moss-cool tree—then sat down a few feet in front of him. When he handed over the canteen of water, Kaden was a bit surprised that he was able to hold it, but he drank his fill before saying, "Tell me who you are."

Ezrah shook his head. "What, you don't even know your history?"

"History was a forbidden subject even in Ashland," Kaden replied. "You never knew who might be listening."

"Not much of an excuse."

"Are you going to talk or not?" Kaden asked harshly.

"I am, I just…" Kaden was surprised to see the other man looking somewhat flustered. "I didn't think I'd have to include a lesson on who I am. I thought you'd know, at least the name."

"Well, I don't."

"Clearly." Ezrah took a deep breath. "King Karatheas had four children. The oldest two, Doran and Elaena, died during the war. The younger two were both presumed dead as well for a long time. You know what happened to yourself by now, of course."

"Bhalla took me from my cradle and saved me," Kaden said dully. *I wish he hadn't, I wish he'd left me, I wish—*

"And the third child watched him leave with you, and was found by Lucient not long after."

It took Kaden far too long to put it all together. "You are my brother?"

"Ezrah Rosenhelm," he said quietly. "But I don't use our last name either. Too many people out there who would be happy to carve it into my skin, then cut it out again."

Kaden's eyes were so wide they stung. "You can't be all that older than me," he whispered. For all Ezrah looked hard as nails, there was a youthfulness to him as well.

"Three years older." He smiled mirthlessly. "Old enough to acknowledge my mistakes."

Kaden shook his head. "What mistakes?"

"Leaving you alone as a baby."

Oh, that was crap. "You couldn't have been more than a toddler."

"I was your brother, and I was told to watch you. Protect you."

"You should never have been given that sort of responsibility."

Ezrah's eyes gleamed with anger. "We were princes," he snapped. "I, at least, knew what that meant by the time our castle was under attack. I knew my responsibility to you, and I failed it. If blame must exist, it rests with me."

That was the most wrong thing of all the wrong things that Kaden had ever heard in his life. "You were a *child*. A frightened child!"

"And you were a baby, and if I'd just stayed with you, we could have been rescued together, and you wouldn't be looking at me now like I'm a stranger!"

All right, that was... too much for Kaden to parse through right now. He was too tired for an argument, too close to the brink of exhaustion. "Our pain isn't a competition," he said, and to his surprise, Ezrah smiled.

"No," he agreed. "It's not. By Orealus, you..." He shook his head. "It's strange, but even when you were a baby, you had a way about you. A presence, a—something that softened arguments and quieted voices. You've been a peacemaker from the day you were born, brother. And I don't want to fight you now." Ezrah leaned forward a bit. "I want to help you."

Kaden licked his dry, cracked lips. He wanted more water, but he didn't feel capable of breaking Ezrah's gaze yet. "Help me with what?" he asked.

"Your quest. The awful, terrible burden that's been laid upon you without you even really knowing why." Ezrah's lip curled with disgust. "It's unconscionable, everything that you've been asked to do for no other reason than that you're the only Rosenhelm Bhalla could find to fulfil our family's destiny." He finally looked down, and Kaden was left feeling breathless.

"I want to destroy Lucient," Ezrah murmured. "I was his prisoner for over a decade. He hurt me, he took my family, he ruined everything good I ever had in this world, and yet I don't want you to lose yourself because of it. This?" He waved a hand around in a general manner. "Everything that's happened to you, everything you've gone through? The fact that you were given no choice at all? I hate that. You deserve better, Kaden, and I'm going to make sure you *get* better."

Kaden was startled by the strength in the other man's—his *brother's*—voice. There was a determination there that he wanted to tap into, a vivacity and decisiveness that he was going to need if he really wanted to survive. "I don't know if I can," he said after a moment. Best to be honest with Ezrah. "Get better. I feel… well. You saw me."

"I did. And I've been there too," Ezrah said. "And no one knows how to get out of a hole that deep better than someone who's done it before. It's taken me a long time to finally rejoin you, my brother." His lips curled in a fierce grin. "But I'll be damned if you're ever taken from me again. Whatever comes next, we'll face it together. I swear it on my soul."

Ezrah's vow was simple and fierce, and its power settled into Kaden's mind like a glowing ember of hope. It was the first he had felt since before returning to Ashland. Maybe, just maybe, there was a way forward for him after all.

CHAPTER 38

Being with Ezrah was both rewarding and challenging. His older brother did not believe in starting slow, and it was still strange and quietly wonderful to think of him that way. Kaden might be half-starved, emotionally destroyed, and mentally on the verge of collapse, but that didn't stop Ezrah from plying him with tasks from the moment he woke up in the morning to the moment he finally went to sleep at night.

He started with deceptively simple tasks. "Fill the canteens at the stream." "Make the fire." They were easy, but also hard, simply because Kaden's body was exhausted. Still, these were things he knew he could do, and although it took him longer than he liked, Kaden was able to handle them.

Ezrah didn't stop there, though. "Can you sharpen a blade?"

"I…" Guilt struck as Kaden remembered leaving Vrangar, and the pieces of Orealus's armor they had bled for, on his mother's grave. "I haven't had to learn. My blade never dulled."

"Then you'll practice on mine." His brother pulled out a truly wicked-looking pair of short swords, handed one to Kaden, then got out a whetstone. "Watch me." He unsheathed one of the blades and inspected it until he found a nick, then laid the sword on his thigh, edge out, and began to methodically work the stone against the metal. The sound was grating, the sight of those killing blades even worse, and

Kaden was only able to watch for a minute before he turned away and vomited onto the ground.

So much blood. His mother, red with it and gray with ash, her dark skin pallid as she bled into the ground…

Ezrah crouched beside him, one hand on Kaden's back, the other offering one of the newly filled canteens. He waited for Kaden to rinse his mouth out before saying, "You can't afford to have an aversion to weaponry."

Kaden's stomach churned, but he nodded. "I know." No future for him didn't include weapons of all sorts, fighting, and death. It made him think, with a brief burst of longing, of how nice it would have been if Ezrah hadn't come. If he could just have collapsed and died and never bothered anyone ever again. His friends could rally around a new hero—Ezrah fit the bill, he was clearly better prepared for a life of war than Kaden—and go on to fight Lucient and all his forces, and know they were worthy of it. While Kaden…

"No." His brother cuffed the side of his head—gently, but firmly. "Whatever you are thinking, stop. Turn around. Sit up. Watch."

Kaden, creaking like he was eighty years old, did so. He watched his brother begin to sharpen again, and this time the visions that came to him didn't hit quite so hard. When Ezrah passed the whetstone over and nodded for him to continue, Kaden's stomach rebelled once more, but eventually he was able to work with the sword.

"There, you see?" Ezrah smiled at him, and Kaden was so surprised by that soft expression on his brother's face that he smiled back. "You just need to keep working at it. That is all living is, Kaden. The will to keep trying in the face of the impossible."

Ezrah had learned that not everyone who served the Light did so in daylight. Some worked where prayers came too late, and mercy only slowed the blade. The Shadowblades did not speak of honor. They spoke of the outcome. They believed the Light did not falter because it was weak, but because it hesitated. Someone had to act where faith could not wait, and so they did. Not for glory. Not for mercy. Only so the world might survive long enough to be redeemed.

"No matter how bad things seem, no matter how bleak, there's always another step to take. Now, come check the snares with me."

Over the course of the next few days, Kaden went from shuddering at the feel of steel and the sight of a dead rabbit to being able to handle a knife to skin their evening meal himself. He didn't like it, but he could do it, and he realized that his brother had been so incremental with him that it hardly hurt at all. Walks became runs. Basic forms became real fights. With food and rest, Kaden's body slowly answered the effort with returning strength.

His mind, or more precisely his spirit, was another matter entirely.

"Faith can't be contingent upon never experiencing tragedy," Ezrah said during one of their evening discussions. "If that were the case, either everyone would be faithful or no one ever would be. Orealus never promised a life without trials."

"Why not, though?" Kaden responded hotly. "Think about it, think about what you went through. What the *king* went through."

"Our father," Ezrah corrected.

"Your father."

"You can include both of yours, and the lesson remains the same," Ezrah replied, unfazed by Kaden's anger. "They died fighting for what was right. Orealus's teachings say—"

"They were better students of Orealus's teachings than I've ever been, and they still died!" Kaden snapped.

"And in so doing have been reunited with him. Just because *we* don't understand Orealus's plan doesn't mean there isn't one, Kaden."

"But they were better than me. More skilled. More faithful. More prepared!" Kaden felt tears burn in his eyes, but ignored them as they began to trail down his face. "Why should I get to live, when I'm such a poor student? Of them, of Orealus, of *all* of it. I'm not any more worthy than anyone else. I'm *less* worthy than my fathers, less worthy than my mothers."

"You're not," Ezrah said calmly. "Orealus has faith in you. You just have to have faith back."

"Then what about you?" Kaden asked, snide and trying to hurt, though he knew he shouldn't be. "How deep is *your* faith these days, after a decade of torture and imprisonment? Why would a loving god leave you to suffer through so much? What did you do to cause him to turn away from you?"

"We're talking about you, not me," Ezrah replied in an unfazed, almost bored tone of voice. "But I don't look back on what I went through and blame Orealus for it."

"No," Kaden agreed. "You blame yourself, and that's worse. You were a child, you weren't even five, how could you have—"

"You're very quick to argue for my forgiveness," Ezrah interjected. "Why are you so unwilling to argue for your own forgiveness?"

And Kaden had no good answer for him.

Attempting to use his yah'zaval again took almost a week, because at first, Kaden was certain there was no point. He didn't feel the light of Orealus inside of him anymore. Heck, the amulet at his chest no longer answered him. It had gone inert on his chest, dead in his presence. If that wasn't a sign that he'd lost the favor of Orealus, then nothing was.

Ezrah didn't buy it, because of course he didn't. He also didn't let Kaden wallow in his sorrow, pushing him to meditate alongside him every evening. "Just let your thoughts pass through your head," he murmured into the darkness behind Kaden's eyelids. "Let them pass right by. There's no need to hold onto them, no need to feel anything about them. Observe them and let them go again."

Meditation was so much harder than Kaden had thought it would be. Letting go of his thoughts? Not feeling anything about the awful images his mind fed him over and over again? Impossible. The first time he tried, he collapsed to the ground, curled in on himself, and wept as visions of his dead parents stared back in silent accusation.

"I hate this," Kaden had croaked to Ezrah as his brother helped him sit up.

"I know," Ezrah replied. "But your mind isn't trying to punish you. It's trying to help you by allowing you to resolve these invasive thoughts so they can't control you again. If you can think these things with enough distance that you don't hurt yourself with them, that's a real improvement. It isn't about forgetting," he added quietly when Kaden shook his head. "It's about remembering without damaging yourself."

Kaden wanted to fight him about it, but he couldn't muster the energy. So he sat there, night after night, and learned to deal with the torment his brain saw fit to inflict on him. The pangs in his heart, the way his breath shuddered and shook in his lungs, the way all his muscles tried to turn to water and collapse around him... the pain never stopped, but he did manage to stay upright by the fifth night.

But accessing his yah'zaval... reaching out and talking to Orealus once more... *I can't. I've failed so badly. I can't do it.*

"You have to try," Ezrah said, reading his thoughts—or more likely, his face—from a ways away.

"I'm not worthy."

"Orealus is a god of forgiveness, Kaden. He will understand."

How can he? But Kaden knew he wasn't getting out of this. He wiped his hands over his wet cheeks, then got into a kneeling position. One shaking hand made the symbol of Orealus in front of his chest as the other grasped the amulet so hard it cut into his palm.

Orealus... I am... He coughed and tried again. *I am a poor son and a poor soldier. I've ruined so many things, but I hope you understand that I tried. I didn't try hard enough to live up to your will, but I swear I tried. If you have any love for me at all, please welcome my parents into your embrace and make sure they know that I tried. It's not enough, I'm not enough, but...*

"Brother." Ezrah's arms came around him, and Kaden's seeping eyes opened. His breath was so ragged that he felt like he was about to faint, but when he finally pried his hand off the crystal, he saw, for the first time in a long time, the faintest light coming from it once more. When he looked up at Ezrah, his brother smiled. "Orealus heard you."

Responding to a prayer was a lot different from accessing the power of yah'zaval the way Kaden used to, but it was something. For the first time since Ezrah found him, Kaden felt a flicker of hope in his heart. It wasn't a big flicker, no stronger than the light at the center of the crystal, but it was something.

Sleep came more easily that night. The little peace he'd found in prayer stretched into his dreams, and before he knew it, he was seeing people he'd given up on ever laying eyes on again. It was his company, the friends he'd run out on, sitting around a campfire at the edge of a ruined village.

Ashland.

"Can't be sure he's not in there somewhere," Bardicus said as he turned the spit he'd made over the fire.

"He's not," Queen Pepper said evenly, not even lifting her eyes from the tea she was portioning out into cups.

"You can't know that."

"I can, and I do."

"She's guided us this far," Ada pointed out, and Kaden's heart ached with longing as he looked at her.

"Hardly needed guiding," Bardicus said. "We knew this was where the lad was headed. What he did once he got here, though…"

"Well, I don't see a big dead dragon anywhere," Eldrin said from where he was standing at the edge of the firelight, staring into the lowering dark. "So he didn't kill Morvar. But we knew that already."

"You put too much store in little pictures."

"And you too little."

"Please," Malacheen begged, "let's nor argue 'mongst ourselves, eh? We came all this way. The only thing to do now is look for Kaden."

"And when we find him, I'm going to give him a piece of my mind," Chum added darkly. "Making us walk all that way when he could have used his power to portal us here in no time, *honestly*, it's like he wants me to suffer!"

In Westramore, the Thieves Guild did not hunt loudly. They waited. Names were remembered long after faces faded, and debts were passed like heirlooms. Chum knew this better than anyone. You did not leave the Guild. You merely delayed its claim.

"Shut up," Petey snapped, and Duke barked at Chum for good measure.

"We'll see what we find," Weylin said, and that was the last of the conversation that Kaden was party to. The vision was lost as his eyes fluttered open, and before he could stop himself, he let out a single sob.

"What?" Ezrah was beside him a second later. "Are you all right? Did you have a bad dream?"

"Not… not a dream," Kaden said once he cleared his throat. "I think it was a vision." "It felt like a yah'zaval vision, not sleep. Like I was standing there with them, only made of light."

Ezrah sat back on his heels, the speculative look on his face clear even in the low light. "What about?"

"My… the people I was with before."

Ezrah smiled. "You can call them your friends, you know."

Kaden sighed. "I don't know that I deserve to, after—ow!" He rubbed his arm where Ezrah had just pinched him. "What was that for?"

"What did I say about deserving?" He shook his head. "We'll keep working on it. Are they coming for you?"

"I think they're already here," Kaden said. "I saw them making camp outside of Ashland. They were talking about looking for me."

Ezrah nodded. "And you're sure this was a vision, not a dream? Because it would make sense as a dream," he added gently. "That you'd want to see the people you care for again."

Kaden knew that, but… "It's not impossible," he said judiciously. "But I've had these sorts of visions before. I'm pretty sure it's the real thing. And even if it's not." He took a deep breath. "I can't stay here forever."

"No, you can't."

There was an unspoken, *but you could take a bit longer* in his brother's voice, but Kaden appreciated him not saying it out loud. Otherwise, he might not be able to resist the urge to hide himself away until he was… what, better? He was never going to be the person he had been before, so strong and so powerful and so *naïve*. That boy was gone forever, lost in the faint puff of Lydia's final smoky exhale. But that didn't mean that Kaden had nothing left to give. He had to atone. He had to face his failures and do his best to remedy them, or what would he be good for? What would be the purpose of his life at all?

A faint wash of warmth came over him, covering him from head to toe like a wave, and the shivers that Kaden had barely noticed went away. His goosebumps faded, and his next few breaths came so much easier that he almost laughed. Ezrah looked at him with a raised eyebrow.

"How far are we from Ashland?" Kaden asked.

Ezrah shrugged. "Not so far we couldn't get there by morning, if you're in the mood to set out tonight."

Kaden already knew he wasn't going to get back to sleep now. "Let's do that."

The walk was a silent one, Kaden following his brother and doing his best to use the woodcraft Ezrah had taught him to move soundlessly. It was funny how much of it he already knew, actually; he'd been watching Eldrin move like this for a year now, effortlessly quiet, and some of it had clearly rubbed off. *Imagine how good you could be at it if you'd bothered to ask him to show you more.*

Kaden was struck by how many opportunities to learn he'd ignored during the quest so far. Not everyone survived by faith or strength alone. Some relied on coin, others on secrecy, others on blades hired without question. Yes, an argument could be made that he'd had enough to learn already, what with the sword fighting and leadership lessons and yah'zaval, but that was a poor excuse when the skills might mean the difference between life and death for someone he cared for. Kaden resolved to reach out more, to ask more questions, and train harder with the members of his company… if they wanted him back, that was.

They would. They'd come so far, surely they'd want him back.

Or they want the you who isn't a broken mess. What good are you to them like this? You don't even have the Armor of Orealus anymore.

Kaden didn't let himself think too deeply about that. He wanted to be able to keep moving, after all, to get this over and done with, so he knew where he stood. Just a few more miles and—

"I see them."

Kaden stopped behind Ezrah and peered into the darkness. It was an hour or so before dawn, and the night had just begun to lighten around the edges. "Where?"

Ezrah pointed so Kaden could follow the line of his arm, and after a moment, he caught sight of the flicker of light that was a banked fire. It could be someone else, but who else would want to stay around the ruins of Ashland right now? Kaden had been breathing through his mouth for the past hour because of the scent of smoke still lingering in the air.

Ezrah's hand found his shoulder. "Are you ready?"

Kaden swallowed. Now that he was here, his vision seemed like a distant thing, unclear at best and taunting at worst. If they didn't want him back, if they shouted at him and confirmed he was every bad thing he already thought about himself, he didn't know how he'd survive it. "I… I don't…"

His breath caught as something bright and diaphanous suddenly rose from the edge of the fire. It floated in the air, twirling and twisting in an invisible breeze, and it took a moment for Kaden to realize it was Pepper. She was alight with power, as though guided by Orealus himself, and—

She was coming straight toward them.

"Steady," Ezrah murmured, not letting go of him, like he was afraid Kaden might bolt.

It was too late for that, though. Now that he saw her, there was no way Kaden could turn away. He waited, frozen with both hope and fear, as Queen Pepper in all her glory flew to him. If she was angry, he didn't know what he was going to do.

Whatever she gives me, I'll stand and take it.

Pepper didn't stop and stare in judgment, though. She came right to him, a smile beaming from her face as brightly as the love of Orealus, and wrapped her little arms around his neck in a fierce embrace.

"Oh, Kaden," she whispered. "We've been so worried about you."

Hesitantly, he brought his own arms up to hold her. "I'm sorry," he mumbled, and to his horror, he started to cry—again. "I'm so sorry, I should never have left you all behind, I only—I had to—my mother, I had to try."

Pepper pulled back just far enough to look at his face. Whatever she saw there must have made it clear that his attempt was a failure. "I'm just happy to be with you again," she said, and Kaden wanted to lean into that comfort, but then the rest of the party was on them, some of them shouting, others laughing, and Duke barking his head off with excitement.

"Where the hell have you been?"

"You look awful, we need to feed you up."

"Are you all right?"

"Did ye stab that big brute a time or two from the rest of us?"

"Thank Orealus, we found you!"

"He found *us*, idiot."

None of it was angry. None of it was accusatory. This welcome was nothing but warmth and gratitude, and Kaden looked at his companions—his friends, his family—and for the first time in far too long, he felt like things were going to be all right.

There was still so much to do. The armor. Ezrah. The quest. But it would be all right, because Kaden would not face it alone.

CHAPTER 39

Sleep never came for the rest of the night. The first thing they did was go and retrieve Kaden's weapons; he got a sound scolding over abandoning them from the dwarves, Bardicus in particular.

"Ye don't go leavin' priceless artifacts where any Daggett, Ironarr, or Jack could snatch them up!" Bardicus chided as he took it upon himself to inspect Vrangar for any signs of wear. "Steel remembers its bearer," he muttered. "And it don't take kindly to being abandoned."

Kaden wasn't ready to put the armor back on, but when Bardicus finally handed over his sword once more, he could at least hold the hilt. He glanced at Ezrah when he did and saw the slight smile on his brother's face, and a quiet warmth settled in his chest and stayed there.

Kaden was surrounded by his friends, ensconced in their care once more, and bombarded with question after question about his precarious journey. Ezrah was less warmly welcomed; not only was he a stranger to them, but the fact that there was another child of King Karatheas still living was hard for them to understand.

It didn't help that Ezrah was unwilling to share the story of his turmoil with them. All he said when asked was that he'd been captured by agents of Lucient for a while, that he'd eventually escaped, and that he had later joined the Shadow Rift Guild.

The Shadowblades did not wear sigils or colors. Their mark was silence, and the places they had passed through learned to fear what could not be seen.

"The Shadowblades?" Weylyn's ears had perked at that. "They're a tough outfit, incredibly insular. You've got to go through fire to become one of them."

"Sounds about right," Ezrah had replied, smiling insouciantly. It was clear the distrust was mutual and unresolved, despite the fact that Kaden was desperate for them all to get along.

Pepper seemed to sense that, and changed the subject quickly. "We retrieved the Greaves Megalos after you left," she said as she heated a pot of water for tea. Kaden looked at the ground, shamefaced, and Pepper reached out and touched his arm. "You did the hardest part for us, my dear. All we had to do at that point was reach out and take them."

"Still, I'm sorry I left you," Kaden muttered. "And it didn't even matter in the end, since I didn't get here soon enough to save my mother."

Ada opened her mouth to say something—what, Kaden didn't dare presume—but someone else spoke up first. "I wonder about that," Eldrin mused from where he sat on a log a few feet back from the flames. "About the timing, I mean."

Kaden shook his head. "What is there to wonder about? The answer was right there, staring me in the face, and I still didn't manage to read it right. I had the opportunity to do something good, and I failed."

"It's your reading of the pictograms that makes me wonder," Eldrin replied. His face was pensive. "What if their intent was never to give you time to confront Morvar at all?"

What else *could* the intent behind it all be? Kaden opened his mouth to argue that very point, but Eldrin held up a hand.

"No, truly, take a moment and consider it. The last time you took on Morvar, we were in an open plain with nothing for him to burn or hide behind and no obstruction to the weapon being fired at him. Even that was barely enough to get him to think twice about attacking.

"Here, though? Surrounded by trees obstructing your view, with incomplete armor and a town full of civilians in peril, not to mention a horde of baby dragons... how could you possibly have expected to defeat Morvar in such circumstances? What could you have done except be overwhelmed by his forces and die right alongside so many of the people here?"

That was… no. "I could have tried to save Lydia," Kaden protested.

"Could you? Or would you have gotten distracted by the cries of a child, or an old friend, or a dying elder, and gone to save them instead? Would you have stood and fought against the first dragonet you saw instead of saving your focus for Morvar, and been taken out by flames from behind?"

Kaden gritted his teeth. "What's your point, that I should have brought all of you along with me, then? I already know that I ruined everything, I don't need you to—"

"No," Eldrin insisted. "That's my point! I don't think you ruined everything. I think that those pictograms might have been showing us what had to happen to keep hope alive for the future. I'm not saying your mother's death was a good thing," he added as Kaden felt his ire rising, "never that. I lost my own mother to war; I know what an awful thing it is. But like it or not, Kaden, *you* are Orealus's chosen defender against Lucient. You're the one who's destined to carry this conflict forward, and so your survival must be paramount. If you had come here earlier, you might simply have portaled yourself to your death."

"It's no use thinking about what *could* have been," Ada insisted, glaring at Eldrin as if she resented him for even bringing it up.

"Even less use in wondering about the motivations of Orealus," Weylyn added. "Gods or monsters, it makes no difference. All that matters is staying alive and staying together. In Westramore, justice was something you rented. No one here has gone untouched by loss," Weylyn said.

Kaden was reminded that Weylyn's own father had lost his life fighting against Lucient alongside King Karatheas.

"The important thing now is to minimize the loss that lies ahead of us. I don't care who we face, as long as we do it together. So, you." He pointed a finger at Kaden. "Don't go leaving us again like that, you hear me? They want to pull us apart so we're easier to pick off, but we're powerful as a group."

Weylyn stepped away from the fire and stopped a short distance off, his hands clenched so tightly the leather of his gloves creaked. He stared at the ground in silence.

"Loss doesn't always come from the blade," he said after a moment, his voice low. "Sometimes the war keeps taking, even after it's finished."

He drew in a slow breath.

"My mother, Ellawyn, survived my father's death," Weylyn went on. "She outlived the fighting. Outlived the fires. But she didn't endure the quiet that followed."

He swallowed.

"She faded," he said simply. "Grief took her where Lucient could not."

The fire cracked softly. No one interrupted.

"Sometimes faith isn't broken all at once," Weylyn added. "Sometimes it just goes quiet."

"Sensible," Ezrah said, the first thing he'd volunteered since meeting the rest of the group. He inclined his head toward Weylyn, and Weylyn returned the gesture without hesitation.

Watching the two of them, Kaden felt a faint, uneasy certainty settle in his chest. If those two ever stood together without question, very little in the world would be able to move them.

The thought barely had time to take shape before everything changed.

Pepper stiffened.

She rose so abruptly that the pot of water beside the fire tipped and spilled into the coals. It struck with a sharp hiss, steam bursting upward as startled voices cried out around her.

"Majesty!" Redfern reached out to steady her, but she was already airborne, turning to the east with a deep frown on her face.

"I see..." she murmured, bringing her hands up as if she were trying to catch something in front of her. "I see... what is that? What... what has happened?" She reached out, flying another few feet into the air and then—

A sudden surge of golden light pierced the darkness, striking Pepper in the center of her chest. She cried out and fell, stricken; only her bodyguards' quick flying stopped her from hitting the ground.

"Pepper!" Kaden knelt beside her, the fears he'd barely begun to put behind him bubbling up in his chest like a volcano on the verge of exploding. "*Pepper!*"

Millicent put a tiny hand on his chest. "Give her space," she said firmly. "The queen is unharmed; she's just lost in a vision right now."

The Light doesn't just show her things," Millicent added quietly. "Sometimes it moves through her."

Once he took a second to really look, Kaden could see the truth of that—Pepper was breathing fine, if a bit fast, and there was no distress on her face, just a bit of confusion as she stared up at nothing.

"Just what we need, another vision stirring trouble," Bardicus said.

"Uncle!" Malacheen smacked his thigh. "Don't go bein' disrespectful!"

"Eh, who's bein' disrespectful to her own king now, huh?"

"You're my uncle first, king second; it's *different*."

"I ought to take you over my knee and—"

"Lumhagen," Pepper breathed out, faint but clear, and everyone fell silent. "Something has happened to Lumhagen."

Kaden went cold. "An attack?" he asked, his palms already sweating at the thought of heading into battle again.

"No... no, not an attack. It's—I can't tell from so far away, but I believe it was Bhalla, reaching through one of his yah'zaval abilities. He wants us to go to Lumhagen to see... something."

"Why isn't he reaching out to Kaden, then?" Petey asked, and Kaden found himself shying away from even thinking about it. Maybe Bhalla knew just how badly Kaden had failed Lydia. Maybe he didn't trust him anymore, and could Kaden really blame him for that? It made sense to communicate through Pepper instead, the fairy queen whose faith had never faltered even in the darkest of times, than to try and communicate with Kaden, who'd proven himself to be so... fallible.

So helpless.

So *wrong*.

"It doesn't matter," Pepper said briskly as she got to her feet, much to Redfern and Millicent's disapproval. "Everyone, pack up. We have to go, now."

Packing was the work of a mere minute—they had barely unpacked in their haste to get this far and seek out Kaden. But going…

Kaden rubbed his chest, feeling only silence where Orealus's warmth used to sit. He could not tell whether his faith was fractured or if he was simply too emptied to hear anything at all. Either way, he felt hollow.

Ada frowned. "Why can't you just make a portal?" she asked Kaden. "Is your yah'zaval exhausted?"

"It isn't just strength," Kaden said quietly. "It's clarity. Faith. Without that… the connection doesn't answer."

"Why don't *you* make a portal, if you like them so much?" Ezrah drawled, and the glare Ada threw at him didn't bode well for the future. He wanted to defend himself, or at least explain why he couldn't do it—he *knew* he couldn't yet, he simply couldn't—but Pepper shook her head.

"We are close to my own lands," she said serenely as she made the symbol of Orealus in front of her chest. Golden light blossomed like a flower around her, sending coiling vines out to touch every member of the company. "To the heart of my people and the power they hold. In this place, I can move us." She closed her eyes, and Kaden felt like he'd been clasped in a warm hand. He felt safe, like he was being held by a parent—by his mother, even—and the sensation brought tears to his eyes even as the world blurred around them.

It was nothing like being portaled. That was instantaneous, gone in a blink. The way they were moving now, he felt the passage of space around him, could almost make out individual trees as they whipped by, faster than sound itself. After a dizzying few minutes of blazing through the forest, they emerged onto a field with a familiar backdrop of mountains. It was a place that should have been filled with the vast and radiant city of Lumhagen, and yet…

The meadow was empty, yet saturated with power. There was no city to be seen here, just a faint glow of holy power illuminating every stalk of grass. Kaden stumbled forward as he was released from Pepper's power, looking at the meadow with wide eyes.

"Where did it go?" Petey asked quietly, coming up beside him. On his shoulder, Bug tilted his cap quizzically. "Where did the city go?"

"I think…" Kaden stretched out with his nascent power and felt the edges of something in front of him, something massive but formless, something that skated away even from his benevolent inspection like oil in water. "I think it's been hidden somehow."

"Great," Weylyn said dryly. "That's fantastic. Just what we needed, for the wizards to turn tail and run when the going gets tough."

"No one wizard could accomplish such a massive work of power," Pepper said, a bit sharply. "It would take every wizard in Lumhagen, as well as the goodwill of Orealus, to hide an entire city from sight. Whatever happened here, it's in accord with Orealus." Lumhagen had always believed that knowledge survived best when it was preserved, not paraded.

That was comforting, and yet Weylyn had a point. "Are we to be cut off from Bhalla entirely?" Kaden asked. "What if we need him?"

"We've got you," Ada said, stubborn and loyal. "You're enough."

Kaden feared she was wrong, but despite that, he would have to try and be enough, no matter what came at them next. If Lumhagen and the wizards needed to be hidden, then that was how it was.

And no matter how much he wanted to be hidden along with them, Kaden knew he had to step up.

No more disappointments. No more regrets. Get your head on straight, get your faith right, and get the job done.

He would try, no matter the cost.

CHAPTER 40

They took refuge in the trees. The empty plain before them felt too exposed and too secret all at once for Kaden to relax. He felt the missing city like a faint vibration under his fingertips, a presence that drew his gaze back to space again and again. After a night fractured by dreams, reunion, and the shock of Lumhagen's absence, exhaustion finally settled into his bones.

He wasn't the only one, thankfully. Petey and Chum both flopped down on the ground the moment they made camp, and even Eldrin looked more fatigued than usual. The dwarves set up a rotating watch, with Malacheen laughing off Kaden's worries with a "Ye're kiddin' me, right? I've gone on week-long watches back at home, y'know! A few days with me eyes open above ground is nothing." She'd patted him on the back hard enough to almost knock him over. "Ye're a sweet one, but we're all right."

"When someone gives you the chance to catch up on your sleep, take it," was all Ezrah had to say when Kaden looked at him a bit uncertainly.

He knew his brother was right, he knew he ought to rest while he could, and yet it felt like one more way in which he was failing his company. He'd left them alone, abandoned them to a dungeon full of monsters and forced them to hunt him down across hundreds of miles and weeks of travel, only to present them with a version of himself who was a far cry from the bold person he'd been before. He was shaky, tired down to the bone, and feeling adrift with the revelation that Bhalla wasn't here for him to seek answers from anymore.

"Lie down," Ezrah said gently, patting the bedroll Kaden had laid out. Ezrah's was next to it. "I'll be here if you need me."

That was the reassurance his body had been waiting for, apparently; Kaden was prone before his brain could muster an objection, pulling his rough blanket over his shoulders and murmuring to his brother, "Wake me if…"

"I know. I will."

Kaden fell into a doze almost immediately. It wasn't a deep enough sleep to make him unaware of what was going on around him, but that was fine as far as he was concerned. It was soothing to listen to Pepper working around the fire as she readied a meal, to hear the sound of dwarven whetstones working over the edges of half a dozen different weapons, to hear Duke turning in a few circles before lying down beside Petey.

It was soothing to hear Ada's voice as well, until he heard what she was saying.

Ada watched the two brothers lying beside each other, a flicker of something raw tightening her expression. Fear, Kaden realized later— fear of losing her place at his side.

"He's too reliant on you."

"He's exactly as reliant on me as he needs to be," Ezrah said, his voice soft but carrying a warning undertone.

"He shouldn't be reliant on you at all. You say you're family, but you've been apart from him his whole life. If you really cared, you'd have found him sooner."

"I found him when he needed me to. When there was no one else around to help him."

"You stepped in when he was at his most vulnerable!"

"Kaden would have died if I hadn't come across him when I did," Ezrah said in a hiss. Kaden tried to rouse, but his body wasn't having it. All he could do was lie there and listen to two of the people he cared for the most take bites out of each other. "You didn't see him when I found him. You think he's skinny now? Underfed, wary, worried? This is *nothing* compared to how he was when I finally reached him. He was less than a day from dying of dehydration and despair, and none of you were anywhere to be seen."

"That's not our fault!" Ada protested vigorously. "We would have been there for him if he'd taken us to Ashland with him!"

"Which he didn't. What does that tell you about whether or not he was comfortable trusting you with it?"

There was a long moment of silence. "How did you even find him?"

"I tracked him better than you."

"*Oh*, you—"

"Stop, before we wake him." The pause stretched on before Ezrah began speaking again. "I'm not here to replace anyone," he said at last, so soft Kaden could barely hear him. "I can never be to Kaden what you and your company are. You helped make him into the person he is; you forged a man from a boy. I know he shares a history with you that I'm not a part of.

"*But.*" His voice got a bit sharper. "That doesn't mean that you and your company have always been what he needed. It doesn't mean there's no room for me in his heart, especially after losing his mother the way he did. I understand what that feels like. I've *been* there. My family was slaughtered, and I was forgotten, but I've never forgotten about my brother. *Never.*"

"We didn't forget about him either," Ada protested, but there seemed to be less anger in her voice now. "We wouldn't do that. We love him."

"Good. He deserves love; he needs it. I'm not here to compete for his love, that's not what Kaden needs." There was a shuffle, like Ezrah was moving closer. "He needs people to believe in him. To help him in the bad times and stand with him in the good. To remember that he's carrying the weight of the world at seventeen, younger than our father ever was when war first came for him."

"I think I understand," Ada said.

"I'm glad."

Their voices drifted into silence, and Kaden finally fell deeper into sleep.

It wasn't a restful sleep, though.

The fire taunted him, flaring in his direction the moment he turned away and then retreating as he looked back. The sky was dark, the stars obscured with smoke that reflected the fire creating it. A fierce wind whipped past him, and he heard a torn banner flapping wildly in it. Tall grasses burned, and the sound of hundreds of hoofbeats echoed across the ground as the centaurs of Wildepointe fled the destruction of their ancestral home.

The Withered Steppes bowed before the might of the great black dragon who suddenly appeared overhead, his bulk so great that he seemed to fill the sky from edge to edge. His silhouette was illuminated by orange smoke and licking flames, and he roared in triumph before lowering his head and adding more flame to the frenzy. Centaurs screamed in fresh pain, a baby cried, and deep in his soul, Kaden knew this was no nightmare.

Wildepointe has fallen. Wildepointe has fallen. Wildepointe—

"—was gone!" he gasped as he sat up. It was dark; he'd slept the day away. On either side of him were Ezrah and Ada, both of them still asleep despite his sudden, lurching wakefulness. Kaden couldn't bring himself to wake them, but he had to tell someone, he had to—

"Oh," he heard Pepper whisper. "Oh, no."

Kaden forced himself out of his blankets and made his way over to the fairy queen, who hovered by the banked fire, her hands pressed to her cheeks, eyes glassy with tears as she stared to the west. "Oh, no," she said again, then turned to Kaden as he joined her. "Wildepointe…"

"I saw it," Kaden whispered. "Morvar destroyed Wildepointe."

"So did I," she replied. "Oh, I hoped it was just a dream, but you saw it as well?"

"I did," he said helplessly. "I'm sorry."

"Kaden, no." She shook her head even as tears fell from her eyes. "Don't be sorry. There's nothing we can do for Wildepointe now, but knowing our enemy is half the battle. You and I dreamed true, I'm sure of it. Now we know where Morvar is, though."

"How's that?" Bardicus called out without any of the thoughtfulness Kaden and Pepper had been using for the sleepy state of their companions. "What'd you say about Morvar?"

Pepper told him and the other dwarves about the dream, and by the time she was done recounting it to them, everyone else was waking up as well. Kaden corroborated her vision with a flat, "It's Morvar. I saw it. He set everything on fire."

"Damn it," Weylyn muttered. "How are we supposed to fight something like that, huh?"

It was exactly what Kaden had been thinking. How could they possibly handle a monster like Morvar, a beast so dreadful his presence made even Lucient feel less deadly? A familiar sense of helplessness rose in him, and he bit his lip as he closed his eyes and, unthinkingly, made the symbol of Orealus in front of his chest.

Holy Orealus, I pray to you, share your wisdom with us. What do we do from here? How can we face this foe? What hope do we have?

THERE IS ALWAYS HOPE, MY BELOVED SON.

Kaden gasped and fell to his knees. The people around him cried out in surprise, but he only gripped his pendant with both hands as he continued to pray. *I thought I was beyond your love!*

MY LOVE IS ETERNAL AND UNENDING. I AM ALWAYS WITH YOU, KADEN. EVEN WHEN THINGS LOOK BLEAK. ESPECIALLY THEN.

He felt a deep sense of purpose filling him then; it was like what he'd felt the first time he communed with Orealus, but more refined, somehow. Kaden wasn't the young, naïve boy he'd been when this adventure began. He'd been tempered by loss, run through with it, and healed once more. He would carry the scars from it forever, but the pain in his heart was slowly replaced with a sense of righteousness.

It was all right to be afraid. It was all right to feel sad. It was all right to doubt his place; Orealus had never left him, and he never would.

Kaden opened his eyes and got to his feet. Yah'zaval surged within him, powered by his renewed faith and his contact with Orealus. The crystal clenched in his fist shone so bright it was like a miniature sun. He turned to look at all his friends, his dearest companions, and smiled. "We are flame shaped by fire. Light forged through loss. We are embers that refuse to die. Let the dark come. Let them march. We will rise to meet them."

He felt their resolve strengthen alongside his, heard it in the rustle of their bodies as they reached for their weapons, saw it as they held them aloft. Every face was set with ferocity and determination.

They weren't beaten. Despite the dark clouds twisting across the sky, the echo of a dragon's roar that still reverberated through Kaden's mind, and the ever-present pressure of Lucient's gaze as he gathered his generals for war, they were unbeaten and unbowed.

As Kaden lifted his blade and the others rose beside him, the storm above crackled with fire. The shadow of dragon wings cut across the sky. From the ashes of grief, a new blaze ignited.

The quest for the Armor of Orealus wasn't over yet. The second Great War loomed, and the threat of dragonfire would follow them with every step.

Their journey, cast in fire, had only just begun.

EPILOGUE

WHAT FAITH LEAVES BEHIND

Baal did not stand where Morvar had burned.

He stood where the fire had already passed.

The land was quiet here. Not peaceful, but spent. Ash lay thin across the soil like a veil, and beneath it the earth still trembled, remembering what it had endured. This was where Baal preferred to listen.

He lowered himself to one knee and pressed his palm to the ground.

The world answered.

Not with sound, but with absence.

"So," he said softly. "You endured."

The faith that answered him was changed. Not blazing. Not obedient. It did not rise eagerly toward the Light the way it once had.

It remained.

Baal's fingers curled slowly.

"That is new," he murmured.

Faith that survived loss without shattering was rare. Faith that bent without breaking was dangerous. It did not obey out of fear. It chose.

He rose and brushed the ash from his hand, eyes lifting toward a horizon he did not need to see.

"He was meant to falter," Baal continued, as though the world itself were listening. "Grief usually finishes what doubt begins. It hollows devotion. Turns prayer into silence."

And yet the silence had answered back.

Baal smiled, not in amusement, but in recognition.

"You prayed anyway," Baal said.

The presence behind him made itself known, vast and cold, pressing against the air like a held breath. Baal did not turn.

"Morvar will burn," he said calmly. "Fire is loud. It teaches fear quickly."

A pause.

"Yes," Baal agreed. "But fear does not end the faithful. It only reveals them."

He stepped away from the scorched earth and into the shadow, already tracing the fault lines forming beneath belief itself.

"Let him gather what remains," Baal whispered, voice almost reverent. "Let him call it hope."

His smile returned, thin and precise.

"Hope always leaves something behind."

The ash settled.

The silence deepened.

And far away, faith reshaped itself for war.

ACKNOWLEDGEMENTS

This book exists because the story was welcomed and carried forward by its readers. *A Journey Cast in Fire* was written with the understanding that the world and its characters no longer belonged to me alone. To everyone who continued this journey, shared it, and believed in it enough to ask for what came next, thank you. Your support gave this book its reason to exist.

I am deeply grateful to Cath for her continued insight, precision, and care throughout the development of this story. Her ability to strengthen what matters on the page has been invaluable. I also thank Kyri for her creativity, thoughtful feedback, and encouragement. Her contributions helped refine this book and sharpen its direction.

I am thankful for the support of my family, especially my siblings Erik, Lamont, Kalinda, and Monica. Each of you has played a part in shaping the person I am today, and that foundation carried me through the challenges of continuing this series. I also acknowledge my late mother, Otherine Preston, whose love, guidance, and belief in me continue to influence the work I do and the person I strive to be.

I also want to acknowledge my son, Calum, whose presence and spirit continue to give purpose to this journey.

I want to thank Skye for her steady encouragement and support during this process. Her belief and kindness meant more than she may realize and helped keep me moving forward when the work felt heavy.

Above all, I give thanks to my readers. Your loyalty, enthusiasm, and belief in this world are what sustained this journey beyond its beginning. This book was written with you in mind, and it exists because you chose to keep walking this path with me.

Finally, I give thanks to Yahweh. Through Him, strength is renewed, purpose is sustained, and this work was made possible.

THE EMPYREAN CODEX

A post-war archival compilation of names, oaths, beasts, coin, craft, and land within Sadunia. Copied from surviving scrolls, guild ledgers, and field accounts.

FOUNDATIONS OF EMPYREA

HISTORY, COLLAPSE, FAITH

Empyrea was once bound under the Rosenhelm line, chosen by Orealus and upheld through covenant, crown, and mutual treaty among the Pillar Tribes and allied realms. In the Great War, Lucient's rise fractured that order. Cities hardened into enclaves. Kingdoms withdrew behind stone, forest, or sea. Roads became borders. Trade became risky. Many who had lived by ceremony learned instead to live by scarcity.

The old feudal structure did not vanish, but it hollowed out. In this age, titles remain, often worn like relics, while true influence gathers around coin, contracts, and those willing to enforce them. The realm's memory is long, but its unity is thin.

LIGHT AND SHADOW

Yah'shavel is the sacred current of Orealus, named as spirit, not sorcery. Its works are recorded as healing, warding, radiant flame, and the shaping of Light Gates. It is treated as a covenant, and its practice is bound to devotion, discipline, and calling.

Dunntaika is the corruption born of Lucient's fall, parasitic upon will and soul. Its works are recorded as curses, necromancy, shadow craft, mind-bending dominion, and the shaping of Shadow Gates. It is condemned as blight, and its use is an invitation to fracture.

ORDERS AND BANNERS

THE PILLARS OF LIGHT

A name given to those who stand against Lucient and bear the burden of restoration. Their ranks include heirs, kings, wardens, wizards, hunters, and unlikely companions. Some are chosen by prophecy, some by oath, and some simply by refusing to kneel.

THE BREAKROOTS

A title for the dark forces that undermine, corrupt, and uproot what remains of Empyrea's order. The name is spoken like a warning: rot does not always arrive as an army. Sometimes it arrives as a bargain.

THE ROYAL EMPYREAN KNIGHTS

Once the sworn shield of the Rosenhelm crown, now scattered after the Great War. Many are tall, scarred, and well-trained across multiple combat disciplines, favoring dark battle armor chosen for function over ceremony. Some have settled into quieter lives of labor and protection. Others have become mercenaries, selling strength to endure.

Their shared inheritance is pride and guilt, and an enduring hatred of Lucient. Though leaderless, many remain oathbound in secret, waiting for a banner worth returning to.

PEOPLE OF NOTE

PROTAGONISTS

Kaden Sheppard, The Heir of Karatheas Rosenhelm

A young man with an unbroken spirit who grows from reluctant and occasionally self-focused into a leader shaped by responsibility and sacrifice. His fiercest instinct is protection, and his destiny draws others into motion.

Petey Elvenshire, The Zany Guardian

A kind-hearted talker who hides fear behind jokes yet proves brave when the cost is real. Loyal to the core, he shares a strange tenderness with Bug, whose light follows him like fate.

Adena "Ada" Davenrich, The Resolute Huntress

A disciplined hunter with a guarded heart and a stubborn sense of right. Adventure calls her beyond ordinary life, and her steadiness makes her a refuge in the wild.

Bardicus Blakenshield, King of Kugdor

A proud dwarf king who rules with strength and celebration, carrying old shame beneath loud confidence. His leadership offers Kugdor a chance to rise beyond the betrayals that marked the Great War.

Eldrin Tolbarg, Prince of the Elves

Prideful and sharp, trained in longbow, daggers, and close combat. His vanity is loud, but his nobility is real, and he learns that honor must be proved in blood and patience.

Cimetes Gallopfoot, Chieftain of the Centaurs

A warrior-leader who wields Windcutter, an inherited spear of oath and lineage. Brave but cautious after the Great War, he guards his tribe while fearing the reach of Lucient's wrath.

Pepper Shinyfawn, Queen of Fayspire

Gentle by nature, formidable by duty. Pepper channels Orealus's blessings to protect her people, preferring peace but prepared to fight fiercely for allies and innocents.

Varun Gadar, King of Nethopolis

A merfolk king shaped by betrayal and loss. Varun safeguards his undersea realm with disciplined resolve, balancing compassion with the hard edge of survival.

Weylyn Echethier, Son of the Wolf

A mercenary driven by vengeance for his father's death. His faith has fractured, but his loyalty to Kaden is iron. He stands between danger and the heir with relentless instinct.

Duke, Loyal Companion

Kaden's hound, found as a puppy near Ashland, is now bound to the road. Duke senses danger early, holds close in grief, and remains constant when the world shifts.

Bhalla Bristlekamp, Protector of the Light

The eldest wizard and a faithful servant of Orealus, known for healing, wards, and guidance. His humor is dry, his power is immense, and he often calls upon Ga'noole, his great eagle companion.

Chum Scruffenhoof, The Cunning Collector

A satyr of wit and opportunism, gathering information and rare goods through stealth and charm. Self-interest often leads him, but the trial reveals a loyalty he would rather deny.

Ezrah Rosenhelm, Shadow's Rift

A silent, lethal guardian who moves like a rumor and strikes like a blade. Hardened by loss, Ezrah's loyalty is absolute, and his presence is often felt only after danger has passed.

Millicent, The Queen's Shield

A towering fairy sworn to Queen Pepper. Disciplined and battle-hardened, she protects with steady devotion and carries loyalty that does not waver under pressure.

Redfern, The Queen's Blade

A calm, decisive fairy guard who reads danger quickly and acts faster. Her loyalty is measured by deeds, not display, and her mind stays clear when others panic.

Thalgrem, The Thunderfist

A gruff dwarf general with a battle-worn presence. He lends strength and hard wisdom to the cause, masking a heart learning again how to trust hope.

Malacheen Hammertoe, The Stonebreaker

A determined dwarf miner and fighter who wields her pickaxe with precision. She balances intellect with raw strength, forging her own path beyond expectation.

Bug, The Frolicking Mushroom

A small fey creature from Fayspire, playful and loyal, timid until tested. Bug's glowing spores can distract, guide, and protect, and its bond with Petey becomes a small light on a dark road.

ALLIES

Marcus Herrington, Captain for Hire

Former Royal Empyrean Naval Officer and captain of the Dawn Light, guiding allies through peril with discipline, honor, and tactical skill.

Asiz Seaspray, The Loyal First Mate

Chief mate of the Dawn Light, defined by unwavering loyalty and growing into leadership beyond grief.

Reginald Sharpey, The Steadfast Officer

First mate aboard the Dawn Light, protecting morale and keeping the crew steady under strain.

Serenya Larethian, Navigator of the Dawn

An elf navigator whose mastery of stars and currents keeps the ship alive through storm and pursuit.

Dinereus Gadar, Queen of Nethopolis

Varun's wife and advisor, blending majesty with empathy, balancing diplomacy and authority in a realm shaped by betrayal.

Seward Grayson, General of the Dragon Guild

Ex-Empyrean Knight and leader of the Dragon Guild, mentoring the next generation while carrying guilt that never fully loosens.

Anika Calder, Captain of the Dragon Guild

Resourceful and independent, balancing authority with personal growth, confronting betrayals and old ties.

Rowden Drakewing, Lieutenant of the Dragon Guild

Charismatic and tense with rivalry, his path bends toward redemption and self-knowledge.

Muk Muk, Centaur Champion

Right hand to Cimetes, fierce and proud, learning leadership that is more than strength.

K'Lani Davenrich, Healer of Whaldalf's Landing

Wise mother of Ada, supporting the cause through compassion and resilience, guiding healers and steadying the fearful.

Ta'la Sundaki, The Shadow Gale

A skilled member of Shadow's Rift, courageous and cunning, growing into leadership without surrendering independence.

Jedrek Veythar, The Iron Scar

Leader of the Shadowblades, evolving into a mentor who values unity, adaptability, and loyalty over pride.

Daven Jones, The Weathered Mayor

The mayor of Whaldalf's Landing, gruff but wise, keeps his community alive through endurance and practical courage.

Regar Ironbeard, The Blind Sentinel

A dwarf miner whose blindness is answered by uncanny awareness, sharp wit, and stubborn bravery.

Lydia Sheppard, Hunter, Farmer, and Merchant

Kaden's adoptive mother, whose warmth and strength shaped his conscience and taught him the cost of love.

Halthro Hammertoe, Master Armorer

Malacheen's father, stoic and pragmatic, equips allies for war while hiding care beneath craft.

Asitra Fenngate, Keeper of the Sacred Scrolls

Master wizard and mentor to Kaden, balancing devotion to prophecy with personal connection and hard choices.

Samantha Pew, Forest Broker

A trader raised among Brightshire's hidden paths, aiding travelers through discretion and knowledge of routes and bargains.

Chip Cherry, The Lantern Trickster

A fairy exile turned storyteller, carrying laughter and secrets through markets like contraband hope.

Gorg Fairweather, Captain of the Coast Guild

Founder of the Coast Guild, cautious and seasoned, rallying fleets when neutrality fails under rising threat.

RENOWNED FIGURES

King Karatheas Rosenhelm, The Last Monarch
The final great king of Empyrea, whose death in the Great War left a crown without a seat and a realm without a spine.

Queen Luna Rosenhelm, The Moonlight Sacrifice
Revered for courage and devotion, remembered for a sacrifice that became a living legend.

Elaena Rosenhelm, The Sapphire Flame
A princess remembered as a compass of courage and compassion, her legacy shaping the hearts of those who remain loyal.

Doran Rosenhelm, The Golden Shield
The eldest Rosenhelm sibling, embodying wisdom and bravery, preserves ideals through heroic memory.

Aelunara Gadar, The Deep Voice
Mother of Varun, a queen of spiritual wisdom and sacrifice whose unseen deeds still shape merfolk's resolve.

Trophorus Gadar, The Tempest King
A legendary Sea King whose assassination shattered Nethopolis, teaching hard lessons about trust and survival.

Khalon Echethier, The Wolf
High Sentinel of the Crown, feared for unmatched skill, whose sacrifice ensured the royal line endured long enough for prophecy.

Ellawyn Echethier, The Gentle Shield
Healer of Westramore and Keeper of Empyrean Lore. Wife of Khalon and mother of Weylyn, her compassion tempered war, and her influence endured beyond death.

Enan Davenrich, The Steadfast Hunter
Ada's father and friend to Karatheas, remembered for discipline, resilience, and devotion cut short by war.

Guildmaster Vellorin, Voice of the Merchant Council
Third Seat of Karnergrien's Merchant Council, shaping trade through restraint, now forced to decide whether coin can stay neutral.

SHADOWED NAMES

Narf Bellyfang, The Sneering Lieutenant
A goblin lieutenant who thrives on intimidation and mockery, feeding on human fear.

Threlka, The Spider Queen
Guardian of the Ancient Empyrean Archives, hunting intruders to protect her subterranean brood.

Malech Cutler, Mad Eyed
Leader of the Sword Brothers and de facto mayor of Westramore, ruling by leverage, charisma, and threat.

Khesza, The Redeemed Captain
An undead Empyrean knight seeking redemption, aiding the cause while haunted by failure.

Gangor, The Forest Colossus
An ancient elemental corrupted by dark influence, a warning that even nature can be poisoned.

Tarel, The Night Prowler
A covert commander under Faldrus, feared for ruthless efficiency and silent kills.

BESTIARY AND LIVING WONDERS

CREATURES

Growlers
Corrupted wolf-like beasts tamed by goblins for war and hunting. Exceptional trackers with night vision, prone to coordinated ambush.

Fallen

Pale-green spirits of slain Empyrean soldiers, wandering battlefields and forsaken places, drawn to life and grief.

Orphidian

Serpentine humanoid warriors with cobra hoods and venomous spines. Once noble guardians, now elite shock troops and commanders under Lucient.

Spider Workers

Dog-sized brood spiders that build, carry, and swarm. Quick, silent, mildly venomous.

Spider Soldiers

Horse-sized elite spiders with thick armor and venomous fangs, serving as Threlka's personal guard.

Sand Wyrms

Giant desert predators that burrow to ambush prey, camouflaging perfectly in sand.

Location: Sizzling Sands

Scorchcrawlers

Heat-adapted predators of the Barren Badlands with leathery hides and sharp claws, capable of brief invisibility.

Scorchcrawler Alpha

A dominant Scorchcrawler coordinating hunts and defending territory.

Scorchcrawler Queen

A massive broodmother, ruling her territory and ensuring the species' survival.

WILDLIFE

Woolymeths

Massive shaggy herbivores, once ridden into war, gentle until threatened, are now rare since the Great War.

Binicorns
Rare horned equines of purity and faith, solitary and wary, dwelling in Binicorn's Farthing.

Giant Eagles
Sacred sky-guardians created by Orealus, few remaining, including Ga'noole the Great.

Empyrean Hounds
Towering war canines of the Rosenhelm line, able to track corruption and defend the worthy.

Catalopes
Small antlered felines, omens of fortune, elusive and gentle.

Glox Fish
Iridescent fish near Whaldalf's Landing, schooling in bright "runs" during certain moons.

Crowned Griffin
A revered river fish with emerald scales and golden crests, blessed by Orealus.

Glow Parrotlets
Small singing birds with bioluminescent throats, sacred to Fayspire.

Fae Lizard
Six-legged translucent lizards are used as wards against corruption, prized in alchemy.

Kaleido Rabbits
Rainbow-furred rabbits born after storms are symbols of renewal.

Fair Fox
A red fox with electric blue eyes that reveal lies, following travelers until honesty is learned.

Gabar
A colossal albino lion was said to mark the destined king's path, its presence banishing corruption.

Fluteds
Blue songbirds whose trills sound like flutes, beloved in Lumhagen.

PEOPLES AND TRIBES

*Extracted as an ethnographic record, compiled for travelers,
traders, and scholars.*

HUMANS

Adaptable and resilient, varied in form and custom. Humans fill the
Pillar Tribes as farmers, soldiers, hunters, wizards, merchants, and rulers. Their strength is versatility. Their weakness is the ease with which
hunger and fear can be weaponized against them.

DWARVES

Stocky, powerful, and exceptionally durable. Masters of stone and forge,
dwarves value workmanship, lineage, and oath. After the Great War,
many withdrew into Kugdor, where craft and warcraft became one
discipline.

WOOD ELVES

Graceful and keen-sensed forest peoples organized under noble houses,
valuing restraint, harmony, and long memory. Their archers are
renowned, and their diplomacy is often as sharp as their blades.

DUNNISS˙

A cursed elven subrace marked by gray to bluish-dark skin and pale
hair, shaped by exile and vengeance. They favor shadow tactics, raids,
and forbidden practices, rooted in Darkvale Valley's cold beauty and
bitterness.

CENTAURS

Swift and disciplined nomads with strong kin-bonds and strict tradition. They guard territory fiercely and trade with caution. Leadership is
earned through strength, wisdom, and service to the herd.

FAIRIES

Luminous fey folk with wings and sacred ties to plant life and grove-health. They serve as healers and wardens under Queen Pepper, cautious after the Great War yet fiercely protective of what still blooms.

MERFOLK

Ocean guardians of reef and current, spiritual and territorial, ruled by King Varun. Their society prizes loyalty, patience, and depth, and their politics can be as dangerous as the open sea.

GOBLINS

Short, cunning raiders and scavengers, often allied with beasts and ambush tactics. Many are cruel and opportunistic. Rare exceptions prove goblins can hold loyalty and kindness, though such souls are often punished by their own kind.

SATYRS

Creative, social, and free-spirited forest folk, known for craft, music, and brewing. Nearly wiped out in the Great War, with few survivors recorded.

FROLICKING MUSHROOMS

Small rabbit-like fey whose glowing spores guide or warn. Ancient guardians that bond to travelers, awakening only for the fated, the gentle, or the desperate.

PIXIES

Tiny luminous fey embodying balance and harmony. Once abundant across sacred groves, now scarce after corruption spread.

TRADE, COIN, AND COMMERCE

THE MERCHANT'S AND BANKER'S GUIDE TO EMPYREA

Compiled under the Authority of the Guild of Scales and Seal-Bearers, with attestations from the Dwarven Mint of Kugdor and the Council of Dockmasters of Whaldalf's Landing.

FOREWORD

Coin is the simplest key to bargaining, and the most honest witness to need. Where coin fails, barter rises, yet barter seldom fits the shape of true necessity. Let the traveler remember this. A starving village prices bread differently from a fat city. A war road turns honest rates into superstition.

By the hand of Guildmaster Vellorin, Third Seat of the Merchant Council of Karnergrien.

ON COIN AND MEASURE

Coin bears weight so that value may be argued less and proven more. Crests and marks matter, yet weight remains the truest test when borders shift, and counterfeiters grow bold.

CURRENCY OF THE REALM

- **Copper Bits** (CB, Rusties): 2.5g copper, crest and wheat sheaf, small trade

- **Bronze Kili** (BK, Brons): 3.5g bronze, crossed hammer and anvil, daily necessities

- **Silver Talons** (ST, Tals): 5.5g silver, falcon and monarch, wages and livestock

- **Gold Chronos** (GC, Crowns): 8.5g gold, sundial motif, rooms, and larger stock

- **Empyrean Gigaments** (EG, Gigs): 11.5g rare alloy, kingdom emblem, and mythical beast, war-scale value

EXCHANGE RATES

1 BK = 10 CB
1 ST = 10 BK
1 GC = 10 ST
1 EG = 10 GC

ON THE FRACTURE OF MINTING

Karnergrien was once the steady heart of coin. After its fall, production splintered and trust thinned. The dwarves ceased broad minting, guarding what remained of their stamps and metals. Coin grew dear, and the art of forgery became a second trade road.

Thus rose the coinwrights, whose work is not to make money, but to prove it, using scales, edge-tests, rune-sight, and the patience that survives threats.

ON COINHOUSES AND CREDIT

Where roads are unsafe, and hoards invite theft, coinhouses keep wealth behind stone and seal. They do not store trust for free. Their price is measured in marks, favors, and quiet knowledge.

Coinhouses are recorded in Lumhagen, Nethopolis, and Whaldalf's Landing, each issuing Promissory Marks to those judged stable enough to be remembered and pursued.

Guild Tokens pass among allied guilds by prior pact.

Ledger Credit exists only where names matter more than blades, and where reputation is guarded like a relic.

Security is often layered. Alchemical seals, dwarven runes, and enchanted watermarks are common among high trade. Still, nothing is unbreakable. Only costly.

ON VALUE BEYOND COIN

Coin is not the only weight. Some goods refuse ordinary pricing and are traded like oaths.

- Gems and commodities hold steady across borders, though theft follows them like a shadow.
- Binicorn Horns are spoken of at 500 GC.
- Woolymeth Tusks are spoken of at 100 EG.
- In hard places, healing, safe passage, and skilled hands outprice silver.

ON THE LIVES OF COMMON HOUSEHOLDS

Scholars argue in neat columns, but the realm eats in rough portions. Still, the Guild keeps numbers for those who must plan caravans, wages, and winter stock.

LOWER-CLASS

- Income: 200 Silver Kili per month
- Typical spend: 195 Bronze Kili
  - Food: 45 Bronze Kili
  - Rent and taxes: 135 Silver Kili
  - Miscellaneous: 15 Bronze Kili

MIDDLE-CLASS

- Roughly double the lower-class income, often held by established households, shop owners, and respected tradespeople.

ON SOCIAL RISE AND FALL

Social ascent is rare and usually purchased by one of three means: exceptional skill, inherited wealth, or cunning that outlasts consequences. The realm remembers the clever. It buries the merely hopeful.

ON SLAVERY AND FORCED LABOR

Lucient's dominion traffics in bodies. Giants, humans, elves, dwarves, centaurs, merfolk, and others have been chained into camps and war-forges. Elderpass Way is recorded as the largest, with Orphidian overseers enforcing forced labor in mines, fields, and forge pits.

Goblins, dark elves, and pirates also supply captives to black markets in Westramore and Nethopolis. This commerce is not merely profit. It is a strategy meant to keep the realm afraid and divided.

ON THE ACTORS OF TRADE

- **Crown and Pillar Houses** regulate tariffs and scarcity when they can, and weaponize them when they choose.
- **Merchant Guilds** move caravans, issue tokens, and keep routes alive through bribes and steel.
- **The Dwarven Mint of Kugdor** is trusted for ceremonial minting and high-value verification.
- **The Coast Guild** holds sea lanes where docks have fallen into politics.
- **The Dunnmark Exchange** persists beneath law, governed by seals and collateral, and rumored to answer to an unseen master.

MARKETS OF SADUNIA

Whaldalf's Landing, Peaceful Exchange

An open port market of salt wind and loud barter, where forest herbs, fishing gear, and imported luxuries change hands.

Merchant Council Member: K'Lani Davenrich

Karnergrien, Sanctuary Square

A ruined marble heart where trade persists under hunger and prayer, contracts and relics passing between the desperate.

Merchant Council Member: Samantha Pew

Brightshire Forest, Lampi Glade
A seasonal glow-market formed when lampi blooms rise, offering forest wares and elven craft beneath drifting light.

Merchant Council Member: Chip Cherry

Kel Tyrion, Flint Exchange
A secluded exchange behind waterfalls, reached by cliffside waterways and known to those who keep its path.

Merchant Council Member: Eldrin Tolbarg

Ashland, Barleyfield Commons
A weekly ring of stalls where bread, livestock, and honest goods trade hands in plain speech and steady measure.

Merchant Council Member: Lydia Sheppard

Wildepointe, Speared Circle
A field announced by hoof drums each dawn, where weapons, leather-work, tents, and trade goods move through centaur hands.

Merchant Council Member: Cimetes Gallopfoot

Nula, King's Crossing
A fortified junction of roads and grain, guarded and wary, living beneath the shadow of the labyrinth's breath.

Merchant Council Member: Vicitious

Nethopolis, Coral Crown Bazaar
A domed undersea bazaar lit by bioluminescence, trading pearls, seafood, and deep treasures beneath quiet currents.

Merchant Council Members: King Varun and Queen Dinereus Gadar

Fayspire, Starlight Market
A treetop market of rope bridges and firefly lamps, offering rare spices, pixie dust, and living flora.

Merchant Council Members: Millicent and Redfern

Westramore, Blackhand Row
A shifting alley exchange where illicit goods and cursed artifacts move by whisper, not stall-sign.

Merchant Council Member: Mad Eyed Malech

Kugdor, Hammer & Groggle
A cavern forge-market where weapons, gems, and grog trade never truly stops, measured by clang and heat.

Merchant Council Member: Bardicus Blakenshield

Lumhagen, Lightspire
A luminous artisan market of travel gear, sacred texts, mechanical devices, and carved staffs, warmed by wards.

Merchant Council Member: Asitra Fenngate

Forgotten Forest, Branchy Oaks Market
A quiet refuge exchange among cabins and hidden fire, trading preserved foods, beeswax, leather, and bows.

Merchant Council Member: Seward Grayson

THE BLACK EXCHANGE, DUNNMARK

A hidden commerce moving beneath law and light, marked by cold bargains and enforced payment.

Leader: Mad Eyed Malech, with rumors of an unseen master

Symbol: a silver coin cut with a serpent fang, cold to traitors

Nodes: Darkvale Valley, Shroudscar Hold, Karnergrien sewers, Charred Caves of Elderpass, Elderpass Way, Talaifotia unconfirmed

Creed: If it draws breath, it can be bought. If it has blood or none, it can be sold. Every purchase carries a cost.

Three Seals: Mark (blood), Price (payment), Soul (collateral)

Collectors: iridescent beings retrieving collateral at night, described rarely and never comfortably

RELICS, ARMS, AND SACRED CRAFT

LEGENDARY WEAPONS

Vrangar, Light-Bringer: Kaden's radiant sword

Alpheon: wolf-guarded blade binding the king's champion

Moon's Eclipse: twin curved shadow blades

Dragon's Fury: short sword of dragon scales, fiery glow

Nightbringer: Lucient's serpent-embossed greatsword

Chaos's Edge: Baal's wavy-blade sword

Decimation: Defyle's bat-winged black axe

Soul Drinker: Ozul's jagged scythe

Loyal Dwingent: Bhalla's dagger for Petey

Great Hammer of Retribution: dwarven obsidian hammer

Windcutter: fearsome oak spear

Storm's Wrath: Varun's lightning trident

Driftwood: Eldrin's green-ore recurve bow

Arcinde and Acantha: Ada's bow and short sword

Thunderfist: kinetic gauntlets

Belegering and Ravenscar: mistwood bows

Lucky Friend: Malacheen's dratonium pickaxe

Skullcrusher: reforged mace of Omak

Mallenir: hexagonal blacksmith hammer

Wave Runner and The Swashbuckler: naval scimitars

Glinting Seas: mechanical revolver

Frenzied End: ivory broad axe

Mountainsplitter: Ogias' massive club

Path's Light: olive-wood staff

Fay's Protection: cherry-blossom staff

Sacred Undoing: dragon-clawed dark staff

Cursed Illusions: reality-warping staff

Jagged Rift: hand-mounted steel claws

Wretched Thirst: zig-zag broadsword

THE ARMOR AND SWORD OF OREALUS

Preserved as a lore summary, with restrained detail.

Ruach, Sword of Truth

A greatsword of rare make, named in dwarven forge-claims and hymn-fragments. It is said to drink force and return it through the wielder's strike. Worthiness is often described as audible, a faint tone heard at first touch.

Justicia, Breastplate of Righteousness

A lion-crested breastplate of white metal, famed for strength without weight. Often paired in memory with doves fastening a red cloak, a sign of protection and authority.

Deimanus, Gauntlets of Strength

Pale gauntlets that fit the chosen as if they were always meant to. Old songs claim they grant steadiness enough to bear burdens others cannot.

Aspis, Shield of Courage

A circular shield bearing the lion motif, remembered for brilliant sun-glint and steadfast defense in fear's press.

Paz, Boots of Peace

White boots of unmatched leather, designed to leave no trace and grant unusual agility to the wearer.

Sozonos, Helmet of Salvation

A shaping helm with a lion-mouth visor and winged crests, its silhouette feared by enemies and revered by the faithful.

Liasti, Belt of Unity

A white belt that adjusts to fit is remembered as a binding symbol for scattered strength gathered into one purpose.

Megalos, Greaves of Stability

White greaves edged in pale steel, worn for sure footing and balance when the ground itself turns treacherous.

RESOURCES AND NATURAL CRAFT

Mercalyptus

Healing plant with glowing blue flowers, used in salves and teas.

Location: Westramore

Branaloy

Rare steel-like material tied to exceptional forging, rumored near Morvar's heights.

Location: Wyvernpeake

Yew Wood

Dense evergreen wood prized for bows and staves.

Location: Brightwood Forest and Ashland

Stonewood

Durable wood from rare Stone trees is used for unbreakable hafts and shields.

Location: Kugdor

Mugasia Longiflora

Purple yearly bloom used in ceremonial grog, dangerous if mishandled.

Location: Kugdor

Bonberries

Indigo berries are used in jams and pastries, a comfort staple.

Location: Ashland

Wanderweedles

Carnivorous tumbleweed plant used as a living barrier.

Location: Darkvale Valley

Nosegye

Small yellow flowers are believed to ward off wandering spirits.

Location: forests and trails

Dratonium

Scarce metal resistant to damage, sources mostly lost.

Location: once in Empyrea, current sources unknown

Soothsage

Calming flower used for clarity and prophecy.

Location: Forgotten Forest

Vynthium

Violet crystalline mineral that hums when struck, used to channel mana.

Location: ancient caverns and sacred sites

ATLAS OF SADUNIA

*Survey entries compiled for navigators, scouts,
and road-worn traders.*

ASHLAND

A rural town of roughly four hundred residents, known for honest labor, plain goods, and the kind of quiet that makes leaving feel like theft.

BINICORN'S FARTHING

A wide plain of open sky and clean wind, crossed by streams feeding a central lake. Binicorns are said to gather here beneath distant mountains.

BRIGHTSHIRE FOREST

A forest of rare life and strange beauty. At night, lampi seeds drift like living lanterns, turning the dark into a moving constellation.

CRAGMAW

An underground ogre realm. Its people avoid daylight, emerging at night to hunt before retreating to cavern depth by dawn.

DARKVALE VALLEY

A mist-bound city between two mountains, home to the Dunnissé. Gray brick streets and mausoleum-like structures lend it a cold, carved beauty.

ELDERPASS WAY

A desert prison where giants are enslaved behind towering clay walls. Chains and heat define the place, and the ground trembles when the prisoners move.

EMPYREA

Once a holy rainforest of abundance, now scarred and ruined by war, its sacred inheritance is remembered more than seen.

FAYSPIRE

A fairy city hidden west of Brightshire Forest, camouflaged so completely that most travelers pass without knowing they were near it.

FEATHERLY ISLES

A sky-realm reached only through hidden portals revealed by the great eagles. Floating islands and wind-veiled cliffs protect the last of their kind.

FORGOTTEN FOREST

A secret refuge for the remaining Empyrean Knights, cloaked by illusion and smokeless fire, heavy with indecision and fading courage.

JUNAGI RIVER

A fast-flowing river through Wildepointe. Centaurs gather along its fertile banks to fish, bathe, and rest beneath the open sky.

KARNERGRIEN

A holy city of gold and marble, where bells and choirs once filled the streets. Even in ruin, ceremony clings stubbornly to stone.

KEL TYRION

An elven city east of Brightshire Forest, politically independent, culturally intertwined, defined by tradition and restraint.

KUGDOR

A dwarven kingdom carved into the Bardok Peaks, famed for metalwork, gemstones, and grog, with forges that never truly sleep.

LANDING'S END

A crowded tavern in Whaldalf's Landing, thick with salt, sweat, and fisherman's noise, where tables fill faster than mugs can drain.

LUMHAGEN

A hidden city of wizards, the seat of Bhalla. Wards and illusions protect it from discovery and judge those who approach.

NETHOPOLIS

An underwater city hidden off the coast near Shrewswell Cove, thriving beneath the sea in domes of living craft and coral light.

NULA

A fearful city built around the Labyrinth of Heham, guarded heavily, its people living under the weight of distant bellows.

THE PRUDENT OCEAN

A dangerous sea is named as a warning. Storms arrive without mercy, and unseen creatures test every voyage.

SANCTUARY SQUARE

A desperate market in ruined Karnergrien where survival replaces civility and trade persists amid dust, smoke, and hunger.

SHROUDSCAR

A fortified settlement housing goblins and mercenaries, serving as a refuge and recruitment for blades that will sell their loyalty.

THE SALTED COD

A rowdy tavern in Westramore, dense with cheap grog and simmering violence, where laughter often carries teeth.

THE BARREN BADLANDS

A scorched wasteland ruled by Scorchcrawlers, where sulfur air and cracked earth make survival a constant contest.

TALAIFOTIA

A volcanic stronghold where Lucient was cast down. Obsidian walls, forge-lit courtyards, and red mist radiate heat and oppressive power.

WHALDALF'S LANDING

A working fishing village built around a small harbor, known for modest craftsmanship, honest trade, and salt-wind endurance.

WESTRAMORE

A grim industrial city crawling with thieves and mercenaries, where coin rules and morality is rented.

WILDEPOINTE

A hilly plain of roaming caravan tents and centaur clans, shaped by movement, trade, and open sky.

WYVERNPEAKE

A high mountain cavern lair of Morvar, marked by bones, broken weapons, and heat that makes every descent feel deliberate.

LEXICON OF EMPYREA

UNIVERSAL TONGUE

Common
Spoken by all races for trade and diplomacy, shaped by necessity and widespread contact.

RACE TONGUES

Faelish (Fairies)

Sylphrin (Pixies)

Wap'Too (Centaurs)

L'eldrian (Wood Elves)

Jonbar (Ogres)

Guktash (Goblins)

Drubata (Dunnissé)

Wyrmtongue (Dragons)

Yumkoian (Trolls)

Khekül (Dwarves)

Ititken, also called Itik (Merfolk)

Choralight (Great Eagles)

Mosswhisper (Frolicking Mushrooms)

S'Durnen, also called Sdurne (Satyrs)

Ancient Serpent Language (Lucient and fallen serpents)

SACRED TERMS

Orealus
Name used for the Light, covenant, and divine authority in the Empyrean record.

Yah'shavel
The spirit-current of Light, named as sacred work, not sorcery.

Dunntaika
Corruption born of Lucient's fall, recorded as blight upon will and soul.

ABOUT THE AUTHOR

B.H. Preston is the author of *The Chronicles of Empyrea*, an epic fantasy series centered on conviction, consequence, and the trials that shape heroes and realms alike. Born in 1983 in Harvey, Illinois, he developed a love for fantasy at an early age through countless hours spent reading at his local public library.

Inspired by the sweeping worlds of J. R. R. Tolkien's *The Lord of the Rings* and C. S. Lewis's *The Chronicles of Narnia*, Bryant focuses on immersive storytelling and deep world-building that invites readers to step fully into Empyrea.

When he is not writing, Bryant enjoys watching movies, listening to music, and playing video games. He currently lives in Duluth, Minnesota, and continues the story of Empyrea with *A Journey Cast in Fire*, the sequel to *A Hero Forged in Blood*.

For more information about the author,
please visit b.h.prestonbooks.com.